Praise for Trisha Ashley:

'Trisha Ashley writes with remarkable wit and originality
– one of the best writers around!'
Katie Fforde

'Trisha Ashley's romp makes for enjoyable reading'
The Times

'Full of down-to-earth humour'
Sophie Kinsella

'A warm-hearted and comforting read'
Carole Matthews

'Fast-paced and seriously witty'
The Lady

'Packed with romance, chocolate and fun, this indulgent
read is simply too delicious to put down'
Closer

'A lovely, cosy read'
My Weekly

'Fresh and funny'
Woman's Own

www.penguin.co.uk

Trisha Ashley's *Sunday Times* Top Ten bestselling novels have twice been shortlisted for the Melissa Nathan Award for Comedy Romance, and *Every Woman for Herself* was nominated by readers as one of the top three romantic novels of the last fifty years.

Trisha lives in North Wales with a very chancy Muse.

For more information on Trisha Ashley and her books, please see www.trishaashley.com or visit her Facebook page (Trisha Ashley Books) or follow her on Twitter @trishaashley.

Trisha Ashley

The House of Hopes and Dreams

BLACK SWAN

TRANSWORLD PUBLISHERS
61–63 Uxbridge Road, London W5 5SA
www.penguin.co.uk

Transworld is part of the Penguin Random House group of companies
whose addresses can be found at global.penguinrandomhouse.com

First published in Great Britain in 2018 by Bantam Press
an imprint of Transworld Publishers
Black Swan edition published 2018

A CIP catalogue record for this book
is available from the British Library.

ISBN
9781784160920

Typeset in 11.5/13.5 pt Adobe Garamond by Jouve (UK), Milton Keynes
Printed and bound in Great Britain by Clays Ltd, Bungay, Suffolk

Penguin Random House is committed to a sustainable
future for our business, our readers and our planet. This book
is made from Forest Stewardship Council® certified paper.

1 3 5 7 9 10 8 6 4 2

To Jen Fishler
Pure Gold

Mossby, 1914

To whoever finds this journal (presuming they do so before it crumbles into dust), some explanation is due.

Having recently, unbeknown to my dear son, Joshua, seen an eminent London doctor and had the verdict I suspected confirmed, it seems to me time to set my affairs in order.

I was in the forefront of women working in the field of stained-glass window making at the turn of the century, including the setting-up of my own workshop here at Mossby during my tragically short marriage. But my achievements in that craft are already well documented, particularly in Miss Cecilia McCrum's recent excellent and exhaustively researched publication, A Brief History of Women Artists in Glass.

However, little has been written about my private life and this journal, which I kept at the time of my marriage, will go some considerable way to explaining my reticence until now in this matter.

Mossby has always held its secrets close, but it will be a relief to me to lay bare the Revell family skeletons at last, even if this book must then be secreted away.

At eighteen, I do not feel that Joshua is ready for the revelations I am about to make, particularly since his aunt Honoria,

1

who dotes on him, has brought him up to idolize the memory of the father he never knew. But perhaps one day he will discover the secret of its hiding place for himself, in the same way I did . . .

1

Fallen Idol

Carey
Late November 2014

Carey Revell lay on his hospital bed, propped in a semi-recumbent position by an efficient nurse and rendered temporarily speechless by the astonishing information his visitor had just imparted to him.

Though Mr Wilmslow was a country solicitor of a prosaic turn of mind and not usually given to flights of fancy, it suddenly occurred to him that with his large frame, gentian-blue eyes, thick, red-gold hair and the stubble burnishing his face, his new client resembled nothing so much as a fallen Viking warrior.

He had the typical Revell looks all right – there was no mistaking his heritage – though on a much larger and more resplendent scale.

Carey's left leg, the flesh scarred, misshapen, patched by skin grafts, and also bearing the marks of the pins that had held it immobile in a metal cage while the shattered bones finally knitted, was mercifully hidden by loose tracksuit trousers. The nerves and muscles still twitched and jangled painfully from his earlier physiotherapy session, but the news his unexpected visitor had brought him had for once

3

relegated this dismal symphony of discomfort to the background.

'Do you have any questions? I know it's a lot to take in at once,' said Mr Wilmslow, breaking the silence.

'Yes, it certainly is,' agreed Carey rather numbly, wondering for an instant if he might be still under the influence of heavy painkillers and dreaming all this. His eyes dropped once more to the letter the solicitor had brought him and he read it through for the third time.

Mossby
April 2014
To Carey Revell,

I will not address you as 'Dear Carey' or 'Dear Nephew' since we have never met and nor have I ever wished to do so. I will not go into the circumstances that led to your father's total estrangement from his family at such an early age, but suffice it to say that we were entirely disgusted when he continued to use our revered and respected family name throughout his stage career.

However, since you are the last of our branch of the Revells, and I suppose retribution for my brother's sins need not be visited upon his son, I feel it only right that you should inherit Mossby in your turn. I am signing a will to this effect today, my ninety-first birthday. My solicitor, Mr Wilmslow, will give you this letter of explanation after my decease.

Do not think I am bequeathing you great wealth, a mansion and a vast estate, for Mossby is a modest country residence, much of it rebuilt in the Arts and Crafts style at the end of the nineteenth century. Besides which, it has not of late received the care and attention it merits, due to the steady decline of my

4

investment income. In fact, I have recently been forced to live on my capital.

On to your shoulders now falls the burden of finding a way to make Mossby pay its own way, before the remaining money runs out. From what I have discovered, you seem to be a young man of some enterprise.

Ella Parry, my stepdaughter by my second marriage, has been pressing me to make a will for some time, assuming, I am sure, that it would be in her favour. Due to the rift with your father, she had no idea of your existence, so was sadly disappointed when I told her of my testamentary disposition. However, I have never considered her as my daughter and, since she and her husband have for many years received handsome salaries for acting as my housekeeper and gardener respectively, besides living rent free in the Lodge, she can have no real cause for complaint. I also paid for their daughter, Vicky's, education.

I hope you will take a pride in your heritage. You will find the family papers in the secret chamber in the Elizabethan wing, which Mr Wilmslow will show you the secret of. I always meant to sort them and write a history of the Revells of Mossby, but never got round to it. Perhaps you will do so.

Your uncle,
Francis Revell

'Secret chamber in the Elizabethan wing?' Carey muttered incredulously, feeling as if he'd strayed into an Enid Blyton mystery. Then he became aware that Mr Wilmslow, who was a slight, be-suited and altogether unremarkable personage to be the bearer of such astounding news, was stuffing papers back into his briefcase as a prelude to departure.

'Among the papers I've given you is a copy of the will. Probate should be granted before the New Year, though you can take up residence at Mossby before that, should you wish to . . . Health permitting, of course,' he added delicately.

'I'll be out of here before Christmas and intended staying with a friend while I decided where I wanted to live. I've put my old flat on the market because carrying things up four flights of stairs is going to be out of the question for quite a while,' Carey said. 'I've lost my job, too – I've been replaced. You know I presented *The Complete Country Cottage* TV series?'

He'd not only presented it, it had been his own idea . . . and being credited in the new series with 'From an original concept by Carey Revell' was not going to be much consolation. He ought to have read the fine print in his contracts more carefully – and so should his agent.

Mr Wilmslow nodded. 'I'm sorry to hear that, but you may find Mossby just the place to convalesce, while deciding what to do next,' he suggested, snapping the lock of the briefcase closed with some finality. 'In the meantime, you have my card, so do contact me if anything occurs to you that you'd like to ask.'

Carey said uneasily, 'This stepdaughter he – my uncle – mentions . . .'

'Ella Parry. Her husband, Clem, is an excellent gardener. Your uncle always thought it worth putting up with Ella Parry's cross-grained ways because he kept up the grounds almost single-handedly. She was the residuary legatee, by the way. Had you been killed in that accident just before your uncle's death, she would have inherited all.'

'Right,' Carey said, thinking Ella Parry didn't sound the most delightful person to have around the house, especially if she was bearing a grudge. But then, as his uncle's stepdaughter, it did seem a little harsh that she had been left with nothing.

When he said so, Mr Wilmslow reassured him.

'Your uncle was *more* than generous to them in his lifetime, but the situation will become clearer to you when you have taken up your residence at Mossby. It's in the Parrys' own interests to make themselves pleasant to you if they wish to continue their employment.' Then he added, after a moment, 'By the way, have you made a will of your own?'

'Oddly enough, yes, because after the accident I lost my feeling of invincibility,' Carey said with a wry smile. 'I sent a friend out for one of those will forms and a couple of nurses witnessed it.'

Mr Wilmslow winced: standard template will forms such as were available at newsagents were obviously beyond the pale. 'Well, those forms are perfectly legal, of course, but you may wish me to draw up a new one in the light of your inheritance.'

'Yes, and in the meantime, I suppose I could add a thing-ummy, making Ella Parry the residuary legatee to the house, like my uncle did?'

'A codicil? You *could* do so, of course, though given that Ella is now about sixty and you a young man in your thirties, we would hope you would survive her.'

'You never know what fate has in store for you,' Carey said darkly, then ran a distracted hand through already dishev-elled thick, red-gold hair. 'It's all a bit *sudden*, to be honest. I keep thinking I'm going to wake up.'

'I'm sorry it took me so long to track you down. It was unfortunate that you weren't in a position to answer any of my communications once I'd found your address.'

'Yes, wasn't it?' Carey said drily.

'And my attempts to contact you via your TV series also failed. I expect it was lost among the fan mail.'

'They've also managed to lose the fan mail itself, now they've replaced me,' Carey said. 'No direct contact at all

7

since telling me they weren't offering me a contract for a new series.'

'Dear me, the world of TV seems remarkably ruthless.' The solicitor's brown eyes showed mild surprise. 'Still, once I'd travelled down and talked to the delightful elderly lady in the flat below yours, all became clear. I hear the driver who knocked you off your bicycle didn't stop and they haven't found him or her?'

'No, and just my luck it was the one square inch of Dulwich Village without any CCTV surveillance! I'd had a minor run-in with another car only a few days before and meant to get one of those helmet cameras, but hadn't got round to it.'

Mr Wilmslow shook his head and made a sympathetic tutting noise. 'I hope you'll make a full recovery.'

'My left leg is never going to look quite the same again, but it was touch and go whether they'd have to amputate it at first, so I'm lucky it's still there. Or what's left of it, because I lost a few chunks here and there and they had to do grafts.'

Mr Wilmslow got up to go. 'I had better get off to catch my train, unless you have any further questions?'

'Not at the moment, though I'm sure I will, once it's all sunk in. If the Parrys could continue to keep an eye on the place, then I should be fit to travel up there soon after Christmas.'

'I'll keep in touch,' promised Mr Wilmslow, shrugging his slight frame into an ancient Burberry and winding a dark, wine-coloured woollen scarf around his neck.

As he left, he nimbly skipped aside to avoid being bowled over in the doorway by the tempestuous entrance of Carey's friend, Nick Crane.

'Who was that?' Nick demanded as Mr Wilmslow disappeared, carelessly tossing an armful of mail on to the bed, narrowly missing Carey's damaged leg. 'Finally remembered to bring all your letters. Sorry,' he added, as Carey winced. 'Leg hurting?'

'Of course it's bloody hurting! It hasn't stopped hurting since some nameless bastard decided to swipe me off my bike – *and* the physiotherapist is a sadist.'

'She's a very attractive sadist,' Nick said, with a grin. 'She can torture me any time she likes, you ungrateful sod! But I'm sure they're sick of the sight of you now and need to get rid of you so someone else can have your bed.'

'And I want to get out of here too, God knows.'

The fact that he would be leaving on his own two feet was, he acknowledged, largely due to the fact that his actress mother had flown back from America immediately the news of the accident had reached her and set about charming and bullying the surgeons into renewed attempts to save the mangled and broken thing that was his left leg.

As if he'd read Carey's mind, Nick said, 'Daisy should have had the same trust in the surgeons that your mother had, not dropped you like a hot potato the moment she got the news.'

'She did go to all the trouble of writing to explain she had a phobia of hospitals and illness . . . and how she'd been meaning to tell me she was moving out of the flat anyway, because she felt our relationship just wasn't working,' Carey said, though at the time his girlfriend's abrupt severance of their relationship had hurt him deeply.

'Lying cow! And I told you she's already shacked up with your replacement on the series, didn't I?'

Carey shrugged. 'Director's assistant perks? And everyone's told me, though I can't say I care any more. How did you get on at the flat?'

Nick had been organizing the packing and storage of Carey's belongings before the sale of the flat was finalized, and Daisy had arranged to meet him there that day to collect a few things she'd left behind and hand over her set of keys.

Nick, who had flung his lanky frame into the armchair, his Converse-shod feet dangling over the arm, suddenly sat upright. 'There was something I meant to tell you the minute I got here and I completely forgot!' he exclaimed. 'Daisy'd already been to the flat and she'd left you this note.'

He pulled a crumpled bit of paper out of his pocket and handed it over.

There was no greeting, or polite wishes for his continued recovery, it simply read:

I can't cope with Tiny any more. Circumstances have changed and anyway, he's become quite impossible. You bought him, so it's up to you to decide what to do with him.

It wasn't signed.

'Terse – and what does Daisy think *I* can do with a dog till I get out of here?' commented Carey, looking up with a frown. Daisy had coaxed him into buying the tiny Chihuahua puppy from a friend of hers, though his novelty had worn off even before he'd begun to show his true nature: no male legs were safe from those needle-sharp teeth. He'd also quickly outgrown the designer dog-carrier she'd bought for him, so it looked increasingly likely that his father hadn't been a Chihuahua at all . . .

They'd been sold a pup.

'She's too self-absorbed to even think of that one,' Nick said, then rolled up his jeans to exhibit a fresh set of pinpoint marks. 'Tiny was shut in the kitchen and when I opened the door, the little bastard got me again.'

Carey stared at him. 'You mean . . . she's dumped him there and *gone*?'

'Yep. And since I couldn't leave him there on his own and there was a plastic pet crate in the hall, I shoved him in that

10

and he's in the car now. I've left the windows down a bit, so he should be OK till I get back. What do you want me to do with him?'

'I suppose I'll have to find him a good home. *You* couldn't keep him till I get out of here, I suppose, Nick?' Carey added hopefully.

'Apart from not wanting my legs to look like I stick pins in them for fun, I'm out all the time, so it wouldn't be fair.'

'True,' conceded Carcy. 'Look, if I give you the address of the kennels we used when we went on holiday, could you take him there? It won't be strange to him and I'll work something permanent out as soon as I can.'

'Yeah, good idea,' agreed Nick, looking relieved. 'They're letting you out of here soon anyway, so we'll think of something while you're staying at mine over Christmas.'

It was lucky Nick had a ground-floor flat. Carey still didn't know if he'd ever be able to walk without limping, but he was determined he was leaving the hospital without crutches and would dispose of even a walking stick as soon as he could.

'Thanks, Nick. And I'll be staying with you only till just after Christmas. Then I'm off up to Lancashire. That visitor you so nearly knocked flat when you arrived was the bearer of some surprising news.'

'Did he want you to makeover a cottage for him?' Nick asked hopefully. 'As long as you delegate all the physical stuff to other people, you could take commissions to renovate cottages again, couldn't you?'

'No, it was nothing like that. He was a solicitor and he'd been trying to track me down for ages. In fact, a couple of those letters you've brought me are probably from him. He came down himself in the end and one of the neighbours told him what had happened and where I was.'

'Not an ambulance chaser, is he? They can't sue anyone if

11

they don't know who the hit-and-run driver was, surely? Unless you've remembered any more details about the car that hit you.'

Carey frowned. 'Sometimes I get a sort of flash and think I can see a big silver four-by-four . . . but that might be totally unrelated to the accident. Concussion can have weird side effects.'

'So, not an ambulance chaser?'

'No, he's a *family* solicitor – in fact, I suppose he's *my* family solicitor now. It appears that my father had an older brother and now he's died and left me everything, because I'm the last of the Revells . . . or the last of that branch of them in Lancashire, anyway.'

'You're an heir!' exclaimed Nick, his deep-set black eyes suddenly burning like coals with excitement. 'You're rich beyond your wildest dreams and can invest lots of lovely lolly in Raising Crane Productions! We'll make a TV documentary series that will blast *The Complete Country Cottage* right out of the water!'

Nick's small production company, in which Carey had an investment, was doing well, but still looking for that big, elusive hit.

'Don't get too excited, we're not talking millions here,' said Carey, damping down his enthusiasm. 'There's a run-down house and not much money. Plus, there's a resentful stepdaughter and her husband living in the Lodge, who expected to scoop the lot.'

'Well, tough,' said Nick unsympathetically. 'How come you didn't know you had an uncle?'

'There was a big family falling-out and Dad ran off to be on the stage when he was still in his teens and never went back.'

The rest was history: Harry Revell, progressing via ENSA on to the post-war stage, had become one of the greatest

12

Shakespearean actors of his generation. He'd married very late and died when Carey was eight.

'Dad never told me anything about his family and if Mum knew, she didn't mention it. I'll have to ask her.'

His mother had been a young aspiring actress when she'd married Harry, and she'd returned to the stage after he died. Eventually she'd gone to America and made her name in the hit series *The Little Crimes of Lisa Strange*. She played a terribly English spinster who travelled round the country solving mysteries, assisted by her sarky female black American driver. It had been going for years and showed no signs of ever stopping.

Carey looked Mossby up on his smartphone, though there were few pictures and little information. It was a white stucco Arts and Crafts house, linked by an old square tower to part of the original Elizabethan building at the back. It was situated on a sort of bluff with terraces leading down to a lake and woodland.

'It's a stately home, all right!' said Nick.

'It's not huge, but it's a little bigger than I thought it would be. The Arts and Crafts houses were mostly built by the wealthy middle classes, and were more like overgrown cottages than anything.'

'Well, it should be right up your street, anyway. And did you say it needed renovating?'

'It sounds as if it's been neglected lately,' agreed Carey, and they looked at each other in sudden mutual understanding.

'This could be just the fresh start you need – and a major opportunity for both of us,' enthused Nick. *'Carey Revell's Mansion Makeover* – a Raising Crane Production!'

'It's not a mansion,' Carey objected, but his friend had the bit between his teeth now.

'I can make a pilot – see who's interested in a series – and I think there'll be a lot of interest, because there's the dual angle of you recovering from a serious accident and the whole unexpected inheritance thing . . . and then all the usual ups and downs of restoration, only on a *huge* scale.' His dark eyes glowed again. 'It could run to more than one series and it'll give us both the break we need!'

'I haven't even seen the place yet,' Carey cautioned him. 'Hold on a bit!'

'Doesn't Angelique live somewhere quite near to this Mossby place?' Nick continued, carried away on a tide of optimism. 'If there are any windows to be repaired or replaced, that'll be really handy!'

'Yeah, I expect she'll think just the same way you do,' Carey said sarcastically. Angel – or Angelique, to give her her full and slightly ridiculous name – was his oldest friend. As students he, Nick, Angel and a couple of others had shared a house together.

'My old gran used to say that as one door closed, another opened,' Nick said, getting up. 'She was right.'

Then he went off to deliver Tiny to Pooches Paradise, after Carey had rung and pleaded with them to house the dog, because last time Tiny had made himself unpopular by biting a staff member. They were going to charge double, and triple over the actual Christmas period.

He couldn't tell them how long they'd have to have him after that. He assumed Daisy had already offered Tiny to all her friends and acquaintances before she'd dumped him, and he didn't rate Tiny's chances of being re-homed if he went to a dog rescue centre.

Carey decided to worry about that later. He got the photos of Mossby up on his phone again and an innate feeling that this was *his* place – somewhere he truly belonged to – tugged at his heart, taking him totally by surprise.

It was ridiculous to feel that way, seeing as he'd never even heard of Mossby till that morning!

Or had he? Now he came to think of it, the name did stir up some very distant recollection . . .

His eye fell on the heap of mail Nick had dumped on the bed and he spotted a letter addressed in Angelique's familiar scrawl and sent via his friend's address, as all her letters had been since the accident. At least Nick had always remembered to bring *those*.

He ripped it open, skimming the enquiries after his rehab progress and smiling at the small caricatures she'd drawn in the margins: himself wrapped up like an Egyptian mummy and one of old Ivan, who worked in Julian Seddon's stained-glass studio, hobbling about with a slopping mug of tea in each hand.

She wrote that she was off to Antigua in a few days to stay with her mother and stepfather, who kept a superyacht in Falmouth Harbour, as well as having a nearby villa. Angel had always spent two weeks with them just before Christmas – he'd gone with her himself a couple of times, when they were students – but last year she hadn't, because her partner, Julian, had been recovering from a stroke.

Carey thought Julian must be making a good recovery if Angel was leaving him to his own devices. Or maybe he had insisted, realizing she needed the break? When she'd been to see him in hospital last time she'd been in London on business, he'd been troubled by how worried and strained she'd seemed.

His conscience suddenly twinged: maybe he should have visited them when Julian first had the stroke, or even rung her more often since? But then, everything had been wiped from his mind by the accident, except recovering and getting out of hospital as soon as he could, preferably on two feet.

He smiled, wryly. Angel always joked that he only remembered her existence when he wanted her to work for free, making or repairing stained glass for one of the cottages featured on his programmes, but that was far from the truth.

15

Since she fell in love with Julian Seddon the summer after she graduated and moved to Lancashire to live and work with him, she might have left the centre stage of his life, but Carey was always conscious of her there in the wings. And he was quite certain she felt the same way about him.

Perhaps I should explain the events that led up to my first, unlikely meeting with Ralph Revell, which took place in my father's glass manufactory in London, in early 1894 . . .

My mother had died early and though my aunt Barbara, who came to take charge of the household, did her utmost to turn me into a young lady, not even her best endeavours could keep me away from the workshop or stop my fascination with the whole art and craft of stained-glass window making.

My father was an intelligent man with a great interest in the arts and well acquainted with William Morris and his circle. Under their influence he had turned away from the modern trend of merely painting pictures on to ever larger pieces of glass, giving a dull, flat effect, and instead enthusiastically embraced the return to the purer artistry of earlier times. Smaller pieces of glass, made in the Antique way, uneven in thickness and containing irregularities, gave life, sparkle and depth to a window. The dark lines of the leading formed part of the design and there was need for only minimal overpainting.

I shared his enthusiasm and it became both my lifelong passion and my profession. My marriage turned out to be a brief, mistaken digression along the way, although in saying this, I realize I will be thought very unnatural. But so it was.

2

Clipped Wings

Angelique
Sunday, 7 December 2014

Eighteen months ago, before Julian had his stroke and our lives changed for ever, he was the owl who stayed up late into the night in his office/studio downstairs, while I was the lark, winging off in the early hours of the morning to the stained-glass workshop at the end of the garden. We were Yin and Yang, two sides of the same coin, and our lives were perfectly balanced and happy.

But all that had changed, literally at a stroke.

Now Julian slept so badly that he was often up before me and, on this particular morning, since I'd found the previous day extra exhausting, it was after eight before I groggily surfaced.

It wasn't yet properly light and looked likely to be another gloomy, cold, grey December day, but Julian's side of the bed was empty. I switched on the lamp and saw that his stick was gone from where it usually hung on the back of a chair within easy reach.

Bathroom? I wondered.

But when I slid a hand between the sheets there was no warmth where he had lain and the house was silent, except for the ticking of the grandfather clock downstairs and the occasional creak of wooden floors adjusting to the fluctuating central heating.

I felt the familiar scrunch of fear in the pit of my stomach.

Was he lying in a heap somewhere in the house? Or had he risen early and made his way to the workshop like he'd done the previous day, so that I'd finally had to fetch the wheelchair to bring him back, totally exhausted, frustrated and angry.

And could I really leave him for over a week to fly off to Antigua, even though, apart from the frustrated anger when his body refused to do what he wanted, his health now seemed quite stable?

He was so keen for me to go that I suspected he longed to escape my anxious eyes as much as the confines of his condition.

When I got up my second guess proved to be right. There was no sign of him in the cottage, but his coat and set of workshop keys were gone and the back door unlocked. When I opened it and looked out, he wasn't lying on the path, and over the hedge I could see the glimmer of light in the large Victorian building that housed the famous Julian Seddon Architectural Glass Studio.

Of course, he could still be lying in a crumpled heap on the floor of the studio, but his condition had been so stable for ages that I didn't *really* think so. In which case, it would be a repeat of yesterday's scene: I'd found him attempting to use his almost useless left hand to hold down a piece of deliciously reamy yellow glass over the white paper cutline he'd laid on top of a light-box, while he ran the wheel over it with his right. But glass slides easily, and you need to exert firm pressure while you're cutting . . .

The scrunch of the wheel incising a firm line across the surface of the glass, then the sharp tap underneath with the heavy grozing pliers, so that the break forms cleanly – these are some of the delights of the craft we both loved so much and took for granted.

His assistant, Grant, or old Ivan, who was officially retired but haunting the studio almost as much as when he was employed there, could have expertly cut the piece for him. As could I, of course, but I knew that wasn't the point. He had begun producing his brilliant designs again, but he wanted to be part of the whole process – the cutting, the painting and silver-staining, the leading-up of the calmes with the smooth caps of solder on every joint . . . even scrubbing the soft, oily black glazing cement into the finished panels, and then polishing the surface with powdered whitening till glass and lead alike were shiny and clean.

He wanted to be part of the whole act of creation, not just the spark that ignited it.

I knew, because I did, too. We recognized that desire in each other almost the instant our eyes met for the first time in a mutual, consuming passion. We'd always been as much in love with that complete act of creation as with each other.

That day was Sunday and we always used to like having the workshop to ourselves at weekends. There was a magic to it, as if Santa's elves had gone home and we'd sneaked in to play. I'd go down and potter about very early, checking on the kiln, if it had been fired, or working on ideas in the studio. Julian would appear later, bearing cheese toasties and I'd make coffee by the sink in the corner, before we settled in amicable silence to our work.

How distant that idyllic life seemed now! I felt weary that morning and found myself hugely reluctant to face whatever the day intended throwing at me. Or whatever *Julian* threw at me – I'd taken him warm *pain au chocolat* the previous day and that hadn't gone down well.

So I had a cup of coffee, spread a thick layer of my own

20

home-made raspberry jam over a doorstep of fresh whole-meal bread, and ate it slowly. I figured I might need the sugar for energy.

My friend Molly, the wife of Grant, who worked in the studio, had made the soft and delicious bread, while the jam tasted of warm summer days. Happier days.

I washed up and hung my mug back on the dresser. Mine had a picture of the Five Sisters windows at York Minster on the side, while Julian's sported a Chartres Cathedral roundel like a brightly hued kaleidoscope.

Then, finally, I shrugged into my quilted coat of many colours and let myself out into the dove-grey day.

The big workroom was lit but empty and I went through the half-glazed door at the end and found Julian sitting at his desk in the studio, writing.

His right side, his good one, was turned to me, and tugged my heartstrings with familiarity. Julian . . . his long, sensitive face had always reminded me of a dreamy knight from King Arthur's round table. He was slender, quietly handsome, his dark brown hair silvered now, but his hazel eyes still shaded by long black lashes . . .

He was more than twenty years my senior, but we'd fallen in love at first sight. Age had never been a factor . . .

The love was still there, though recently I'd come to accept that the nature of that emotion had changed. It had happened subconsciously over many months, until the knowledge finally presented itself as a fact. Until then, it had been better *not* to think, just to scramble through each day, looking after Julian, while keeping the business going as best I could.

As our relationship had changed from that of lovers to reluctant dependant and carer, I knew Julian had found the situation just as hard as I had – more so, for he was such a private person and resented each indignity of illness. And it brought anger — I'd never seen him angry in all our time together, until one day frustration welled up like a volcano and he shouted at me. Just for a brief moment his eyes had held the hard gaze of a bitter stranger. Since then, I'd learned to dread that look.

But there *had* been some physical improvement in the first months after the stroke. He could walk to the workshop, supervise Grant and old Ivan, design a window or glass installation, take on more of the running of Julian Seddon Architectural Glass again.

But he wanted to be the man he had been and by now he must have realized as well as I that things would never be the same again.

The role of nurse and then carer had not come easily to me and in the first months I'd been thankful for Molly's help. She'd previously been a nurse, though she now made her living filling the freezers of select clients with healthy home-cooked meals, and Julian seemed to find her brisk, impersonal no-nonsense assistance more acceptable than mine.

But I was sure that love in some form still existed between us and would eventually settle into a new pattern — and if it that was more a thing of shared interests and long association, then that was the way most marriages probably went . . .

Though actually, we *hadn't* married because I'd never wanted to, even though after ten years Julian had teased me about my having become a common-law wife, whether I liked it or not. I suppose I might have changed my mind if there'd been a child to consider, but we had been so happy and fulfilled together that we'd kept putting off starting a family . . .

I must have made some small noise, for Julian lifted his head and, to my relief, gave me a slight, lop-sided smile.

'Hi, Angel. I'm making notes for my will.'

I could feel the answering smile freezing on my lips and my heart began to thump. 'Your *will*? Are you feeling—'

'Don't panic,' he interrupted impatiently. 'I'm not doing it because I'm feeling worse. It's just that I've been putting it off because it always seemed like tempting Fate, but now I think Fate already knows where I live, so I might as well sort things out.'

He gave another slightly twisted smile. 'Anyway, I heard something on the radio the other day that set me thinking. It appears that if you die without making a will, it can lead to all kinds of problems and delays.'

'But you're so much better now that you really don't need to think about that kind of thing—' I began.

'Yes, and I'm also twenty years older than you are, so the chances are I'll die first, one way or the other, aren't they?'

This seemed to be a rhetorical question, so I didn't point out that life was a lottery and you never knew when your number would be up. The Grim Reaper had his random moments.

'I want to make some provision for you, but to be fair to Nat as well.'

I have a tendency to live in the moment so I'd never given the future a lot of thought until recently, but I'd vaguely assumed that Julian's only son by his long-ago marriage would inherit everything at some nebulous future date. I'd been building up a little nest egg from my wages and the occasional prize or commission, but it had stayed little because I so often broke into it to add to my magpie's shiny store of Antique glass that was stashed away in one of the outbuildings.

I didn't have a lot of outgoings, because the cottage was Julian's, as was the business. I was still an employee, though I took design commissions of my own sometimes, too, if they were to be made elsewhere.

23

'You've always been fair to me, Julian,' I assured him. 'But Nat is your only son, so naturally *he* should inherit everything.'

Nat had followed in his father's footsteps and worked with him in the studio, until my arrival on the scene had led to an estrangement between them. I felt guilty about that and over the years I'd done my best to heal the rift.

Julian had overheard Nat accusing me of being a gold-digger, muscling my way into the workshop by sleeping with the boss, and he'd told Nat that if he couldn't accept the situation in a civilized manner, he'd have to go elsewhere. The upshot had been that he'd found Nat a job in London in a friend's stained-glass workshop and he'd made his life down there ever since.

I don't think the problem was ever really about my relationship with his father, who'd been a widower for several years when we met, it was Nat's realization that although he was a great craftsman, he hadn't got a spark of originality when it came to designing windows and installations . . . and *I* had.

'You haven't thought it through,' Julian told me, recalling my wandering mind. 'The cottage has been your home for years and the business is becoming as much about you now, as me.'

That was a slight exaggeration, but I was beginning to make a name for myself and there was a whole Angelique Arrowsmith section on the Julian Seddon website. I'd won a major competition a couple of years previously, too.

'Besides, the cottage and business really go together, so I'm leaving both to you,' he continued, not waiting for any comment. 'Everything else – and there's quite a lot of money invested – goes to Nat.'

I knew Julian had inherited money from his mother's family, not to mention what he earned himself – and his work was still as much in demand as it was when he blazed on to the scene with his first major commission, the spectacular Tidesbury Abbey west window.

'But . . . if you *must* leave me something, couldn't it simply be a small amount of money, enough to buy a tiny cottage with?' I suggested. 'And everything else to Nat. I'm sure that's what he'd expect.'

'He seems to have made a life for himself in London, but my investments would give him enough money to set up his own workshop, if he wanted to,' Julian said. 'I want you to carry on the business here, which is what you've been doing since the stroke anyway. In fact, we'll change the name to Julian Seddon and Angelique Arrowsmith Architectural Glass as soon as you get back from Antigua, and I'll make you an equal partner. I don't know why I didn't think of it before.'

'I'm perfectly happy with things the way they are,' I protested. 'And we're going to live to a ripe old age together, working and having fun like we used to. Look how much better you are now.'

'I hope we do, darling, though let's face it, I'm never going to be the man I was,' he said. 'I want you to have security if anything should happen to me, because there's a whole bright future ahead of you, while my glory days are all in the past.'

'From someone who's just designed a spectacular rose window for Gladchester Chapel, that's a bit rich,' I said, and he laughed, like an echo of the old Julian.

'Do change your mind about this will business,' I coaxed him.

'I know what I want – and what's fair,' he insisted. 'I'll get Mr Barley to draw up the will and then bring it over to be signed.'

I was still deeply troubled, but he had that stubborn

expression and I didn't want to provoke him. I made some coffee and got out the biscuit tin, then changed tack.

'Julian, I really don't think I should have let you persuade me to go off to Antigua, leaving you alone,' I began. 'What if—'

'We've already had this conversation, Angel,' he broke in impatiently. 'A break will do me as much good as it will you.'

A break from me, he meant, since he hated hot countries and had never been to Antigua with me. I felt hurt. We were both private people, but we'd lived and worked together in perfect harmony. In fact, my annual December visits to Mum and my stepfather had been the longest periods we'd ever spent apart.

'Don't tell me you haven't already asked Molly to check on me every five minutes while you're gone, because I won't believe you,' he added, with just enough of the ghost of his old, familiar smile to reassure me.

And of course I had done just that, though it still seemed wrong that I should leave him.

'Julian, why don't I cancel the flights and have a break nearer home?' I said impulsively. 'Or we could both have a little holiday in a hotel somewhere lovely, like Cornwall or—'

The smile vanished and I caught a glimpse of the alien, slightly dangerous fire of anger that the stroke had somehow lit inside his mind.

'No, and we're not discussing it any more,' he snapped, and I turned away.

The only consolation was that this time I'd only be absent for a mere nine days, not the usual fortnight. What could possibly go wrong in so short a time? Especially with Molly, Grant and old Ivan watching over him for me.

When making a window, any details that needed to be painted on to the glass were applied in a vitreous enamel that fused with the surface when fired in a kiln. As I had some skill with the paintbrush, this became one of my earliest tasks.

At this time, the men Father employed tended to specialize in certain areas of the glassmaker's craft, rather than having experience of the whole process, but this was not what I wanted. I was consumed by the desire to learn everything there was to know, from start to finish . . . Or as much of the process as Father would allow: for though he frequently forgot I was a mere female, he did draw the line at letting me attempt to blow molten glass into a cylinder that could be cut and flattened into a sheet, or spin great discs of it.

Nor would he let me help heat and mould lead to be milled into the long H-shaped strips called calmes that held the pieces of window glass together. Even then, though, I was unfortunately of small stature and slight in build, so perhaps he had a point.

3

Rum Punched

So there I was en route to Antigua a few days later, luxuriating in business class and with a glass of bubbly clasped in a hand somewhat battered, scarred and workmanlike from years of making stained-glass windows for a living. I don't think I quite realized how emotionally and physically stretched and exhausted I was until I settled into my seat: it was if I were a puppet and someone had cut my strings.

My stepfather, Jim Dacre, was *totally* loaded, so he always insisted on paying for my flights. I suspected he was trying to make up for having married and removed Mum to the other side of the Atlantic when I was ten, after first depositing me in boarding school, like left luggage you might want to reclaim at some future point.

Since I'd already lost my childhood friend Carey the previous year, when his actress mother had taken him back to live in London after her husband died, the last vestiges of my happy childhood ended right there.

Up till then, we'd lived in a small Bedfordshire village and Mum taught art in a nearby grammar school. She took a casual attitude to motherhood, had a circle of bohemian friends, a busy social life and a succession of boyfriends. (My father died before I was old enough to remember him.) I thrived on a diet of casual affection and neglect, growing up to be self-reliant, happy and consumed by painting and drawing the world around me.

I suppose I might have felt lonely if Carey, who was almost exactly the same age as me, hadn't lived next door. Mum said when Carey's parents bought the pretty thatched cottage as a weekend retreat, it was the most exciting thing to hit Little Buddington since the Black Death. For although Carey's mum was merely an aspiring young actress, his father was Harry Revell, the great Shakespearean actor. He was very much older than his wife and late fatherhood can't have agreed with him, because Lila and Carey were soon living permanently in the cottage with Harry an increasingly rare visitor.

Carey and I were both artistic, fiery Aries characters and often struck sparks off one another; but at bottom, we were best friends right through infants and junior school. Mum and Lila had become friends, too, and the first time Mum visited her in London after the move – having parked me with the postmistress – she somehow hooked herself a rich, early-retired millionaire at a party and life as I'd known it *totally* ended.

It wasn't that I disliked Jim when I met him, but he'd been married before and had handed his business over to grown-up sons. He wanted to carry Mum off to the Caribbean where he was now based and *I* was surplus to requirements.

So, I ended up in boarding school among strangers, my home was sold and, apart from a couple of weeks a year when I flew out to Antigua, I spent my school holidays with Granny in Lancashire, where she had a neat semi-detached council house in Formby.

Mum never came back, not even for Granny's funeral. She had a fear of flying, though never in the Erica Jong sense, and, having got out there, stayed put.

Life based between a superyacht and a villa on a Caribbean island seemed to suit her perfectly . . . and the responsibilities of motherhood had never weighed heavily on her shoulders anyway.

I became withdrawn and solitary at my new school, for after losing Carey it seemed safer not to make new friends. Instead, I spent all my free time in my own little world, drawing and painting.

Then, with miraculous serendipity, Carey and I chose the same university and met on the first day of term. He was scanning the accommodation notices on the board and though the boy I remembered had turned into a tall, well-built man, the set of his shoulders and the blaze of his red-gold hair were unmistakable.

'Of all the universities in all the world, you had to choose this one,' I'd said slightly huskily.

He'd turned quickly, his gentian-blue eyes blazing with surprised delight.

'Shrimp!' he'd shouted, then swept me off my feet and swung me round and round until we were both laughing and dizzy. The lonely, unhappy years between nine and eighteen had dissolved in a tide of happiness . . .

'Ice cream and cookies?' suggested the stewardess brightly, breaking into my reverie. She seemed to have been programmed to offer the passengers something to eat or drink about every fifteen minutes and if I accepted everything I'd be so fat by the time we landed I'd have to be prised out of my seat with a crowbar. I closed my eyes, hoping she'd stop tempting me if she thought I was asleep.

And sleep I did, drifting off to the thought of Carey, always there at the back of my mind like a six-foot-four comfort blanket, spun from soft red-gold fleece. His leg was healing well and he'd be out of rehab any minute, so perhaps he could come and stay with us in the New Year. Julian liked him, even though they were chalk and cheese, and the company would perk him up no end.

The knot of tension and anxiety that had inhabited my stomach for so long was quickly unravelling, taking with it some of the guilt and relief about leaving Julian. Slowly I sank into a deeper sleep, only barely conscious of the stewardess's voice suggesting, hopefully, 'Pretzels?'

I rang Julian that evening, sitting in a rattan chair on the shaded decking of Jim's villa, which overlooked Falmouth Harbour. Nearby was a telescope permanently focused on his pride and joy – his vast and glossy superyacht. It might not be *quite* as super as some of the other floating palaces moored there, but to me it was still impressively enormous.

I had the remains of a rum punch in my other hand and I wasn't sure if I was suffering from jet lag, or Jim had ignored my request to go easy on the rum, but I felt limp and spaced out.

I wasn't too worried about Julian, because I knew Molly would already have popped in to make sure he was all right and had eaten something – and she wouldn't take any nonsense. And then Nat was driving up to visit Julian next day – he would only stay at the cottage when I was away and had even booked into a hotel when Julian had his stroke, despite my urging him to stay with me.

But this visit would be different, because he'd married two years ago and was bringing his wife, Willow, for the first time.

Willow was a freelance graphic artist and I hadn't yet met her, though I'd insisted Julian go down to London for the wedding, even though I hadn't been invited. In the pictures she was tall, blonde, leggy and long-nosed, and reminded me of nothing so much as a heron. I did a little cartoon of her like that, standing on one leg . . . which I now remembered was lying around in my sketchbooks in the studio. I hoped Willow was not of an inquisitive nature.

Julian's voice on the phone, with that hint of a slur, still didn't sound quite like him, but he brushed off my enquiries about his health.

Then he added that I could call Molly off, too, because Nat and Willow had arrived a day early. 'Or maybe I got the date wrong? Anyway, they got here a couple of hours ago.'

'Oh? What's she like?' I asked interestedly, for he'd barely had a chance to speak to her at the wedding reception.

'Girly and gushing,' he replied. 'Went into rhapsodies about the cottage, especially the oak beams and the old-fashioned kitchen.'

'It's not *that* old-fashioned, just comfortable. Shabby chic,' I added vaguely. Molly was into all that upcycling and distressing furniture stuff and we'd acquired several of her pieces. 'Anyway, Carey's the expert on cottage makeovers and, if you remember, he said it was fine as it was, the perfect eclectic mix of furnishings.'

'Willow said we should update it with a red Aga and a giant pink Smeg fridge/freezer. I think she said something about cement kitchen units, too, but I must have got that wrong, because it sounds so unlikely.'

'Cement-coloured?' I suggested. 'All the interior decorators on TV programmes, except Carey, seem mad about grey lately. A red Aga is a total cliché, too, and there's nothing wrong with our fridge or the freezer.'

'She had a look at what was in both of them, before announcing they were vegetarians.'

'Really? I can't believe Nat's turned vegetarian! But anyway, since we don't eat meat, she can't have found anything particularly awful in there, other than a bit of fish. If they want anything else, then they should have warned us.'

'Well, she seems to have brought a lot of their own food with her, so I expect that's why she was rooting in the fridge and freezer, trying to find some space among all the stuff you and Molly seemed to think I'd get through in nine days.'

'*And* Nat and Willow, because we thought we were catering for three,' I pointed out. 'What are they doing now?'

'Nat's taken her to look at the workshop . . .' He paused and then said, 'I got Mr Barley to draw up that will, but I'm not going to mention anything about it to Nat.'

That was probably a good idea, because if Julian had stuck to his guns on his intentions and Nat found out, then the fat really would be in the fire. He'd expect to inherit everything and, really, I still thought he should. But while I didn't want to look ahead to a time when it might be an issue, if it ever came to it, then I supposed Mr Barley would help me sort it out.

Julian seemed reasonably cheerful, though he told me not to keep ringing him up after today, because I'd hear soon enough if he wasn't feeling well. I was to relax and enjoy my holiday.

Then we talked about the work in progress for a while – a big rose window is quite an undertaking – before Nat and Willow came back and he rang off.

I thought about phoning or emailing Molly after that, but just then Mum came out on to the decking, her curling hair freshly rendered a shining but improbable chestnut brown, followed by a group of equally brightly dressed and tanned friends. It was like being surrounded by a flock of noisy parakeets.

'Guess what, Angelique – we're all going to sail to Anguilla tomorrow! Jim's gone to make the arrangements, because they're *so* fussy there about moorings and things,' Mum said brightly, and wouldn't hear of my staying put quietly in the villa. Jim's superyacht would be one loud floating party and I was not, and never had been, any kind of party animal.

Mum, Jim and several of their crowd went to dine and

whoop it up at the Purple Conch and then returned in the early hours and kept up the revelry for ages, so my attempts to sleep and let my body clock catch up were doomed to failure.

Next morning, hollow-eyed and functioning only because of large amounts of good American coffee, I hurriedly repacked my small case, and soon Jim's yacht, with its deck full of inexhaustible revellers and one reluctant one, set sail for Anguilla.

I was a party-pooper, immediately retiring to my cabin where, with the help of airline ear plugs, I went out like a light for several hours.

When I finally woke up, I discovered that in the rush to get off I'd left my phone behind – not that it would have done me much good out at sea, but I could probably have talked to Julian when I was on Anguilla. I could still have got round that and contacted him, of course – but he'd been so insistent I didn't keep checking up on him. Willow and Nat would have left by the time we set sail back, but Molly would resume visiting him the moment they'd gone. It was only a few days . . .

Anguilla was beautiful and for a jam-packed forty-eight hours we piled into local taxis and explored, swam and ate wonderful local food. It was a world away from home and I have to say I was totally chilled and relaxed by the time we sailed for Antigua again. Everyone else finally seemed pooped out and retired to cabins and sun loungers to recover, but I'd caught up with my sleep and felt fine.

In fact, my Pollyanna gene kicked in and I was filled with a rush of sudden optimism for the future. I'd been letting things get too much on top of me and this break would do both me and Julian good. We'd get things in perspective and be able to move on into a different, but more relaxed, future.

Though of course, that wouldn't stop me ringing Julian the very moment I got back to the villa and perhaps by then he wouldn't be cross, but instead tell me how much he was missing me, the way he used to.

Later I attended some classes at one of the art schools that had opened their doors to young ladies, in order to broaden my skills in painting, drawing and design. I felt sorry for some of the other girls, for they would never know the joy of painting with light as I did, not just with flat pigment.

Many of them, like my great friend Lily Stavely, hoped to learn skills that would enable them to earn a respectable living. Lily, the fifth child of a poor parson, had a flair for embroidery that she hoped would release her from the obligation to take a post as a governess or companion.

Not all our time was spent working or studying, and London offered many opportunities for entertainment. Together with some of Lily's brothers and sisters and, often with my cousin Michael, whom Father was training up into the business, we spent many happy Sundays on excursions to the parks, and there were boating expeditions in summer and skating in winter. My girlhood was a very happy one.

4

Lost Voices

But when I finally tracked my iPhone down behind a sofa cushion, I discovered that Julian had been incapable of telling me anything since the Sunday we sailed for Anguilla, when he'd suffered a final, catastrophic stroke.

I knew there must be bad news the moment I plugged the phone into the charger and a million missed calls and text messages from Molly popped up, even before I listened to her voicemail gently breaking the news.

I called her straight away, cold and shivering with the shock, and she picked up as quickly as if she'd been standing by the phone waiting. Perhaps she had.

'Molly – it's me, Angel. I've only just heard your voicemail . . .' I swallowed, unable to continue.

Her voice sounded thick and husky, as if she'd been crying. 'Oh, Angel, I'm so sorry you had to get the news this way. I was afraid your phone might be broken and I couldn't find another number to try.'

'Jim suddenly decided we were sailing to Anguilla and in the scramble my phone got left behind . . . but Julian told me on Saturday not to keep checking up on him, so I decided to take him at his word,' I said, only half aware of what I was saying.

'Of course you did. He seemed fine, so there was no reason to think this would happen,' she said comfortingly.

'It takes around twelve hours to sail to Anguilla but the contact details for Jim's yacht are in the big address book for emergencies, though I don't suppose you knew that . . . and you didn't know I was on it, anyway.' I broke off, realizing I was gabbling inanely.

Then I took a deep, shaky breath and said, 'I can't believe it's true. Please tell me what happened, Molly. Julian – didn't *suffer*, did he?'

'No, not at all. The doctor said it must have been instant-aneous,' she assured me quickly. 'It seems he'd gone down to the workshop very early on Sunday morning, but it never occurred to Nat and Willow that he wasn't still asleep in his room until he hadn't appeared by lunchtime. Then Nat rang us up to see if we knew where he was and Grant and I went over there and suggested we look in the workshop . . . And there he was, in the studio. He must have been sitting in his chair at the desk and just slipped down on to the floor. He'd been gone for hours by then, there was nothing that could be done.'

'Déjà vu,' I said, because it had been Grant who'd found him early one morning the first time, when he'd arrived to open up. Julian had been worrying about whether the kiln was firing properly and we thought he'd probably gone down in the early hours to check it.

'He said he felt fine and could manage perfectly well without me. And all that medication he was on should have stopped him having any more strokes.'

'It would help, but don't forget they told you the outcome after the initial stroke would have been better if he'd been found quickly enough for him to have that special treat-ment,' she reminded me. 'It has to be administered within a short time after the stroke.'

'Yes, I was just fooling myself recently that there was still some improvement, but I'm sure he knew it and that's why

38

his frustration was making him angrier every day. I *knew* I shouldn't have left him,' I added, anguished.

I felt transfixed with guilt. I hadn't been there the first time he'd needed me, because I'd been in London, having won a competition to design a glass screen for a museum. And now I'd failed him again.

'If I'd been home, I'd have known where he was,' I said, though of course I'd have assumed he'd gone down there to get away from me again, and perhaps waited a while before following him. 'I might have been in time to save him.'

'Angel, they said even if someone had been there with him when it happened, he couldn't have been saved,' Molly said gently.

'And think of poor Nat, finding his father like that,' I said, suddenly. 'I wonder if I should ring him. I mean, I know he's always resented me, but at a time like this . . .'

'I wouldn't,' she said. 'I gave him your phone number and email, so I'd leave it up to him to contact you, but I'll tell him I've broken the news.'

'Do, and if you could say that I – I'm so devastated by Julian's loss and understand how he must be feeling, too. I'll be home as soon as possible. I suppose he's still there, organizing everything, till I get back?'

I suddenly realized that it was already Thursday morning, so he'd had to cope alone since Sunday.

'He's here, but Willow had to return to London.' She hesitated, then added slowly, 'Angel . . .'

But I'd heard the villa door slam and the sound of Jim's voice calling to Mum. 'Look, Molly, Jim's just come in so I'd better go and get him to book me a seat on the first flight home. I'll let you know when he's done that.'

'Yes, do, and I'll meet you off the plane,' she offered.

'Bless you,' I said gratefully.

*

39

But it was Friday before Jim could get me on a flight, by which time I was almost beside myself with desperation to get home . . . even if that home would now be an empty shell.

Somehow, though, I felt as if Julian would be there waiting for me, and perhaps he would, his presence in the workshop and cottage, where we'd been so happy together for over ten years, lingering to comfort me.

By the time the plane landed at Manchester airport, I'd slept little and eaten almost nothing for over two days, though I hadn't really cried. I think that was because I couldn't accept Julian had gone until I was home and saw for myself.

As I came out into the bright arrivals lounge, it seemed like a shaky stage set that might tumble down at any moment, until I spotted Molly's familiar, stocky figure, clad in jeans and a loose quilted lumberjack shirt, her round rosy face under its mop of greying curls unwontedly serious. She was solid enough to anchor me back to reality.

We hugged and then she grabbed the handle of my larger case, leaving me with just my small carry-on one. 'Come on, the car's in the short-stay car park. We can talk when we're on our way.'

Everyone seemed to be leaving the airport at the same time and in a hurry, but once Molly had negotiated her way out and we'd joined the motorway, she said, 'Did Nat finally get in contact with you to update you on what's happening?'

'No, not a word. Has he gone back to London, or is he still at the cottage?' He might not have previously wanted to spend a night under the same roof as me, but I assumed our mutual grief and loss would change that.

'He got leave from his job and now Willow's come back again, too,' she said. 'I rang him to say what time I was collecting you from the airport and he told me he'd organized the funeral for next Tuesday.'

'Already? And without discussing it with me?' I exclaimed, shocked.

'I know it seems a bit fast, but actually it's been six days now since Julian died, Angel,' Molly said gently.

'I suppose it has,' I said numbly, 'and I expect he felt he had to start making the arrangements, though he could have *consulted* me about them! But perhaps he's waiting till I get back to finalize things.'

'Um . . .' said Molly, and lapsed into silence until we left the motorway and headed into a maze of increasingly narrow country lanes.

'Not far to go now,' Molly said, and I realized the warmth of the car had almost sent me to sleep. I roused myself and asked what was happening with the workshop. 'I suppose it's been shut all week?'

'No, Nat told Grant to open up as usual last Wednesday. He's trying to take charge and throw his weight about already.'

'I suppose someone had to run things till I got back.'

And Nat probably assumed that the workshop would be his and he had a right to do so.

'Julian would want the work on hand to be finished on schedule. We'd only factored in the usual break from Christmas Eve till just after New Year,' I said.

'There's running things, and there's taking over – and the way Nat's started lording it about, I've been expecting to find your bags outside the cottage door any time!' Molly said indignantly.

'Oh, I'm sure he wouldn't do anything like that, Molly, even if he could. Julian told me before I went to Antigua that he was making a will to leave things divided between us, even though I tried to persuade him out of it, and Nat must surely have been in touch with the solicitor by now.'

'You have to be the least materialistic person I know!' She turned her head and gave me a brief, affectionate smile. 'Nat hasn't mentioned a will, even if he knows about it. But then, he wouldn't be likely to discuss anything with those he thinks of as employees! I'm glad Julian thought of making a will, though, because things can be tricky without one.'

I wondered if perhaps Nat hadn't mentioned the will because Julian *had* changed his mind and left the lion's share to him after all. I hoped so, for Nat's sake, but I was sure in any case we would be united by the depth of our loss and able to work things out fairly. It didn't seem important at that moment.

'Whatever happens, you've always got me and Grant to fall back on,' Molly assured me rather ominously.

Despite the warmth from the car heater, I gave a sudden shiver.

I'm certain that in taking Michael into the business, Father hoped that he and I would make a match of it one day. However, from the first moment Michael set eyes on Lily, who is as tall and fair as her name, my father's hopes were doomed.

As for myself, I had at that time no interest in beaux and was still much the same thin, sallow, brown-haired little thing that I'd been at eleven. If I occasionally sighed over stories of knights in shining armour and beautiful damsels, it was not in the hope of such a man sweeping into my life and carrying me off. In fact, had this happened, I suspected that in no time at all I'd have been rendered witless with boredom away from the workshop and begging to be returned thence.

In retrospect, my life up to the point where this journal begins seems like an idyll and I was ill prepared for the events that were to follow.

But I will let the voice of a younger self I barely now recognize take up the tale.

Jessie Kaye Revell

5

Cold Front

By the time we turned into the drive, the short December day had already descended into cold darkness, but there were no welcoming lights switched on in the porch to greet us, as there would have been if Julian had been at home.

I felt the first unsettling intimation of catastrophic change, and suddenly I didn't want to go in.

'They'll probably be in the kitchen,' Molly said encouragingly as I got out and hesitated, shivering in the cold air. 'I'll come in with you.'

I'm sure she guessed how I felt and realized how hard this first meeting with Nat – and his unknown wife – would be, yet I was still convinced that this tragedy would finally bring us together, because surely he would be feeling as devastated as I was?

We dumped my bags in the hall and she'd been right about where they were, because we could hear voices from the kitchen – Nat's low, even tones and a high-pitched female twittering that must be his wife, Willow. They suddenly ceased talking as Molly pushed the door fully open, letting light and warmth flood out into the hall.

'Here's Angel – didn't you hear the car?' she said, in her best, brisk Nurse Molly manner. 'I hope you've got the kettle on, because she's freezing.'

44

Two faces looked back at me, though my eyes were immediately drawn to Nat, sitting at the long oak table, because he was a smudged and pale imitation of his father, like the last lithograph in a too-long print run.

'Oh, Nat, I'm so sorry about Julian!' I exclaimed. 'It seems so much worse that he . . . he should have gone when I wasn't here, too . . .'

I faltered to a stop, my initial impulsive move towards him to offer a comforting hug stifled at birth, for he made no move to rise to his feet and his expression remained cold and remote.

'You're finally back, then,' he observed brusquely.

'I told you she was getting the first flight back she could,' Molly reminded him. 'She'd have been here sooner, if she hadn't been out of phone contact when it happened.'

'Yes, and I feel so bad about that, but it's a busy time of the year for the Caribbean, so I was lucky to get this cancellation,' I gabbled, only half aware of what I was saying, for this was so not the scenario of my homecoming I'd envisaged. 'Otherwise, I'd have had to wait till my original flight back on Monday.'

'There was no rush anyway, Monday would have done,' he told me, and I looked at him blankly. The feeling of being trapped in a nightmare that I'd had since Molly had first broken the news to me was increasing by the moment.

'What a stupid thing to say!' Molly told him forthrightly, putting her arm around me. 'Of course she needed to get home as soon as she could.'

He shrugged. 'She chose to go on holiday and leave him on his own.'

'But he *insisted* I go to Antigua even though I didn't *want* to leave him,' I said.

I choked, looking at him for some sign of empathy that didn't seem to exist. 'Oh, Nat, it really does feel so much worse because I wasn't with him when it happened.'

Willow, a tall, slender creature with smooth margarine-yellow hair framing her long, beaky face, regarded me curiously out of pale-blue eyes. 'It wouldn't have made any difference whether you were here or not, you know. The doctor said he just dropped like a stone and that was it.'

'Oh, tactfully put,' Molly snapped sarcastically, and Willow flushed.

'Well, it wouldn't have made any difference, would it, Nat?' she appealed to her husband.

'None at all.'

'But it would have made a difference to *me*,' I told them. 'Besides, I could have helped you to organize everything. Molly told me you've booked the funeral, but we'll need to discuss the service and—'

'It's next Tuesday. It's all fixed,' Nat said flatly.

'Oh . . . I suppose it's at the village church? I know Julian wasn't a *regular* churchgoer, but he did like to slip into evensong and—'

'No, it's at the crematorium, though the vicar's doing the service,' Nat interrupted. 'We were lucky they could fit it in so quickly, this close to Christmas.'

'But Julian and I discussed it once and he wanted to be buried here in the village churchyard – we both did.'

Nat gave me a savage look, so clearly expressing his wish that he could inter me there immediately, that I was quite taken aback. It was blindingly clear that the tragedy, instead of healing old wounds and bringing us together, had instead made him even more inimical towards me, though I had no idea why that should be.

In any case, right at that moment I was too jet-lagged, exhausted and emotionally drained to deal with it. In fact, I turned so dizzy that I might have fallen if Molly's arm wasn't still around me.

'You look pale. You'd better sit down,' suggested Willow, as if

46

she was the hostess in my own kitchen, and even in my present state I was starting to be irritated by the way her fluting voice went up at the end of every sentence as if it was a question.

I ignored her, for the first time taking in the alien signs of their occupation: the strange coats on the rack behind the door, a raspberry-pink Mulberry Bayswater handbag occupying the top of the dresser. Willow was drinking out of Julian's mug, too, the one with the Chartres Cathedral window roundel on the side.

Everything else in the room was so familiar and yet so subtly changed, as if I'd time-slipped into an alternative version of my life.

'I don't need to sit down,' I said finally, the whirling in my head ceasing, so that I stood firmly again, shell-shocked but myself. 'I'll . . . just take my things upstairs and wash my hands.'

Suddenly I was desperate to be alone for a few minutes, to gather myself together.

'Good idea – and *I'll* put the kettle on,' Molly said pointedly as I turned for the door.

Willow's voice arrested me as I was reaching for the handle. 'We've put you in the back bedroom.'

I spun round and stared at her, wondering if I'd heard aright. '*What?*'

'Well, it was stupid the two of *us* squeezing into that box-room when you didn't need the big one, so we've changed over,' Nat said, with something in his eyes that told me he was relishing the situation.

I felt as sick as if I'd turned over a stone and found something repulsive under it. I hadn't realized *quite* how much he hated me.

Molly gave them both a look of searing disgust. 'This is Angel's home, so who gave you the right to take over as if you owned the place?'

47

'Because I do – or I soon will,' he stated. 'Julian was married to my mother and since I'm their only child, I inherit everything. Angel might as well get used to that from the start.'

'You're jumping the gun, Nat,' Molly said. 'They'd lived together so long that Angel was Julian's common-law wife.'

'Oh, but that has no status under the law of inheritance,' Willow said brightly.

'Well, status or not, Julian told Angel he'd had his solicitor draw up a will that divided things fairly between you,' Molly said.

I staggered to a nearby chair and sat down before my knees gave way. I'd hoped Mr Barley, Julian's solicitor, might already have told Nat how things had been left, but perhaps he'd been waiting for me to return first.

Nat's next words disabused me of this notion. 'So Mr Barley said when I asked if there was a will. Unfortunately for dear Angel, it appears that Dad died the day before it was due to be signed.'

'Oh – of course,' I said. 'He spoke about signing it the day before he . . .' My throat closed up.

Molly was frowning. 'But if Julian had had it drawn up, then it's a statement of his wishes and must be taken into account.'

'I'd hoped he would have changed a few things before he signed it,' I said. 'I wanted him to leave the lion's share to you, Nat.'

'Yeah, right,' he sneered.

'You can believe it or not as you like, but anyway,' I added wearily, 'we can discuss it with the solicitor on Monday, can't we?'

'*You* can, if you want to, but it's all cut and dried, so there's no point in us going, too,' Nat said shortly.

'That's right, because if there's no signed will and you

48

weren't married to Julian, then Nat inherits *everything* under the laws of intestacy and you're not entitled to a thing,' Willow agreed. 'I mean, you were living in his house without contributing to any of the expenses and you were just a paid employee in the workshop, weren't you? Just like Grant and that awful old man.'

'Ivan's retired, he just likes coming in and helping – and he's not awful,' I said automatically.

Molly was looking gobsmacked. 'What you've said about Angel not being entitled to anything at all can't be right. They've been more like partners in the business since Angel began making a name for her designs – and what's more, she ran it alone for months after Julian had the first stroke, besides looking after him.'

'But there was no official partnership, and though it was clever of Angel to talk Dad into writing the will, I'd have challenged it on the grounds of undue influence while he was mentally incapable, even if he had signed it,' Nat said, and I looked at him astounded.

'There was never anything wrong with Julian's mind and I didn't talk him into anything. In fact, I tried to talk him out of leaving me so much, because I didn't think it was fair.'

I was wasting my breath. Nat was bloated with gloating, while Willow had assumed a spurious expression of sympathy that I would have liked to have smacked off her face.

'Don't worry about the cottage, because we won't want you to move out of it straight away,' she assured me. 'So long as you're gone by the time the workshop reopens on the fifth of January it'll be fine. Nat's handed his notice in and he's got unused holidays to take into account, so we'll move up the weekend before. I work freelance, so there's nothing to hold us.'

'Move out . . . ?' I repeated blankly.

Willow looked scathingly round the room. 'I've got some lovely things in the flat, so a lot of this tat can go to make

49

room for it. I hate clutter – like all that junk on the dresser. I expect there are odds and ends of yours scattered round the house that you'll want to take, though?'

'I can't believe you two!' Molly said, finally finding her voice. 'You make it sounds as if Angel's been an occasional visitor for the last decade and more, not Julian's partner – *and* you owe her a debt of gratitude for running herself ragged the last eighteen months, nursing him while keeping the business going!'

'I don't know who asked *your* opinion about anything,' Nat told her. 'In fact, nobody even invited you in, so I think you ought to go – and maybe think about how secure your husband's job in the workshop will be if you keep sounding off about things that are none of your business.'

'*I* invited Molly in,' I said. 'She's my friend and there's no call to threaten her – and if you fired Grant you'd be an even bigger fool than I think you are, Nat.'

'You'll soon find I'm no kind of fool, and there'll certainly be some changes when I take over in the New Year,' Nat said darkly.

But I was now beyond thinking that one through and I got up unsteadily. 'I-I've changed my mind about going upstairs. I need to go down to the studio on my own first for a bit.'

I went across to the rack by the door and reached for my set of workshop keys, which always hung there next to Julian's, but neither bunch was there.

'I've got all the keys to the workshop now, except Grant's, seeing he's the one who opens the place first thing and locks up in the afternoon most days,' Nat said. 'I've applied for permission to administer the business, so you can all carry on with the current commissions for the present, while the estate is sorted out. The workshop's always closed from Christmas Eve till after New Year anyway.'

50

'But Julian and I work in the studio even when it's shut, because it's a good quiet time . . . and we were going to paint and fire the rest of the glass for the Gladchester Chapel rose window over Christmas . . .'

My voice broke and I turned away so they couldn't see the tears in my eyes and went upstairs, dumping my case and bag in the small back bedroom. I didn't even want to open the door to the one that had been ours.

Then I splashed my face with cold water until I was more or less in my right mind, before going back down, determined to get those keys even if I had to threaten Nat with the bread knife to do it. Bereavement seemed to be bringing out a violent streak in me.

But there turned out to be no need, for evidently there had been a brief skirmish in my absence and Molly handed me the keys as soon as I appeared, along with a lidded Thermos mug of coffee.

'Better take this with you, because you still look frozen,' she said. 'Shall I walk down to the studio with you?'

'No, it's OK, I know the way blindfold,' I assured her. 'You get back to Grant – and thank you so much for picking me up at the airport, Molly!'

'It was the least I could do,' she said, with an unloving look at Willow and Nat, who glowered back. 'Ring me any time if you need me.'

'Willow and I are off out for dinner shortly, so I expect we'll see *you* tomorrow,' Nat told me, making it sound like a threat.

'I can't tell you how much I'm looking forward to that,' I snapped, the old sarky version of myself suddenly resurfacing. I was glad to see she hadn't left the building permanently.

Outside in the cold, starless darkness, Molly hugged me, said I was always welcome to go and stay with her and Grant, and

51

then went off round the cottage towards her home in the village, while I made my way down the familiar path, edged with lavender and rosemary bushes I'd planted myself. In summer the heady fragrance as you brushed against them on your way to the workshop was heavenly.

Once I was through the wicket gate the security lights on the large, brick-built Victorian workshop came on and I let myself in through the small side door and flicked the switches on the board inside, illuminating the interior.

The familiar, warm smell immediately and comfortingly enfolded me: the mingled scents of wooden flooring, the treacly cement used to seal the finished window panels . . . perhaps a hint of vinegar from the acid used in etching glass and the earthy sacking wrapped round the smaller bundles of lead calmes. It was a combination of all of them, instantly recognizable to anyone who'd ever worked in the trade.

The original purpose of the Victorian building had been the same as its current one, but Julian had altered and extended it, so that there was now also a small office, a room with an air filtration system, for cementing the leaded panels, and a separate studio, as well as the main workshop area.

The latter was furnished with long, scarred wooden tables with half-leaded panels of the rose window still pinned by horseshoe nails over their white paper cutlines. The cut pieces of glass for another panel had been stuck with blobs of plasticine on to a sheet of heavy plate glass on a rack over the window.

There were troughs full of lead calme strips in various widths and a wall of wooden shelves holding sheets of Antique glass, but none of the mechanically produced Cathedral Rolled, which Julian and I, both purists, abhorred.

I passed the stairs that led up to the loft storage area and through into the roomy studio that Julian and I had shared.

We had a desk each and a pair of long tables, unscarred this time, used for drawing up cartoons – the full-sized designs for windows – and the simpler black-and-white working drawings, the cutlines . . .

I shivered, feeling chilled to the heart, then remembered the coffee I was still holding and unscrewed the lid, releasing the hot fragrance in a puff of steam that unfurled like ectoplasm.

I sat in Julian's wooden swivel chair: this had been where they'd found him, after he'd slid down on to the floor.

'Are you there, Julian?' I asked, for the first time feeling his presence close by. 'You might have waited for me to get back.'

On the desk in front of me was a drawing of an angel's head that he must have been working on in his last moments. My own face looked back at me – pointed chin, obliquely slanting eyebrows over slightly almond-shaped eyes, and the away-with-the-fairies expression I wore when working on a new design.

I set the coffee cup carefully to one side, then laid my head on my arms and wept.

March 1894

Ralph Revell paid a visit to Father's glass manufactory today, in order to see for himself the progress of the leaded windows destined for the porch of Mossby, his house in Lancashire, which were the last of the exterior glazing to be completed. I had been absent during his previous visits, but of course I had heard all about the commission and indeed cut some of the glass for it.

Mr Revell had inherited the property some few years previously and had since pulled down half of it, before embarking on an extensive programme of remodelling and extending in the new style. Everything, including the interior furnishings and fittings, had been designed especially for it, down to the smallest detail.

Father, upon first accepting the work, had travelled up to Lancashire to view the house for himself, then again to oversee the installation of the main windows and described to me how Mr Revell's architect and good friend, Mr Rosslyn Browne, had incorporated what remained of an existing Elizabethan wing and an ancient tower into the new house, which stood on a terraced bluff above a small lake and woodlands. He'd been surprised to find both the new building and the ancient tower rendered in white stucco, such as he'd seen favoured in the Lake

District, *rather than leaving revealed the honest workmanship of the grey local stone.*

However, the house was very light, airy and modern and the effect pleasing.

6

Spelt Out

It was late when I finally went back to the dark and silent cottage and let myself into the kitchen, switching on all the lights. I didn't hang up the workshop keys, because I'd put them on the ring with my house ones, and if Nat wanted them back he'd have to fight me for them.

There was no sign of the Terrible Two and the house felt empty, so I assumed they had not yet returned. I sort of hoped one of those sudden and hungry sink holes had opened up underneath their Chelsea Tractor and swallowed them whole. Not that you'd get much meat off Willow: she looked all hair and gristle.

The kitchen was still littered with dirty mugs and crockery, evidently from Nat and Willow's breakfast and lunch, which I ignored, though I did thoroughly scrub out my and Julian's mugs before hanging them in their right place on the dresser.

By now I was so spaced out with weariness that my head seemed to float above me attached only by a string. I felt hollow, too, but then I couldn't remember when I'd last eaten anything. I can't say I felt hungry, but I heated some soup from a tin and had that with a hunk of strange, dark bread from the end of a loaf that was in the fridge. I washed it down with cocoa, laced with a slug of dark rum. It didn't exactly shiver my timbers, but I didn't feel quite so shaky after that.

When I went upstairs I automatically walked into the bedroom I'd shared for so many years with Julian – then immediately recoiled, feeling as if I'd been both burgled and invaded simultaneously, for there were belongings scattered everywhere, and none of them mine. The makeup littering the dressing table, the stiletto shoes kicked off by the bed, the jacket hooked over the back of a chair – they were all alien.

I went out again, closing the door behind me, and along the landing to the boxroom, where I'd dumped my luggage earlier. I'd been too overwrought to notice anything then, but now I saw that the clothes from my wardrobe had been heaped on a padded ottoman under the window, while the contents of my chest of drawers and my personal effects were in a cardboard box on the bed.

Not only did I now feel burgled, but as if someone had also struck me a very low blow, one that just then I had no resources left to deal with.

I found clean pyjamas overlooked in the airing cupboard on the landing, then pushed the box on to the floor and tumbled into bed, where, despite the turmoil in my mind, I fell deeply and instantly into an abyss of sleep.

Something woke me from the depths of a comforting dream of my early, happy childhood. Carey and I had been sitting at the newspaper-covered dining table in our tiny cottage, each absorbed in our different interests. I was drawing a dead mole I'd found in the garden, the small black velvety corpse laid out to show the pink palms of the shovel-shaped front feet, while Carey was carefully taking a clock to pieces and making notes as he did so.

He had a passion for knowing how all kinds of things worked, so if he wasn't avidly watching someone lay bricks,

repair a car, or shoe a horse, he was taking things apart –
and even sometimes managing to put them back again, in
working order.

One advantage of having a carelessly bohemian mother
had been that she'd had no objection to our doing this kind
of thing in the house, despite the possibility of germs and
mess. Carey's mother, Lila, would have banished the mole to
the garden and the clock dismembering to the workbench in
the shed.

Reluctantly surfacing from this golden dream, I opened
my eyes to find myself in the back bedroom of the cottage –
and only then did the full recollection of yesterday's
nightmare homecoming rush in upon me like a dark and
unsavoury tide.

I'd slept much later than usual, for already daylight filtered through the sunflower-yellow curtains, but something
had woken me up and I wondered what it was.

Maybe it was the back door slamming, for now two car
doors did the same thing, like synchronized pistol shots.
Then came the roar of an engine and the heavy scrunch of
gravel under the tyres of Nat's four-by-four. Julian and I
could never imagine why they would need a monster off-
road vehicle when they lived in London.

The house was now silent again, as if holding its breath. I
padded down to the kitchen in my pyjamas and bare feet
and found the debris of breakfast had been added to the
remains of the previous day's dirty crockery. Did they think
we had a servant popping in and out to clear things away?
Or were they expecting *me* to take up that role, banished
like Cinderella to kitchen duties?

As I put the kettle on I spotted an envelope propped up
against the teapot on the table, with my name on it. Inside
was a brief note from Willow and several folded sheets of
thin paper.

She'd written:

We've gone out, but here's the inventory I made of the contents of the house. Perhaps you could circle whatever is your own personal property on both copies so we can go through it together later. Nat will be doing the same in the workshop tomorrow. He's been too busy with all the arrangements to do it sooner.

Laters,
Willow

PS Please do not eat the rest of my special spelt bread – it appears to be impossible to buy it around here.

So that was what the weird loaf was.

I hoped they got back very *much* laters. In fact, the laters the better.

I read the note again with a sense of disbelief, before glancing at the inventory: she certainly hadn't let the grass grow under her feet. But then, last night they'd seemed totally certain that Nat would inherit everything and I nothing at all, not even, it appeared, the common courtesy of giving me time to come to terms with my loss and make arrangements for my future.

I found it hard to believe that Julian's intentions and our long relationship, not to mention all the years of hard work and happiness we'd invested in the business and our home, counted for nothing. For a start, was it right that I could be turfed out with so little warning? Maybe it was something I could ask the solicitor about tomorrow.

I had coffee and muesli, though the only milk I could find in the fridge was soya, which tasted . . . different. I expect it's an acquired taste, like the spelt bread. Further exploration revealed a lump of vegan cheese and there was a thin layer of vegetarian ready meals in the freezer on top of the home-made wholemeal bread and perfectly healthy dinners prepared and put in there by Molly.

There were boxes of things called 'paleo bars' in the cupboard, too. I expect palaeolithic people spent *hours* beating their nuts and seeds into neat little rectangles before they ate them.

I lifted a wholemeal loaf out to defrost and then went back upstairs to shower and dress in my workaday jeans and a warm, fleecy green sweatshirt. After that I unpacked, cramming my dumped belongings away in the wardrobe and chest of drawers in the boxroom.

I was just loading the washing machine with incongruously bright, summery holiday clothing when Molly rang to see if I was OK.

I assured her I was. 'Actually, I haven't seen Nat and Willow since we got back last night and now they seem to have gone out for the day.'

'I can't believe how callous and unfeeling they're being,' she said indignantly. 'I mean, even if they're right about Nat inheriting everything, which I doubt they are, that wasn't the time or place to discuss it. And the way they spoke to you was disgraceful.'

'It did totally take me aback that they were so relishing being vindictive,' I agreed. 'But I'm seeing Mr Barley first thing tomorrow morning so I'll see what he says.'

'I suspect they're jumping the gun, because they must have to wait till probate is granted before they can do anything. But Mr Barley will tell you your rights – I'm sure you're entitled to some provision from the estate – and then make sure they behave themselves,' she said confidently.

'I hope so,' I said, and told her about the inventory. 'I think she's listed the entire contents of the cottage down to the last teaspoon! And though they're just inanimate objects, some of them have memories attached.'

'Of course they have. And what do you do about the things you bought together, or that Julian bought for you?'

Julian and I used to enjoy going to car-boot sales on sunny summer Sunday afternoons; it was one of the things we did together. Julian loved to rummage among the books and also had a thing about carriage clocks, while I adored buying pretty pieces of old china for my dresser and unusual plates that I displayed on one kitchen wall. Who paid for what hadn't been something we'd given any thought to.

I also collected old samplers, though you didn't often spot those in car-boot sales. My most valuable ones were those that Julian had bought me as Christmas and birthday presents and they'd literally have to kill me to get their hands on those.

'I'd ignore the list till you've seen Mr Barley,' she advised. 'Cheeky cow!'

'That was my first thought, but since I expect I'll have to move out at *some* point, I might as well do it now,' I said. 'It'll keep my mind occupied for a bit, because I don't know quite what to do with myself.'

'There is that,' she conceded. 'And if you start by crossing off everything that was already in the cottage when you moved in, that'll speed the job up.'

'Good thinking – and that's most of the furniture, for a start, though there are a few good pieces that belong to me, like the Welsh dresser, the rocking chair, that funny dark wood corner cabinet with the twirly barley-sugar columns . . . oh, and the black wood triangular chair with the rush seat. Those were all Gran's.'

'I wish I could come and help, but we're going over to Grant's mum's for Sunday lunch today.'

'It's kind of you to offer, but I don't mind doing it alone,' I told her and, since it was better than sinking into a black hole of misery over Julian and wondering what the future held, I got right down to it as soon as she'd rung off.

I went through the small cottage methodically, room by room, starting upstairs. There wasn't anything in the box-room of mine, except for the luggage and clothing recently dumped there, but I circled the Lloyd Loom chair and laundry basket in the bathroom. I'd bought them from a junk shop, resprayed them white and made a new padded lid and cushion from a small remnant of fifties fabric printed with jolly poodles and the Eiffel Tower.

There was a matching cushion on the chair in what had been our bedroom and a few pieces of bric-a-brac. In pride of place on one wall hung a framed seventeenth-century sampler that had been my thirtieth birthday gift from Julian, though the rest of my collection was in the sitting room.

Julian's personal effects, like his watch and cufflinks, were still in his top drawer and though I cried over them, I left them where they were. They seemed to have pushed his belongings aside, rather than cleared them out like mine.

Downstairs, the oak settle, the mahogany hallstand and the splendid carpet runner up the polished floor of the hall had already been crossed off, but I'd bought the yellow Chinese pottery umbrella stand recently, because I'd been drawn to sunny, cheerful things during the dark days after Julian's first stroke.

The cloakroom held nothing of mine except coats and boots, and the tiny room next to it had been solely Julian's studio and den. But the sitting room, cosy and cluttered, was the one I was putting off.

Time slipped by as memories were evoked by the things

we'd acquired together, even though I firmly crossed them off the list, one by one, denying Willow any opportunity to do a Judgement of Solomon and divide them into two useless halves.

The soft ticking of Julian's row of carriage clocks on the mantelpiece kept me company, once I'd wound and reset them.

The bureau held my personal paperwork in one of the drawers. I hoped they hadn't been through that, but I wouldn't put it past them.

There were boxes of photographs in there, too, mainly of windows, occasionally with either me or Julian in the foreground, as well as the annual workshop Christmas pictures: me, Julian, Grant and old Ivan. Ivan's grandson, Louis, had taken the last one. He'd hoped Julian would take him on as an apprentice when he left sixth-form college next summer, but now his future, like mine, was obscured by uncertainty.

Willow had listed every single sampler in my collection, all the antique plates hanging in the kitchen and even the bits of pottery on my dresser. It must have taken her *hours*, and was entirely pointless because I ringed each and every one.

How I'd loved my kitchen, with the big old wooden table and the rocking chair near the inglenook fireplace, which was big enough to take whole logs. A jewel-bright rag rug lay in front of it, made by Molly. I'd added to the crockery and utensils over the years, but who cared so much about those that they would carefully list and describe each potato peeler and mixing bowl?

Willow, apparently.

I was flagging, but on to the last page, and Willow must have felt the same by this point, because the larder seemed largely to have defeated her. The jams, pickles and chutneys lined up on the shelves were clearly labelled with mine or Molly's names and the dates we'd put them up and I wasn't about to come to blows over who owned the vegetable rack or the large cake stand with a glass dome over it.

'*I think Willow's head would look nice under that,*' said Julian's clear, cool and amused voice, and I turned quickly as if I expected to find him there. But of course he wasn't, even though I'd felt his occasional presence ever since last night's visit to the studio, and been comforted by it.

At the bottom of the final page Willow must have had a sudden last burst of enthusiasm, for she had even listed the gardening tools in the shed, not to mention the pots and bags of bark chippings in the old outhouse. Was there no part of my home she hadn't inquisitively sifted through? It was as if she was trying to pull out long threads from the tapestry of my life, so that it fell into holes before my eyes.

By now, hours had slipped by and the short day was fading, as I suppose the sense of Julian's presence and his voice in my head would slowly vanish over the coming days, for they were no more than an echo of the past.

It occurred to me that my life was falling into a kind of pattern: the idyllic near-decade of golden childhood with Carey, the lonely wasteland of boarding school, the joyful reunion at uni, and then the happy years with Julian. Now it was time for another lonely wasteland bit, though this time I still had Carey.

I was suddenly desperate to ring him and hear his familiar, dear, deep warm voice. I thought he must be out of rehab and staying with Nick by now, but he had had so much to endure that I didn't feel it would be fair to burden him with my woes just before Christmas.

Anyway, he'd be totally frustrated that he couldn't rush up here to support me through all this, and that was the last thing I wanted.

But still, it was comforting to know he was there. In the New Year, when things were more sorted in my mind and I knew where I stood, I'd talk to him. I might even go down and stay with him and Nick for a couple of days – but not while Willow was poised like an albino vulture over my precious possessions.

I went back into the kitchen and highlighted all my stuff in bright pink, then propped Willow's copy against the teapot, before forcing down a meal I didn't want and setting off for the workshop. I felt I could work again, now. I *must* work.

The comfortingly familiar and beloved environment folded round me like downy wings as I settled to cutting out a roundel of clear glass and grinding black enamel paint on a slab. Then I placed Julian's drawing of the angel with my face on the light-box and traced it on to the roundel, using a long, fine brush. When that had dried I added a little stippling detail with a fatter and stiffer badger-hair one, to give depth.

When it was completed, I put it in a tray in the rack ready to be fired and then carried on and painted some of the pieces of the rose window that were laid out ready, too. You can't think about other things while painting glass: you have to concentrate.

I had coffee at some point and a couple of the fig roll biscuits from the tin, which were Julian's favourite, then later dozed off in my office chair for a while.

When I woke, I felt reluctant to go back to the cottage, so it was very late when finally I locked up and set off under a cold, silvery-sequin-starred sky.

Nat's car was in the drive and as soon as I entered the kitchen, I spotted that Willow's copy of the inventory had vanished.

It would have been too much to hope that Nat and Willow would have done the same.

When Mr Revell arrived, I was engaged in painting the face of the Virgin Mary on to a piece of clear glass over a cartoon of my own design. I had been determined that she should not wear the self-satisfied and even smug simper so common in ecclesiastical windows.

I looked up as Father ushered our visitor through the room where I was working and my brush momentarily stilled, for he was the embodiment of how I imagined an angel would look – tall, slender and with burnished red-gold hair, pale skin and eyes of an unusual blue with a hint of purple, like harebells or violets . . .

He also appeared much younger than I expected, though that might have been his air of boyish enthusiasm. I learned later that he was in fact thirty-four, more than ten years my senior.

7

Clear as Glass

I got up just after five, as I used to before Julian's illness, though then my mind was always buzzing with ideas and I was eager to start each new day. That seemed a very long time ago.

But there was still work to be done. The painting and silver-staining of Julian's final window commission must be completed in the way he would have wanted.

Luckily Nat and Willow didn't seem to be early risers, so I ate my toast and drank my coffee in peace, before going down to the workshop. The theme of the window was Noah and the Flood, and I put on Julian's CD of Benjamin Britten's *Noye's Fludde* to play in the background, just as he would if he'd been there. And actually, it felt as if he still was . . .

By the time Grant arrived at half past eight, I'd painted the rest of the glass for one of the few remaining panels, ready to be fired in the kiln along with the angel's head.

I made us both coffee and, after he'd said how sorry he was about Julian, we turned to discussing the work in hand, before I glanced at my watch and told him I'd better get off to see the solicitor.

'I need to know how I stand, because Nat seemed so certain he was entitled to take over the workshop and everything straight away.'

'Perhaps he is, though it doesn't seem right to me,' Grant said, shaking his head. 'Molly told me how they treated you when you got home on Saturday, too. They should be ashamed of themselves and I'd like to give that Nat a thick ear!'

'They *were* very unpleasant, but please don't say anything to Nat,' I begged him. 'He's spiteful enough to sack you if you do, even though he'd be cutting his nose off to spite his face. He couldn't run the workshop without you.'

'Well, he's a good enough craftsman in the field himself – he's got on well at that big leaded light firm in London – so he might think he could. Still, let's see what the solicitor says first, then we'll know where we all stand,' he said sensibly. 'I've been here since I left school and didn't think I'd ever work anywhere else, but if it comes to it, then there are other firms who'd take me on in a flash.'

'I'm certain they would,' I said, because he was an excellent craftsman with years of experience. 'But let's see what I find out.'

I left him loading the trays of painted glass into the big kiln, which lived next to a smaller version in the back room.

Outside, the winter sunshine was low and dazzling and I almost collided with Nat, who glowered at me in his usual appealing fashion.

'I'm just off to see Mr Barley,' I said. 'Grant's loading the kiln.' I didn't mention the angel's head roundel, my own personal small project, which Grant would slip in with the rest.

'I suppose you're taking the whole day off?' he said disagreeably.

'No, of course I'm not,' I snapped. 'There's work to be done and I've been at it since six. I'll be back in a couple of hours. I expect you'll be starting the inventory of the workshop while I'm out,' I added. 'Grant knows what's what, but I'll discuss it with you later.'

Nat muttered something about Willow wanting to talk to

me first, probably about *her* inventory. I was starting to feel as if a *pair* of vultures was circling over me, so I brushed past him and walked briskly off. I'd intended changing the old fleece and jeans I was wearing for something cleaner and smarter, but instead bypassed the cottage and headed straight for my car.

It was an ancient dark green Citroën hatchback (paid for, owned and insured by myself, so Nat and Willow could keep their talons off it), and was reluctant to start after standing in the cold for over a week. But eventually it roared into life and I took a roundabout route to the solicitor's office, in the next village, in order to charge the battery up a bit.

Mr Barley had visited the cottage a few times and we'd also frequently met at local social events, so I knew him quite well.

He was a large, plump, hearty man, with lint-fair hair, a ruddy face and slightly protuberant grey eyes. After some obligatory but sincerely meant expressions of condolence, his secretary brought in coffee and biscuits and we settled down to business.

'This is a sad homecoming for you, Angelique, and I'm afraid there are also some difficulties to face regarding the disposal of Julian's estate,' he began. 'I've already talked to Julian's son, Nat, of course. In fact, he rang me last Monday morning, the day after the . . . unfortunate occurrence. Then he called to see me that very afternoon.'

'He didn't let the grass grow beneath his feet, did he?'

'No,' Mr Barley agreed, and then asked, 'I suppose he and his wife are still staying with you?'

'They are, though oddly it feels the other way round and that I'm the visitor, there under sufferance,' I said wryly. 'They're returning to London right after the funeral, but say they'll be back for good in the New Year.'

It was only as I said the word 'funeral' that I fully realized that it was actually taking place tomorrow and the thought hit me like a blow. I hadn't even had any input in the order of service, or the music to be played . . . nothing. I'd been written out of Julian's life.

I blinked back a sudden rush of tears and said, 'Mr Barley, I need your advice, because Nat told me he would inherit Julian's entire estate and he doesn't even have to wait for probate before taking over the cottage and business.'

Mr Barley steepled his fingers and looked seriously at me over the top of them. 'That must have given you a considerable shock, but I'm afraid things *have* fallen out rather unfortunately. You knew that Julian was making a will?'

I nodded. 'He told me just before I went to Antigua. He said he wanted to make sure I was provided for if he . . . went first and so was leaving me the business and the cottage. I didn't think that was fair to Nat and argued about it.' I smiled wryly. 'That seems a bit ironic now, me fighting Nat's corner!'

'I drafted the will along those lines, but since Julian was leaving all his quite considerable investments to Nat, in my opinion it would have been a most equable distribution.'

'I tried to persuade him to leave me a much smaller legacy, perhaps enough to buy my own house, though actually I never thought it would come to that: I always imagined Julian and I growing old together and working as long as we could.'

'One never knows what fate will bring,' he said. 'But it's a great pity Julian didn't have time to sign the will, because unfortunately it means that Nat was correct and you are quite left out of any inheritance.'

'But doesn't Julian's intention to provide for me set out in the will mean anything?' I asked, surprised.

'No, the expression of intent has no legal validity, I'm afraid.'

'Right . . . And Nat also said that my being a comr
law wife didn't give me any rights in law, either.'

'That's so. Indeed, I'm sorry to tell you that you have r
legal claim on anything other than your personal goods anc
chattels.'

'So Nat and his wife were quite correct, though they took
great delight in telling me so, as if I was all out for Julian's
money,' I said. 'But our relationship was never about money.
We loved each other and we adored our work. We were . . . *very*
happy,' I added, with a catch in my voice.

Mr Barley looked uncomfortable at this sign of emotion.
He gave a dry cough and said, 'I suggested strongly to Nat
that he himself should make some provision for you from the
estate, but unfortunately he didn't take kindly to the idea.'

'No, I'm sure he didn't, because I can see now that he's out
to get his pound of flesh for all his imaginary grievances.
Though so far as I can see, my only crime was that I lived
happily with his father for over a decade and looked after
him while keeping the business running after his stroke.'

'That's exactly how I put it to Nat myself, but he was
adamant. Of course . . .' He paused and gave me a speculative
look. 'We could ourselves apply to have provision made for
you from the estate, as a dependant, though there would be
no guarantee of success, since you were also a full-time
employee and there were no children of the relationship.'

'I'd rather beg on the streets,' I said adamantly. 'And I
don't care about the money – but I thought at the very least
I'd be entitled to a couple of months' grace, while the legal
side was sorted.'

'In common decency, Nat certainly ought to give you
time to get over your first grief and find somewhere else to
live, but didn't you say that they'd told you they were moving into the cottage in the New Year, when the workshop

ns after the Christmas break? They surely can't expect to have moved out by then?'

'They've made it very clear that they do, and Willow had already drawn up an inventory of the contents of the cottage before I got back, so she could check I only take what belongs to me personally,' I said bitterly. 'Nat is doing the same thing right this moment in the workshop.'

'It beggars belief that they should behave in such a vindictive way for no good reason,' he said sadly. 'Do you have anywhere to go to until you decide on your future – a relative, perhaps?'

'No, there's only my mother and stepfather in Antigua, though I could stay with Molly and Grant Long for a few days – that's Grant from the workshop. I'll have to pack over Christmas and put my things into storage until I know what I'm doing, and what Nat intends doing with the workshop.'

'Since he immediately applied for permission to continue the business until the legalities are completed, it appears he intends running the workshop himself. This will obviously put you in a difficult position when he becomes, to all intents and purposes, your employer.'

'I hadn't really considered that aspect of it yet,' I said. 'Whatever happens, it's my intention to finish off Julian's final commission as quickly as I can. I was painting some of the pieces for it early this morning.'

I paused and thought it through. 'Nat won't want me working there, but he hasn't got an artistic bone in his body, so he'll need to find someone to replace me. I mean, he can carry on making new windows in Julian's *style* indefinitely, but it will all get very stale. He can't very well accept new commissions as Angel Arrowsmith, though.'

'Very true,' Mr Barley agreed.

I ran my fingers through my short, tangled mop of brown curls. 'It'll be best if I pre-empt Nat by handing in my notice

when he comes back after Christmas, but for Julian's s
I'll tell him I won't leave until he finds someone else.'

'Could you afford to set up on your own?'

'No, not really, because I don't have a huge amount o.
savings and I'll need to rent somewhere to live, too. I mean,
Julian paid me generous wages and also let me take some
private design commissions, so I've got a little nest egg, only
I tended to break into it whenever I heard of anyone selling
up and putting their stock of Antique glass on to the market. Julian said I was like a squirrel storing up nuts against a
rainy day – and here it is, a perfect storm!'

I sighed. 'I expect I'll have to move away in order to get a
job with another firm, probably somewhere down south. And
I really don't want to do that, because I love this area of Lancashire. This is where my grandparents lived and where my
roots are, even if I wasn't brought up here.'

'Couldn't your mother and stepfather help you in these
circumstances?' he suggested.

'Mum doesn't have any money of her own, and though I
like my stepfather, I've never felt I had any claim on him,
and he's already forked out for my school fees and put me
through university. No, I'll find another job.'

'I wouldn't imagine you'd find that difficult, because
Julian told me your work was increasingly in demand.'

'I have had a couple of job offers from firms who haven't
realized Julian and I were a couple and I wasn't just working
for him.'

I'd always valued my independence, which was probably
why I hadn't wanted to marry. I liked earning my own wages
and in fact I *more* than earned them, for I worked longer
hours than those I was paid for: you do, when you love your
profession. Julian and I were never happier than when we
were together in the studio, working separately, but attuned
by our mutual passion for what we were creating.

mind you, that idyll had come to an end after Julian's ...t stroke, though I counted myself lucky to have had those ...ars.

I sat up straighter. Time for decisions. 'Thank you for making everything so clear to me and being so kind,' I told him gratefully. 'I'll pack up my things over Christmas, put them into storage, then move in with Molly and Grant while I finish off the commissioned work and look for a new job. It will at least stop me thinking too much.'

'I'm sorry I couldn't do more to help,' Mr Barley said, getting up and shaking hands.

'At least I've got it all clear in my mind and a plan of action. And now I'd better get back and make sure Nat hasn't added my stock of glass to his workshop inventory!'

It was still barely mid-morning and though I didn't feel hungry – I was starting to think I'd never feel hungry again – I thought I'd better have something now because I had a couple of short visits to pay before my return to the workshop.

So I had a large, warm and buttered cheese scone and coffee in the village café, while making a few notes before I set off to call on the vicar who would be taking Julian's service tomorrow, followed by the undertakers. Nat was going to have one or two surprises . . .

When I arrived home and parked at the side of the cottage, Nat's car was gone and there was no one about. He wasn't at the workshop either; there was just Grant and old Ivan sitting in the studio, finishing their lunch.

'Have a Chelsea bun,' Grant said, offering an old biscuit tin. 'Molly baked them this morning and brought some down.'

'Where's Nat?' I asked, automatically taking one and

then wondering if I could actually eat it after my scone: they were quite big.

'That Willow wafted in earlier and dragged him off somewhere,' Ivan said. 'Just as well, because he'd poked his nose into every corner of the place by then and his face was enough to curdle milk.'

'How did you get on with the solicitor?' asked Grant.

'Mr Barley said Nat was right and he will inherit everything. I have no legal status because Julian and I weren't married, so he can take over the house and business whenever he likes.'

'Well, that don't seem fair,' Ivan said, running a gnarled hand through his thick thatch of silver hair. 'And even if it's true, he shouldn't be throwing his weight about even before the burial. It ain't decent.'

'He may be legally in the right, but he doesn't have to be so unpleasant about it,' Grant said.

'No,' agreed Ivan. 'And he told us he and that pale streak of tallow he's married to are moving into the cottage in the New Year, putting you out of your home.'

'It doesn't really feel like my home now, anyway,' I said. 'Did Nat finish his inventory of the workshop while I was out, then? He said he was going to.'

'Went through the place like a dose of salts,' Ivan confirmed. 'He wanted to know what was in the locked outhouse too, but we told him it was your personal property – all those tea chests full of Hartley Wood glass you bought when Williams & Gresham in Chorley closed down.'

'I said there was only one key to the outhouse and you had it,' Grant added.

'Thanks, both of you,' I said gratefully. 'I paid for those with my own savings, though practically everything else in here will be part of the estate.'

I looked round the studio. 'My sketchbooks in the

75

cupboard and box of art material are my own . . . and my personal set of tools, of course, in the workshop.'

It was a rite of passage, buying your own pair of grozing pliers and then shaping a lathekin – the smooth piece of wood used to open up the leads to receive the pieces of glass. Then there was the sturdy oyster knife, a circle of thin metal nailed into a coronet on top of the wooden handle and filled with lead, which was used to tap in the horseshoe nails that held everything together until it was soldered. Ivan had helped me make that.

'There are your experimental pieces of stained glass up in the loft,' Grant reminded me, 'and your college pieces and portfolios and stuff.'

'Oh, yes, I'd forgotten those were up there. All the rolled-up cartoons and cutlines, too, though I suppose only the ones I did for personal commissions belong to me.'

I found I'd nibbled half the Chelsea bun without realizing it and hoped the sugar on top would wake me up a bit, because I was starting to feel dazed again.

'I don't know what's going to come of us all,' Ivan said ruminatively. 'Nat don't like me much, for a start . . . and *I* don't much like change.'

'No, nor me,' I agreed, and in my head I could hear Bob Dylan's rather Yogi Bear voice singing that the times they were a-changin'. He sounded so melancholy that I'd have given him the other half of my Chelsea bun if he'd been there.

76

*Father was so used to my presence that he did not think to intro-
duce me and I don't suppose Ralph Revell even noticed me – or
if he did, he must have assumed I was a boy, with my cropped
curls and slight figure enveloped in a sacking apron.*

*Later, Father told me that Mr Revell had been pleased with
the windows that had already been installed – and so he should
be, for they were all exactly as he wished, made to frame and
enhance the enjoyment of the vista beyond the house, rather
than impede any view of it.*

77

8

Sketchy

I'd worked on for a bit after Ivan and Grant had gone home, but there'd still been no sign of Nat and Willow when I returned to the cottage, so I assumed they were eating out again.

I had one of Molly's healthy home-cooked ready meals from the freezer, a lentil and vegetable curry with rice, though I barely tasted it because all my thoughts were on the funeral tomorrow.

It was a hurdle I had to get over, but at least I'd put my own stamp on the proceedings, now I'd thrown off the semi-acquiescent daze I'd been in when I first arrived home.

The old Angel, who let no one walk over her, had bounced back.

I was in the sitting room, sifting through the mail that had piled up while I was away, with the TV twenty-four-hour news channel on for company, when Nat and Willow finally returned. They must have heard the TV and I hoped they might have left me in peace. But no, after a few minutes they both came in, and Willow was holding her copy of the cottage inventory in one hand.

I'd wrongly assumed that even they wouldn't have the brass neck to start going through it on the night before the funeral, but Nat's first words proved me wrong.

'I'm glad you're here, because we're going straight London after the funeral tomorrow and there are a things you've ringed on the inventory we need to query.

I pushed the rest of my unopened mail back in the box was using as a temporary in-tray and gave them a scathing look. 'Well, if you're greedy and insensitive enough to think this is a good moment for that kind of discussion, fire ahead.'

Willow flushed and looked at me with pale, startled eyes. I expect she'd thought I was some weak push-over, but she was about to learn her mistake.

'We only want what's ours, there's no question of greed,' Nat said, scowling at me, which was not a good look. He was becoming more like a really badly smudged carbon copy of Julian, rather than the last lithograph off the block.

'There are several valuable items you've marked as yours, including some furniture?' fluted Willow.

'Yes, my granny left me those and I don't recall either you or Nat being mentioned in her will.'

'There's no call to be sarcastic,' Nat snapped. 'And your grandmother lived in a council house in Formby – what would she be doing with valuable antiques?'

I looked scornfully at him. 'She worked in an antique centre for years and her hobby, even after she retired, was going to auctions, house sales and car-boots. She had a good eye for quality and gave me the first sampler in my collection, an early Regency one.'

'Oh, yes, there are a lot of framed samplers about and some of them are very old,' Willow said. 'Are you saying they're all yours?'

'They certainly are, and I have the receipts for most of them to prove it. Julian gave me a few for my birthday and Christmas presents, too, but any gifts made to me are my property. I checked that with Mr Barley.'

Willow, thwarted, abandoned that tack and pointed at

ll display cupboard in the corner instead. 'There's
hole cabinet of Poole pottery.'

'Julian and I collected that together from car-boot fairs,
'cause we loved the shapes and colours, but if you feel I
might be stealing away with something worth a few pounds,
by all means cross it off the list,' I said, then pushed back my
chair with a grating noise and got up.

'I don't own anything else of any value, except my antique
green jade earrings and necklace, which Julian also gave me.
And if you want those you'll have to fight me for them after the
funeral, because I intend wearing them then – they match my
dress.'

'Green for a funeral?' Willow said, easily diverted by my
fashion faux pas.

'Green's a colour Julian loved: the symbol of spring and
rebirth and renewal. He hated black.'

I turned for the door and Nat demanded: 'Where are you
going? We haven't finished going through the list yet!'

'I suggest you stuff it up a place where the sun don't
shine,' I said pleasantly, and went out.

I felt in need of a breath of less poisonous air and shrugged
into my coat before leaving by the kitchen door. My first
thought was to walk round to Molly and Grant's terraced
house, but realized it was quite late and I didn't want to dis-
turb them.

So instead, I took a walk round the deserted village green
and then bypassed the cottage and made myself some coffee
in the studio.

I put it on my desk and then opened the cupboard where
I kept my sketchbooks – years of them, with the dates they
were begun and finished on the spines, going right back to
my teenage years. I'd decided to edge the roundel of the
angel's head with an Arts and Crafts-style flower border and

I knew I'd once drawn something similar . . . if I
my hand on the right book.

I'd left them neatly arrayed in rows in date order, t
glance at the shelves showed me that someone had rumn.
through the lot, pulling them out and then leaving tl.
stacked on top of others, or shoved back in any old place.

*'You'd better pack all those up the minute they leave tomor-
row,'* said Julian's voice. *'Otherwise they'll insist they belong to
the business and could carry on using your ideas after you've
left.'*

'Yes, I'll do that,' I said, then realized I'd spoken the
words aloud, because he'd sounded so close, so very, very
near . . .

'I wish I could take your sketchbooks when I leave, too,
Julian – and leave I must. But we'll make a splendid job of
the Gladchester window first.'

'I should hope so,' he said, though his voice in my head
seemed fainter, as if he were moving away . . .

Perhaps I was going mad, having these conversations
with Julian? But if I was, then it was a comforting kind of
madness.

To be honest, the funeral passed by in a blur, interspersed
with bizarre vignettes, like Willow attired in dead black
from head to foot, a tall, skinny raven of doom.

They went ahead in the big, sleek hearse with the coffin,
which I expect was meant as a calculated insult, though I
was much happier following in the second car with Molly,
Grant and Ivan. That was the complete cortège, though
other friends and acquaintances, including Mr Barley, were
already waiting at the crematorium. He and the vicar both
came to say a few kind words as I got out of the car.

To have the service in the crematorium was *so* not what

uld have wanted, though ironically, the windows
his making: sunny and hopeful scenes in the Garden
n, before the fall.

was never entirely happy about that snake,' Julian's amused
ce said very faintly. Then I sensed the empty space where
e had been and knew he'd left me for ever, a second
bereavement.

The vicar's eulogy, which now included a reference to me
as his beloved partner and an anecdote I'd given her that
illustrated just how special a person Julian had been, caused
Nat and Willow to stiffen and turn as one to glare at me. I
expect it was lucky that, unlike a wedding service, there was
no point at which a member of the congregation could stand
up and object to the proceedings. And by the time we were
being wafted out of the building by a booming blast of
Britten's *Noye's Fludde*, which certainly hadn't been Nat's
choice, there was nothing they could do about it.

There was no funeral feast, and Nat and Willow didn't hang
about, but got straight back into the car and left without a
word to anyone.

But I lingered, talking to the vicar and some of the guests,
so it was a little while before I followed them.

Molly came back with me, to keep me company for a
while – or act as a buffer zone between me and the Terrible
Two – but we discovered that Nat and Willow had already
changed and were stowing their bags in the car ready to
make a quick getaway to London.

Nat got into the driver's seat without a word to us: I
expect he was still seething because I'd dared to put my
stamp on Julian's service. Willow lingered long enough to
whisper that I'd made Nat very angry.

'Well, tough titties,' I said vulgarly, and she looked really
shocked, though when you spend your days in an all-male

work environment, these turns of phrase tend just to s... naturally.

'I'll let you know if the move is definitely fixed for third of January once I've booked the removal company,' s... said coldly. 'I'm hoping so, because Nat will want to be here when the workshop reopens on the Monday.'

'We'll be counting the days till you get back,' Molly said.

'Yes, but we'll try and struggle on without you until then,' I added, and Willow gave us both an uncertain look before hauling her skinny frame up into the four-by-four and slamming the door.

'If only this was all a bad dream,' Molly murmured, as the noise of the engine faded into the distance.

But as the Queen song says, there's no escape from reality.

Ralph Revell seemed to take a keen interest in the making of his windows, for he soon visited the workshop again. He much admired an interior leaded panel that was in progress for another customer, which had a design of tall, swaying red tulips against a background of light-green rippled glass.

This prompted Father to remember my existence and he introduced me to Mr Revell, informing him that I had not only designed the panel, but also cut the glass, painted it for firing and then leaded it up.

'Is that not unusual in a young lady?' he asked, looking at me with amusement and a keen interest that, being small and boyish in figure, I rarely invoked in young men.

'Oh, Jessie can carry out all aspects of the business,' Father said. 'I've never managed to keep her out of the workshop and, indeed, she's more useful than many of the men.'

'Young ladies do seem much taken up with arts and crafts these days,' he observed, giving me a very charming smile. 'I think it is quite admirable – especially when they are as talented as your daughter.'

I blushed at this compliment, for Father was never fulsome in praise, even when I knew myself to have done a piece of good work. He was called away for a few moments on some matter of business and I soon found myself chatting quite easily to Mr

Revell and telling him about the classes in drawing, desig.
painting I was taking.

When I said that, unlike my best friend, Lily, I had no s
in the more womanly occupations such as the embroidery an
tapestry in which she excelled, he remarked that I was a much
rarer creature.

I think he meant it as a compliment, but it seemed a strange
way of putting it.

9

Alchemy

Molly made us sandwiches and tea, before popping home to fetch the supply of cardboard cartons, tape and large marker pens I'd asked her to buy for me when she did her shopping.

She and Grant were going to spend Christmas with their daughter and her family in Keswick, setting off after the workshop closed at noon next day, but Molly was worrying about leaving me on my own.

'Why don't you come with us?' she suggested. 'I'm sure Rosie wouldn't mind in the least.'

'Oh yes she would, because I'd be like the spectre at the feast!' I said. 'Really, Molly, I don't even want to *think* about Christmas. What I really need right now is a few days alone here in the cottage, to come to terms with everything.'

She looked unconvinced, even when I told her I'd be occupying myself by packing up my belongings and working in the studio, but I was adamant and in the end she had to accept it.

After she left I suddenly became overtaken by a kind of restless energy and so for the next few hours I went through the cottage like a dose of salts, scrubbing, polishing and generally expunging every last trace of Nat and Willow, so it was as if they'd never been.

Then I moved my things back into the front bedroom,

while the cold late December air whirled in through open windows and carried off the last lingering whiff Willow's obtrusively musky perfume.

Finally, boneless with exhaustion, I sank into Granny's old rocking chair. The gentle ticking of Julian's carriage clocks from the other room was soothing and the old house creaked, as if heaving a sigh of relief that the usurpers were gone.

In fact, the only evidence that they'd ever been there were fresh copies of the cottage and workshop inventories, with several things I'd marked as mine now highlighted in orange, with crosses next to them.

That was helpful: I'd make damned sure those were the first things that went into the storage boxes.

I was in the studio before dawn next day, then when Grant, Ivan and his grandson, Louis, came in, we carried on working till eleven.

On Christmas Eve we usually closed the workshop at that hour until the New Year and adjourned to the pub for an early turkey-and-trimmings lunch, but this time none of us had the heart for it.

Instead, Molly brought food in and spread it out on one of the tables in the studio, like a mini version of the funeral feast we didn't have yesterday.

The future was an uncertain thing, but we were all agreed in our determination to finish the rose window as soon as possible. To that end, I intended painting, silver-staining and firing the last of the glass for it over the break, which would make a pleasant change from the packing.

By twelve, everyone had gone and I locked up and went back to the cottage to email my stepfather, Jim. I'd kept him and Mum updated on what had been happening and Jim was convinced I was being done out of my rights and wanted to engage a good solicitor to fight for part of Julian's estate.

as I told him, I didn't care about the money and I was moving on, both literally and figuratively.

He offered to bankroll me himself next and I gratefully but firmly declined that, too.

As soon as it was light on Christmas morning I drove to Crosby and walked along the beach, something I'd often done with Granny when I stayed with her during the school holidays. I don't know what she'd have made of the tall Gormley sculptures of figures gazing out to sea, but I suspected she would have liked them.

There were a surprising number of other solitary walkers, though most had dogs. Later, I knew, families would appear, intent on walking off their Christmas dinner excesses.

On my way back to the car, a message pinged into my phone from Carey, wishing me and Julian a happy Christmas. He was, as I expected, out of rehab and staying at Nick's flat and they were about to go to Nick's parents for Christmas dinner.

It was odd to think he knew nothing of what had been happening to me, but then Julian's passing had made only the local TV news, plus one small obituary piece in the national press that Molly had cut out and kept for me. I longed to talk to him, but he too needed a respite from everything that had been happening to him, so I resisted the urge and instead wished him a happy Christmas back.

'See you in the New Year, Shrimp,' he returned. It would be time enough to tell him then.

At home the clocks busily ticked away the remaining hours of my old life as I packed fragments of it into the boxes, a task I continued over the next couple of days. It all took a lot longer than I expected.

And how odd and bare the cottage looked without my stuff in it, not like my home any longer, though I supposed

that would make the moment I finally left much less c
wrench.

Having completed that task, on the Sunday after Christmas I
started on the workshop, which I didn't expect to take very
long. But it was surprising how much that was personally mine
was stored there and in the end I had to fetch a couple of old
empty tea chests from the outhouse to take the overflow.

Into the boxes went my years of sketchbooks, the rolls of
cartoons for private design commissions and competitions,
along with a few small experimental leaded panels I'd stored
in the loft. Nat had padlocked the cupboard the cartoons
were kept in, but since the keys were hung in the office, that
had been a pointless exercise.

My crazy magpie hoard of glass in the outhouse was still
packed up – I'd only opened the tops of the tea chests so I
could gloat over the contents – so they were good to go.

I'd finished the roundel with the angel head, giving it a
bright flower border and a hanging loop, and that was carefully bubble-wrapped and stowed away.

Other than that, there was just my current sketchbook,
the huge plastic toolbox with tiers of trays in which I kept
my art materials, and my own set of tools, which I would
need until Julian's final commission was finished.

And now, everything else was out of the way, I spent the
remaining solitary days absorbed in painting and staining
glass.

Oddly, many people assume we paint the colour on to
clear glass – but no, apart from any details added in dark
vitreous enamel, the glass is usually coloured in the making
of it – pot metal glass.

But sometimes one deep shade, like red or blue, is thinly
flashed over a thicker layer of clear or pale glass. This means
you can acid etch some of the top layer away, so you have

colours in one piece. And then you can vary it even ore, because if you apply a coat of muddy ochre silver stain o the back of some areas and fire it in the kiln, by a kind of clever alchemy it turns into a clear bright yellow. Or green, if it's painted over blue, orange if over red . . .

Pure magic.

I'd booked a small storage unit at a nearby depot and, once I'd got everything packed up, I engaged two men with a Transit van to move my stuff into it on the Wednesday after Christmas.

Luckily, Molly and Grant had come home the previous night and helped with a couple of the really heavy and awkward things, like the dresser and the tea chests of glass.

It looked a bit dismal in the cottage after that, with all the empty spaces and the memories, so after I got a brief message from Willow saying she and Nat were definitely moving in on Saturday the third of January, I packed my bags and decamped to Molly's house, leaving my door keys – though not my keys to the workshop – on the kitchen table.

I'd already started sending out feelers to friends and contacts about a new job but, of course, right after Christmas wasn't the best time for that.

Grant generously texted Nat offering to give them a hand with the move, but got a one-liner back saying, 'No need.'

Gracious as always.

I avoided the cottage that day, going early to the workshop by way of the separate drive from the lane. I took out the last of the painted and stained glass that had been cooling in the kiln and stuck it up with blobs of plasticine on a sheet of plate glass over the window, so once the sky grew light enough I could see how well it looked: the last interpretation of Julian's vision fused into the glass and ready to be leaded up.

Even though it wasn't a work day, Grant came in later to see how the last panels were looking, and brought me a hot cheese and onion pasty from Molly.

He reported that a large removal van was parked by the cottage and in the process of being emptied.

'I'm glad I've managed to get the last of the rose window panels ready to lead up,' I said. 'I wanted to do it myself and chances are that when the workshop reopens on Monday, Nat will put me in my place by telling me to sweep the floor, or something like that.'

'I suspect you're right, and though I know you'd prefer to stay long enough to see Julian's last commission completed, he may make it impossible for you.'

'Even if by some miracle he's stopped being childishly vindictive, I really couldn't work with him now,' I said. 'Though for Julian's sake I'll hang on till he's found someone to replace me. Perhaps I'll have had some response to my emails about a new job after the weekend when everywhere reopens.'

Stained-glass work was very specialized, but now I'd put the word out that I was looking for a move, I was sure something would turn up.

'I saw Nat briefly and said you'd finished painting and staining the glass for the chapel and I was popping in to see if you needed help unloading the kiln, and he said he wasn't paying either of us overtime,' said Grant.

'Nice. Not that I've ever been paid overtime, but Julian always gave you extra if you came in to see to the kiln, or we were working flat out all hours, didn't he? Still, at least Nat didn't come straight down and tell me to clear off!'

'I've a horrible suspicion that's what he's going to say to Ivan on Monday,' Grant said gloomily.

'But Ivan's really handy! Besides, the few quid Julian used to slip him to supplement his pension would hardly break the bank.'

'He's opinionated, though, is old Ivan,' Grant pointed out.

'Well, so are you sometimes, Grant, and I don't want you to lose your job, defending me or Ivan.'

'Oh, don't worry about me,' he said. 'I've decided I'll look for another job, though it will have to be near enough to drive to, because Molly and I don't want to move. Or then again, I might just set up on my own to do leaded light repairs. There's always a big call for that and I'm not arty like you and Julian, so I don't care much what I'm leading up, as long as I get paid for it.'

'Yes, that's an option,' I agreed. Julian hadn't been interested in repairs, only in creating new works of art, but if Grant, one of the best craftsmen in the business, chose that more mundane use for his skills, then it was a sad loss.

'I'd not take on the restoration or conservation of old glass – that's a matter for experts,' he said thoughtfully. 'But goodness knows, there are enough damaged front-door panels and broken chapel windows in that pink, yellow, blue and white machine-rolled glass that reminds me of Molly's Battenburg cake. If there's enough business, Ivan can come and be *my* right-hand man.'

On Sunday I furtively skirted the cottage and popped into the workshop, because I'd left my sketchbook behind and didn't want it lying around with Julian's drawing of the angel's head tucked into it.

As soon as I opened the door I could tell that someone – presumably Nat – had been in there. It was in the air, rather than in anything different, though one or two objects had been slightly displaced. I think he'd been checking on what I'd taken.

My sketchbook was still in my desk drawer, though, with the drawing safely tucked inside.

I wasn't looking forward to tomorrow, when the workshop

reopened under the new regime. But nothing mattered now: the cutting, painting and staining – the interpretation of Julian's genius – was completed and whoever leaded up and cemented the remaining panels of the rose window couldn't change that.

When Father returned, Mr Revell looked again at the window panel I'd made and said that he thought something similar would look very well in the inner hall at Mossby, to replace the plain opaque half-glazing.

'It would be extra expense,' Father pointed out, but Mr Revell simply shrugged.

'Also, it would make the hallway darker,' Father added, 'though since you told me you'd had most of the interior painted white since I visited, that should not be a great issue.'

'Perhaps later Miss Kaye might also design something for the window on the landing above the main staircase too,' Mr Revell suggested.

'I . . . should be very glad to,' I stammered, dazzled by those strangely beautiful purple-blue eyes. Lavender, I thought confusedly. Yes, that's the colour. Fresh lavender flowers . . .

'Good!' He gave me a beguilingly boyish smile, then turned to Father. 'Mr Kaye, perhaps you could revisit Mossby to discuss the new changes — bringing Miss Kaye, too, of course, since she will wish to see the setting for her design.'

'Well . . . I suppose that could be arranged,' began Father, as taken aback by this unprecedented suggestion as I was myself. He was quite used to paying such visits by way of business, but

94

Mr Revell being very much the gentleman, the social niceties of taking me with him were somewhat complicated.

'Excellent: you must spend a weekend with us! My sister, Honoria, will be delighted to welcome you,' he said, which made all clear.

And that was that: we were soon to travel north to Lancashire and I would see Mossby for myself!

10

Designs

Next morning the workshop officially reopened and I'd meant to turn up with Grant at half past eight, his usual time and now, presumably, also mine. But the previous night Nat sent me a terse message (did he ever send any other kind?) telling me to take the morning off in lieu of overtime and go in after lunch.

My first impulse was to ignore it – I mean, what would I do with myself if I wasn't working, except grieve and worry? – but Grant persuaded me not to.

'Let the dust clear a bit first. He'll see the huge amount of work you've done over Christmas and realize just how important you are to the business. Then he might change his tune a bit.'

'I doubt it,' I said, though perhaps he had a point, and now Nat had gained possession of both the cottage and workshop, maybe he'd mellow a bit and be slightly more magnanimous in victory. But if I turned up anyway, he might take it as a sign I was still trying to assert my authority.

So instead I spent the morning watching Molly prepare a batch of Lancashire hotpots and vegetarian curry puffs for her freezer-filling service.

After that, fortified by the excellent Spanish omelette we had for lunch, I walked down to the workshop . . . and my feet began to lag, the closer I got to it.

My Pollyanna gene curled up in a corner and whimpered the moment I opened the side door because I knew, as I walked into a heavy air of discord, that things weren't going the way Grant had hoped.

He and Ivan were leading up panels of the chapel windows on adjoining tables, and the sixth-form college term mustn't have started yet, because Ivan's teenage grandson, Louis, was busily stretching lead calme on the workbench, ready for use.

They all looked up at the sound of my Doc Martens clumping across the floorboards and I raised my eyebrows questioningly. They grimaced like unpractised gargoyles, nodded at the studio door and made thumbs down gestures.

Through the heavily ridged greenish glass top of the door, distorted shapes moved like large fish in an uncleaned aquarium.

'Ructions,' said Ivan in a conspiratorial hiss, made more sibilant by his badly fitting top teeth. 'Nat and that Skinny Minnie of his are in there and he's just fired me – only he couldn't really, because I've already retired. But he told me not to come round here again after today.'

'The way he's heading, I think he's going to cut his nose off to spite his face and *you're* for the chop next, lass,' Grant said quietly. 'He's seen me and put my wages up,' he added with a twisted smile. 'Though if he gets rid of you *and* Ivan, then I'll be doing most of the hard graft and it should be double.'

While Julian and I carried out all the designing and artwork, we'd also worked alongside the others in every aspect of the process, and when there was a commission to be completed to a deadline, it was often all hands on deck. To be part of a team, working together to produce something wonderfully beautiful – there was no feeling quite like it.

'So you really think he's going to hand me my notice today?'

I asked, surprised. 'I thought he'd want to find someone with design skills to replace me first. And I was *really* looking forward to pipping him to the post by resigning, even if it did mean I wouldn't get my redundancy money.'

'I don't suppose he realizes how much you'd be entitled to. But I told him if he had any sense he'd persuade you to stay and make you a partner, because your name's been pulling in the commissions almost as much as Julian's lately,' Grant said.

'Well, we all know *that* isn't going to happen!'

'Yes, but he must know he's got no original ideas of his own,' Grant said. 'And that's what the studio's got a name for.'

'That's right. And what does that Willow know about making a window, I ask you?' demanded Ivan. 'Nowt!'

'*Willow!*' I exclaimed.

'Yes, he told Grant that he and Willow were going to design the windows from now on.'

'I know she's a freelance graphic artist, but I didn't know she's worked in this field.'

'She hasn't,' Grant said.

'Well, actually, I suppose quite a lot of artists have designed successfully for stained glass – think of Matisse and Chagall,' I offered.

'Matisse and Chagall she ain't,' said Grant.

'How do you know?' I asked.

'Because she was talking to me at lunchtime,' Louis chipped in, looking up from the workbench. 'I was reading a manga book and she said she did a lot of illustrations for them. Graphic novels, too.'

'Manga are sort of strip cartoons,' Ivan explained to me seriously, so I must still have been looking blank. 'Like *Batman* comics.'

'They're nothing like *Batman* comics, Granddad,' Louis said long-sufferingly.

'I do know what you mean,' I told them. 'And maybe there's a market for manga-style windows? Or she might do other kinds of illustration, too.'

'Perhaps she might, but you've worked hard to get to where you are now,' Grant said. 'You're on the website and everything. When it comes to creating something modern and outstanding, Nat wouldn't know where to start and Willow's just going to have to make a name for herself like you did. She can't use yours.'

'No, though I suppose they might cannibalize the cartoons and cutlines I've had to leave behind in the loft, because they belong to the business. But not under my name. And my style is distinctive enough to be recognized.'

'Nat was rooting about to see what you'd taken when I got here this morning,' Grant told me. 'He seemed to think those sketchbooks of yours belonged to him, but I told him you only stored them there; he'd no entitlement to them.'

'Cheeky bugger!' Ivan said. 'I told him you'd only taken what belonged to you and he should be ashamed of himself.'

'They'd certainly only get my sketchbooks over my dead body,' I said grimly. 'Oh, well, I suppose I'd better go and get fired – unless I can get my resignation in first!'

When I opened the studio door, the first thing I saw was Willow, sitting at my desk, sifting through the drawers, though she wouldn't find much left in there unless she was interested in my collection of odd bits of Conté crayon, dried-out putty rubbers and shrivelled elastic bands.

The big blue plastic toolbox containing my art materials was open on the desk, the tiers of compartments pulled out to each side like wings.

'Did you want to borrow something, Willow?' I asked politely. 'Only, I'm a bit fussy about my personal pencils, paints and brushes, so it would be better if you used Julian's. You'll find them in the cupboard by the window.'

'I assumed these were just common to the workshop for anyone to use,' she said.

'Yeah, that would be why my name is stencilled in big letters on the lid,' I said sarcastically, and went over and closed the box with a snap.

She recoiled slightly, the wheels of the chair squeaking. 'I've got my own things anyway – why would I need yours?'

'Ah, yes, I've heard you're going to try your hand at stained-glass design.'

'Willow's going to be our new designer,' Nat said from behind me.

When I turned he was standing by the corkboard on which was still pinned Julian's initial design for the rose window.

'Once I've shown her how to do a cartoon and cutline, she'll soon get the idea of what works and what doesn't. I can handle the more traditional commissions myself.'

'Well, no problem then,' I said brightly. 'She'll pick it up in no time and you won't need me then, will you?'

'I don't need you now,' Nat said bluntly. 'The place is overstaffed and I've already told Ivan I don't want him hanging around after today, let alone that grandson of his. Grant and I can do everything between us.'

'So, you're giving me my notice?'

'Making you redundant, shall we say? We don't want any tribunals for unfair dismissal, do we? But we won't expect you to work a month's notice.'

I shrugged. 'I was going to tell you today that I was handing in my notice anyway, though for Julian's sake I wouldn't have left you in the lurch before you'd found someone to replace me.'

'And I already have – Willow,' he said triumphantly, obviously not realizing that if he hadn't been so quick to fire me, he'd have saved himself a whole lot of redundancy pay.

'As soon as we've sold our flat, we're going to build a big

100

extension on the cottage, including a studio space for me, so I can carry on with my other graphic work, as well,' Willow said.

'So, there it is, and I'd be glad if you removed yourself from the workshop as soon as possible – *without* taking any more of my property.'

'You know very well that I wouldn't take anything from here or the cottage that didn't belong to me.'

'I think that's debatable,' Nat said unpleasantly. 'Anyway, we're off to the cottage for our lunch now and you can clear off before we get back.'

They went out, slamming the door behind them, and though I was vaguely conscious of voices in the workshop, I was struggling to get control of myself. I thought of all the hard work Julian and I had put into the business, the happy years of working as a team . . . the difficult eighteen months I'd spent trying to nurse him back to health while keeping the business running, always hoping that he'd get better and life would resume its happy pattern once again . . .

The door must have reopened without my hearing it, for behind me a voice like dark heather honey trickling over gravel suddenly said, 'Hello, Shrimp!'

I turned quickly, thinking I must have conjured up Carey's voice, just as I had Julian's, but no, there he stood, tall, pale and gaunt, but more or less upright, propped up by the doorframe on one side and a black walking stick studded with shiny silver skulls on the other: the witchdoctor will see you now.

I told Lily all about it at the first opportunity and she teased me, saying that the handsome Mr Revell must have been motivated by a romantic interest in me. But I told her roundly that it was no such thing, for apart from my lack of inches, figure and beauty, he is very much the gentleman, while I am a tradesman's daughter – and working in the business.

He had been very friendly, it was true, and talked with great enthusiasm about his new house, having been involved in every aspect of the design, both inside and out. Everything, from the fittings, furniture and soft furnishings, right down to the smallest details such as door handles, must be unique and fit in to the Grand Plan. He had a true understanding of the workmanship that went into the various crafts involved.

A day or two later, as I was coming away from one of my art classes, I was surprised to see Mr Revell passing by, and as soon as he saw me he stopped and raised his hat. Lily and one of her numerous younger brothers had called by to walk home with me, but Mr Revell, after some conversation, somehow became one of the party.

When the same thing happened again a few days later I knew it could not be coincidence, but that he had sought me out for some reason. I invited him into the house that time to meet my aunt Barbara, which threw her quite into a flutter.

Unfortunately it also seemed to have awoken the most uncalled-for romantic ideas in her head, just as it had in Lily's, though if they could only overhear my conversation with Mr Revell when we are alone, they would soon change their minds. It is entirely concerned with architecture, art and especially glass, with nothing lover-like at all about it! In fact, I think he forgets that I am female during these lively discussions, much as Father and my cousin Michael often do, which is very refreshing.

Cursed Windows

'Carey?' I gasped, before doing something totally out of character: I threw myself on to his broad chest and burst into a Niagara of tears.

Even under the onslaught of my slight weight he staggered slightly, before gathering me in against his hand-knitted cream Aran jumper and patting my back with one large hand, in a reassuring kind of way.

'Angel – Grant's just told me about Julian and I'm so sorry! It was quite a shock because I thought he was getting better.'

'Yes, we all did . . . or that he was stable, at least,' I said, my sobs having quickly subsided to the odd hiccup and snivel.

I released myself, feeling rather embarrassed at my display. I expect I had the intricate pattern of his jumper (probably knitted for him by one of his many adoring fans) imprinted on my damp cheek. I fished out a tissue and blew my nose.

'Sorry to cry all over you. I don't know what got into me.'

'Well, it wasn't like you, but I don't mind,' he said amiably. 'In fact, it's good to be useful to someone after all these months of being a crock.'

'That's a point – how on earth did you get here?' I asked,

my mind beginning to work again. 'You surely didn't drive yourself up, when you've only just got out of rehab?'

'I wish people wouldn't keep saying "rehab" as if I've been drying out, or getting over a drug problem at some posh private clinic, rather than being stretched, pummelled and bullied back on to two feet by the NHS.'

I picked up the walking stick, which he'd dropped on the floor when I threw myself at him, and handed it back. He seemed to be leaning heavily against the doorframe now, as if he needed its support, rather than just unconsciously falling into a naturally photogenic posture in the way he usually did.

'I drove myself up,' he admitted. 'But it's OK, because I've swapped the old Land Rover for an automatic car, so I can manage without using my left leg. And I'd have been here sooner if you'd told me about Julian. Why didn't you? After all, we've swapped several messages and you've never said a word about what's been happening!'

'Since you'd only just escaped from hospital, I didn't want to cast a cloud over your Christmas. You deserved a bit of fun after everything you'd been through, Carey.'

'So did you after the time *you've* had recently! I assumed you'd chilled in Antigua and then come back with your batteries recharged to spend a quiet Christmas with Julian.'

'And *I* assumed you were going to stay with Nick for a few weeks, so now I feel guilty that you've driven all the way here to see me. I mean, I've only managed one visit since your accident.'

'Don't feel guilty, because I knew you'd been looking after Julian and, anyway, your letters kept me entertained and cheered me up. After the last one, telling me you were going to Antigua, I thought Julian must be feeling a lot better or you wouldn't have left him.'

'He'd seemed stable, or I wouldn't have gone. Though

actually,' I added wryly, 'he really *wanted* me to go, he was so desperate to be on his own for a while!'

'Poor Angel. And now Grant and Ivan were telling me you've been shoved out of your home and the workshop, too – though I overheard some of that bit myself,' Carey said.

I shrugged. 'I'm past caring and I meant to hand my notice in today anyway. I just wish I'd got it in first. Nat and Willow must have been surprised to see you – did they say anything on their way out?'

We'd both vaguely known Nat at college, though he'd been in his final year when we started our first. The fact that his father was the famous Julian Seddon, designer of the Tidesbury Abbey Heaven and Hell window, gave Nat a sort of reflected glory. I suppose it might have been why it occurred to me later to apply to Julian for work experience. And then when I landed both Julian *and* a job, Nat put me down as a gold-digger.

'Nat assumed I'd come to persuade you to do some more work for me for another programme. He doesn't seem to be up to speed on my having been dropped for the new series. He said you weren't employed here any more, but he'd consider doing it himself for some publicity. I said he could get lost, I'd only come up to see you.'

'That probably went down well.'

'He looked a bit taken aback, to be honest, and walked out without another word. But his wife – did you say she was called Willow? – was still staring at me as if I'd dropped in from another planet. Then she said, "Aren't you Carey Revell from *The Complete Country Cottage* series? I thought you'd been killed in an accident!"'

'Tactful,' I commented, though grinning at his imitation of Willow's fluting voice with the questioningly raised endings to every sentence.

'I told her the rumours of my decease were grossly exaggerated, and then Nat shouted for her and she shot out.'

'Didn't you like her? She's a leggy blonde – I thought she'd be just your type.'

'She's more like an albino stick insect than a woman, and anyway, I've given up leggy blondes,' he told me.

'Again? That's just what you said in our last year at uni.'

'I should have stuck to my guns.'

'So ... if you didn't know about Julian before today, what *are* you doing up here so soon after you got out of hospital, Carey?' I asked. 'Usually it *is* because you want me for something.'

'Not always,' he said, looking hurt. 'And I did tell you I'd be up in the New Year, didn't I?'

'Yes, but I took it as a general sometime-during-the-year kind of thing – and you always let me know when you're going to stay with us. But even if you were fit to go back to work on a new TV series, which I don't think you are, they've replaced you with that actor who fronted a series about historic houses in Scotland. I've forgotten his name – the one with dark hair and crossed eyes.'

'Seamus Banyan, and I don't think his eyes *do* actually cross, they're just very close together.'

'Does he know anything about interior design, the history of domestic architecture, or traditional craftsmanship? Has he had your years of experience, learning new crafts and skills and making contacts with experts in all kinds of relevant fields?' I demanded indignantly.

'I doubt it. I heard he mugged it all up from a script for the Scottish series, so I expect they thought they could do the same when he took over mine – not to mention persuading all the specialist craftspeople and tradesmen they needed for the project to work for them for nothing, like I did.'

'But that's your particular forte. They come because you

appreciate their skills and often they're people you've hung out with and learned from in the past. Or, like me, they do it from friendship and for the fun of being part of an interesting project, not for the publicity.'

The format of the series was that over six episodes Carey worked on restoring, renovating and redecorating one dilapidated cottage, learning new skills along the way, or inviting specialists like me to help out. In the final programme he refurnished the cottage in an eclectic manner, ending up with a beautifully restored cottage that looked as if it had been occupied by the same family for generations, each adding a layer of their own to it. The owners always cried tears of joy and amazement. Add in the factor that Carey was enthusiastic, energetic, big, strong, handsome and *very* charismatic – not to mention having that wonderfully sexy voice – and you can see why *The Complete Country Cottage* was such a winner.

'Most of my contacts told Daisy exactly that, when she got in touch with them for the new series,' he agreed, grinning.

Daisy, his ex-girlfriend, was the director's assistant on the series.

'When she moved out, she took my address book with all their contact details in,' he said. 'But they're all in my laptop, too, of course, *and* on my phone.'

'She didn't get in touch with me. Maybe there wasn't any stained glass involved in the new series.'

'Or it was because she knew we were best friends and you'd just turn her down flat? They've finished shooting the new series and it should be out in early spring,' he added.

'I don't think it's going to be that popular without you,' I said dubiously. 'For a start, it was based on your ideas, after you'd restored that first cottage you bought as a wreck and wrote a book about it!'

'Not according to the minute print in my contract, I discovered. I'm to get one mention in the credits saying the series is "from an original concept by Carey Revell", and that's it.'

'That's completely unfair!'

'It's certainly taught me to read the whole of any document before I ever sign anything again – and my agent's still in the doghouse,' he said. 'Did I tell you that Daisy's been shacked up with Seamus Banyan for months?'

'No! She didn't hang about, did she?'

'The moment she saw me lying in a hospital bed after the accident, she decided to cut her losses,' he said, his wonderful, almost violet eyes darkening slightly. 'I'm trying *not* to hope the new series bombs and she regrets dumping me, especially when she discovers what I've got up my sleeve . . . if it's a success, of course.'

'I knew it! You're really only here because you want me for a new project!' I joked, though shaken by the slight note of self-doubt in his voice. He was usually so full of confidence and practically incandescent with energy and enthusiasm.

But then he grinned at me and I saw the old Carey was still there. His face might have been etched by recent pain, but it was all the more attractive and buccaneering for it.

'I wanted to see you anyway, but something surprising *has* come up, and I'm going to need your help. And it seems my timing couldn't be better, because it sounds like you need *me* just as much as I need *you*. Everything could work out really well for both of us.'

I looked at him blankly. 'I've no idea what you're talking about, Carey,' I said patiently.

'Oh, no – so you haven't,' he agreed. 'Well, just before Christmas I unexpectedly inherited a house from my father's older brother, who I didn't even know existed until his solicitor tracked me down.'

'Now who's been keeping secrets?' I demanded. 'So, the lost heir of the Redclyffes rides again?'

'Not quite, because there's very little money and the house is in need of some serious TLC.'

'Is it a spooky Gothic mansion with a resident ghost and a ghastly secret?'

'No, it's not huge and the main part is relatively modern, though one wing *is* Elizabethan and there's an ancient tower and some cellars that are even older.'

'That sounds pretty substantial to me.'

'It's rambling, but it's no stately home, and it's been very neglected for years.'

'I'm beginning to see where you're coming from,' I said resignedly.

'It was Nick's idea. As soon as he heard about it, he persuaded me to let him shoot a pilot for a series he wants to call *Carey Revell's Mansion Makeover*. And after all, it's what I've been doing for years on a smaller scale, so it makes sense.'

'Yes, I can see it would be an intriguing challenge, but should you be taking on so much work so soon?' I suggested, even though I knew I was wasting my breath.

'Nick already has footage of me hobbling out of rehab and on Friday he came up with the crew to film me pretending to see the place for the first time, even though I'd been shown over it by Mr Wilmslow when I arrived the previous day. He's coming back on Wednesday, too.'

'Who, Nick?'

'No, Mr Wilmslow, the solicitor. Nick's bringing the crew back later, when I've settled in a bit.'

His eyes suddenly glowed with all of his old enthusiasm, as if the sun blazed behind them. 'The house is wonderful and it's *mine*. Just wait until you see it! But I'll have to make it pay somehow if I want to keep it, and the series would be a start, if Nick can sell it.'

'So, am I to take it there's lots of stained glass there that needs renovating, repairing or replacing and that's where I come in? Because if so, you're out of luck: I not only have nowhere to live, I've also lost my job and urgently need to find another – a paid one.'

He brushed these minor quibbles aside like so many cob-webs. 'Never mind all that, just wait till you see the place! There's some really old heraldic glass in the Elizabethan wing and an unusual seventeenth-century window that needs repairing, only it can't leave the house because of some weird family curse. The newer part of the house is Arts and Crafts and' – he paused, as one about to announce the clincher – 'one window and some interior panels were made by that woman you used to rave about when you were writing your dissertation on early female stained-glass artists, Jessie Kaye.'

'Jessie Kaye?' I repeated, astonished. 'You don't mean you've inherited *Mossby*?'

'Got it in one,' he said. 'I didn't realize you knew about the connection with Mossby, though. It only dawned on me when I got there and remembered you commenting on the coincidence of her having married a man called Revell.'

'Yes, I did know. There wasn't a lot written about her pri-vate life, but I found out that after her marriage she'd set up a stained-glass workshop in the grounds of Mossby and there was some of her work in the house. In fact, when I first moved up here, I wrote to the owner asking him to let me see the Kaye windows, but I never got any reply.'

'That must have been my uncle Francis, but I think only the Elizabethan wing was ever opened to the public, and that only rarely and to pre-arranged parties,' Carey said. 'But never the Arts and Crafts house, which was always a private residence.'

'I've actually seen the old part, because Grant's wife, Molly, wangled me on to a WI trip. I heard the story about Lady Anne's ghost and the cursed window, too, though not *why* it's cursed.'

111

'Mr Wilmslow only mentioned it in passing, along with a potted family history, but perhaps he'll tell me more when he comes back on Wednesday. He's going to show me the way to open a priest-hole, where there's a chest full of family documents. There might be a hint in there somewhere about why the window's cursed. It would make a good story for the series.'

'It all sounds like the start of an Enid Blyton adventure book!'

'You know, that's exactly what I thought,' he said.

I cast my mind back to my visit and the windows above the stairs in the Elizabethan wing. 'I seem to remember the windows I saw were all in reasonable repair, though they'd need checking over, especially the tie bars. The Lady Anne window was fine, too. I spent a lot of time looking at it because it was so unusual in design for the mid-seventeenth century. The motifs in the quarry panes were more like a sampler than anything I'd seen before in a window of that age.'

'There's been some recent damage to the top of it since you saw it, I'm afraid. I'm told a large bird flew into it.'

'Well, if so, it's a job for a skilled conservator,' I said firmly.

'You're forgetting the family curse,' he reminded me.

'No I'm not, but you can't just patch up a unique historic window on the kitchen floor, you know. And even if you decided to risk the curse and persuaded me into mending it, I've got nowhere to work on it now.'

'But, Angelique . . .' he began, in a cajoling voice I recognized of old, and I tried to harden my heart.

'I'm staying with Molly and Grant, but I can't be their lodger for ever. My priority is to find a job and somewhere to live, and the chances are it will be London or the south. But . . . I'd love to see the Kaye windows before I leave,' I added wistfully.

'And so you shall, Cinderella. In fact, think of me as your Fairy Godfather, ready to grant all your wishes and solve all your problems,' he announced.

'Yeah, right!'

'No, I mean it. You can come and stay at Mossby, because there's enough room for a dozen people to rattle round in. And even better, there's a stained-glass workshop in the grounds ready and waiting for you!'

'What do you mean, a stained-glass workshop?' I stared at him, and an incredible suspicion slowly formed in my mind. 'You can't possibly mean that—'

'Yes, the workshop Jessie Kaye's husband set up for her when they married is still there. I believe it was in use by a local leaded light maker until the thirties and has been shut up ever since.'

'*Really?*' My mind was whirling – it was like discovering the Secret Garden and Tutankhamun's tomb all rolled into one.

'I've simply *got* to see it,' I declared longingly.

'And so you shall!' he declaimed, still in Fairy Godfather mode. 'I've only had the quickest of looks myself, to see if you might be able to mend the window there. It's in the grounds, so I thought the family curse might not kick in and I know there's electricity and water connected, because it backs on to the stables and garages. You could set up your own business there, though it might all need a little updating, of course.'

I thought that was probably the understatement of the year. 'If it hasn't been used since the thirties it would take a lot of money to turn it into a modern workshop and I don't have much saved.'

'I think you're being a bit pessimistic – and it would be rent free,' he said enticingly. 'Your bed and board, too.'

'Oh, yes, so long as I worked night and day helping you renovate the house for nothing, as well as repairing the windows?'

'Please come, Angelique,' he said simply. 'I realize I can't manage to do everything I used to on my own yet, and anyway, it'll be more fun if we do it together!'

I thought there was genuine appeal in his eyes: he really did need me. And then, there was a strange serendipity about it all, as if it was meant to be . . .

'Why don't you come and look at it now and then decide?' he suggested. 'You could stay at Mossby till you know where and what you're going to do – have a holiday, cut yourself some slack!'

'Look who's talking,' I said. 'But . . . I suppose I could.'

'Good, because I really *do* need you,' he said, and I protested no more.

Mr Revell returned to his home in the north. The arrangements for our visit were made and soon we followed him, travelling by train to Liverpool, which to me was an adventure in itself.

A carriage had been sent to convey us to our destination and although at first it seemed to me that Lancashire consisted of mills, chimneys and rows of mean houses, we were soon out in the countryside and the ground slowly began to rise.

Father had described Mossby, but it was still quite a surprise to see the white house sitting so boldly above us on a kind of bluff, with an artfully designed series of terraces leading down to the lake and woodland below. Weak sunshine sparkled off Father's windows, with their central pattern of large octagons and smaller squares, and the plainer glazing of a kind of veranda between two curved bays.

The carriage stopped for a moment so we could admire the vista and Father informed me that the square tower at one end was of great antiquity and now connected the Elizabethan wing, which lay behind it, to the new house.

'Mr Revell told me that he demolished a hotchpotch of later additions to clear the way for the new building, but retained the major part of the Elizabethan house, since he much admired the craftsmanship of the construction.'

'And perhaps he was also swayed by the story you repeated to me on the way here, Father, suggesting that the most awful doom would befall the Revells should they remove a certain ancient stained-glass window from its place there!'

'Now, my dear, you know my opinion of such things, even though Mr Revell and his sister seemed to set great store by it,' he said. 'But the window is unusual – you will be interested to see it, for not only is it of great antiquity, it is unusual in that it was designed by a woman – Lady Anne Revell.'

'Yes indeed,' I said eagerly.

12

Caged Beasts

I told the others where I was going, and before we left I wrapped my personal set of tools in a piece of sacking and Grant promised to take those and my other stuff back to the cottage later, when he finished work.

'How's the leg?' I asked Carey, though his limp, as we walked to where he'd parked his car up the lane, made me suspect I already knew the answer.

'OK.'

I stopped and gave him a look. 'Don't try and fob *me* off, Carey Revell! I want to hear the truth, not some über-macho lie.'

He capitulated, running one hand ruefully through his thick, red-gold hair in a familiar gesture. 'Well, if you really want to know, the physiotherapy was excruciatingly painful, but I know I'm lucky the bones have knitted so well and I haven't come out of it with one leg shorter than the other, which might have happened.' He paused, then added, 'It doesn't *look* a pretty sight, with all the lumps and bumps and patchy skin grafts, but at least it's still there.'

'Yes, that's the main thing, and you'll just have to be patient and build the strength back up in it *slowly*,' I said pointedly. 'Literally, don't run before you can walk!'

He grinned. 'I know, and I realize doing too much too

soon would only set me back. I've accepted my leg is never going to be quite as good as it was, either, but eventually I'll be able to get rid of the stick and lead a normal life.'

'Your version of normal isn't everyone's, but I'm sure you will.'

'The physio gave me a set of exercises and I'm supposed to do them every day.'

'Then you'd better!'

He draped his free arm around my shoulders and gave me a hug. 'There you are, you see – I need you to boss me around, now I haven't got the nurses and physios to do it.'

'I'm not bossy,' I protested and he gave a derisive snort.

'Assertive, perhaps,' I conceded. 'But when you've got the bit between your teeth on some project or other, Carey, *someone* will have to stop you overdoing it.'

And at least, I thought, my role if I moved into Mossby wouldn't be that of a carer, as it had been with Julian after his stroke. Instead of coaxing Carey to do things, I'd instead be trying to prevent him doing too much.

'I'm going to get plenty of exercise just going over the house and grounds, getting some idea of what's there and what needs doing, even before I start work on restoring it,' he said, confirming my thoughts. 'I've only had a quick look so far, but the house is on different levels, with lots of stairs up and down in the old part, not to mention the attics and cellars. I haven't explored those yet, apart from the first cellar with the boiler in it.'

His strangely coloured eyes glowed with enthusiasm and Hendrix's 'Purple Haze' started playing in my head. He had that effect on me sometimes, usually when I was about to be swept into one of his crazy schemes whether I liked it or not.

'Along with the tower, the cellars are supposed to be the remnants of the earliest building that stood there.'

'Wasn't it because there were too many stairs that you decided to sell your flat?' I asked.

'Partly. I mean, I knew four narrow, steep flights would be a bit much for quite some time, but I never wanted to live permanently in Dulwich anyway, it was Daisy's idea,' he said. 'And actually, my uncle had a small lift put into the tower that goes up to the bedroom level, so I can use that if my leg aches. Or aches more than usual,' he amended honestly.

Carey had spent the money he'd inherited from his father to purchase a tiny old cottage in Devon, which he'd used as a base while he moved around the country, working with stone masons, blacksmiths, thatchers, carpenters, upholsterers . . . learning myriad skills. Then he'd renovated and restored his own cottage, and the book he wrote about that led to commissions to restore and make over other cottages, and finally to his hugely successful TV programmes.

'Have you sold the flat now?'

'Yes, it went almost instantly and I'm about to complete on the sale, so that will give me some capital to use to start restoring Mossby, along with the bit my uncle left me. I'll have to find some means of making the house pay its own way eventually, though. Maybe Nick will sell the pilot about the restoration and a new series, that would be a start. And I expect we'll come up with some more ideas,' he added optimistically.

I noted the royal 'we'.

By now we'd reached the lay-by and he opened the door to a large, nondescript estate car in an odd shade of limey-gold.

'This is a bit different from what you usually drive, Carey?'

'The old Land Rover wasn't going to be easy until my leg was stronger, or any manual car, so I looked for an automatic. This will still be roomy enough for when I need to transport bulky materials about.'

'The colour reminds me of those chocolate lime sweets we used to get from the village shop when we were little—'

119

I began, settling into my seat, then broke off abruptly as I registered an ominous low, rumbling growl right behind me. Turning quickly, expecting to be facing an angry lion at the very least, I found myself instead almost nose-to-nose with the most ill-favoured black Chihuahua I'd ever seen in my life.

It was staring at me through the mesh front of a pet carrier, which had been strapped to the back seatbelt fittings. Its eyes glowed like dark coals and two over-long front canine teeth stuck out as it lifted its lip to growl again.

I'd seen more prepossessing animals, but then I'd always had a soft spot for an underdog, and it was kind of cute in a little-demonic-gremlin kind of way.

I cast a questioning gaze on Carey.

'That's Fang, the dog Daisy pestered the life out of me to get her last year. She's dumped him back on me because she can't cope with him. The breeder must have lied about him being a pure Chihuahua, too, because he outgrew his chichi designer dog-carrier in about a month. That seemed to be the decider for Daisy.'

'She can't possibly have called him Fang!' I'd met Daisy a few times and she hadn't struck me as having a mind capable of being even remotely original. Or a sense of humour.

'No, she called him Tiny, but Fang suits him better. He's a vampire.'

'He does look a bit like one.'

'He bites like one, too – mostly men and on the lower leg, because that's as far as he can reach,' he explained. 'Not me, though, because we came to an early understanding that it wasn't a good idea to bite the hand that usually remembered to feed you and fill your water bowl.'

'Right,' I said, turning to look at the little dog again. I'd always wanted a dog, but in addition to Julian having an allergy to them, I couldn't have taken one to work with me.

No matter how well you cleaned up a stained-glass work-shop, there were always sharp bits about to cut unwary paws.

'I think I chose the wrong puppy from the litter,' Carey said. 'The bitch's owner assured me he was the best, but she probably just wanted to get rid of him. Daisy dumped him in the flat for Nick to find, after she'd arranged to meet him there to pick up a couple of things and give him her set of keys.'

I already thought Daisy was totally callous: first she'd dumped Carey at the very moment he needed her most, and then her dog! Mind you, I'd never really taken to her: she might be stunningly pretty, but she had a brittle veneer and I wasn't quite sure what would be underneath if it cracked. Nuts, possibly.

'Poor little thing! Did Nick look after him till you got out?'

'No, he'd already bitten Nick, so he wasn't very keen. I had to put him in kennels, but even they asked me to take him away again a few days later, which is why I've had to bring him with me. I'd like to re-home him, but I'll need to get a dog psychiatrist on to him first. Dog rescue centres don't want pets that bite.'

'You should keep him for company,' I suggested, and peered into the cage again. 'Hello, Fang. Who's a cute little boy, then?' I cooed.

Fang stopped growling and fixed me with an incredulous stare from his slightly protuberant eyes, as did Carey (though happily *his* eyes aren't protuberant).

'Has this nasty man misunderstood your deep, dark and troubled soul?' I continued, and Carey snorted with laughter as he drove out of the village and set off down the network of small lanes as if he knew the way back to Mossby by instinct. Some people just have the ability to glance at a map once and they know where they are – not a knack I possess myself.

121

We finally emerged on to a larger road I recognized, which connected the village of Middlemoss with Great Mumming. We passed a large hotel and a petrol station by the turn to Halfhidden, a hamlet that had been in the local news quite a bit lately. I was going to tell Carey about it when, round the next bend, Mossby itself suddenly appeared like a mirage: a white, strangely modern stucco façade perched high above us, a square stone tower forming the left corner. A steep series of terraces dropped down to a lake below, where there was an old boathouse. Even though I'd been there once before, it was still dramatic enough to make me catch my breath.

Carey pulled in, so I could get a good look at it.

'Picturesque, isn't it?' he said. 'Mind you, the natural stone would have fitted into the landscape better, but there are a lot of white Arts and Crafts houses in the Lake District, so it's not that unusual for the time. You can't see the Elizabethan wing and the servants' quarters – they're behind it.'

We set off again and passed through a pair of open wrought-iron gates. In fact, they didn't look as if they were capable of closing, for weeds grew up around them and one was leaning at a distinct angle.

'Does the Lodge belong to you, as well? It looks quite big, as they go.'

'It is part of the estate and it's surprisingly large. Apparently Ralph Revell had it built for his friend, the architect of Mossby, Rosslyn Browne. It was completed before the house itself.'

'You know a lot about the place already,' I said as he stopped so I could get a good look at it. It was a sort of no-frills mini-Mossby, the two small bay windows linked by a porch rather than a veranda.

'That's because the solicitor, Mr Wilmslow, started to drip-feed me the family history the moment I stepped through the door last Thursday. Wilmslow & Parbold have been the Revells' solicitors for generations, so I expect he knows all our secrets. Ella and Clem Parry live in the Lodge,' he added. 'She's my uncle's stepdaughter by his second marriage. He employed her as housekeeper and Clem as gardener and let them live there rent free.'

'What are they like?'

'He's very pleasant and an excellent gardener, but she's a bit grim and unwelcoming. Mr Wilmslow said she persuaded my uncle into making a will last year, assuming she'd inherit Mossby, so when I came out of the woodwork it must have been a nasty surprise.'

'Didn't your uncle leave her *anything*?'

'No, apparently he'd never liked Ella and felt he'd been more than generous in offering the Parrys employment and a roof over their heads. Clem lost his previous job due to an alcohol problem about fifteen years ago but he hasn't fallen off the wagon since. And my uncle needed someone to run the house, because his health was deteriorating even then. He must have been a creaking gate, though, because he was ninety-one when he died.'

'She being his stepdaughter, I can see why Ella would be upset that he hadn't acknowledged that in his will,' I suggested.

'That's just what I thought at first, but it's not quite so cut and dried: he'd never adopted Ella and she was seven when her mother died and she was sent to live with an aunt. He continued to support her financially through school and college, too, so Mr Wilmslow said she didn't have any grounds to claim against the estate.'

'Julian's solicitor said *I* might have a claim on his estate as a dependant, but I wasn't one; I've always earned my salary,' I said. 'Are the Parrys going to stay on?'

'I don't know – I'll need to have a discussion with them about that when I've found my feet. Clem's more than worth his generous salary as a gardener, but I don't need a house-keeper and she doesn't seem to do much. She does act as tour guide on the rare occasions when the Elizabethan wing is opened up for a coach party.'

That rang a bell. 'Oh, I'm sure she was the one who showed us round when I came on that WI trip! Tall, dark hair and eyes, long beaky nose – reminded me of Mrs Danvers, the evil housekeeper in *Rebecca*!'

'Yes, that sounds like her – she made me think of Mrs Danvers, too.'

I looked at him curiously. 'I thought you only read non-fiction and Terry Pratchett?'

'I ran out of anything to read in the hospital and it was that or a lot of ditsy novels about cupcakes and fairy-wing repair shops by the beach.'

'I don't think I've come across the fairy-wing repair shop one,' I mused.

'Probably not: I made it up.'

'Maybe you should write it?' I suggested, then reverted back to the subject in hand. 'So, you have a gardener and a housekeeper. How about a butler and two footmen?'

'Ho, ho,' he said.

A movement caught the corner of my eye. 'The curtain in one of the front rooms just twitched. I think someone's watching us,' I said uneasily. 'I suppose it is rather nosy of us to park opposite the Lodge and stare.'

'I can park anywhere I like on my own estate,' Carey declared grandly, but started the car again and drove up the hill, between banks of overgrown rhododendrons. Paths seemed to dive off down small dark tunnels of undergrowth towards the lake on the left, but we carried on until the drive started to level out a bit.

'Here's the stained-glass workshop coming up on the right,' he announced, slowing. 'I've got the keys with me,

124

because when I found out about the Jessie Kaye connection I thought you wouldn't be able to resist coming back with me for a quick look. Do you want to see it now?'

'Of course I do!' I said. 'I can't wait!'

The day was drawing in as we passed through a pair of wonderfully ornate and gilded wrought-iron gates, guarded by a substantial lodge.

The drive curved uphill and passed some outbuildings, including what looked incongruously like a small mill, or something of that kind. Father told me the present Mr Revell's father had built it in order to employ some of the local people in the making of hosiery, or some such thing, though it was not now in use.

'Except as a workshop by those employed in building and furnishing Mossby. But now all is nearly completed, I believe Mr Revell intends to demolish it. The stables and a walled garden lie behind.'

Little did I know then that it would one day become my place of refuge and solace, or I might have paid more attention to it. But we had passed on towards the house and I felt an eager sense of anticipation.

13

Love at First Sight

The building was not too dissimilar to Julian's workshop – low, brick built and with long windows to let in as much light as possible. It was partly concealed behind a beech hedge that still bore a few tattered bronze leaves.

'If we followed that branch of the drive behind the workshop, there's an extensive range of old stables and outbuildings round a courtyard, but we'll stop here.'

Once he'd pulled in, I insisted Carey get poor Fang out of his carrier and he must have been desperate for a pee, because he shot off and watered a nearby bush for about five minutes. After that, though, he trotted back to Carey.

'Won't he run off if you don't put him on a lead?'

'No, he prefers hanging around my feet, trying to trip me up,' he said, which seemed to be true because Fang followed him as closely as a tiny shadow.

I thought the poor little creature was probably clinging to Carey as the only familiar thing in an uncertain, ever-changing and threatening world, but I didn't say anything.

I waited impatiently while Carey unlocked the workshop door and led the way into a big, light room full of dust motes and cobwebs.

'It's got electricity,' he said, demonstrating by flicking on and off the series of dim bulbs that hung down the centre of the room in metal cages, 'and running water. It backs on to a stable they turned into a garage with a flat over it for the chauffeur, in the days when they had such things.'

'Those lights look a bit more recent than the thirties,' I said, gazing round.

'My uncle had thoughts of renting it out again at one time, but in the end I think he decided it would cost more to renovate it than he would get back.'

'It was obviously lit once by gas,' I said, surprised. 'See, there are the old brackets on the wall.'

'Mossby actually had its own private gas-making plant – one of the earliest in the country,' he told me. 'My ancestors seem to have been very innovative.'

'I prefer a gas soldering iron to an electric one,' I said. 'But I can always run it off a cylinder.'

'Or we could have a storage tank outside and pipe it in,' he suggested, but by then I was exploring.

In addition to the main area, there was a collection of smaller rooms with plenty of space to house everything I needed. The final door I opened even revealed a freezing cold cloakroom, with a white Victorian loo and no washbasin.

'All mod cons,' said Carey enticingly, like an overeager estate agent. 'Just needs a little updating.'

I gave him a look, then returned to examine the main workshop area more carefully. It was all very familiar, for nothing much has changed in the way leaded windows have been made over the centuries. And Jessie Kaye would actually have stood and worked at one of these long, wooden, dust-laden tables! I brushed the furring of ages from the top of the nearest one and revealed the indentations where the horseshoe nails had held the glass pieces together during the leading-up process. One of the tables would be smooth-surfaced, though, for drawing cutlines and cartoons. In the days before light-boxes, glass would always be cut on the

128

table, laid over the cutline, the drawing that marked the position of the leads.

There were deep stone sinks and wooden work surfaces with tall, leather-topped stools. In fact, now I'd had a chance to take it all in, I thought it resembled a time capsule, for there were still crusted jars of pigment, a large pestle and heavy glass grinding tile, a pair of rusted grozing pliers tossed down on a bench and a tall and deep wooden rack that would once have held the store of coloured sheet glass. There was even an old hand mill for producing lead calme from cast blocks. I couldn't imagine why the last leaded light maker to rent the place hadn't sold those off when he retired, though there was no actual lead or glass, so presumably everything of real value had been removed by the last tenant.

'So, what do you think?' Carey asked finally, sounding amused. 'Will it do?'

'It's wonderful!' I sighed. 'And it's in a much more workable state than I expected, too.'

'Great, I knew you'd love it!'

'I do – but by workable I didn't mean I could move right in and set up shop. It needs so much doing first – the electricity updated and extended, for a start, and a heavy-duty cable for the kiln installed. And hot water as well as freezing cold would be good.'

'Minor details,' he said dismissively.

'*Expensive* minor details,' I said firmly. 'And I'd have to have an air filtration system in one of the other rooms.'

'What for?'

'The cementing process generates a lot of dust, because you clean the panels off afterwards by brushing powdered whitening over them. You don't really want to be breathing that in.'

'I wish I'd got round to learning more about the leaded light process when I used to visit you,' he said. 'I always

129

meant to – but then, I had you to help me with the programmes when I needed it.'

'It's not exactly something you can do at one end of the garden shed, either,' I said. 'Or not on any kind of professional level.'

I shoved my hands in the pockets of my padded coat for warmth, mentally doing a rough calculation of the costs and comparing them with my modest nest egg.

'The air filtration system will be pricey and so will a kiln. I'd need more wooden racking for glass and lead calme storage, and, of course, lots of Antique glass and lead . . . big rolls of cartridge paper, light-boxes, silver stain, glass paints, brushes, glazing cement – you can buy that ready-made these days – acid for etching, horseshoe nails, soldering irons, tallow, solder, resin . . .'

'That's going to be one hell of a big shopping list,' he said.

'Renovating and updating the actual structure of the building will be your part of it: a washbasin in that toilet would be good, for a start. I don't suppose you're on mains drainage?'

'We are now, though until fairly recently there was a cesspit, or a septic tank, or whatever.'

'Oh, right. I suppose Mossby isn't really cut off from civilization. Not that it matters if my workshop is out in the sticks,' I added.

'There aren't many houses nearby, other than the Lodge and Moel Farm up above the house. There's a gate to that, but it's kept locked and never used, because my uncle fell out with the current tenant of the farm. Before that, you could drive over the tops and come out in the middle of Halfhidden, the village in the next valley. I'm told it has a couple of shops.'

'*And* ghosts,' I said.

'Ghosts?'

'I was going to tell you about it before, when we passed the turning on the road. Someone enterprising has created a ghost trail right round Halfhidden to attract more visitors and there was already a haunted Roman spring, with healing properties. It used to be a popular local spa in Victorian times and people would come and drink the waters and stay at the Spa Hotel – which is that one we passed on the road just before we got here.'

'I thought that was called the Screaming Skull? I noticed it, because they do food,' he said. 'But the name seemed weird. We'll have to look into this ghost trail – it could make a good angle for the series, because we've got a family ghost, too.'

'Do you mean the Grey Lady, thought to be Lady Anne, the seventeenth-century chatelaine who designed that window? She was mentioned on that tour of the Elizabethan wing.'

'Yes. Allegedly she paces round one of the bedrooms, moaning and wringing her hands. Then sometimes a young girl runs screaming along the gallery.'

'Nice,' I said appreciatively.

'I must tell Nick about Halfhidden and the ghost trail – he'll love it. Maybe Mossby can even become part of the tourist trail eventually. I'll have to think about that,' he mused.

Fang returned from an exploratory foray under the work tables and jumped up at my legs, though not in a savage kind of way. I got the message and picked him up. A small pink tongue licked my chin.

'Free dog with every workshop,' Carey enticed me, back in ingratiating estate agent mode. 'Free dog with every *free* workshop.'

'If you mean Fang, I've had more tempting offers,' I told him. Fang looked at me in a hurt way, so I cuddled him. 'I didn't really mean it, poppet. You're cute.'

'I'm cute, too,' Carey said appealingly, 'though I draw the

line at licking your chin after that dog, just to persuade you into agreeing to move in.'

'I'm immune to your charms,' I told him, though actually, when the full force of his enthusiasm and charm was turned my way, I tended to be putty in his hands. Just thinking of some of the scrapes he got us into as children made me shudder.

'Come on, Shrimp, let's go up to the house, thaw out over a hot drink and discuss things,' he suggested and, though I was reluctant to leave the workshop, I realized I was partially glaciated and reluctantly allowed myself to be ushered out. I glanced at his face as I passed him and he was looking annoyingly smug.

He knew he had me: I'd never be able to resist taking over Jessie Kaye's workshop.

The carriage turned into a circular gravel sweep with a central fountain and drew up in front of the porch.

I had little more time than to cast an astonished glance at the white and black ornate intricacy of the ancient wing to the right, for both our host and his sister had come out to greet us.

For some reason I had imagined Miss Revell to be younger than her brother, but she looked to me much closer to forty than thirty. She was very tall and unfortunately had inherited only a watered-down version of the family colouring, with sandy hair and pale-blue eyes.

She welcomed us with cold civility and I had the impression she had taken me into instant dislike. But perhaps it was just that she considered herself to be a cut above entertaining tradesmen and their daughters as weekend guests and particularly a tradesman's daughter who worked in the glass manufactory.

Ralph, however, held my hand for longer than was due to mere politeness and told me with a warm smile that he was delighted to see me and looked forward to showing me his home.

The glow in his eyes was, I was certain, entirely due to the prospect of showing Mossby off to someone who would appreciate every detail . . .

14

The Dust of Ages

When we got back into the car, the short January day was as faded as an underexposed photograph.

The white façade of the Arts and Crafts house might front boldly on to the drop down to the lake and woods, but the main entrance was to the rear, as I knew from my coach trip.

Carey turned left into a gravelled courtyard, circled a small knot garden with a lichen-stained stone fountain at its centre, consisting of a bizarre sea creature disporting itself above a large scallop shell, and finally scrunched to a halt before an imposing entrance porch flanked by lollipop-shaped topiary. The Elizabethan and servants' wings on either side formed a squared-off U shape behind the new building and the tower, but the white stucco blended well with the black and white intricacy of the older building.

It was several years since I'd made that brief visit with the WI, but I remembered the coach had parked in a level area on the other side of the drive, just above the workshop, and we'd been ushered along a small pathway to a side door, where the rather grim-faced guide I now knew to be Ella Parry had awaited us. At the time, I'd been more interested in seeing the windows than the rest of it, which was probably why my memory of anything else was a bit patchy.

'Here we are, welcome to the House of Revells.'

'My little place in the country,' I said sarcastically, and Carey grinned.

'The central part really *is* just an overgrown cottage, you know, Angel. Unless you count the servants' quarters and the Elizabethan wing, there are only six bedrooms.'

'Only six? How on earth will you manage? Won't Fang want a lordly chamber of his own?'

Fang was sitting on my knee, looking at the sea creature looped about the fountain with narrowed eyes. He was either an outraged art historian or suspected it might leap off and attack him.

'I expect I'll survive with a mere six bedrooms, because if I have a houseful of visitors they can overflow into the servants' wing. Arts and Crafts houses were generally built for the well-to-do middle classes, so they were usually fairly modest,' he added.

'Go teach your grandmother to suck eggs,' I told him rudely. 'Don't forget that I know all about the Arts and Crafts movement from writing that dissertation on the rise of the female stained-glass craftworkers in the late Victorian era.'

'So you do, my little in-house expert.'

'Not yet,' I said. 'Anyway, I assumed the Revells were gentry, not middle class? There were lots of family coats of arms in the windows I saw on my visit.'

'Originally they were minor gentry – there's a portrait of one who is supposed to have briefly made a hit with Elizabeth I – but the last of the line was female and married a plebeian, but extremely wealthy, factory owner in the middle of the nineteenth century, so I'm afraid my blood probably isn't even a watered-down blue.'

'I suppose he was the Revell who built the workshop?'

'That's the one, giving employment to the locals,' he agreed, then reached over for his skull-studded stick. 'Come on, I'm dying for a cup of tea.'

I put Fang down and we followed Carey as he limped away from the porch to a small side door into the service wing. Inside was a stone-paved passage with several intriguingly closed doors off it, which led to a large kitchen.

It was a strange hybrid: you could see the remains of what must have been the last word in modern kitchen furnishings and appliances at the end of the nineteenth century, overlaid with the changes and additions of ensuing generations. There was a large, ancient and well-used table and two shiny benches up the middle of the room, while one long wall was fitted with modern units, an electric oven and hob and a very large fridge.

Actually, when I came to think of it, it already resembled the eclectic effect of one of Carey's finished cottage makeovers!

Fang made a beeline for a cushioned basket next to the huge range set in an inglenook, which was radiating warmth.

'This is nice,' I said appreciatively. 'It wouldn't need much to make it quite cosy and home-like.'

'True, though all the electric wiring in the house could do with an overhaul to make sure it's safe, because it's been put in and extended piecemeal. This servants' wing has a lot of old wiring, especially in the bedrooms and some of the rooms off the passage.'

'I was dying to open all those doors when we came in,' I confessed.

'There's nothing terribly exciting behind them if you do: a utility room, scullery, boot room, a little parlour for the housekeeper . . .'

He looked at me, the familiar enthusiastic glow lighting up his eyes. 'I haven't really checked them out properly yet. There's still lots to explore. Maybe we can have a good look round together tomorrow, when you move in.'

He seemed to be taking that very much for granted.

'*If* I move in,' I corrected him.

'Of course you're moving in, Shrimp,' he said. 'I need you and you need the workshop. Anyway, how could you resist being here on Wednesday, when Mr Wilmslow comes back to reveal the hidden chamber containing the family secrets? You don't want to miss that!'

'But what if there's a skeleton in the family cupboard, one so terrible that no one but a Revell must ever know anything about it!'

'I sincerely hope there is, because then you can help me decide how best to exploit it for filthy lucre, starting with giving it a starring role in the *Mansion Makeover*,' he said flippantly.

I sat down at the dark wooden table that had been worn and marked by centuries of use, while he made a pot of tea and got out mugs and a wooden biscuit barrel with tarnished silver fittings.

'I'm afraid there are only arrowroot biscuits on the premises and they're a bit limp,' he said, offering it to me. 'My uncle seems to have been on a bland diet for the last few months of his life, because the freezer in the scullery is full of mushy stuff like mince and mash, fish pie, macaroni cheese and that kind of thing. And the cupboards are stacked with tinned soup, rice pudding and semolina.'

'Lovely. You need building up a bit, but I don't think that kind of stodge is going to tempt your appetite.'

'Mrs Danvers' not very strenuous duties included preparing dinner – by shoving it in the microwave from the look of things – but apparently the nurses took care of breakfast and lunch.'

'I'm not surprised, if they had to eat the same pap for dinner as your uncle. I expect that's all he could digest, though,' I suggested. 'What else did your very own Mrs Danvers do for her extravagant salary?'

'So far as I can see, not a lot. She ordered supplies, arranged for the cleaners and carers to come in, and sorted out the laundry for collection: nothing terribly hard or time consuming. But her husband, Clem, seems to do the work of five men in the garden, so I suppose it sort of evens out.'

'*Is* there much actual garden?'

'The way the land rises behind the house means there isn't a formal garden, other than that small knot in the courtyard and the shrubbery round the parking area and down the drive, mostly rampant rhododendrons. But the terraces going down from the house to the lake have rockeries, stone troughs and flowerbeds on every level, so that keeps him busy.'

'Yes, those terraces must take a lot of work,' I agreed.

'Clem told me there's an old walled kitchen garden behind the garages and stables, but it fell out of use before he came here. I haven't found the key to the door yet, but there's a tin box of them in the boot room to go through.'

'Nick will be entranced by the idea of a secret garden!'

'It's not secret, just unused and overgrown. But yes, he's going to be delirious with pleasure when he finds out about it.'

'Let's hope he's just as delirious when he and his film crew find themselves hacking their way in and digging vegetable beds while they're at it,' I said tartly, and he grinned.

'You won't need Mrs Danvers to cook because you can do that yourself, and Grant's wife, Molly, runs a business filling freezers with her own lovely home-cooked and healthy dishes, so you could have some of those for back-up when you don't feel like doing the catering.'

'Sounds good – especially since I know your cooking skills of old.'

'I *can* cook!' I protested indignantly. 'It's just that there's usually something more interesting to do.'

'We'd have to get rid of Mrs Danvers' ghastly frozen stodge before we could refill the freezer,' he said. 'Seems a pity to throw it out, though. She's going to come as usual this Friday to let the cleaners in and so on, till I decide what's happening.'

I looked round and noted all the signs of neglect in the kitchen, like the dull range, the dusty ceiling light, and the tarnished silver mountings on the biscuit barrel. 'The cleaners don't seem to be putting a lot of effort into their work.'

'They're only here for a couple of hours once a week and they strip and make beds and do any ironing in that time, too, so vacuuming the floors, cleaning the bathrooms and having a quick dust is probably all they've got time for. But the panelling in the old wing is immaculately polished: Ella said she cleans that herself and it's obviously a labour of love.'

'Well, that must be worth part of her wage, at least – and she shows visitors over it, too.'

'Once or twice a year? Big deal!'

He put down his mug and smiled at me, his wonderful purple-blue eyes glowing in the way that I sometimes think makes him look slightly loopy, but in a good way.

'You have to find somewhere to live and work and I've got the space and the workshop – plus, I need you.'

'To mend the cursed window and as general dogsbody?'

'No, as my best friend. I think you're the only person I could bear having around me the whole time just now,' he said honestly. 'We know each other so well and we've even lived together before.'

'But with Nick and some of the others,' I pointed out. There had been quite a group of us renting the student house together when we were at college. It had been chaos, in a fun kind of way.

'Well, when Nick, Sukes and the rest of the unit are staying here, it'll be just like old times, won't it?' he said.

'You mean, you cook vats of spaghetti bolognese, nobody washes up for a week, there's an endless party in the living room with empty bottles everywhere and someone's new girlfriend is throwing up in the only bathroom?' I asked.

'Well, no, perhaps not quite like that.' He gave me the borderline loopy grin again. 'Come on, Shrimp, what do you say?'

He knew the answer: after the last couple of weeks I needed a safe haven, and he was it.

'Equipping the workshop will take all of my savings,' I said cautiously. 'You'd have to be responsible for the fabric of the building – any repairs, structural work, plumbing and electrics.'

'Of course, and you can have it rent free until you're in profit, plus live here rent free for as long as you like,' he said. 'Nick can come and film us cleaning the place up and planning what you need – but there's no rush to start on it, is there? You could do with a couple of days' break and *I* could do with someone to bounce ideas off.'

'I expect you mean someone to follow you round noting down endless lists of things to do to the house and grounds,' I said resignedly.

'It'll be fun,' he coaxed.

I wasn't sure, after the last couple of years, that I remembered what fun was like.

'Oh, well, I am actually longing to go over the whole house, and *dying* to see all the glass. But not today, because it's getting late and dark so I ought to get back to Molly's.'

'I wasn't going to let you see it today anyway, because I knew all that Art and Crafts glass would draw you back like a magnet.'

'You know me too well,' I admitted, getting up.

'Before we go, I will just let you have a quick look at the bedroom you'll have. Come on, we'll go up the backstairs.'

The steep flight of wooden stairs came out by a baize-lined door to the family's quarters, which matched one in the passage below.

140

'Separating the riff-raff from their masters,' Carey said. 'The nursery suite and servants' bedrooms are to the right, but we go this way.'

He opened the baize door, revealing a corridor on a grander scale, with a plush red carpet down the middle. The walls were a dark, soupy brown.

'The interior of the house was originally almost all painted a soft white – there are some photographs downstairs that show it like that,' he said. 'It's going to be some job getting it back to how it should be. I mean, this dark varnish is bad enough, but why on earth comb a wood-effect pattern into it, when it *is* wood underneath?'

'I think that's a fairly recent addition. Wasn't it a popular look in the fifties?'

'I don't know, but it's not popular with me,' he said. 'The main staircase comes out further along. There's a half-landing with a stained-glass window you'll see when you come back tomorrow.'

'Tease,' I said.

'The best rooms face over the lake and woods, and there's a big bedroom at either end of this corridor, each with a bathroom next door. We have all mod cons at Mossby: there's a cloakroom downstairs off the hall and the servants have one in their wing.'

'You could soon be known as "Four Toilets Revell",' I suggested.

'I'd rather not. You'll love the toilet off the entrance hall, by the way – it's got an amazing blue glazed print of Windsor Castle inside the bowl.'

'I can hardly wait to see it and I'm sure it'll become my favourite,' I said gravely.

'My room was my uncle's, so it has a connecting door to the bathroom of fairly recent date. There's a sort of little kitchenette affair in a small room across the landing, too, where I assume the nurses brewed the tea and that kind of thing. I thought I might be able to turn it into a shower room eventually. The tower's next to my room and connects to the Elizabethan wing on both floor levels and the lift is in there, too.'

He opened the first door we came to, on the left. 'This is the corresponding room to mine, so when no one else is staying we'll have a bathroom each.'

The room was very large and I was drawn immediately to the window, though it was too dark to see much of what must be a stunning view out of it, down the terraces to the lake and woods.

Carey said musingly, 'I have no idea what's under that horrible wallpaper above the panelling. And why paint the woodwork dark green? It's the sort of municipal shade they use on park benches.'

'Who knows?' I said. 'But the bed is lovely, isn't it? Very Arts and Crafts! And that tapestry, too . . .'

I peered at it. It was a little faded, but seemed to be the Lady of Shalott.

'The room will look so much better when I've finished with it,' Carey said, which it would. Carey's art in transforming houses always made me think of the way diamond cutters could reveal the beautiful gem inside a dull pebble. He was not the kind of historical purist who wanted to strip a house right back to the probably hideously uncomfortable and impractical original, just pare back the worst excesses from successive periods, without removing its character.

He felt that a cottage that had been occupied for generations should show signs of it – layers of individuality, but with the original bones of the house showing through. It was an art I really admired, along with his unquenchable thirst for learning new skills.

Of course, the downside was that he got bored quickly

and moved on to the next thing, but he didn't forget anything he'd learned to do, it was just added to his extensive repertoire.

When we were children, this succession of short-lived enthusiasms used to drive me mad, but I came to understand how they fused together later, in his work.

'If the rest of the house is like this, then it will need some extensive TLC – starting with a damned good spring clean!' I said. 'Someone could at least have polished the furniture and the windows occasionally!'

'If Mrs Danvers had expended only a fraction of the care she's taken on the Elizabethan wing to this part of the house, it would have made a difference,' he agreed.

'If we keep calling her Mrs Danvers, we'll do it to her face one day,' I pointed out, and he laughed.

'Do you fancy this room, or would you like to see the others?'

'No, I love this one,' I told him.

'Come on, then. The rest will keep for tomorrow.'

'Yes, to be honest, I'm starting to wilt. It's been a long and eventful day.'

'Of course it has. Just have a quick look in here at the bathroom, and then I'll take you home.'

Through the open door I glimpsed a large, chilly Victorian bath and loo, the white tiling making it look even colder. I shivered.

'Does it come with hot and cold running polar bears?'

'There *is* central heating,' he said indignantly. 'I've got it turned low, to save money, because it runs on oil and costs a fortune. And at least the kitchen is always warm,' he added as we headed back down there.

I shivered and followed him, glancing back only once along the long corridor, half expecting a ghostly figure to emerge from the heavy shadows . . .

Then I shook myself free of tiredness-induced fancies, for any ghostly apparitions would surely haunt only the old wing, and scurried after Carey through the swinging baize door.

The porch led into the half-glazed inner hallway where my designs, if they found favour with Mr Revell, would replace the plain opaque panes currently installed.

By now it was almost dark outside, but the white-painted walls and panelling, together with several gas lamps of interesting design, made everything seem quite light and airy.

Father was much interested in the lights and Mr Revell explained that he had his own gas plant adjacent to the stables.

A housekeeper showed me up to my room, which looked out over the courtyard – I could just make out the black and white of the Elizabethan wing – and was furnished beautifully. Lily would have loved the tapestry with its scene taken from the story of King Arthur, the colours and theme of which were echoed in the bed furnishings and the tiles of the fireplace, in which bright coals burned.

I washed in the warm water provided, unpacked and changed into my best dress, though I feared I would look very unfashionable next to Miss Revell, who though in no way modish, at least showed that she had more interest in her clothes than I had. In any case, I don't suit the fuss and frills that so become Lily, so my plain amber evening dress would have to do.

My eye fell on the small enamel clock that ticked away on

the mantelpiece and I snatched up my shawl and hastened downstairs. I didn't feel at all nervous, but was instead enjoying all these new experiences to the full, for they might not again come my way.

15

Sudden Appearances

When we came back from inspecting the bedroom, Fang was still curled up in his basket by the stove, though his snores came to an abrupt halt as we went into the kitchen and he eyed us balefully.

'He's not daft – this must be the only warm room in the house,' I said. 'If you want anyone to come and help you renovate Mossby, you might have to offer them free thermal underwear as an incentive.'

'It's not that bad, Angelique! And I promise to turn the heating up a bit when you move in, though I expect we'll be so busy most of the time that we'll be warm enough anyway,' Carey said optimistically.

I gave him a look. 'I'm not prepared to freeze to death in order to save you money and if I spend all my savings on setting the workshop up, I won't be able to afford to rent somewhere else to live for ages. So, if you want another free pair of hands to help you, that's the deal.'

'You know you're more than just a free pair of hands, Shrimp – and it'll be hard work but fun!' he said enthusiastically. 'Remember how great it was when we spent all our time together, the last two terms at uni, when I gave up leggy blondes and your only passion was dead female glass artists?'

'I suppose we did have fun,' I admitted.

'Every weekend and the hols I drove you round all the places with windows you wanted to see, not to mention glass museums I never knew existed.'

'And *you* made me go on that weekend course in stone carving,' I said. 'My lump of stone looked much the same as it did before I gave myself a blister chiselling at it, but you came back with a gargoyle.'

'I'm naturally talented at these things,' he said modestly. 'Nick's coming up next week with the gang to do a bit of filming and he'll probably want you to pretend to see the workshop for the first time.'

'I'm not very good at acting, but I'll do my best.'

'Whenever you've appeared in the series before, Nick's always said the camera loves you and you're a natural.'

'I think what he means is that after a few minutes I just naturally forget I'm on camera, because I'm looking at interesting windows or making one.'

'It works, whatever it is,' he said. 'I'll get a spare set of the main house and workshop keys cut for you, so you can make yourself at home and come and go as you like.'

Until my workshop was ready to vanish into, I was more likely to come and go as Carey pleased, probably loaded with tools of one kind or another. But we'd be company for each other while he literally got back on his feet again and I built up my own business.

'My workshop – we'll have to have a long discussion about that,' I said, then stifled a yawn.

'Yes, but that can wait until after you've moved in tomorrow.'

'Tomorrow?' I echoed, slightly startled out of impending stupor.

'Yes, why not? There's nothing to prevent you, is there?'

'I suppose not. Everything I've taken to Molly and Grant's will fit in my car, but I've got lots of things in storage.'

148

'Then we'll get it out again, because you don't want to be paying for storage when there's all this space here,' he said practically. 'I'll hire a van and bring it over—'

He stopped dead as the realization hit him that hefting boxes and furniture about right now wasn't a good idea.

'It's OK, I can sort that out,' I said quickly. 'I hired a couple of local men with a Transit van to take everything to the unit, so I'll get them to move it here. There are several pieces of furniture – my gran's Welsh dresser, for a start.'

'There's certainly enough room for that in here. I had my things from the flat put in storage too, and it's being sent up in a day or two.'

He looked around the kitchen. 'Things tend to find their own space eventually and soon it will all look a lot more homely.'

It suddenly occurred to me that I shouldn't feel *too* much at home here, because one day he'd marry another Daisy and I'd have to move out, if I hadn't done that already. Really, before I got too settled in, I ought to go and look at that chauffeur's flat over the garages behind the workshop that he'd mentioned, to see if it could be made habitable again fairly easily. Then if my business flourished, I'd be able to rent it and I'd be living right near the workshop, but not in Carey's pocket.

Meanwhile, I'd stay here with Carey while he needed me – while we needed each other – enlivened by the sporadic invasion of friends and acquaintances roped in for a few hours or days to help with various parts of the project.

'I'll pack up and drive over first thing tomorrow, then,' I said.

'Great! Then I can give you the whole guided house tour. I bet you can hardly wait to start planning out the alterations to the workshop. I know *I've* already begun to prioritize what wants doing in the house even though I've only been here five minutes and—'

He broke off as the door creaked open like something out of a horror film, and there stood a tall, dark-haired, lugubrious woman. She was handsome, in a slightly reptilian way – I mean, if you liked lizards, you'd be really taken with her – and she looked vaguely familiar, though of course I knew who it was before Carey introduced us.

'Ah, Mrs Dan— Ella,' he corrected himself hastily. 'I wasn't expecting you till Friday!'

'I'm used to popping in and out, but say so if you want me to stop, and maybe give you back my keys?' she said belligerently.

'Not at all . . . I mean, we'll talk about all that in a few days, when I've had time to work out what I'm doing,' he said, though it was obvious to me, at least, that he didn't want someone with the charisma of a female version of the Grim Reaper appearing at unexpected intervals.

'This is my friend Angelique Arrowsmith. She'll be moving in tomorrow for a long stay, so while you *are* here, could you make up the bed in the big room with the bay window and the cabbage-rose wallpaper, while I'm driving her home?' he asked.

There was an ominous silence, broken only by a low rumbling growl from Fang. As he arose from his basket and lifted his lip at the new arrival, I scooped him up.

Ella Parry gave the dog a dirty look before transferring it to Carey.

'I suppose I *could,* though it's not part of my job. The cleaning service changes the beds Fridays, when the laundry calls. I only came up to give you the list of things you're short of in the house, since you said you'd do your own shopping over the internet.' She pronounced the word 'internet' as if it was grossly improper.

I thought she'd just made that up as an excuse, having been consumed by curiosity after spotting us through the Lodge window.

She plonked down a folded list and then unearthed a winter cabbage and some carrots from a wicker basket.

'Clem sent you these.'

'Oh – thanks,' Carey said. 'Clem's got a vegetable patch at the back of the Lodge,' he explained to me.

'If you're going out now, I hope you're taking that creature with you,' she said, giving Fang the evil eye, and then stomped off towards the backstairs.

'Friendly,' I commented.

'Yes, and she seems to haunt the house at random – I never know when I'll open a door and find her on the other side.'

'Not a cheery thought, though I suppose she's used to having the run of the place, as she said.'

He was frowning. 'I think she listens at doors. I'm pretty sure she hadn't just arrived when we saw her. And when Mr Wilmslow was here the day I arrived she was waiting to meet me and offered to make coffee and bring it through into the sitting room. I suspect she hung about outside afterwards, while we were discussing a codicil to my will I'd asked Mr Wilmslow to draw up, making her the residuary legatee to the house if anything happened to me. But by then I'd decided I needed a bit more time to think about it.'

'Do you really think she was listening then, too?'

'Yes, because I heard a noise in the drawing room and when I went out into the hall, the baize door was swinging.'

'If she overheard you say that about leaving Mossby to her, she'll probably be slipping weedkiller into your coffee from now on. You'd better write another one quickly, leaving everything to a dog's home and then leave it lying around where she can see it.'

'I'll discuss it with Mr Wilmslow again on Wednesday. He's pretty keen I make a whole new will, because the one

I've got is just something I drew up myself after the accident,' Carey said. 'I'm hoping to survive till then.'

'I don't see that there's such a huge hurry. He might let you settle in first.'

Carey shrugged. 'I think we've both learned recently that you never know what might happen. For instance, I must have had my accident just a week after my uncle signed *his* will, so if that hit-and-run driver had made a better job of it, Ella would have copped the lot when he died not long afterwards. Come to think of it, I'd already had a near miss only a couple of days before. London's getting dangerous for cyclists, even in the suburbs. All I was doing was heading for my usual lunch at Gino's Café.'

I shivered. 'Oh, don't! I'm just grateful you got out of it more or less in one piece. And speaking of which,' I said firmly, 'you're going to have to pace yourself more. I'm sure you've already been doing way too much.'

'Yes, but from tomorrow I'll have my very own personal assistant to run about for me,' he teased.

'In your dreams, buster!' I said. 'Now, take me back to Molly and Grant's house, so you can rest up for a bit. I wish I'd thought to follow you in my own car, so you didn't have to go out again.'

'Oh, I'm OK,' he assured me, though I could tell he wasn't really from the way he limped and leaned heavily on his stick as we headed for the back door.

'Come on, Fang,' he called to the little dog, who I'd put down when Ella Parry vanished upstairs, and we went out into the chilly, dark late afternoon.

When we got there, Grant had just arrived home from the workshop and invited Carey in, though I'd wanted him to get straight back and have a rest.

It worked out OK, though, because Molly, who had a

strong maternal streak, took one look at him and instantly went into feed-and-cosset mode.

While we ate, I told them that I was moving into Mossby next day and would be renovating an old stained-glass workshop on the estate. Grant was keenly interested.

'And Carey wants you to restock his freezer, Molly, because it's currently full of all the bland stodge his uncle was eating. That will all need getting rid of first.'

Molly asked Carey what sort of things he liked to eat and started jotting down a few ideas, though he said I should have some input too, since I'd also be eating them.

'Well, I don't eat meat any more,' I told him. 'I eat fish and eggs, though.'

'You've gone semi-vegetarian?'

'Yes. It was odd. One day I just felt I couldn't eat another living creature . . . not even a hen. Julian said he didn't mind going meat free with me, though neither of us had quite the same cuddly feeling about fish, or eggs, so long as they're from happy, free-range hens.'

'Which mine are,' said Grant, since he kept leghorns on the patch of land he owned at the end of his garden.

'I can give meat up, too; I don't eat much these days myself,' Carey said. 'That'll make it easier for Molly to cater for us both. And often I'll have a few people staying in the house, Molly, helping out with things, so some meals that will feed several people would be useful. I enjoy cooking, but I'll be too busy or tired to do it all the time.'

'I'll get some ideas together and maybe come up and discuss them one day soon?' she suggested.

'I'd love to see this old workshop some time,' Grant said. 'Ivan will probably want to come with me. I don't know what he's going to do with himself now Nat's told him not to turn up any more. And Julian was going to take Louis on over the summer, when he left college.'

'Louis is Ivan's grandson and keen on a career in stained glass,' I explained to Carey. 'You probably saw him earlier, in the workshop. It's such a shame Nat doesn't want him, because he's a nice boy.'

'When he helped out in the holidays, he was starting to get useful, too,' Grant agreed.

'Now there's only you and Nat to do all the work, Grant,' I said.

'Well, if he expects me to do three people's jobs for one wage, he can think again,' Grant said. 'I left on the dot of five thirty tonight and that's how it's going to be from now on.'

'I suppose there might not be as much work without Julian to draw in the big commissions,' I suggested. 'Are you still thinking of finding another job, or setting yourself up to repair stained glass?'

'I'm tending more to the idea of setting myself up, because working on your own doorstep's convenient. I've got a big outbuilding I could convert, and if I got a little van I could do small repairs on the spot.'

'There's always a call for leaded light repairs,' I agreed.

'Ivan might come and help you out, once your workshop gets going?' he suggested.

'I think it's going to be a long time before I can pay myself, let alone anyone else,' I said ruefully.

'Oh, I don't know. If the basic workshop's there it won't take you that long to get it up and running. And the commissions will come in, all right. You entered that competition to design a glass installation for a shopping mall in Brisbane, didn't you?'

'Yes, and another to design a transom window for a children's library, though I'm not holding my breath about either of them. But I must set myself up a website quickly, so people can find me.'

'Nat remembered to look at Julian's website this afternoon,'

154

Grant said, 'and saw you'd taken all your details off it. He was mad.'

'I don't know why he should have been: he wanted me to leave. He can replace me with Willow and make any other changes he wants – the password's in the top desk drawer in the office.'

'I'll tell him. I expect he'll keep the studio name and trade on his dad's reputation, so the work will still come in, though he's not going to get any major commissions without someone of your or Julian's calibre to design them.'

'Unless Willow turns out to be amazingly good at it – though it takes time to make a name for yourself,' I said. 'Or perhaps he *will* see sense and employ someone else.'

'Well, it's not your problem any more,' Molly said. 'You never did anything to harm him, he just couldn't stand you and his dad being happy together.'

'Got it in a nutshell, from what I've seen and heard,' agreed Carey. 'And he's likely to be even madder when he finds he's going to be competing for work with the Angelique Arrowsmith Art Glass Studio.'

'Too much alliteration,' I said with a grin.

'I like it,' Grant said. 'Rolls off the tongue.'

'Maybe miss off the "Studio" bit: Angelique Arrowsmith Art Glass,' Carey said.

'What do you think, Molly?' I asked.

'I think it's just perfect!'

'Then – it looks like I have the name before I have the workshop!' I said.

It was late when Carey finally set off back to Mossby, though he looked much better, and Molly had given him a box of home-baked pastries, in case he could squeeze another bite in later.

The evening had been only slightly marred earlier by

155

Fang's waking from a stupor induced by consuming a large bowl of leftovers, and fixing his teeth into Grant's ankle, like a small, furry piranha. He'd been banished to the car after that, in disgrace.

I wondered if you could buy muzzles that small?

The family gathered in a vast drawing room off the inner hall before dinner where, as well as the usual arrangement of comfortable sofas, armchairs and small tables, there was also sufficient space for a billiard table and a pianoforte!

The main staircase came down into it and since the others were already gathered there, I felt a little ridiculous making a grand solo appearance when I was such an insignificant snip of a thing!

I almost giggled, but luckily managed to repress it. I admired the room very much and Miss Revell showed me the veranda between the two bay windows, where one could step out on to the terrace and look out over the lake and trees. I looked forward to doing so the next day – in fact, I could hardly wait to see the rest of the house!

We went into dinner, which was what my aunt Barbara would have described us fancy and wasteful, for there was far more food than any four people of normal appetite could possibly eat. But perhaps the remains were finished off by the servants?

While we were eating, Father asked after Mr Browne, who was both Mr Revell's great friend and the architect of the house, and had been present on his last visit.

'He's in the Lake District, having recently accepted another commission to design a house there,' Mr Revell said. 'He will be

157

sorry to have missed you – and I would have liked to have introduced him to Miss Kaye, also.'

I looked up in time to catch the strangest expression on Miss Revell's face: I could not interpret it. But then, it vanished so quickly, I was inclined to think I had imagined it.

When we retired for the night, Miss Revell accompanied me to my chamber to ensure I had everything that I needed, though I assured her I was most comfortable.

Then she lingered, as if she had something to say, before finally remarking that her brother was looking forward to showing me around the house upon the following morning. Then she paused before adding that it was a pity I should not meet Rosslyn Browne on this occasion.

'He and my brother are very great friends, you know, quite united in their enthusiasm for building and furnishing Mossby. Mr Browne has tenure of the Lodge, which was completed before the new house. Indeed, they lived there together while it was being built.'

'I suppose that was the most convenient arrangement. Did you also live there?' I ventured curiously.

'No.' Her lips seemed to tighten and the paleness of her skin gave her an insubstantial, ghostlike air. 'I stayed in the old wing for some of the time and occasionally with relatives in London and Tunbridge Wells.'

Then she bade me goodnight and left me to my comfortable fire and inviting bed. I decided that there was definitely something about Mr Browne she did not care for. In fact, she seems to favour him even less than she does myself, for I can see that her civility is but a veneer over her true feelings.

Perhaps, as I surmised on our arrival, she is annoyed that she must entertain a tradesman and his daughter. But I did not fail to catch her doting expression when she looked at her brother, so it may be that she's simply jealous of anyone else who might enter into his interests.

158

16

Moving

It had been a long and emotionally eventful day and, unsurprisingly, I was so totally exhausted I fell into a deep sleep the moment my head hit the pillow.

When I awoke it was without the awful feeling of disconnection and emptiness that I'd felt every day since I knew I'd lost Julian. Instead I was filled with a new sense of purpose.

When I went down the narrow twisty stairs, Grant had already gone off to work and Molly was baking a large batch of lattice apple tarts and marmalade cakes.

I made us both a cup of coffee and popped some bread into the toaster, before sitting and watching her crimp tart edges while I ate my breakfast.

'I'll have to come and empty those ready meals out of Carey's freezer so I can restock it,' she said. 'And I've had an idea: I know several local elderly people who'd love all those easy-to-digest dinners and the cans of rice pudding and so on. I do a small portion size and special deals for my senior citizen customers, but it's often difficult for them to eat well on a pension.'

'What a great idea!' I enthused.

'I've made a menu of all Carey's favourite meals and desserts – and yours – so you can choose from it when you want to order.'

'Carey's not a fussy eater and he likes to cook when he has time, too – though I don't want him to do too much standing about while his leg is still healing,' I said. 'I can cook rice or pasta, though, so if you make lots of portions of curry, pasta sauce and chilli, I can whip up a meal in no time.'

She wiped her hands on her apron and made a couple of notes on the list.

'I'm looking forward to seeing the house when you've settled in,' she said. 'Carey said you're taking a few days' holiday before you start on the workshop?'

'By that, he means I'm spending a few days following him round the house, outbuildings and grounds, taking notes and being the sounding board for his ideas.'

She laughed. 'He must know he can't keep you away from that workshop for long! You probably won't be able to keep Grant away, either. I'm sure he'll want to give you a hand at weekends, setting everything up.'

'I think he'll have enough on at the moment, doing three people's work – not to mention his garden and the hens.'

'I bet Ivan will want to help you out, too, and he won't care if he's paid or not,' Molly said, and then added thoughtfully, 'I like Carey! You've mentioned him so often that it was good to meet him at last, though of course I've seen him on the telly and Grant knows him from when he's been up.'

'That new series of his programme, with that actor fronting it instead, will be starting soon, but I don't know if it will be as popular. Carey has an awful lot of fans.'

'Yes . . . Carey's so big, splendid and charismatic, even though I can see he's not a hundred per cent well yet,' she said. 'Now I know what people mean when they say someone is "larger than life"!'

'I always think he's so glowing with enthusiasm that he sort of lights up inside! He's been like that since he was little

160

and sometimes it used to drive me mad, though it seems to come over well on the TV.'

'The poor man's obviously had an awful time with that leg, so inheriting Mossby couldn't have come at a better moment for him – for both of you. A fresh new start.'

'True, though I hate the thought of leaving everything Julian built up over the years in Nat's hands, including his reputation . . . It wouldn't surprise me if he kept on turning out windows in a pale imitation of Julian's style for ever! And Willow's designs are a bit of an unknown quantity.'

I poured us both some more coffee from the fat, speckled blue Denby pot. 'I mean, even if she turns out to have a knack for it and her designs are brilliant, she'll have to get her name known before she gets the big commissions. I don't know what will happen to the studio . . .'

'I know, but you'll simply have to let it go, because there's nothing you can do about it now. And people who are interested in *your* designs will find you wherever you are, won't they?'

'They will once I get organized with a website. I'll have to notify the British Society of Master Glass Painters, the Crafts Council and a few other places of my change of address and that of the new studio. I saved my pages from Julian's website, so it shouldn't take too long.'

Deleting all mention of myself from the Julian Seddon Architectural Glass website had felt like unpicking major threads out of my life, leaving gaping holes in the fabric: all warp and not enough weft. But now I'd have to weave a whole new pattern of my own.

The morning was advancing and I didn't want to hold Molly up, so I booked the two men with the van to collect my belongings from the storage unit in a couple of days, packed everything else into the car and set off for Mossby.

I didn't look at my old home as I passed it . . .

*

161

It was a gloriously sunny though chilly day, the sky a pale duck-egg blue, modestly veiled by a few white wisps of cloud. I drove past the workshop – *my* workshop! – and parked in the gravel circle in front of the porch . . . where I found Carey, standing next to a large, sturdy golf buggy, with Fang tucked under his arm like a shiny black package.

This was presumably to stop him biting the person he was talking to – a burly, weather-beaten man of about sixty with a head of wiry, silvered fair hair, who had 'gardener' written all over him.

'Good timing, Angelique,' Carey said, as I got out. 'This is Ella's husband, Clem. I've been updating him about what we're going to do with the workshop.'

Clem said he was pleased to meet me in a pleasant, slow voice with a hint of Devon cream in it. 'It seems a good idea to use the old workshop again, seeing it's there. I know Carey's uncle had some idea of letting it out to a local business at one time, but it came to nothing in the end.'

'Where did the buggy come from?' I asked.

'Clem told me about it. My uncle used to get around the grounds in it before his final illness, so he brought it up from the garages behind the workshop and we've filled it with petrol. It's just the thing for getting up and down the drive and round the grounds, till my leg's up to more hiking.'

'What a great idea! Hello, Fang,' I added, stroking the little dog's head. He curled his lip at me slightly, but didn't growl, so I was sure it was meant as a smile.

'Mr Revell had a shed with double doors put in at the end of the kitchen wing to keep the buggy in so it was handy. It's behind that bay hedge, so you've probably not noticed it's there yet,' Clem said. 'But after he passed on, I thought it would be better stored in the garage in the stable block.'

'Yes, that was a good idea, but it's certainly just what I

need at the moment,' Carey said, climbing into the driver's seat while still holding Fang. 'Come along, Angel – hop on.'

'Why, where are you going? I've only just got here and my car's full of stuff!'

'Only for a quick tour of the grounds. I haven't felt up to it before, but now there's nothing to stop me.'

'But—'

'You can settle in later,' he said impatiently. 'Your things will be safe in the car for a bit.'

'If you leave me your car key, I'll put everything in the kitchen wing for you,' offered Clem. 'It won't take me a minute.'

'That's very kind, but—'

'Thanks, Clem,' Carey interrupted. 'We won't be long. Come on, Angel, give him your keys and let's get off!'

'Oh, OK,' I capitulated. There's no stopping Carey when he's got that look in his eyes. 'But only if you move over and let me drive!'

'It's hardly strenuous,' he objected. 'That's the whole point of it!'

'I know that, it's just that I've always wanted to have a go with one of these things,' I told him, and he laughed and shifted over.

'See you later,' he said to Clem, who was already hefting boxes and suitcases out of the back of my car.

I trundled sedately round the knot garden. In fact, I did it twice to get the feel of the thing, before setting off down the drive.

'I hope it gets us back up this slope to the house afterwards,' I said doubtfully. 'It's steep lower down.'

'If not, you can get out and walk,' he suggested.

'Thanks. Always the true gent.'

Carey directed me to branch off to the left behind the workshop and through a large arch into a cobbled square, where I came to a halt. It was surrounded by a substantial range of out-buildings. There was another arched entrance directly opposite, though closed by a wooden gate with a Judas door in it.

'There's still an old Mercedes saloon in one of the garages, which Clem used to drive my uncle about in,' Carey said.

'He's clearly a man of many talents.'

'I'll leave checking that out and seeing what else is in the various buildings till later. That arch on the other side leads on to the car parking area your coach must have used when you visited, and then through that small passage to the right, you get to the walled garden I mentioned.'

'That's *definitely* something for another day,' I said. 'We might even have to mount an expedition.'

'Yes, Clem says he hasn't been in it for years and the key to the padlock on the gate is lost. If it's not in that tin box with the others up at the house, I'll have to bring bolt cutters down one day.'

'I can see why your uncle thought it was worth paying Mrs Danvers a good wage, even though she didn't earn it, because Clem seems to have been doing several jobs at once.'

'He does seem willing to do anything he's asked to.'

'Or even *not* asked to, like moving my luggage about. He's so different from his wife! I wonder where they met.'

'Oh, he told me that. She was working at a National Trust property as some kind of resident custodian-cum-housekeeper and he'd nearly worked his way up to be head gardener when he got the drink problem and was fired. That's when Ella asked my uncle if he could help and he offered them jobs and the Lodge. I don't think that's quite what she had in mind. I suspect she was hoping they could just move in and freeload.'

'Maybe being married to an alcoholic soured Ella's soul?'

'It was probably fairly tart to start with,' Carey said. 'Clem told me losing his job shook him up, and he's stayed on the wagon ever since.'

'You know, on the whole, your uncle seems to have been quite generous to them, doesn't he?'

'Considering all the circumstances, now I know them, I think Uncle did more than I would have expected. He paid for Clem and Ella's daughter, Vicky's, education, too.'

'I didn't realize they had a daughter. Does she live with them?'

'No, she's an actress and lives in London, though I've never heard of her so I don't think she can be doing very well – and her choice of occupation probably didn't go down too well with my uncle.'

'All these undercurrents of family history to get the hang of,' I said, turning the buggy on the rather weedy cobbles of the yard and heading back to the main drive. Further down, I took one of the branches on the other side and emerged from a tunnel of rhododendron bushes to a view of the woods and lake.

I stopped so we could see the lie of the land. To the right, the steep terrain rose to the house in a series of steps and terraces. Below it, on the edge of the lake, was a very ancient-looking stone boathouse.

The thin strip of potholed tarmac seemed to go right round the lake as well as taking a circuit through the woods.

'Clem says my uncle had the old paths tarmacked over when the drive was resurfaced years ago, though it's in need of repair. He goes round with the brush-cutter once a year, to keep it clear. Let's see what it's like.'

I trundled the buggy rather doubtfully past the lake and down the unkempt dark snail-trail through the trees, which made a loop and brought us back out by a bluff of rock next to the terraces. It had been an obstacle course of potholes and fallen branches, but not too bad. Most of the trees were bare at this time of year and the woodland wasn't extensive.

Near the boathouse was a pretty, columned summerhouse with stone seats, built against the wall of the lowest terrace. A rose twined up the front of it. It was probably quite enchanting in summer.

'According to Clem, there's a rowing boat and a couple of punts in the boathouse, but I think we'll explore that another day, too – it's hardly punting weather,' Carey said. 'They could well be too rotten to use by now, anyway.'

'Well, I certainly don't want to risk an icy dip,' I agreed, for the winter sunshine was now rapidly vanishing behind heavy pewter-dark clouds and the wind had an icy edge. 'Let's go back. I want to unpack and I'm dying to explore the house. Besides, I'm freezing!'

'Why don't you walk back up the terrace steps to the house and meet me there?' he suggested. 'It'll warm you up and I can take the buggy up without your heavy weight to hold it back.'

'Ho, ho,' I said, since he was about three times my weight. 'But I think I will. I could do with some exercise.'

Carey put Fang on the seat next to him and drove off, while I began to climb the stone steps. Each level was planted and maintained beautifully, with lion heads spouting water into half-moon pools full of flickering orange-gold fish. There were climbing shrubs, rockeries, great stone planters and narrow rose beds. I suspected the terraces got at least eighty per cent of Clem's attention as they were evidently his labour of love.

On the top terrace, which was neatly set out with rose beds, gravel walks and a hexagonal gazebo, I came across the man himself, cleaning out yet another fountain.

'Hi!' I greeted him. 'I walked up to admire the terraces. You've kept them looking wonderful.'

'Do you like gardening?' he asked eagerly.

'I love gardens,' I said truthfully, 'but I'm afraid I'm not a gardener. My friend Molly's husband has a big vegetable and fruit garden and keeps his own hens.'

'I haven't room to grow much fruit behind the Lodge. I'm more a vegetable man,' he said, and I suddenly had a vision of him as Mr Potato Head.

'This terrace must be lovely in summer when the roses are out, but time consuming to keep up.'

'It is, so it's just as well there's nothing by way of a formal garden anywhere else,' he said. 'Carey's uncle used to get some men in once a year to cut back all the shrubs along the drive and clear the trail through the woods, but he started economizing a few years back.'

'Carey would probably have been straight out with a chainsaw himself by now, sorting out the fallen trees, if it hadn't been for his accident,' I said ruefully. 'He can turn his hand to pretty much anything.'

'I know he had that series on the telly doing up cottages, because our Vicky told me.'

'That's right, and he actually did a lot of the work involved himself. But the new series is being presented by someone else.'

'If that's his bent, there's plenty for him to do here at Mossby.'

'There certainly is,' I agreed. 'Well, I'd better get going – and thank you for taking my luggage in for me. That was kind.'

'No problem,' he said, and started scooping slimy brown leaves out of the bottom of the fountain again, so I left him to it and joined Carey, who had appeared round the corner of the house.

'Would madam care to enter for a spot of lunch?' he suggested when I was within earshot.

'What's on offer?' I asked, suddenly hungry. I'd tended to forget about eating regularly lately, and I suspected by his gaunt aspect that Carey had been just the same.

'Dish *du jour* is cheese on toast – and come on round this

way to the kitchen door, because I'm not letting you near any windows until we've eaten.'

I'd been casting lingering glances at the leaded windows in the façade but capitulated. 'Sounds good to me . . . and Molly sent an apple tart up – I'd forgotten. It must still be on the back seat of the car.'

'No, Clem left it on the kitchen table with your car keys. Come on!'

Next morning, as soon as we had breakfasted, Mr Revell took us all over the house. Father's windows looked very fine, with central large octagons and squares in clear glass and borders in a woven strap effect, which I knew he had copied from some old heraldic windows in the Elizabethan wing. Looking out, I thought the view over the lake and woodland was perfectly delightful.

It was a bright day and the house was now quite flooded with light, so that I could imagine how my windows would look in the inner hall. When he conducted us up the wide, curving staircase, I longed to design something to replace the tall, narrow, plainly glazed window on the landing, too.

Father had not seen the finished house, so he was just as interested as I in all the details of furnishings and fittings that had been so carefully designed for their situation. We saw one or two of the principal bedrooms, which were very fine, and then passed through a dark wooden door of some age into the old tower.

I observed that glass had been inserted in the narrow window to keep out the weather, and a seat built into the embrasure underneath, but otherwise the walls of roughly dressed stone, the large hearth and wooden floor must surely be original to the building.

Our host did not pause here, but led us through another door into the Elizabethan wing. I was hard on his heels, because now I knew that it contained a window designed by a woman of a bygone age, I was quite agog to see it! First, though, we must tour the upper part of the house. Mr Revell played the guide very well, telling us that this first bedchamber was that supposed to be haunted by the ghost of Lady Anne Revell and had been kept locked up during her lifetime . . . and unused since.

Mr Revell's new gas lighting obviously had not yet reached this far, so it was very gloomy, not helped by all the old linenfold panelling. There was another of those vast hearths and a massive and ornately carved bed of wood so dark it seemed black.

'The old house has many ghosts besides Lady Anne, who commissioned the stained-glass window I know you are so eager to see, Miss Kaye,' our guide said with a smile.

'I have no patience with such imaginings – old tales told round a fire to frighten children!' said Father.

'I admit, I have never seen any ghostly apparitions myself, so I expect you are quite right,' Mr Revell admitted.

But I did not feel the same, for there seemed a dark, brooding atmosphere in the chamber, as though something bad had once happened there and it would not have surprised me if someone – or something – had stepped out of the deepest shadows . . .

With a shiver, I hurried after the others.

17

Let the Revells Commence

'It's surprising how parts of the old house have been joined into one fairly harmonious whole with the new,' Carey said, as we drank our coffee after lunch and prepared for what he kept referring to as 'The Grand Tour'.

'You seem to have picked up an awful lot of information about it already, considering you've only been here a couple of days.'

'That was Mr Wilmslow's crash course in Revellry, the day I arrived,' he said. 'He seems especially interested in how the building evolved through the centuries. Then Ella insisted on showing me over the house again the next day, but *her* conversation was confined to terse statements like, "Here's the linen cupboard," and, "That stair goes up to the attic." She only waxed lyrical about the Elizabethan part, in a strangely proprietorial way.'

'And now you're going to give *me* the quick guided tour . . . followed, if I know you as well as I think I do, by an in-depth inspection lasting a couple of days, where I follow you round with a notebook, tape measure and camera.'

'Yes, I'm really looking forward to getting stuck in properly,' he agreed happily. 'The best way of discovering the secrets of an old house is to restore it.'

'Then film the whole ongoing restoration and write a book about it, like the previous series.'

'There's so much more to do here than I expected that I'm starting to think this might be the basis of several TV series.'

'I suspect you might be quite right, and there'll probably be all kinds of spin-off magazine articles and that kind of thing,' I said, then got up determinedly. 'Come on, I want the tour now. Where shall we start? With the servants' wing as the aperitif, the Arts and Crafts part as the main course and the Elizabethan wing as dessert?'

'If you like, but the attics and cellars are a bit too substantial to be an *amuse-bouche* between courses, so we might have to snack on them tomorrow, instead.'

'*Amuse-bouche*? That's right posh,' I said, in my grandmother's Lancashire accent, and then followed Carey as he picked up his stick and headed for the first of the small rooms off the passage outside.

' "Begin at the beginning and go on till you come to the end: then stop," as the King said to Alice,' he said, throwing open the door. 'These steps lead down to the cellars. I've only really looked at the first, which has the central heating boiler in it, but the rest of them seem to go on and on.'

He moved along the passage, opening each door briefly. 'These next three were sculleries and larders and that kind of thing. Here's the one with the giant freezer.'

'I'll get Molly round soon to empty that,' I said, and told him about her brilliant idea for disposing of the contents to some of her more elderly clients, which he thought an excellent scheme.

Next came a utility room with an old-fashioned drying rack hanging from the ceiling, but also a large washing machine and tumble dryer lined up along one wall. There was a heap of bags stamped with a laundry logo, too.

'Snowball Laundry – that's original,' I said.

We moved on to a small spartan cloakroom and a few random hidey-holes little bigger than cupboards, before returning to the kitchen by way of the housekeeper's parlour.

'This is where the information leaflets and postcard stock for the coach parties visiting the Elizabethan wing are currently stored and arrangements made. Not that it's exactly a money-spinner at the moment, but we can think about that one later.'

It was a tiny, slightly gloomy room, with a soupy brown chenille tablecloth over a claw-footed pedestal table, some deal shelves laden with small cardboard boxes, a tin cashbox and a ledger.

'If you expand that side of things, you could turn this into a proper office, with a computer and desk and so on,' I suggested.

'I've got another room earmarked as an office-cum-studio,' he said. 'I'll show you in a minute.'

The kitchen by now felt like my second home, especially with Fang snoring like a miniature buzz saw in his basket, but I hadn't yet been in the servants' hall that led out of it. It had a window to the front of the house, as well as one at the side, so was quite light and airy . . . or it would be, if the shrubbery was pruned back a bit.

'It isn't used because there haven't been any servants living in for years, and of course it's quite plain – none of the Arts and Crafts touches in here!' he said. 'Perfect for making a studio/office once the table and random chairs are taken away.'

'If you can get that big table out!'

'Easily, because it's in sections. You can remove leaves till you end up with something really small, that's no problem. We could share this space, if you like, unless you'd prefer a room of your own to work in?'

'No, a corner in here would be fine, because I'll have a studio area in the workshop, too: that big back room with the sink that looks as if someone has used it as a tool shed.'

'I thought I'd have a door knocked through into the main part of the house – the formal family dining room is next door – then if we want to, we can always expand into there, or have a room each. There's enough space to get at least twelve people round the kitchen table, so I don't need a separate dining room.'

'But it might be nice for Christmas dinner, or celebrations,' I pointed out.

'Yes, I suppose you're right. There's no rush to make any major changes anyway . . . and your eyes have glazed over,' he added. 'I didn't think I'd have bored you already.'

'No, I've just had a brainwave: you know I ended with tons of material about female glass craftswomen of the Victorian era when I was writing my dissertation? Well, I'm going to turn it into a book, with an expanded new section about Jessie Kaye.'

'That's a great idea, Shrimp!' he enthused. 'And being at Mossby is bound to inspire you.'

'I'd be even more inspired if you finally let me see some of her windows!' I said, and he laughed.

'OK, come on!' He headed back out to the kitchen. 'Until I get that door knocked through into the dining room, we have to go this way and up the passage through the baize door . . .'

But he'd lost my attention the moment the door swung closed behind us, for I was gazing, entranced, at the half-glazed inner walls of the long narrow entrance hall. Light filtered in from the room beyond, enough to make out the shapes of bending leaves and rippling grass, enhanced by the clever use of reamy and seedy glass, while the rich amber roses on tall stems swayed against the palest of blue skies. The effect was like a bright garden under water . . .

'Wow!' I whispered finally. 'These are so beautiful – and technically *really* clever.'

'They'd look much better if all the woodwork in here was repainted white, instead of this dark green. You can see the original colour where it's chipped at the corner.'

'Yes, that would make it much lighter in here,' I agreed, running a finger lovingly over a piece of seedy ochre glass, feeling the tiny bubbles nearest the surface. You have to be so careful not to break into them when you're cutting and leading-up, or the cement seeps into the bubbles and it doesn't look good.

'If you could possibly bear to tear yourself away, there's more house to be seen – and after all, now you're living here, you can come and gloat over them any time you like,' he said finally.

'I suppose so,' I agreed reluctantly. 'Where next?'

'This way, madam,' he said, back to his tour guide role. 'On your right is the cloakroom I mentioned, with the picture of Windsor Castle in the toilet bowl.'

'Every home should have one.'

'The porch has the same plain octagonal and square patterned windows as the rest of the house, though the ones in the bays also have quite intricate borders – as you can see,' he added, throwing open a door in the half-glazed wall, revealing a vast room with two curved bay windows looking out on to the front, with a door to the veranda between them.

'Ella calls this the drawing room, though it seems to have been intended to be multi-purpose, what with the billiard table and the veranda.'

The billiard table was at the far end of the room, across an acre of original carpet, but round the hearth was an arrangement of slightly faded and shabby period seating. A grand staircase vanished upwards and the whole effect was a bit like a stage set for an Agatha Christie play.

175

'It wouldn't be exactly cosy, unless you'd got lots of people staying, but it has a sort of charm to it,' I commented.

'If you want cosy, have a look in here,' he said, opening the door to a small sitting room with a TV, bookshelves and rubbed, squishy velvet sofas and armchairs.

'That's more like it. You could relax in here,' I approved. 'What's through the teeny-tiny door?'

'The ancient tower that links the two parts of the house,' he said, opening it. He had to duck his head to avoid knocking it as he went through, but it was just the right height for Hobbit-sized me.

'My uncle had a lift put in, as you can see, and though the cage looks a bit antique, the workings have been modernized and regularly serviced.'

The tower's narrow window had been glazed and the large stone fireplace was obviously original, but probably not the plastering and panelling on the walls, or the polished wooden floor.

'The bookshelves in the sitting room are sort of an overflow from the library, which is in the muniment room next door, the only part of the old wing the family regularly used. But we'll go upstairs first and work our way down to it.'

With some trepidation, I let him take me up in the lift and I could tell from the way he operated it that it was a new toy, though at least that meant he would sometimes use it while his leg was mending.

'You can explore the bedrooms in the new part on your own later,' he said as we stepped out into a room that was a replica of the one below, except that the stone fireplace was carved with a battered coat of arms and there was a glass-lidded curio cabinet.

It was lined in dark velvet, so it was hard to see what was inside. I'd just begun to lift the lid when Carey said, impatiently, 'Never mind that! This is supposed to be a quick overview of the whole place, so you can get your bearings: we haven't got time to faff about with curios. Aren't you dying to see Lady Anne's bedchamber?'

I reluctantly lowered the lid and followed him through another Hobbit-sized door . . . and stopped just inside the bedchamber, shivering.

In the ancient tower I'd had no sense of the pressing presence of past centuries, yet as the chilly darkness of this room heavily enfolded me, it felt as though I was stepping back into another age.

Politeness made me hide my impatience while we admired the paintings of Revell ancestors in the Long Gallery, but it was soon rewarded when we descended the stairs, for on the half-landing were five narrow rectangular windows.

The two on either side of the central one were of great antiquity and consisted of diamond panes in uneven greenish glass, inset with brightly coloured heraldic devices. They were bordered with the woven strap pattern Father had copied in his own work.

The middle window was constructed in a similar style, with the woven border and quarry panes, but the central device in this case was a painted and silver-stained depiction of the old house, with two women standing on one side, and a girl kneeling in prayer on the other. Below, a Cavalier seemed to be striding through a cornfield, while high above, a spiked sun shone down on all.

The diamond panes of clear glass surrounding these figures each contained a central circle or square painted with a different and seemingly random motif. At the bottom had been lettered:

Lady Anne Revell caused me to be made: let no man remove me.
To God, all things are clear.

178

'You seem quite dumbstruck, Miss Kaye!' said Mr Revell, amused.

'I told you it was remarkable, Jessie,' Father said. 'What do you make of it?'

'Why, it reminds me of nothing so much as a sampler,' I said. 'You know, where one sews little bits of pattern or flowers and other motifs to see the effect.'

'I had not thought of that before, but you are quite right,' Father agreed.

'There are samplers hung in the muniment room below, some of them of great age, so perhaps she drew inspiration from those,' Mr Revell suggested.

He led the way downstairs, through a huge and impressive hall, hung with pikes and halberds and mutely attended by empty suits of armour, then along a short passage to the muniment room.

I would have liked to have lingered to examine the samplers there, though they hung on a dark wall and were difficult to make out – but time had scurried by on silent mouse feet and as we returned to the light and airy new house, the gong sounded for luncheon.

18

Dimly Illuminated

Carey switched on wall lights, which had been made to look like candle sconces, but the bulbs were dim and only faintly illuminated the room.

'The blinds are usually kept down in here to stop the sun fading the seventeenth-century bed hangings,' he said. 'You can date when the electricity was put in by the fact that all the sockets are two-pin brown Bakelite ones. If those coach parties ever visited on dark days, it must have been like playing blind man's bluff.'

'I seem to recall it was quite gloomy upstairs, though we weren't shown this room.'

I'd have remembered the large stone fireplace, which must back on to the one in the tower, the dark linenfold half-panelling and the intricately moulded white ceiling. The bed was vast, with a heavily carved headboard.

'What are those figures carved into the bedhead?' I asked, peering more closely.

'Hard to say, though it looks like a man and a woman. But presumably this was the nuptial bed of the Revells. I'll open the blinds and bring a torch next time we visit and you can have a better look. Not all the soft furnishings in this wing are as old as these, though there are a couple of really ancient tapestries in the Great Hall and a collection of framed samplers in the muniment room.'

'Samplers?' I asked, interested.

'Oh, yes – I'd forgotten you collect them. The Revell ladies all seem to have been industrious needlewomen.'

'I'll look forward to seeing those,' I said, then shivered. 'There's a strange atmosphere in here, don't you think?'

'There's certainly a *cold* atmosphere. The central heating doesn't extend this far, so there are just a few ancient electric storage heaters dotted about to keep the damp away. This wing wasn't used once the new building was completed, apart from the muniment room, which was my uncle's library and office until he became bed bound.'

'New storage heaters would be more cost effective, but maybe when you've had the old electric sockets replaced,' I suggested. 'Those sound dangerous.'

'There are adaptors, so you can use three-pin plugs, but it's a bit of a deathtrap at the moment,' Carey agreed. 'A lot of the furniture was removed soon after Ella came here fifteen years ago, when my uncle decided to allow the occasional coach party to visit. I don't think there's anything later than the eighteenth century in here now.'

'I wonder what he did with it. After all, practically everything in the new part was designed and made for it, so none of it's there.'

'I wondered that, and I'm sort of hoping it's in one of the attics,' he said, his eyes gleaming. 'Though not in this part of the house, because there isn't much of a roof space.'

'How have you managed to stop yourself from searching the other attics?'

'Because I feel just like I did when there was a present under the Christmas tree and I was afraid to open it in case it wasn't what I really wanted.'

'But there might be nothing there at all, if your uncle got rid of anything he thought redundant. Or else he kept it, but it's all monstrously huge and heavy Victorian mahogany.'

'What a happy thought,' he said, closing the door behind us and then leading the way into a wooden-floored gallery that ran along the back of the house. There were wall brackets that might once have held burning torches, but now were fitted with funny little curly light fittings, like whipped ice-cream cones.

A warren of small rooms led off it, including one set out as a nursery that I remembered seeing on my last visit, with an ancient cradle standing near the hearth.

The windows were all diamond paned in thick, greenish, uneven glass that distorted the view and there were unexpected steps up and down, and twists and turns, in the bewilderingly random way of many such old properties.

Finally, we arrived at the top of the main staircase, which was unusual in that the flight up from the hall divided into two at a half-landing, where the real attraction for me lay: the five leaded windows.

They were quite narrow, with pointed tops, and started at about the level of my chin. 'I'll need a stepladder . . .' I muttered, standing on tiptoe to see what I could: it looked as if they had been made in three panels, the top triangular one being the smallest. There was a plastic margarine tub on the ledge under the central window, containing a few broken fragments of glass. I squinted up again, trying to make out where the damage was.

'You shall have a ladder and yours truly to hold it steady . . . *later*,' Carey promised. 'As part of that great big survey of the whole place we're going to make, remember?'

'Oh, yes – that "break" you said I needed,' I said snarkily, going down the bottom flight of stairs for the long-distance view of the windows.

'Nice pair of heraldic crests in the two windows on the left,' I said. 'Probably contemporary with the building of this wing. The two on the right are a little later and I'd say a new panel with an escutcheon was put in at the top to replace a clear section, sometime in the seventeenth century. Those look like strawberry leaves, so that should mean someone of rather nobler blood marrying into the family,' I added.

'I think Lady Anne *was* of noble birth – she wouldn't be addressed as Lady Anne, otherwise – but an impoverished widow, which is probably why she was happy to marry into the minor gentry.'

'The Lady Anne window has the date it was made at the bottom,' I observed. This was lucky, for it was nothing like any other seventeenth-century windows I'd ever seen, having a design of painted motifs in circles at the centre of each diamond pane. It was that that had made me think of a sampler, the first time I saw it. Now I was further away I noticed something had been taped over the damaged section at the top. 'What did you say happened to it?'

'An unfortunate bird flew into it – or at least, the remains were found below, so it was presumed so. Clem stopped up the gap to keep out the elements and the pieces were collected up and put in that box.'

'The window was probably weakened already. I suspect the tie bars on all of them need some attention,' I said absently. Each panel would originally have been tied with wires to a metal bar set horizontally across into the masonry, to keep it from sagging or bulging over the centuries, but they did tend eventually to break loose.

'The Lady Anne window will definitely have to come out,' I told him. 'And as I've said before, you really should send it away to be professionally restored or conserved, because it's a rare example of a seventeenth-century window. It's *really* different from most glass of its time.'

183

'No way is it ever leaving Mossby, or some dreadful doom will fall on the House of Revell,' he said flippantly, but with an underlying seriousness.

'Then you'd better hope the ghost counts the workshop as part of Mossby. Otherwise, no dice.'

'I'm hoping I can loosely interpret Mossby to mean the whole estate, but if Lady Anne should pop out of the wainscoting while you're removing it, perhaps you could assure her you'll have it back in pristine condition in no time.'

I gave him a look.

'Will you have to cut and paint new pieces of glass to repair it?' he asked.

'Absolutely not!' I exclaimed, horrified. 'I hope to reuse the broken pieces, leaded together with narrow ribbon calme. A specialist would have a lot more techniques to offer, like edge-bonding the pieces back together with clear resin, but I'm just going to conserve what's there, not try and restore or renovate it.'

'Sounds tricky, anyway,' he said.

'It will be . . . and I may have to take the whole window apart and re-lead it, while I'm at it.' I mused over it for a moment and then added, 'I might ask advice from a friend of Julian's who works in glass conservation at York, before I start.'

And suddenly I really wanted Julian to be there to talk it over with. He'd have been as interested as I was in the design.

'Come on, there'll be plenty of time to moon over the windows later,' Carey said briskly. 'Let's finish the whistle-stop tour.'

I think he was tiring, for his limp was more evident as we crossed the flagged Great Hall. The walls were decorated with ancient arms and vacant suits of armour . . . or at least, I *hoped* they were vacant.

'There's a kitchen of sorts at the other end and a few more

rooms, but the rest of the service wing was demolished once the new house was finished,' he explained.

'Back in the days when your home was your unlisted castle and you could knock it about to suit yourself?'

'Yes, you'd certainly never get away with it now, not even the lift in the tower. But I'll restore it really sympathetically, in my usual wonderful way,' he said modestly.

We passed through a dim parlour and along a passage to a door he had to unlock.

'The muniment room,' he said grandly, bowing me in. 'This way, my lady!'

'I have no idea what a muniment is,' I confessed.

'No, me neither. But somewhere in here is the secret hidey-hole that Mr Wilmslow will reveal tomorrow. There's a priest-hole in the Great Hall somewhere, too, just big enough to hold a man, but that one is common knowledge.'

'I vaguely remember we were shown that. It's about the size of a glorified linen cupboard.'

'They discovered another upstairs when they were knocking down the service wing. Behind a cupboard there was an entrance to a stair leading up to a room in the eaves. There are probably others too, because the family were originally Catholic at a time when that wasn't a great idea.'

'Didn't you say the hiding place in here is full of family papers?'

'Apparently they've just been stuffing them into an old chest for centuries.'

'Sounds fascinating. Nick's certainly going to want that in the series! The Mossby Secrets could be a whole chapter in your first book about the house, too.'

'*Books*. The more I see, the more I realize that restoring and looking after Mossby will be my life-work.'

'But will you be happy staying in one place for very long?' I asked.

'I would here, because this is *my* place,' he explained. 'I expect I'll take commissions to work on other properties later, but I'll always want to come back home.'

The muniment room was a long chamber which, despite the dark panelling and large fireplace, was not entirely in period with the rest of the house. There were several fairly recent additions, like a lamp, a roll-top desk, a large Turkish rug and a wall of bookcases, some glazed.

'My uncle liked to hang out here before his last illness. He was allegedly writing a family history, but he was working back and had only got as far as the wealthy but plebeian mill owner who married the last Revell in the middle of the nineteenth century and changed his surname to hers.'

'That would be . . . the father of the Ralph Revell who married Jessie Kaye?' I ventured.

'I think so – I'll have to go into it later. There must be a family tree in here somewhere.'

I looked round. 'Don't you have *any* idea where the secret hiding place is, then?'

'No, not even a hint. I'll have to contain myself till tomorrow. Usually the secret is passed directly down from one heir to the other, but in this case, Mr Wilmslow is the middleman.'

But now I'd spotted the samplers on the darkest wall, some framed and some simply on stretchers, and Carey had to drag me away.

'Like the windows, those will have to wait for another day,' he said firmly. 'It feels like hours since lunch and I'm ravenous!'

I was sure he was also tired, so I didn't protest, and we returned via the turret to the twenty-first century.

'I don't know about you,' I said, 'but I'm bushed and I want to unpack a few things and then just chill for a while.'

'OK, but why don't we go along the road to that

186

pub – hotel – whatever it is, and have dinner, in a bit? I noticed a sign saying they served food.'

'The Screaming Skull? Yes, we could do that. I'll drive so you can get legless.'

Then I realized what I'd said and looked at him, appalled at my slip of the tongue.

Carey grinned wryly. 'Laugh, and the world laughs with you.'

During luncheon we discussed what might be the subject of the windows in the inner hall and Miss Revell suggested roses. They appear to be her great passion and, though at this time of year there was nothing to show me in her rose garden on the first terrace, she described each variety that grew there in great detail.

Father, who is not much interested in horticulture, went off with Mr Revell to view the gas-producing plant, which was in a building near the stables, and I confess I had an unladylike interest in seeing it for myself.

However, Miss Revell has inspired me with ideas based around her beloved roses and I will have some designs ready to show her brother on his next visit to London.

For the rest of our stay, Mr Revell barely left my side and even accompanied us to the station when we departed after lunch the following day.

Of course, I completely understood his passion for Mossby and his striving to have everything perfect, down to the very smallest detail, so we had much to talk about. This does make one lose track of the time . . .

I don't think Honoria shared his interests, but behind her severe façade she clearly doted on her handsome younger brother — even more than on her beloved roses!

While Mr Revell had shown me great attention during our visit, it had merely been on the friendly basis we had established in London. If sometimes my breath caught and my heart beat a little faster when he turned those wonderful eyes on me, glowing with enthusiasm, that was hardly to be surprised at.

But I could see Father was uneasy as we travelled home and after some harrumphing warned me not to put the wrong interpretation on to Mr Revell's attentions to me during our stay.

'Oh, no, Father,' I assured him briskly. 'I am sure that with his friend Mr Browne away, he was simply missing a sympathetic ear to discuss his grand schemes with. In fact, Miss Revell more or less told me so, soon after we arrived.'

I did not add that since he was tall, handsome and a member of the gentry, while I was an insignificant dab of a tradesman's daughter, it would have been silly indeed for me to cherish hopes in that direction!

'I thought that you and Michael would make a match of it,' Father said.

'I love my cousin like a brother and am delighted that he and Lily are to marry,' I said. 'They are perfect for each other – and as for me, I love my work and am entirely contented with my single state.'

Which I was, especially since I had begun to take a much greater role in the business. Few husbands, I fancied, would be likely to tolerate such involvement from their wives.

19

The Screaming Skull

'How could you possibly forget that there was another Jessie Kaye window above the main staircase?' I said, not for the first time, as I drove us to the Screaming Skull.

He shrugged. 'I just did. Anyway, you've seen them all now.'

'Are you quite sure there isn't another one somewhere that's slipped your mind?' I said sarcastically and he laughed.

'No, that's the lot. I think I forgot that one because it doesn't look like the panels in the hall.'

'It's a much later window – the rose theme again, but stronger and less stylized.'

He gave me a sideways look and a grin. 'Come to think of it, there *is* a bit more stained glass in the nursery – the small top lights of the windows. But that's totally different again and I'm sure it was made by someone else.'

'I'll see for myself tomorrow. I don't think I trust your judgement or your memory!'

We'd arrived at the pub and I parked the car near a large information board. It welcomed us to the start of the Halfhidden ghost trail which, according to the map, began at the bottom of a nearby path and led up through the Sweetwell woods to the Lady Spring. A biting wind drove us indoors at this point, past a deserted beer garden that would be lovely in summer.

I was sure Carey would be able to walk there easily by then, and maybe even up to that spring and on to the other spectral delights of Halfhidden.

Once inside it was surprisingly warm, noisy and crowded, and we pushed our way to the bar to see if we could eat in the restaurant . . . and came face to face with a grinning, red-stained skull in an alcove between rows of bottles. It was wearing the sort of thin silver cardboard crown you find folded inside a cracker.

'That's Howling Hetty, that is,' explained the plump young woman who came to serve us.

'So, this must be the Screaming Skull the hotel is named after?' Carey asked.

'That's right, and the rest of her roams the Sweetwell woods at night, trying to find her head.'

The barmaid was now looking at Carey as if she thought she ought to know him from somewhere . . . or if not, as if she'd *like* to.

'We wondered if we could eat in the restaurant without a booking?' I asked, and she reluctantly unpeeled her eyes from Carey and shouted round a partition into another bar. 'Lulu! Can you fit two more people in for dinner?'

There was an indistinguishable reply and the barmaid said, 'Lulu will come and sort you out in a minute.'

This sounded slightly ominous, but a nearby door opened and a pretty woman of about my own age, with curling dark brown hair, came out. She was wearing a most sumptuously patterned tunic in jewel colours and I immediately wanted to ask her where she got it from.

The barmaid indicated us with a flip of the hand before moving off to serve clamouring customers.

'Hi, did you want a table in the restaurant?' Lulu asked us.

Carey gave her his best smile. 'We haven't got a booking, but we wondered if you could fit us in for dinner?'

'I could in about half an hour, if that suits?' she said. 'Would you like to follow me through to the lounge? It's much quieter.'

It was indeed, for the only other occupant was a fair, slight, handsome man who was seated at a small table and totally absorbed in something on the laptop in front of him.

'That's better, we can hear ourselves think.' She gave us a friendly smile. 'I'm Lulu Tamblyn. My parents own the Screaming Skull and I help out when it's busy. The rest of the time I run the Haunted Holidays and Haunted Weekends – you may have heard of them?'

'I was telling Carey about the ghost trail only today,' I said. 'I'm Angelique Arrowsmith and this is—'

'Oh, I know who *you* are, from the telly!' she said to him. '*And* I know that you've just inherited Mossby.'

'The local grapevine must have been working overtime,' he said ruefully.

'Nothing stays a secret round here for long. And after all, you are a celebrity, so it's quite exciting.'

'*Minor* celeb at most,' he said modestly.

'Cam!' Lulu called imperatively to the blond man, and he tore his eyes away from the screen and looked up.

'This is my husband, Cameron. He's an artist and owns the Hidden Hoards gallery in the village.'

She introduced us and told him to move round so we could all sit down. 'And let me get you both a drink on the house, to welcome you to Mossby. That is,' she added, 'if you *are* staying and not intending to put the place straight on to the market?'

'I'm definitely staying,' Carey told her. 'And Angel's moved in today, too. She's going to renovate and reopen the old stained-glass workshop in the grounds.'

'*That's* where I know your name from,' Cam said to me

192

with interest. 'I've seen that window you did at the White-wood Library.'

'Yes, I . . . worked with Julian Seddon for over ten years,' I said, a lump suddenly and unexpectedly forming in my throat.

'I saw that big piece about him in the local paper. It was a sad loss. His work was brilliant,' Cam said. 'What's happening to his workshop now?'

'His son has taken over. Carey and I are very old friends, so when he discovered there was a disused leaded light workshop already at Mossby, it seemed an ideal opportunity for me to start up on my own.'

I'd skimmed lightly over the surface of the events that had led up to my move, but that seemed to cover the essence of the situation.

Anyway, Cam seemed more interested in me as a fellow artist than in my past life. 'If you want to make any individual hanging pieces, I'd be happy to display them in my gallery. You should come up when you've settled in and see it.'

'I'd love to,' I said. 'In fact, we're both really interested in the way Halfhidden has turned into a tourist hotspot, so we want to explore.'

'Yes, especially the ghost trail,' Carey agreed.

Lulu turned from the bar next to us with a drink in either hand and set them in front of us before sitting down next to Cam. 'Well, funnily enough, *we're* interested in you for the same reason. We know you've got ghosts and we want them!'

Cam fished a couple of glossy leaflets out of a canvas satchel that was on the floor at his feet and handed them across. 'This is the official trail — so far,' he said significantly.

'You want to extend it?' I asked, as we studied the map on the back. 'It looks quite an extensive trail already.'

'Or *trails*,' Carey said. 'I see there are some suggested

short walks around the village, or longer ones taking in all of the spooky bits.'

'It's quite a hike if you want to do the whole thing in a day, especially if you start here at the car park and go uphill through the woods to the spring,' Lulu admitted. 'But most day-trippers just do part of it, and the visitors who stay here for the weekend or longer go round it in a more leisurely way. Almost everyone wants to see the Lady Spring, though.'

'I've heard about that – wasn't it a spring running into a Roman bathhouse?' I asked.

'The healing properties of the water were known about centuries before that and it's always been an important site,' Cam said.

'Carey's recovering from a bike accident – he had a badly broken leg. Maybe it would do him some good?'

'It definitely would, especially if he swam in the pool,' Lulu agreed.

'Not in early January it wouldn't,' Cam pointed out. 'He'd freeze to death!'

'Well . . . perhaps not,' she admitted. 'But he could drink the waters, couldn't he?'

'I'll give it a go as soon as I can,' Carey said. 'Or I'll send Angel up to fetch me some in a bottle.'

'The spring enclosure is only open in the afternoons at this time of year: the opening times are on that leaflet,' Cam said. 'There's a small charge for entry, but if you tell my uncle Tom I sent you, he'll waive that.'

'Cam was just designing a new leaflet for the coming season. That's what he was so engrossed in when you arrived,' Lulu said. 'We're expanding the ghost trail and planning out the new route – an extra loop.'

She pointed to a spot on the map near the central village green. 'There's a single-track lane here that serves a couple of cottages and Moel Farm, which is just above Mossby. The farm is the newest ghost attraction and they've recently diversified into alpacas, so there's going to be a little shop selling everything alpaca-related – the daughter and a friend are running that and weaving things out of the wool to sell, too – and the farmer's wife will provide refreshments in the summer.'

'Alpacas? That sounds a bit different,' I said. 'What kind of ghost have they got?'

'Actually, they've come up with a haunted well,' Cam said. 'On nights when there's a full moon, you can see the face of a maidservant killed and thrown down there, looking back at you.'

'Or possibly it's just a reflection of your own face?' Carey suggested.

'That may have given them the idea . . .' admitted Lulu. 'There is a bit of free licence, in the way of ghostly goings-on in Halfhidden.'

'Why not?' I said. 'I'm all for a bit of imagination.'

'On the way to the farm, the visitors can make a small diversion over a stile and across a field to an outcrop of rocks where the Mossby Worm used to hang out,' Cam continued. 'Some kind of dragon.'

'Every village should have one,' Carey said gravely.

'Unfortunately, the new trail is a dead end at the moment,' Lulu said, 'so the visitors would have to walk back the way they came. But there used to be a way from the farm track down to Mossby, though it hasn't been used for a long time, so I wrote to Mr Revell, asking if he might be interested in being the next destination on the ghost trail.'

'I bet that went down like a lead balloon,' Carey said. 'My uncle seemed to prefer living like a hermit, and under sufferance only let a couple of coach parties a year have a look at the old part of the house.'

'Yes, he told me that in no uncertain terms! It was such

a pity, because I know there's a real ghost legend there. And if people will be able to visit Mossby, then they could carry on down the drive and along the road back here afterwards.'

'*I* wrote twice to Carey's uncle soon after I moved to Lancashire, asking for permission to view some stained glass in the Arts and Crafts part of the house, which I had a particular interest in, but he refused me, too,' I said.

'Never mind, Angelique, you can drool over the Jessie Kaye windows as much as you like now,' said Carey.

'Might *you* be interested in making Mossby part of the ghost trail, then?' Lulu asked him hopefully.

'It's a possibility, because I need to make the place pay its own way. I already have plans to turn the renovations into a new TV series, a bit like my old one, but on a much bigger scale.'

'That sounds like fun,' Lulu said. 'We loved your cottage series, didn't we, Cam?'

He nodded. 'The new series, with that actor bloke presenting, just isn't going to be the same. People liked watching you get stuck in and work, not ponce about waffling about architecture.'

'That's what I liked doing, and I don't mind being filmed working on the house, but I don't want to open the Arts and Crafts part to the public, because it's my home, after all.'

'Some places on the ghost trail open only from Easter to late September,' Cam said. 'That's when Lulu's Haunted Holidays and Weekends run. There aren't so many visitors the rest of the year.'

'The ghosts are in the Elizabethan bit, too, Carey,' I pointed out. 'And you could rope off the parts of the grounds that you didn't want people to wander down on opening days.'

'Good idea. I wouldn't want them drowning themselves in the lake, or getting brained by a falling rotten tree branch in the woods,' he said. 'And I suppose the house only needs to open part of the week, too.'

'Thursday to Monday, say two till four in the afternoon, to get the long weekenders?' I suggested. 'And Mrs Danvers could show people round and sell them postcards and souvenirs.'

'Mrs Danvers?' repeated Cam.

'She's Mrs Parry really; that's just a silly joke,' Carey explained.

'She and her husband live in the Lodge. He gardens and she used to housekeep for Carey's uncle.'

'We know them by sight, but they don't come to the pub,' Lulu said.

'You'll both have to come and see the Elizabethan wing,' Carey suggested. 'The main ghost seems to be a seventeenth-century one, Lady Anne Revell, who hangs out in the haunted bedchamber, and there's a family legend that if the stained-glass window she had made is ever removed, some sort of doom will fall on the family.'

'It's a very unusual window for its time anyway,' I enthused. 'Well worth seeing.'

'The first thing Angel's going to do when her workshop is up and running is mend the Lady Anne window, because a bird flew into it,' Carey told them.

'Reluctantly, because it should really go to a specialist glass conservator.'

'No way! I'm definitely not risking the family curse. I feel I'm dicing with death just having it taken to the workshop.'

'Is it badly damaged?' asked Cam.

'Some of the small panes at the top are cracked and one shattered. It might be a bit tricky preserving as much as possible of the original.'

'I wouldn't know where to start,' Cam said, so I described

197

some of the techniques that were used to conserve and repair old glass.

'Couldn't you just stick the fragments of the original panels to a piece of clear glass, with resin?' he suggested, interested. 'I've seen whole windows made like that in churches – appliqué glass, they call it, don't they?'

'They do, and it had a real vogue at one time. The effect could be quite stunning, but there turned out to be a drawback. When the windows were exposed to outside temperatures, the glass and the resin tended to expand and contract at different rates. It wasn't unusual for pieces of glass to drop off and fall on the congregation.'

'Bit of a drawback,' Lulu said, laughing. 'Maybe the old techniques are best!'

'They're certainly what I prefer to work with. I know a lot of glass conservators use resin these days, but even the best yellows after a time.'

Carey had been lost in thought but now suddenly exclaimed, as one seeing a vision of Paradise: 'You've got broadband!'

'Yes, all of Halfhidden has it now,' Cam said.

'I wonder if it could extend to Mossby? If I'm stuck with dial-up much longer, I'll go stark, staring mad.'

'Talk to the people at Moel Farm – they're about to get it, too,' suggested Lulu, and then our table in the restaurant was ready, so we swapped phone numbers and went in, feeling we'd made new friends and opened up some interesting possibilities.

On our return to London I threw myself back into my work and, most particularly, into my ideas for the Mossby hall panels. I was pleased with the final design, which featured the roses so beloved of Miss Revell, and I had already sought out a plantsman specializing in these blooms, who had dispatched to her what he assured me was an unusual rose, as a thank you for her hospitality. To me, it had looked like a small bundle of thorny twigs, but I was told this is the most propitious time of year for the planting of roses.

Mr Revell was not long in following us back to London and approving my designs . . . and that was not all: to my total surprise I found myself caught up in a dizzying, intoxicating, whirlwind courtship, which ended with his asking Father for my hand in marriage.

My normally logical thought processes deserted me and so, I fear, did my common sense. I had fallen in love with Ralph, as I now called him, but yet I also loved my work and knew that I could not be truly happy unless I was engaged in it.

However, when I explained my feelings to Ralph, I found he perfectly understood me, for he immediately suggested that he turn the disused small mill at Mossby into a workshop. What is more, he promised to have it ready by the time we married in the New Year, if Father would lend him some of his men to set it up.

He told me it was to be my wedding present and I felt truly I had found a soulmate. We had been friends first and out of that had grown love.

If I occasionally felt that what was happening was quite unreal, or that I couldn't bear to leave London, my friends and especially Father's workshop, I also felt swept up in the train of something pulling me inexorably along, aided by Aunt Barbara's enthusiasm for the match.

Miss Revell sent me a chilly, formal note saying how delighted she would be to welcome me to the family and thanking me for her gift.

It was evident that it would take more than the present of a few roses to make her love me like a sister.

20

Good Will

On my way to breakfast next morning I went into the nursery to check out the stained glass Carey had mentioned the previous evening and found the top panels of the windows glazed with charming scenes from Aesop's fables: 'The Town Mouse and the Country Mouse', 'The Tortoise and the Hare' and 'The Lion and the Mouse'. There was a beautifully worked embroidered hanging on the same theme, too.

I went down the backstairs to the kitchen and found Carey leaning on to the long table, doing leg exercises, like a ballet dancer limbering up for *Swan Lake*.

Fang was sitting upright in his basket watching him with an expression of faint astonishment.

My hand delved into my bag for my phone, but Carey said evenly, 'If you film me doing this and put it on social media, I'll kill you.'

'Just checking for messages,' I said quickly. 'Anyway, I'm not on social media and you know I wouldn't do a thing like that!'

Carey stood upright and stretched himself. 'There, that's the last one. Some of them you can do lying flat, so I get those over with before I get up in the morning.'

'Good idea,' I said, then began rummaging in the fridge to see what there might be for breakfast. As I buttered toast and Carey poached eggs, he told me that his mother had called him early, waking him up.

'Mum has even less idea than I have about the time difference between wherever she is in the States and here. She's on location somewhere.'

'She didn't say where?'

'I'm not sure she knew.'

When her husband died, Carey's mother had reverted back to being Lila Carey – which is where he got his Christian name from – and was now based permanently in the States, co-starring with her best friend, Marcie, in the long-running cosy crime TV series.

'I told Mum about Julian and that you'd moved in here. She sends you her love and says she hopes you'll stop me doing anything stupid.'

'Fat chance,' I said, watching him neatly deposit a poached egg in the centre of each rectangle of toast. 'How did she feel about your inheriting Mossby?'

'Surprised, but pleased. She's dying to come over and see it, but she can't till the new series of *The Little Crimes* is in the can. When she does, she'll probably bring Marcie with her.'

I liked Marcie, who was tall, slim and just as sassy as the character she played, while Lila had grown laid-back and comfortably plump over the years.

'Eat up, because Mr Wilmslow will be here soon,' Carey advised me.

'Have you fed Fang?' I asked. 'Only he's looking at me ravenously.'

'Ages ago. I'm thinking of taking shares in that upmarket and overpriced dog food he favours.'

'You'll have to keep him out of the way when Mr Wilmslow arrives. I should think biting a solicitor would be a *really* bad move.'

'Biting anyone is a really bad move. He's coming at half

past nine and he's the punctual type, so we can take him into the small sitting room. Fang hasn't learned to open the baize door yet.'

'It swings, but I think it might be too heavy for him. I'll make coffee and bring it through when Mr Wilmslow's here. And by the way,' I added, 'I had a quick look at the nursery windows and I'm not entirely sure, but I think they might also be early Jessie Kaye: they're certainly beautifully made. I'll have a better look later, when there's more light.'

When the solicitor arrived I gave him and Carey time for some private discussion before taking the coffee in.

Mr Wilmslow stood up politely to shake hands, saying he'd been hearing all about me and my plans for the workshop.

Carey knew all my secrets, so I sincerely hoped not . . .

The solicitor was a pleasant man who probably wasn't as old as his manner suggested. His face was plumply wrinkled, much like a good-quality prune, and his eyes were a soft brown.

'We've been talking about my will, Angelique,' Carey said cheerfully. 'Do you remember I said that last time we were just discussing a draft codicil leaving Mossby to Ella, I heard a noise outside the door and I'm sure she was trying to listen in?'

I nodded.

'Your uncle always suspected that she snooped whenever she had the opportunity,' said Mr Wilmslow. 'He kept the door to the muniment room locked except when the cleaners went in, and he had the key of his roll-top desk on his watch chain.'

Carey said, 'She won't be hanging about this time, because the back door's bolted and, anyway, Fang would bark at her.'

'She does creep in very quietly, though,' I pointed out. 'Remember yesterday when she suddenly appeared in the kitchen while we were talking? She could have been there for a while, before Fang started growling.'

'I believe she has only the back door key – and those to the Elizabethan wing, of course,' Mr Wilmslow said. 'She spends a lot of time there. Your uncle said she had a fixation with it.'

'He could be right,' agreed Carey. 'But she can't get into this part of the house that way, because the door from the muniment room into the old part is locked on this side, as is the one from the turret upstairs into Lady Anne's bedchamber.'

I thought Ella could have lifted the bunch of spare house keys off the hook any time, and had them copied, but I said nothing. I probably have a nasty, suspicious mind.

'After our last meeting, you decided to think further about making a new will entirely, instead of adding a codicil. Have you come to any decision?' asked the solicitor.

'Yes, now I understand that Ella only lived here for a couple of years as a small child, I think my uncle was very generous to her and her family.'

'Then you do not wish to leave Mossby to her now?'

'No. It's not even as if she seemed to care about the place, other than the old wing. So I'd like you to draw up a new will along the same lines as the other, leaving a few bequests to friends and my mother and the remainder, including the Mossby estate, to Angel.'

I nearly dropped my coffee cup. 'To *me*?'

'Yes: why not? I haven't got any near relatives, apart from Mum, and she's well off and settled in the USA. You're my very best friend and if anything happened to me, I know you'd look after Mossby.'

'Yes, but, Carey—'

'Have *you* made a will?' he broke in.

'No, of course not! I've never had anything much to leave.'

'Everyone should make a will. It simplifies the proceedings for those left behind,' Mr Wilmslow said.

'Come on, Angel, if you made a will, who would you leave your worldly goods to?' Carey asked, putting me on the spot.

'A few small bequests to friends and Mum, and the rest to you, of course,' I admitted.

'There you are, then. And anyway, my will would only come into effect if I died unmarried and without issue. Even if I was a cat, I'd still have seven lives left.'

'Seven?' Mr Wilmslow queried.

'I had an earlier slight bump on my bike,' Carey explained.

'Oh, yes, I believe you did mention it.'

'Cycling in London seems increasingly dangerous,' I said, but I hoped Carey would be safe enough here . . . And then one day he'd marry and fill the house with little Revells.

'Going back to the will question, I think I'd like to leave some money to Ella and her husband,' Carey said generously. 'I may not like her, but my uncle did support her over the years and I feel a certain obligation to carry on.'

They discussed how much and Mr Wilmslow scribbled a few notes.

'I'll draw up a new will accordingly and let you know when it's ready, so you can come in at your convenience.'

Business done, he turned to his hobby and began to discourse with enthusiasm on the history of the Revell family and the constant remodelling of the house.

'There are many mysteries and stories connected with Mossby,' he said, getting into his stride. 'For instance, Cecil Revell, whose portrait hangs in the Long Gallery, briefly found favour with the first Queen Elizabeth. She bestowed on him a magnificent baroque jewelled ornament – always referred to in family documents as the Jewel of Mossby – which was suspended from a chain of huge rubies. He's wearing it in the painting, but of course these adornments went out of fashion and the Jewel itself vanished, probably during the seventeenth century.'

'Could they have sold it?' I asked.

'Possibly, though it would fetch such a sum that you would think the coffers would have swelled considerably and there was no sign of a sudden influx of wealth. One theory is that the Cavalier Revell, Phillip, had it sent abroad during the Civil War for safekeeping and perhaps to provide for himself should he need to flee the country, as many did once the tide of success turned in the Parliamentarians' favour. But he died in battle and presumably took the secret with him. His body was never found,' he added. 'He was seen to fall wounded, so after a time his death was presumed and his posthumous son, Edmund, inherited in due course.'

'And handed down the estate to his descendants – ending in you, Carey,' I said to him.

'True, though of course the Revell line would have died out at Mossby, had it not been for Joshua Winterbotham,' said Mr Wilmslow.

'He was the wealthy factory and ship owner who married the heiress in the middle of the nineteenth century and changed his name to hers, wasn't he?' Carey said.

'Yes. The fortunes of the house had dwindled and all the farmland had been sold off, so materially it was a good match for her.'

'And he built my workshop, to give employment to local people,' I said.

'For some form of cotton manufacture – hosiery, I think,' he agreed. 'I have forgotten now and, of course, it fell into disuse after his death. His son was brought up a gentleman and his interests lay elsewhere.'

'Until he married Jessie Kaye and she set up her stained-glass workshop there,' I said.

'And that was really serendipity,' Carey told Mr Wilmslow, 'because now Angel can work there.'

After the coffee and biscuits we set off for the muniment room, where I tactfully turned my back and studied the samplers on the wall, while Mr Wilmslow revealed to Carey the mechanism that opened the concealed cavity.

'It's not a particularly difficult one, as they go. It pivots when pressure is applied to the right place, much like the entrance to the priest-hole in the Great Hall,' explained Mr Wilmslow. 'Of course, the existence of that one has been known for many years.'

But by this point, I was not really paying attention, because I was fascinated by the samplers, some of which were long and narrow strips of linen on stretchers, while others were framed and of the alphabet-and-house type.

Behind me there was a sort of click and a sliding noise. Carey said, 'Come and look at this, Angel! I don't know why you're being so tactful, because if I can't trust you, then I can't trust anyone.'

I turned and saw that the doors beneath the deep window seat had been opened and the floor inside appeared to have vanished, revealing a sizeable cavity containing an extremely ancient chest.

'They call those Spanish chests, don't they?' Carey asked.

'I believe so, though this one doesn't have a locking mechanism, as some do,' the solicitor agreed. 'It must have been quite difficult to get it into the space, since it's a close fit.'

'It does have those handles at the side, though,' said Carey. 'They probably lowered it in with ropes.'

It was dark under there, but Carey had had the forethought to equip himself with a torch. When he lifted the lid back, we saw the chest was stuffed almost full with bundles and rolls of papers, packets and ledgers.

'Well, you did say that the family had just shoved their papers in there for generations,' Carey said ruefully.

'And no one's ever gone through them properly, so far as

I know, so the earlier layers at the bottom could prove most interesting,' Mr Wilmslow said, his eyes gleaming.

'You wouldn't be able to get the chest out unless you emptied it,' I said. 'That probably had something to do with it never having been sorted.'

'I know that at one time your uncle had some idea of writing a family history, because we often discussed it, but it didn't come to anything,' the solicitor said. 'Despite his long life, he was never a well man: rheumatic fever in childhood, affecting his heart, I believe. He was exempted from active war service.'

'Wouldn't it be great if the Jewel of Mossby was lying forgotten at the bottom of the chest?' Carey said, staring absently down into it.

'I think we'd have to be beyond optimistic to expect that no one else had thought of that,' I told him. 'That's probably why it looks such a jumble in there! I'd give up any idea of treasure hunting: it's long gone.'

'At some point I'll empty it all out and catalogue what's in there,' said Carey, 'but that's a job that will have to wait. It'll make an interesting episode in a later series, if the first one is a success.'

'Of course it will be,' I told him firmly. 'Nick will want to film you pretending to see the secret treasure chest for the first time when he hears about it.'

Mr Wilmslow looked at us enquiringly and Carey explained about basing his new TV series on Mossby, to be filmed by Nick and his company.

'There are so many different aspects of Mossby to draw into the series – like the workshop and the legacy of the original artist who worked there, Jessie Kaye. Angel's going to write a book about her and the other early stained-glass craftswomen of the Arts and Crafts era,' Carey said. 'Her final university dissertation practically turned into one, she was so into it.'

'And when Carey's built the strength back up in that leg, he can start taking commissions to restore old cottages, like he did before,' I said.

'But until I begin earning money again, the proceeds from the sale of my flat will pay for the urgent expensive repairs and renovations to Mossby: the electrics and plumbing and anything structural.'

'Dear me, I don't know what your uncle would have thought about Mossby being filmed and on television! Would that be one of those so-called "fly-on-the-wall" documentaries?'

'Sort of. Nick and his crew will dash up and film for a day or two every so often, which means some of it has to be staged to look as if it's happening on camera. And my uncle *did* want me to find a way of keeping Mossby in the family and knew what I did for a living,' Carey pointed out.

'The Elizabethan wing is probably going to become part of the Halfhidden ghost trail from Easter, and open to the public, too,' I said. 'So that'll be another source of income.'

'I'm starting to see you've got many irons in the pot, Carey, and I'm sure you'll infuse new life into the place.'

We went up to the Long Gallery to see the Elizabethan portrait of a slender young man, who looked like an attenuated version of Carey. He was wearing a whopping baroque pearl-centred medallion, jewelled and enamelled. I think it was supposed to be St George and the Dragon, with the pearl forming the body, and it was suspended on a heavy chain of huge square rubies linked with gold.

You could break a wrist, pulling a cracker with that in it.

The artist was mediocre and the portrait flat and uninspired, though the Jewel at least must have stirred his enthusiasm, because he'd lovingly captured every detail of it.

'It's extremely ugly and must have weighed a ton,' I said.

'Maybe, but having seen it, perhaps I'll have a rummage about in that chest after all,' Carey said, staring at it. 'That monstrosity would pay for all the renovations on its own – and possibly the running costs up to the next century!'

Then he sighed. 'I expect it was broken up, reset and sold on centuries ago.'

I was sure he was right, but having a quick look wouldn't hurt.

'Could it have been hidden in another priest-hole and the secret lost?' I suggested. 'Perhaps the Cavalier Revell hid it before he went off to his final battle, but didn't tell anyone where it was?'

'That possibility has been thought of,' Mr Wilmslow admitted. 'But despite extensive searches, it hasn't come to light.'

On the way downstairs again we paused to look at the windows and I told him my theory that the design of the Lady Anne window was based on samplers of the time.

'Now you've said it, I can see what you mean,' he said thoughtfully. 'I expect she would have used motifs and patterns that she was familiar with, even though it does seem an odd fancy.'

'The so-called curse really isn't one, is it?' I suggested. 'I mean, it doesn't specify what will happen if the window is removed.'

'I think that's left to our imagination,' Carey said. 'Something too terrible to contemplate.'

We carried on down to the hall where, like the rest of the old part of the house, Ella had polished the panelling to a high gloss, while ignoring the grime and cobwebs adorning the ceilings and furniture.

This must have made Mr Wilmslow think of her, because he asked, 'Have you decided what to do about the Parrys' employment, Carey?'

'I have: my ideas for Mossby's future are coming together and I can see that things will have to change. I'm going to suggest to them that they continue to live rent free at the Lodge and I'll substantially increase Clem's salary to reflect his hard work. But I don't need a housekeeper, so Ella's employment will cease.'

'That seems a fair and practical solution,' he approved.

'She doesn't seem to have earned her salary and while everyone has told me how she insists on cleaning this wing herself, she hasn't even done that properly.'

'Very true. I had noticed. But of course, making her redundant isn't likely to go down well,' he said drily.

'I can't help that – I have to be practical.' Carey's strong jaw set in a way I was familiar with. 'I'm going to keep the cleaning firm on and I'll get them to do a thorough spring clean through the whole property.'

'I suspect Ella won't like that either, if they're going to come in here too,' I said.

'Then she should have made a better job of it herself. I'll probably give her first refusal of the position of seasonal tour guide if we open to the public at Easter, though.'

'If Clem's salary is substantially increased, then there will be no radical drop in their income, so I think your solution is a very fair one,' Mr Wilmslow said.

He left soon after that, promising to ring once the new will was drawn up ready for signature, and as soon as his car vanished Carey turned to me.

'I feel like going for a rummage through that chest in the muniment room, even though I'm sure the Jewel won't be there. But then, there's so much I'm dying to look at, explore and work on, that it's hard to know where to start. I mean, we haven't even *seen* the attics yet, so why don't we—'

'Why don't we have lunch and take Fang for a little airing, before we do anything else?' I interrupted firmly.

And we did: up the weedy, unused part of the drive behind the house to where an old wrought-iron gate was

211

fastened by a huge chain and a padlock that looked as rusted solid as the rest of it.

'Bolt-cutter,' Carey suggested, examining it. 'These gates and the front ones will look splendid when they're restored. The wrought-iron work is really fine.'

'There's an old stone stile in the wall over there you could replace with a small wicket gate for the visitors to use.'

'Or put a gate in next to it, for those who can't climb over stiles?'

Beyond the gate you could just see where the old drive had continued and joined the narrow farm track, which skirted the walls of the estate and headed off downwards. It had been tarmacked, but a Mohican ridge of tufty grass had grown up the middle.

'So, if you reopened these gates, you could drive up past the farm and come out eventually in the middle of Halfhidden village?' I said.

'You could, though I'm not sure it would exactly be a shortcut, because I bet there are two or three gates or cattle grids on the way.'

We could see the roof of Moel Farm above us with a plume of blue-grey smoke winding up into the sky, and suddenly, over the stone wall opposite, the inquisitive heads of two alpacas popped up like furry periscopes.

'Are those the ones that spit, or is that llamas?' I asked.

'I don't know. I thought it was camels. But if they can spit, they'd have to be Olympic champions to get you from there, Shrimp,' he said, laughing.

When I first told Lily of our engagement, she gently pointed out that though Ralph and I seemed to be on the friendliest of terms, his manner to me was not at all lover-like. But of course I did not heed her, for I was dazzled by the sun of Ralph's splendour and if my wings got singed, it was entirely my own fault.

So it was that soon after Christmas we were married and spent our honeymoon in Paris, one day taking an exceedingly interesting excursion to Chartres, to see the cathedral windows. I wrote reams back to Father and Michael about it: I was quite overcome. Looking back later, I could see that I mentioned the stained glass I saw on my honeymoon with much more frequency than I wrote of my husband. Of course, I adored Ralph, who was gentle and kind, but the feeling of excitement receded fairly quickly and we were soon back to being the companionable friends we had always been. I was happy in Paris, though I soon saw that Ralph longed to get home to Mossby – and I too began to miss my work and looked forward to viewing my very own workshop.

For the first few days at Mossby, relations with Honoria proved very difficult, until finally I spoke my mind bluntly to her and we came to an understanding that she should continue to make Mossby her home and keep house as she had always done. I had no experience or interest in running a household and, in any case, I had barely unpacked before I was running down to see how the transformation of the old mill into a glass workshop had turned out.

In fact, with its tall windows in the main area, it might have been built for the purpose and the two men Father had sent to set it up said they would be happy to settle in Lancashire, if asked. Since Father seemed from the start to regard it as an off-shoot of his own business, I could continue to do work for him, the train making a convenient link between us for the transportation of painted glass for firing and finished panels.

But I was quite sure that I would soon be accepting, and carrying out, commissions of my own.

21

Spats

After lunch Carey handed me a large torch and swept me off down the cellar stairs, which were near the back door.

At the bottom lurked the boiler, ticking quietly to itself in the manner of its kind. A long, whitewashed passage led out of it, off which were a series of cellars furnished with old empty packing cases, broken suitcases and other rubbish. One contained an almost empty wine rack and the last one a strange, stone-topped table like a pagan altar, which Carey thought might have been for cutting up carcasses.

A low wooden door at the end of the passage took us into what was clearly a more ancient part, held up by a series of arches and dimly illuminated by single light bulbs hanging from cables loosely looped across the ceilings.

I was just thinking that it was as well it was dry down there, when in the very last cellar (which we assumed to be next to, or under, the old tower) we found there was a stream in a deep stone channel running right across it.

'Oh, look – all mod cons,' I said. 'Cold and cold running water.'

'This is interesting!' Carey squatted down to examine the stonework. 'I've seen this sort of thing before in old farm-houses and it must have been a luxury not having to go out for water in the middle of winter. I'm sure this is what's feeding the fountains and fish ponds on the terraces below the house, too.'

He looked around, shining his torch into the darker corners. 'The shape of the arches and the construction of the roof gives the place a slightly ecclesiastical air, doesn't it? I wonder if there might originally have been an early church, or hermitage or something like that on this site.'

I shone my torch down on the huge slabs under my feet, looking for carved lettering or crosses, or whatever. 'I sincerely hope this isn't a crypt, with burials!'

'No, of course it isn't,' he assured me, though sounding quite disappointed about it. 'There's a lot of space down here, but I can't imagine what I'll do with it, other than set up a workbench and tool rack in one of the first rooms . . . though maybe we could have parties down here later?'

'Not the sort of parties *I* go to,' I said firmly, remembering the odd stone slab table, which had looked a bit sacrificial. 'Mine tend to involve nibbles and drinks *above* ground.'

'Is that the kind of social life you've been leading up here, Shrimp? It sounds like a round of total dissipation.'

'Well, it was until Julian had the stroke. Before that, we were invited to lots of little drinks parties by the solicitor, our doctor, the vicar and a few other professional people. They were all nice.'

They'd all been about Julian's age, too, but, unlike him, rather boring. I expect they thought much the same about me . . .

'Right, time to explore the attics,' Carey said, his energy and enthusiasm undiminished. 'We'll go up the backstairs and start in the servants' wing. The nursery suite occupies half the first floor, so I presume the upper staff had the remaining bedrooms there and the unfortunate lesser orders were housed in the attics.'

He was right, too, for up there were several bleak, chilly

chambers with cast-iron beds and washstands that were much more utilitarian than Arts and Crafts. Ralph Revell's beautiful vision did not seem to have extended beyond the baize doors.

There was no connection to the rest of the house on that level, so we had to go down and back up again, but once there we saw the attic ran the full width of the house and had been crammed with unwanted possessions like an illustrated guide to Junk through the Centuries.

'Every time they modernized, or knocked down and rebuilt a bit of Mossby, the unwanted stuff must have been stored away somewhere – and eventually they brought it all up here,' I suggested.

'I think you're right, but goodness knows why they would want to hang on to most of it,' Carey said, regarding the ranks of monstrous dark furniture with dislike. 'Unfortunately, the pre-Arts and Crafts Revells appear to have gone in for the worst excesses of mid-Victorian mahogany in a big way.'

He picked his way through the stacked piles and flashed his torch about. 'I think there are some nice earlier pieces hidden behind all this stuff. Perhaps some of it would look interesting in the house.'

'You're not sticking to the pure Arts and Crafts ethos, then?'

'You know how I feel about restorations: every generation should leave their stamp on their homes and no one seems to have done that to Mossby. Even in the Elizabethan wing, everything later than the eighteenth century has been removed. I'll just put a few pieces back here and there, where they seem to fit.'

It was what he was good at and it had always worked in the past, though that, of course, had been on a smaller and more domestic scale.

'At least the roof looks fine,' he said, looking up. 'What little my uncle spent on Mossby appears to have gone on

217

vital repairs to the fabric of the building, which makes sense.'

'Let's hope that extended to the outbuildings, including my workshop, then,' I said, opening an old leather-bound trunk and removing an empty top tray so I could shine my torch inside.

'I'm sure I can sell all the dark, ugly furniture to a dealer I know,' Carey mused. 'He's stockpiling it under the misguided belief it'll come back into fashion eventually. Once it's all gone, we'll be able to see the wood from the trees.'

'And the Sheraton from the Chippendale?'

'You never know,' he said, but by then I was rooting in the trunk.

'Oh, look, these must have come out of the old nursery!' I said. I pulled out a doll with a waxen and ghastly face, and a small toy crib. 'There's a wooden top and some of those roly-poly figures that bounce up again if you knock them over, and I think there's a Noah's Ark, too.' I looked up. 'They'd add a bit of interest to the nursery in the Elizabethan wing, wouldn't they?'

'They certainly would, though I think I've seen a doll just like that one in a horror film . . . And that's a thought: maybe we could rent out the old wing as a set for horror films.'

I wasn't sure if he was serious or not: I wouldn't put it past him and Nick to know people who *made* horror films. I suddenly remembered the sinister stone table in the cellars . . . and so did Carey.

'The cellars would be good for that, too. Just think of that stone table!'

'Oddly enough, I just did.'

'Two hearts that beat as one, Shrimp.'

A horrible image flashed into my mind and I gave a shudder. It was all going a bit *Frankenstein*.

*

When we'd removed the cobwebs and washed the grime of centuries off our hands, Carey rang the Parrys and invited them up next morning to discuss their future employment.

Since he had cold feet about how they would take his decisions, especially Ella, he wanted me to be there too, but I thought they'd resent an outsider sitting in on a private interview.

So we decided that when they arrived he'd take them straight through into the big drawing room, where the chairs and sofas were arranged around the hearth and a log fire could be lit to make it cosy. I'd take tea and biscuits through, then retreat to the kitchen and make sure Fang didn't get out. His biting Clem, Ella, or both would only make a difficult situation worse.

In any case, Molly was coming over first thing, because we were going to empty the contents of the freezer so she could take the frozen mush.

Molly arrived first and we'd just finished ferrying in her stack of cold boxes when someone hammered on the back door.

'That must be the Parrys, though I'd expected Ella to just waltz in,' I said, surprised.

Carey pulled a comically terrified face and said, 'Here we go – lights, camera, action!'

He shut the kitchen door behind him, and Fang, Molly and I all listened to a murmur of voices and then the tramp of feet past the door.

I had the tea tray ready and quickly poured boiling water into the pot before following them.

They were just settling around the fire when I took it into the drawing room and to my surprise, there was a stranger there with them: a tall woman in her late twenties or early thirties, slender, with curling fair hair and round, wide-set, baby-blue eyes that made her look a bit kittenish. Her figure was set off by a white off-the-shoulder jumper and an extremely short skirt that revealed legs about ten feet long, ending in nude stilettos.

Since she looked like a miscast actress, I wasn't surprised when Carey introduced her as the Parrys' daughter, Vicky, up for a visit.

'Oh, yes, you're an actress, aren't you?' I said.

She nodded and arranged her long legs for Carey to look at, crossing one over the other with a silky slither. It was just as well she was wearing tights, because she was the type Granny would have referred to as all fur coat and no knickers.

'I'll just fetch another cup for you, Vicky, and then leave you all to have your talk,' I said, before dashing to the kitchen, pulling a face at Molly and zipping off again.

As I approached the door from the hall into the drawing room, which I'd left open, I heard Ella announcing loudly that she'd had enough pussyfooting around and wanted to know exactly where they stood.

She broke off the moment she saw me and I put the cup and saucer down on the coffee table, smiled and exited stage left.

Back in the kitchen I told Molly what was happening, and that the Parrys' daughter had unexpectedly turned up with them.

'I knew she was an actress. I was surprised when I saw her because I assumed she'd be dark like her mother, but she must take after Clem's side of the family.'

'What's she like, then?'

'Tall, slim, fair curly hair, big blue eyes, a cute face and legs that go on for ever – just Carey's type, in fact,' I added gloomily. 'She couldn't take her eyes off him, either, but he really doesn't need another Daisy in his life right now. Daisy was his last girlfriend, who dumped him after the accident and shacked up with that actor who took over his TV series. Daisy works on the show,' I explained.

'How mean of her! But I'm sure Carey must be used to women chasing him, because of being on the telly, and he won't take any notice.'

I didn't feel quite as sanguine about it, but since there was work to be done, we finished our coffee and some of the excellent coconut pyramids Molly had brought with her as a housewarming present, and started emptying the huge freezer.

Once all the food was packed into the insulated boxes, Molly produced a couple of those fast-defrosting sprays and we blasted the positively Siberian ice layer with them before beginning to chip it away. It was so thickly encrusted, I wouldn't have been at all surprised to find a baby mammoth at the bottom, permafrosted in.

While we were working, I outlined the ideas we'd come up with for making Mossby pay its way.

'If you open the Elizabethan wing regularly, you'll need special insurance. Public liability, I think it's called,' she suggested. 'I mean, not only to insure against theft and breakage, but in case any of the visitors sue you because they've tumbled down the stairs, tripped on a step, or gone for a stroll down a path marked "Private" and fallen into the lake.'

'You know, I think you're right. I must tell Carey, in case he hasn't thought of it.'

'If you do become part of the Halfhidden ghost trail, when would you open to visitors?'

'Lulu Tamblyn, the girl I was telling you about who thought the trail up, said they were adding the farm behind Mossby as a new attraction from Easter, so we'd want to do the same. That's early April this year.'

'That would give you only a couple of months to get organized – it's not long.'

'Carey can get on with that. He's roped me in to help him do a big inventory over the weekend of what needs doing, but after that I'm going to be busy setting up the workshop and drumming up commissions.'

'Well, let me know when Grant and Ivan can come over and see the workshop, because they're champing at the bit to have a look and give you lots of advice you don't need.'

'I'll do that. I do miss them already and I loved working as part of a team, so it's going to be odd being on my own.'

'I'm sure you'll soon be able to employ someone to help, so I wouldn't worry about that,' she said. 'Didn't you enter designs for a couple of competitions before you went to Antigua? When were the closing dates?'

'Some time soon, I think. One was for an installation in a mall in Australia and the winner gets an all-expenses-paid trip out to Brisbane to see the finished work.'

'That would be fun!'

'Yes . . . though, of course, I much prefer designing windows when I know I'm actually going to be making them myself, even if they do have the cartoons to work from.'

'But Julian let you take those as private commissions, didn't he? While if they were to be made in his workshop, if you won then they would be part of the business. And if those had been, then I suppose the prizes would belong to Nat!'

'That's true. Thank goodness both of them were just for the design. Not that I'm likely to win either of them,' I added. 'Any news on the Nat and Willow front?'

'Nat's following up a couple of enquiries and trying to give Willow a crash course in stained-glass window design.'

'Let's hope she's a quick learner, then,' I said.

We'd been too busy at our task to notice any sound of departure, but when finally the freezer was clean, dried and switched back on and we returned to the warmth of the kitchen, we found Carey slumped in a chair by the table, looking as if he'd gone three rounds with a grizzly bear.

'The Parrys have left the building?' I asked brightly.

'Brilliant deduction, my dear Watson,' he said. 'Hi, Molly.'

'So, how did it all go?' I asked, putting the kettle on and removing the almost empty box of coconut pyramids from his reach.

'Sticky and sometimes explosive. Clem was pleased I was putting his salary up and I've promised we'll get people in to see to the trees and cut back the undergrowth and shrubbery. I'll look into buying a sit-on-and-ride mower too, to keep the grass around the lake neat.'

'Sounds like a good idea to me,' I said. 'There were lots of fallen trees round the lake, so you could build up quite a log store to season for next winter.'

'Yes, that's what I thought: we'll have a log-burning stove or two, neat small ones that will fit in. I'd better make sure the wood axe is kept well out of Ella's reach, though.'

'That bad?'

He nodded.

Unsurprisingly, she'd not been at all happy about losing her job and became angry when Carey told her that he was going to ask Dolly Mops to carry out a big spring clean, including the Elizabethan wing.

'In fact, she flew into such a rage that I never really got round to telling her about opening it to tourists and that there might be a seasonal job there for her when it does. She said she'd worked her fingers to the bone single-handedly running Mossby for the last fifteen years,' he added gloomily.

'There isn't a lot of sign of it,' I said.

'No, but they don't seem to have noticed that. Vicky said her mum loved the Elizabethan wing so much that she cleaned it herself once a week and Clem told me I didn't appreciate all the hard work that involved.' He sighed and ran his hands through his thick, red-gold hair. 'I really don't think she or Clem have the least idea that Ella's cleaning amounted to a manic desire to polish every inch of the panelling till you could see your face in it and neglect of everything else. Vicky did a nice line in gentle reproach – you can tell she's an actress.'

He paused and a faint smile touched his lips.

'So, how long is Vicky staying for?' I asked tartly, before I could stop myself.

He grinned at me. 'No idea – and no interest, either, Shrimp. I told you I'd given up the Daisy types, they all turn out to be candy-coated with hard centres.'

'Yes, you *told* me, but then I distinctly remember you said something along those lines during our last year at university.'

'Well, at the time *you* said you weren't going out with any more losers, you were just going to concentrate on writing your dissertation,' he countered.

'And that's exactly what I did!'

'Don't I know it! Remember, it was *me* who drove you all over the country looking at obscure Victorian stained-glass windows. And then you met Julian the moment you graduated and vanished.'

'Well, you couldn't call Julian a loser! You know you liked him.'

We somehow seemed to be on the edge of an argument, but suddenly he relaxed and smiled at me. 'Yes, I did. He almost deserved you.'

'Don't be daft!' I told him.

Molly had been listening to our spat in a startled kind of way, having never heard us bicker like Grant had. Now she got up and said she had to go and I thanked her for helping me defrost and clean out the freezer, when I was sure she was really busy.

Then we helped her load the cold boxes of food into her

little van and she left for home. She was going to stack it all in one of her freezers until she could deliver it to the local senior citizens, a sort of free frozen version of Meals on Wheels. And rice pudding on wheels too, since all of the tinned goods had gone with her.

I tried to remember: is tapioca the one that looks like frogspawn? And semolina the smooth paste you could fill wall cracks with?

After she'd driven off, Carey went to ring the cleaning agency, followed by a prolonged discussion with his internet provider of choice about installing it at Mossby.

After that we went out to do some food and drink shopping and have a couple of complete sets of keys to Mossby cut, as well as extra spares to the back door and Elizabethan wing, for the cleaners.

On the way back we stopped at an office supplier and bought clipboards, pads, pens, highlighters, tags . . . Carey meant business.

And so did I, adding a big fat notebook and a clipboard of my own, just for the workshop. I was champing at the bit to get started on it, and only Carey could have kept me away from it for even a moment.

During our engagement, I had become aware that there had been some kind of falling-out between Ralph and his friend Mr Browne, who certainly was absent from our wedding. The cause remained unclear to me and I did not like to question him or Honoria about it. Having never met Mr Browne, I did not miss his company and the Lodge remained empty.

While I threw myself into my work, Ralph was engaged in improving the design of the grounds and having a base laid in the woodland where a gazebo to Mr Browne's design could be built. We had much to discuss every evening, companionably entering into each other's interests.

Honoria, her position as chatelaine unassailed, and with my backing against Ralph in the matter of increasing the number of rose beds on the terraces, had unbent somewhat. In fact, she now tended to look on us both like an indulgent parent!

I felt quite settled and happy . . . and then one morning, about a month after our return to Mossby, Ralph came in to breakfast and informed us that Rosslyn Browne was returning next day to the Lodge.

He seemed pleased about this, so I assumed that their argument, whatever it was about, had been made up. Honoria, however, did not seem to share her brother's delight in his friend's return, so the impression I'd gained on my first visit that she did not like him would appear to be true.

When Ralph had gone out, I asked her what Mr Browne was like and she said that she did not care much for him and considered him a bad influence on my husband.

'In what way?' I asked, and I thought for a moment she wasn't going to answer.

'He encouraged Ralph to spend too much on the house and I expect will soon be persuading him to embellish the grounds with all kinds of expensive follies and other schemes,' she said finally.

I'd assumed Ralph to be very wealthy, for he spent freely and insisted on the best of everything. Honoria, however, was quite thrifty in the manner of housekeeping, so perhaps she would have preferred to rein in his spending on the house somewhat?

22

Small Creatures

We knew Friday was going to be non-stop busy, because
Carey's removal firm had chosen the same day to bring up
the things from his flat as my two men with a van had to
fetch mine from the storage unit.

One good thing was that there was no sign of Ella,
because we'd been unsure if she might not just keep turning
up on Fridays from sheer force of habit, or until the end of
her month's notice had been reached.

Mrs Bartlett, one of the co-owners of the Dolly Mops
agency, had come along to talk things over in person with
Carey, while her team of cleaners set about their usual work.
I was in the inner hall, carefully polishing the Jessie Kaye
windows to a sparkle with a soft cloth when she emerged
with Carey.

She was a small, cheerful, grey-haired woman of perhaps
sixty, who shook my hand before popping upstairs, where
we could hear her exhorting her ladies to get a shift on,
because Mr Revell wanted all the spare beds made up, since
he expected a constant flow of visitors helping him renovate
Mossby.

Then, with a spurt of gravel, she swooped off in her red
Suzuki Swift, leaving them to it.

'I've given her a key for the back door, so the cleaners can let themselves in after today – lots of her clients are out when they clean for them,' Carey said. 'And the lady doing the ironing will put out the laundry to be collected and take in the clean stuff.'

'That's good. It was hardly one of Mrs Danvers' more onerous tasks, was it?'

'Mrs Bartlett is sending in a bigger team next Friday to spring clean the whole house. She says she's been dying to "bottom" it, as she put it, for the last few years.'

'Including the Elizabethan wing?'

'My uncle used to get them to clean the muniment room sometimes, though he kept it locked up otherwise when he wasn't using it, but she hadn't seen the rest of it so I took her round. The good news is that they have a married couple who specialize in cleaning historic properties, because apparently this part of Lancashire is peppered with them. They're very careful, use specialist products that won't damage anything.'

'Sounds brilliant! I bet they cost more, though.'

'They do,' he admitted, 'but once they've given the wing a good going over, it won't take them so long every week. I told her where the spare set of keys to the wing are: in the key cupboard in the housekeeper's parlour.'

'It's all getting organized, but you're going to have some big monthly bills!'

'Tell me about it. Maybe we should have a treasure hunt for the Jewel of Mossby after all!'

Just after the cleaners had had their elevenses in the kitchen and gone back to work with tea-restored energy, my belongings arrived. I got the two young men to stash most of it in the housekeeper's parlour next to the kitchen, handy for unpacking, but Granny's Welsh dresser and the rocking chair went straight into the kitchen.

I asked them to carry the Lloyd Loom chair and laundry

basket to my bedroom, where they didn't look out of place against the Arts and Crafts ambience, unlike that dreadful blowsy flowered wallpaper.

I'd started picking bits of it off in passing the moment I moved in, so it was starting to look a bit scabby.

The heavy tea chests full of sheet glass were the last things in the van and Carey took the men down to the workshop so they could be unloaded straight into one of the back rooms.

He must have gone for a rummage round the outbuildings after that, because by the time he returned, I'd put the jewel-bright rag rug down in front of the stove, wiped the dresser and was unpacking and arranging china.

He sank into the wide, comfortable wooden rocker and sighed. 'It already looks more like a real home in here – and any minute now, my stuff will arrive from the flat and we can spread that out a bit, too.'

Carey had furnished his flat with the carefully collected antique furniture he'd bought for the country cottage that had been both his first home and restoration project. Since both cottage and flat had been tiny, there wasn't a huge amount of it and I was sure it would fit in.

The removal men must have stopped for lunch on the way up from London, for it was after two and the cleaners had long gone before they appeared.

We watched anxiously as they reversed carefully into the small courtyard, only inches from the grimacing sea creature disporting itself in the fountain, then carried everything in.

Carey's desk went into the old servants' hall that was to be our combined office/studio, along with bookcases, a sturdy kitchen table for me to work on and several boxes. The rest was stacked in the nursery suite upstairs.

When the removal men were tipped and departed we both felt totally exhausted, and Fang was about to spontaneously combust with thwarted rage because he hadn't been allowed to bite anyone.

He'd been so good with the cleaning ladies earlier, too, apart from pestering them for biscuits . . .

After a cup of coffee and a toasted teacake apiece, we revived enough to start sorting out the studio. I stacked the boxes of sketchbooks, portfolios, rolls of cartoons and cut-lines, my old easel and everything else I needed in the corner near my worktable and put my laptop on the end.

'We'll have to fight over the plug sockets till I can have more put in,' Carey said. 'And we'll have a hunt in the attic for more bookshelves and perhaps a couple of cupboards when we've got some nice strong visitors to carry them down.'

There was enough wall space to have a giant corkboard each, and I suddenly thought how useful it would be to have a whole cork wall in the workshop on the windowless side of the wide double end doors. I could pin up entire cartoons, even of very large windows.

Later, while Carey was starting to prepare dinner – nothing fancy, just pasta and a ready-made sauce from a jar – and I fed Fang his gourmet portion of Canine King Salmon Surprise, someone knocked at the back door.

'I hope that's not Ella with more bloody carrots, or we won't just have good night vision, but X-ray eyesight,' Carey said ungratefully.

'If it is her, it must be some kind of peace offering, though,' I suggested. 'Or maybe poisoned, like the apple in *Sleeping Beauty*.'

He went out and returned a moment later with Vicky in tow, who had now poured herself into skin-tight leather trousers and another off-the-shoulder top with a big floppy bow over one boob, as if she'd awarded it a prize.

A booby prize?

231

'Vicky's brought us some potatoes and more carrots, isn't that kind?' he said blandly.

'Lovely!' I agreed. 'You can never have too many carrots. Perhaps I'll batch bake a lot of carrot cakes tomorrow.'

'I wish I could eat cake, but I daren't, because you have to be soooo slim in my business,' Vicky said, giving me a pitying look, as though I was the size of a minke whale. 'But of course, it doesn't matter for you.'

'When Angel isn't wearing those big boots, I have to tie her to something to stop her floating away,' Carey said, and she gave him a puzzled look. I'm not sure she has a sense of humour, or if she has, it's withered from lack of use.

Fang had been gulping down the last of his dinner as if he suspected Vicky of coming to steal it. Now he'd finished, he began his slow-stalking, lip-lifting and growling routine – and after he'd been so nice to the cleaners, too! I'd started to think that, apart from Ella, he was fine with women, it was just men he hated.

Vicky recoiled. 'Mum warned me you had a vicious dog. He's very ugly, too, isn't he?'

'*I* think he's cute,' I said, picking him up and holding him on my knee, where he continued to vibrate with temper, like an idling engine.

Seeing he was secured, Vicky sat down opposite, uninvited, and cast her big, baby-blue orbs around the room.

'Gosh, it looks so different in here now!'

'Of course, you must have been in and out of the house all your life,' I said.

'Not really. I was about fourteen when Mr Revell offered Mum and Dad jobs and somewhere to live, and I'd never seen the place till then. He didn't encourage me to come to the house, either, because he didn't like teenagers, especially female ones. In fact, Mum said he didn't really like women, full stop, so how he came to be married twice, I don't know!'

She gave Carey a melting smile, but he'd gone back to chopping onions and garlic to jazz up the ready-made pasta sauce and missed it.

When he did look up, through slightly watering eyes, he said to her, frowning, 'You know, the minute I saw you I was sure I'd seen you before somewhere and it's still puzzling me.'

For a moment, her face went strangely blank, and then she said, 'Really? But I'm sure you haven't seen my blink-and-you'll-miss-them appearances in *Casualty* and *Coronation Street*, so it must have been in Dulwich Village.'

'Do you live there?'

'I did, and I used to catch sight of you cycling around occasionally – and once you were going into Gino's Café just when I was leaving with some friends. I didn't think you'd noticed me, though.'

Not for want of trying to catch his attention, I suspected. I bet she'd tried everything bar throwing herself to the ground and clinging to his knees.

'I suppose that must be where I remember you from,' he agreed, though still frowning, as if trying to grasp some distant and elusive memory.

'Of course, I'd no idea you were related to the *Mossby* Revells until your uncle made a will not long before he died, and told Mum you were his estranged brother's son and he was leaving everything to you. It was a bit mean of him, I thought, because she'd assumed she was his only relative.'

'She wasn't really related to him at all, though, was she?' I pointed out. 'She was the daughter of his second wife by her first marriage.'

'She looked after him like a daughter, anyway,' Vicky insisted. 'And when he told her about the will, she was so upset she jumped in the car and drove straight down to my place. Dad had no idea what had happened to her till I rang him to say where she was.'

It was odd to think of Ella, Vicky and Carey all being in Dulwich Village at the same time, though perhaps by then Carey had already had his accident and was in hospital.

'I've sold my flat in Dulwich now,' Carey said.

'I'm not there any more either, because I lost my flat share after the other two got married within a month of each other, so I'm back with Mum and Dad for the minute. My agent's sniffing around, so if any auditions or work come up, I'll crash on a friend's sofa till I find something else I can afford. I'm getting more work as an extra these days, though I usually get the roles with a couple of words to say,' she added.

'It must be a hard profession to make a living in, unless you're really lucky,' I said.

'Or you know someone useful, who will give you a hand up.' She directed a languishing glance at Carey, though what she thought he could do to boost her to stardom, goodness knows. He doesn't have theatre directors or film producers in his back pocket.

'Mum says *you're* an old friend of Carey's, down on your luck and staying here till you're back on your feet again,' she said, making me sound like a bag lady that Carey let sleep in the doorway out of charity.

'No, *I'm* the one trying, quite literally, to get back on my feet again,' Carey said. 'Angel and I have been friends all our lives and we just happen to need each other's support at the moment.'

'Friends from our cradle days, when we threw our rattles at each other,' I agreed. 'And I wasn't so much down on my luck, Vicky, as bereaved – I lost my partner before Christmas.'

'Oh, really?' She perked up slightly. That made me practically a grieving widow and so no competition at all. 'I mean, that's sooo sad,' she commiserated.

'Angelique is a well-known stained-glass artist and she's

going to reopen and use the old workshop by the stable block,' Carey said.

'Angelique? Is that really your name?' she asked rudely, staring at me. 'It's a bit weird.'

'My mother used to love a series of novels with a heroine called Angelique, so that's how I ended up with it.'

I was seriously thinking of having the explanation tattooed on my wrist, so I could just hold it up for people to read whenever I was asked.

'Is she dead?'

'Mum? No, alive, kicking, married to a millionaire and living in the Caribbean.'

Though of course, there was a chance that Mum could at this moment be dead drunk and out for the count on rum punch.

'Really – a millionaire? *I* was all set to holiday on Branson's Necker Island with my boyfriend a couple of years ago, because he was a well-known actor and he got invited, but then he dumped me just after I'd bought a whole load of sarongs and bikinis.'

'How tragic,' I commiserated. 'Did you get your money back?'

Scanning my well-worn black jeans, Doc Marten boots and a Grateful Dead sweatshirt I'd bought at a car-boot sale, she said, 'You don't look like a millionaire's daughter.'

'I'm not.'

She glanced uncertainly at me through spider-leg eyelashes and gave up any further attempt to suss out what my relationship with Carey was.

There had been times when even *I* hadn't been too sure about that . . . or even what I wanted it to be.

I mean, when we'd bickered in front of Molly about that last year at college, it had made me remember how we'd briefly seemed to come even closer than ever before . . . until

235

I caught him snogging a former girlfriend at a party and realized he hadn't really changed his ways. And then, almost immediately, I'd met and fallen head over heels in love with Julian, so it was probably just as well.

The next time I'd seen Carey he was going out with the first in a new line of dazzling blonde beauties with velociraptor instincts wrapped up in pink fuzzy coatings.

But there was no denying he would always be special to me: take the way my heart had leaped at the sound of his voice when he'd turned up in the workshop to rescue me, and the feeling I had that I wanted to wrap myself around him and never let him go . . .

Vicky was obviously keen on working up to that position, for she'd moved her chair nearer to his and was now employing every flirtatious trick in the book and, what with all the fluttering, I was surprised her eyelashes hadn't dropped off. If she'd had a fan, she'd probably have rapped him over the knuckles and told him he was very naughty.

'Mum was upset all over again, when you told her she was going to lose her job and salary,' Vicky told him. 'Of course, since you're putting Dad's wages up, they won't be that much worse off, only she's so attached to that stupid old wing of the house, she seems to think it's her life-work to look after it. She's batty.'

If she'd cleaned everything else the way she did the panelling, I'd have suspected Ella was OCD, rather than batty, but I didn't say so. I'd obviously been relegated to the back of the audience and Carey was occupying the Royal Box.

'She seems to love polishing the panelling in the old wing and I don't really mind if she carries on doing that, so long as she doesn't wear it away,' Carey said good-humouredly. 'But I can't afford to pay her that large salary any more, and what I save in the difference after increasing your Dad's wages will go to pay the cleaning company for the extra hours they'll put in to get the place up to scratch.'

'Oh, well, I'll tell her she can still haunt the old wing if she wants to, and that might cheer her up a bit,' she said. 'You wouldn't catch me in there on my own, because it really *is* haunted. When she lived at Mossby as a little girl the old nanny used to tell her stories about the ghosts. Lots of people *died* there.'

'That goes for all old houses,' I said. 'And after all, Carey's uncle died here only last year.'

'He doesn't seem to be haunting me, though,' Carey said. 'Or not yet. Maybe he will when he sees Mossby on telly and hordes of visitors swarming round the old wing.'

'Is Mossby going to be on telly? Like in your *Complete Country Cottage* series?' Vicky asked eagerly, so Carey gave her a short, edited description of our plans for a new series.

'I'd *love* to be in it,' she sighed wistfully, and pointedly.

'It's not a film, it's a fly-on-the-wall documentary,' I said, but I could see she was already imagining herself into a starring role – maybe as chatelaine, if she could nudge me right out of the picture.

I thought we'd never get rid of her after that, until my eye caught Carey's and he gave me a wink.

'It's getting late,' he said, standing up and tipping his onions and garlic into the pan with the sauce. 'Angel, if you put some water on to boil for the pasta, I'll just run Vicky back home in the golf buggy: it's so dark out there, we don't want her breaking anything, do we?'

She went eagerly enough, probably assuming he wanted to get her on her own. And perhaps, despite that wink, he did, for even though I disliked her, I could see she had sex appeal – and a great technique.

I went and looked in the age-mottled mirror on the far

wall and a small creature with a pointed face and mossy grey-green eyes under obliquely slanting dark brows looked back at me, like something slightly feral peeking out of the undergrowth.

Perhaps something, like Fang, that might suddenly bite.

On the day Mr Browne was to return, Ralph set out to meet him and was no more seen again that day, presumably dining with his friend. And since we had separate bedchambers at Mossby (something I assumed to be the way of the gentry) I had no idea what time he came home.

Next day I spent in the workshop. Father having approved a design I had made for a customer, I was engaged in drawing up the cartoon to send down to him, along with some trays of glass ready for painting and firing.

I was quite occupied and happy, so that I entirely forgot the time until Honoria sent a servant down to remind me to return for lunch. Ralph very often called in so that we could walk back to the house together, but today he had not done so and Honoria told me he and his friend had gone off somewhere, but would both be back in time to dine that evening.

Rosslyn Browne came to dinner and somehow the whole atmosphere changed, though I couldn't understand why. He was an elegant, slender, bearded man with eloquent dark eyes and of middle height. He and my husband seemed to share many interests and indeed engaged in similar conversations to those

239

we had shared. But when I joined in, both looked at me as if surprised that I had interrupted them.

It quickly became clear that Mr Browne resented my presence: he was of the jealous variety of friends and wanted to be the centre of Ralph's attention.

I did not like his dismissive – almost sarcastic – attitude towards Honoria either and she, unsurprisingly, was very cold towards him.

I hoped Mr Browne's work kept him frequently away from home.

23

The Vital Spark

We spent practically every waking moment of the entire weekend exhaustively going over the interior of the house, making not only a complete inventory of what was there, but a list of what needed repainting, renovating, renewing or restoring. Carey took a million photographs and made notes, too.

Only one of us really enjoyed this experience. I was limp as a wet rag by Sunday evening, but though Carey was hobbling like an actor auditioning for a bad spy film, his enthusiasm and energy were undiminished. After dinner, he downloaded all the pics he'd taken on to his big laptop and could hardly wait to input the reams of notes, and various lists, not to mention email his many useful contacts.

Even running on about seventy per cent of his normal self, Carey had twice as much vitality as most people. That black and silver stick would soon be worn down to a nub, at that rate.

Fang had shadowed us throughout the weekend, though he tended to lie down and sigh a lot, and also inadvertently get shut into rooms and have to be released after a lot of highly aggrieved barking.

On these occasions, Carey would mutter something about re-homing the daft creature, but we both knew he didn't mean it because we'd grown fond of Fang.

Of course, his antisocial tendencies where ankles were concerned made life a bit difficult, and if the internet wasn't taking all year to connect, I'd have already looked online for miniature dog muzzles.

Nick and the rest of the film crew were due to arrive on Monday morning. They were setting out from London before dawn, intending to shoot loads of film before leaving some time on Tuesday, but even so, we were surprised to see the big white van with 'Raising Crane Productions' along the side pulling into the courtyard just after ten.

They all piled out, stretching in the chilly sunlight. Nick enveloped me in a big hug, followed by tall, red-headed Sukes, who for once was not trying to ram something that looked like a muff on a stick under my nose.

Jorge, the cameraman – though Nick also could double up in this capacity – shuffled his large feet shyly and gave me a smile from somewhere between his beard and fringe, while Nelson, who had black dreadlocks all the way down to the tattered jeans that hung off his almost non-existent hips, said in a deep, plummy Oxford accent, 'Hello, darling!'

You could make a documentary about the documentary makers! They had worked as a team for so long that they tended to act like a flock of Midwich Cuckoos: if one knew something, then they all did. Sukes, Nick and Nelson had once shared the student house with me and Carey, while Jorge had joined them soon afterwards and was now living with Sukes.

Nelson smelled of full cooked English breakfast when he kissed me on the cheek: but come to that, they all did.

'Carey said you'd turned vegetarian, so we thought we'd better get some protein while we could,' Nick explained. 'If you only eat beans, it's going to be like a re-cast of *Gone with the Wind* by the time we leave.'

'You're thinking of vegans, but we're not even totally vege-tarian, because we're still eating fish and eggs and dairy stuff,' I said. 'There was no need to clog your arteries up with saturated fats, because we wouldn't have let you starve.'

I made a big pot of coffee and they sat down to discuss what they were going to do and look at some footage Nick had taken of Carey leaving the physiotherapy unit, with a flotilla of nurses in attendance.

Of course, they'd already had a flying trip up to Mossby the day after Carey moved in, so they had some preliminary shots of it.

'The last time we were here, the weather wasn't so bright,' Nelson said, dunking an iced ring biscuit into his coffee, so that the topping bubbled slightly. 'We still got some good shots of Carey stopping at the bottom of the drive to look at Mossby for the first time and then the sun suddenly coming out just as he reached the courtyard. Couldn't have staged it better.'

'Jorge wants to take some more footage from the bottom of the drive and try a few outside angles with Carey wander-ing round the place,' said Nick. 'Then we'll move on to Angel seeing the workshop for the first time and talking a bit about what it'll mean to her to be working there.'

'Carey told you it was where one of my greatest heroines, Jessie Kaye, worked at the end of the nineteenth century? She was one of the leading female glass craftswomen of her day.'

'Yes, he updated me, though anyone who'd lived with you while you were writing that dissertation knew all about Jessie Kaye and the Arts and Crafts movement, whether they liked it or not!'

'I must have been a monumental bore,' I said apologetically.

'I expect we all were, on our favourite subjects,' Sukes said, pouring herself another mug of coffee.

'I'll go down to the workshop and pretend to see it for the

'first time whenever you want me to,' I promised, because at least Nick hadn't asked me to talk about Julian's illness and death, and how and why I'd moved to Mossby, even though it would make just the sort of angle he'd have liked to introduce.

They fell into a discussion about the various strands that were going to be important when they'd sold the pilot, which they seemed convinced would happen very quickly. On the list of topics that could be woven into the series, along with that of the restoration itself and my setting up the workshop, was the family history, ghosts, legends and secrets, and Carey's determination to make Mossby pay its way.

'And Fang, the little werewolf of Mossby, will be your co-star, Carey,' Nick added.

Unfortunately, all those male legs had been just too tempting for Fang, who was in disgrace again. He was now tied by a longish lead to a hook in the wall by the stove, which was probably once part of some kind of archaic spit – maybe even the sort powered by a little dog. He should thank his lucky stars he wasn't born in an age when they used those.

When the light had gone, the crew and Carey went down to the cellars and amused themselves by pretending they were shooting a horror film. Strange screams and moans floated up through the open door at the top of the stairs as I got out a couple of giant pasta dishes from the freezer. Fortunately, Molly had dropped off the first batch of new food very early that morning before dashing off to do the rest of her round.

Once the pasta was cooked and the wine opened, I called them back up and we all retired to the small sitting room with our plates and glasses, to watch the first of the new *Complete Country Cottage* series without Carey starring in it.

I wasn't sure how good an idea this was, but they all seemed hellbent on it and booed loudly when the new

presenter, Seamus Banyan, appeared, as if he was a panto-
mime villain. He proved to be polished, charming and
enthusiastic, but not remotely hands-on. It just wasn't the
same – how could it be? Carey was knowledgeable about so
many skills that craftsmen loved to talk to him and help out,
and he wasn't afraid to get his hands dirty by mucking in
and working with them, either.

'It's a bit . . . dead,' Jorge said finally, and we all agreed.

'They've got the shape of the old programme, but there's
no heart to it any more,' said Sukes.

'I didn't know any of the people working on the cottage,'
Carey said. 'And what they did to that wattle-and-daub wall
was criminal! Having uncovered that section, they should
have put glass over it and kept it as a major talking point in
the new scheme.'

'It's so unfair. The whole thing was your baby, yet the
only mention of you was that bit in the credits,' I said angrily.

'Serves me right for not reading the small print in the
contract – and my agent should have noticed, too.'

'It was an Immaculate Concept,' sighed Sukes. 'The new
series is just a bastardized production.'

'Never mind, it'll be how it should be in the *Mansion
Makeover* series,' Nick reminded us.

'Well, where's this pub you mentioned?' Nelson said
briskly, changing the subject. 'Let's all go and have a drink.'

Jorge drove us – he always drew the short straw, being
teetotal – and we had a convivial evening in the public bar,
playing darts with some of the locals. Due to a slight under-
estimation of the strength of the local beer, things got a bit
fuzzy, but I do recall Lulu and Cam joining us for a drink
later, together with some friends called Izzy and Rufus. By
then, though, the bar was so full and noisy we could hardly
hear ourselves speak.

If you want to know why the countryside in west

Lancashire is deserted on dark winter evenings, it's because the entire population is in the Screaming Skull.

Under the influence of several pints of Old Spoggit Brown, Nelson got into a rather one-sided conversation across the bar with Howling Hetty, just as we were leaving, and he wanted to take her back with us, but we managed to drag him away.

When we got home, I took Fang out into the courtyard on his lead, since Nick was still out there leaning against the fountain, having a sneaky fag.

'You've got dark sky and stars here,' he said, gazing upwards through circling smoke.

'No streetlights to pollute the night sky, that's why. I expect I'll appreciate it all more when Carey stops running me ragged and calms down to his ordinary semi-manic mode.'

'I'm sorry about Julian, you know,' Nick said awkwardly. 'We all are. We just don't know what to say.'

'I know. It's all right.'

'We heard what a bastard Julian's son turned out to be, but you'll be OK with Carey. And I'm not worried about him, either, now you're here. You're like twins, always happier together.'

Then he flicked his stub into the bowl of the fountain and went off to bed.

What he'd said was insightful for Nick: it must have been the booze talking!

The fountain wasn't on, so I could see the faint last glow of the cigarette stub in the bowl and fished it out. I wasn't having my sea monster poisoned by nicotine.

Not usually the earliest of risers, the crew all found their way down to the kitchen eventually, even if one or two looked just slightly the worse for wear.

I cooked up a big breakfast which, though it might have been lacking in the bacon and black pudding department, had some delicious vegetarian sausages and free-range eggs, guaranteed to be from happy hens.

After following that with an acre of buttered toast and jam and gallons of tea and coffee, they were ready for action.

We went down to the workshop so they could film me seeing it for the first time . . . again. Then it was Carey's turn.

After that, they decided to take some arty shots of the rusted entrance gates and views of the house looking up at the terraces from the lake. Carey not being required for those, he went off in the buggy to look at his uncle's car in the stables, while I walked back to the house and spent a quiet couple of hours in the studio next to the kitchen, sorting out my stuff and starting my list of things I'd need for my new workshop. Since I was beginning almost from scratch, it grew longer and longer.

Carey was in by the time the crew straggled back for lunch and Jorge said that a nosy blonde had suddenly appeared and kept getting in the way of the filming.

'She said you'd told her we were coming, Carey, and since she was an actress she'd be happy to help if we wanted her in some of the shots,' Sukes added.

'Yeah, so I said we weren't making a bloody film so we didn't need extras,' Nick said. 'She was gardening outside the Lodge when we drove past . . . in full makeup and stilettos. I didn't think people gardened in January. Isn't everything dead?'

'Not dead, only resting,' said Carey, sounding a bit *Monty Python*.

'That was Vicky Parry and she's staying with her parents at the Lodge,' I explained. 'But we certainly didn't suggest she should help, or appear on film.'

'No, we didn't think you had,' Nelson said. 'She seemed to be irrelevant.'

Call me mean, but I quite liked hearing the lovely Vicky described as irrelevant!

'That's right. Unless she's got hidden talents in roofing, plumbing, plastering or anything else useful to the programme, I can't see that we'd want her wandering around in the background,' said Sukes.

'She was only a lodge keeper's daughter . . .' murmured Jorge, then got stuck for a second line until, by concerted effort, the crew came up with something amazingly filthy.

'Doesn't quite scan,' Carey said critically, lobbing more rounds of his standby – cheese on toast – on to a plate in the centre of the table.

After lunch, Jorge gave Carey a crash course in the finer arts of filming, since they were loaning him a camera so that he could shoot anything interesting between their visits. Now I'd never know when he was going to suddenly pop up and immortalize me in glorious Technicolor . . .

Then they quickly packed up and we followed them down to the gates in the buggy, where we stood waving them off.

They weren't going straight back, but detouring to Liverpool to shoot some tall ship that was moored there. We could hear them getting in the right mood by discordantly belting out, 'Yo, ho and up she rises!' as they vanished round the bend.

'It was fun, all the old gang together, wasn't it?' Carey said, draping one long arm across my shoulders.

I turned to look up at him, smiling, and that was when I suddenly noticed the stone ball on the top of the tall gatepost next to us move.

Without conscious thought, but with a strength I didn't

realize I possessed, I gave him an almighty shove, pushing him backwards and then, overbalancing, falling on top of him.

The stone ball missed us by about a foot, landing with a soggy thud that shook the ground, and then rolling into the ditch.

Carey clasped me to his chest and then planted a decidedly un-platonic kiss on my lips.

'Did the earth move for you, too, darling?' he said finally, sounding shaken.

'Oh God, you could have been killed!' I exclaimed, staring down at him. My heart was still racing.

'We both could,' he said, then scrambled up, pulling me with him. Then he stooped with a grimace to rub his bad leg.

I picked his stick up and handed it to him. 'Did I hurt your leg? I'm sure I landed on it.'

'A bit, but it was certainly better than a stone ball landing on my head – and I'm sure you just saved my life, Shrimp.'

'It was instinctive. I just happened to catch sight of the movement out of the corner of my eye.' I felt a bit shaky suddenly at the thought of what might have happened.

Carey peered down at the stone ball in the ditch. 'That'll take a bit of getting out.'

'I could have sworn I heard something crashing about in the shrubbery afterwards, while we were lying there,' I said. 'Did you hear anything?'

'No, I was too stunned, though birds and squirrels can make a surprising amount of noise if they're startled. Let's go round and have a look.'

A small path came out of the shrubbery by the gate and the ground was hard under its covering of dead leaves. Despite my protests, Carey climbed far enough up the open rusted gate to examine the top of the column.

'It looks as if the cement holding it on had loosened over the years . . . though why it should suddenly roll off just at

moment, when there wasn't a breeze, or even the vibra-
on of a heavy lorry passing to cause it to, is anyone's guess.
Unless the squirrels are conspiring to kill me and got together
to push it?'

'Don't be daft,' I said.

Carey checked the other column, which seemed firm
enough, before we got back in the buggy and headed towards
the house. It struggled a bit up the steep part, but my legs
were feeling jellified and there was no way I was walking.

The Lodge curtains didn't even twitch as we passed, and
the only sign of life was Clem, doing something horticul-
tural with a spade on the lower terrace.

The house seemed empty and quiet without the others, just
Fang dozing by the stove. Carey made us both coffee and
spiked it with the remains of a bottle of dark rum.

'I think you just lost another of your nine lives – how
many does that make?' I asked.

'Three used, six to go,' he said. 'Cheers!'

But I wasn't entirely cheered, even after the rum, because
I suddenly remembered that when he was a little boy he'd
fallen out of a tree and the back of his jumper had caught on
a branch, slowly throttling him.

Mum, who did have her practical moments, saved him by
bashing the branch with the long wooden clothes prop,
though he was badly bruised from the fall and half asphyxi-
ated. I reminded him of this.

'Five lives left, then,' he said. 'Perhaps I'd better stop having
near-death experiences, even if the kiss of life was enjoyable.'

I looked at him uncertainly, but he gave me his familiar,
loopily brilliant smile and pushed the biscuit tin in my
direction.

'Sugar's good for shock,' he said.

In the ensuing days, I saw little of my husband and missed our easy comradeship. I was much occupied in the workshop, of course, and I now decided to make a full-size cartoon of the Lady Anne window, which fascinated me.

And the more I worked on copying the design, the stranger the whole thing struck me. Some of the diamond panes were painted with repeated sequences of motifs of no apparent significance, while others were filled quite randomly, sampler fashion. The man dressed in Cavalier fashion below the house I had at first supposed to be walking through a cornfield, but on closer inspection I thought it resembled more a bed of flames!

It was all very curious.

24

Connections

Carey's mind soon turned to practical matters and he wondered if the people up at Moel Farm might know how to get the stone ball out of the ditch. It would in any case give him an opportunity of meeting them.

Having cut the rusted padlock off the back gate, we dragged back one side, squealing and protesting, just far enough to get the golf buggy through.

Clem, alerted by the noise, appeared out of the shrubbery with a wheelbarrow and was shocked when we told him what had happened yesterday.

'I haven't been down the drive since then and the tops of the rhododendrons hide that gatepost from the Lodge, so I hadn't noticed the stone ball was missing.'

'It was very odd it should choose the exact moment when Carey was standing next to it to roll off,' I said.

'But perhaps the post has sunk a little, so that it might not be level any more,' Clem suggested. 'In that case, if the mortar loosened enough, it could roll off any time.'

'Angel thinks it was pushed off on purpose,' Carey told him, and Clem's ruddy face blanched. He glanced at me uneasily and then away again.

'Surely not? Who'd do such a thing?'

'Homicidal squirrels – that's my theory,' Carey said with a grin.

'Something big crashed away into the shrubbery right afterwards,' I insisted stubbornly. 'I was shocked, but not so shocked I didn't notice a noise like that.'

'I had other things on my mind,' Carey said innocently, and I shot him an uncertain look.

That kiss had certainly been far different from our usual friendly exchanges . . . but then, shock affects us all in different ways, so it probably had no other significance.

Carey got into the buggy and suggested to Clem that he might like to oil the gate hinges and pull out some of the weeds and ivy that were trying to take over, then he drove off up to the farm. The buggy jolted over the rough and unused bit of track, then trundled off along the tarmac.

I went back into the house and worked on my equipment list in the studio for a while, with Fang curled companionably at my feet, but I was making coffee in the kitchen when Carey returned. He was carrying a box of freshly baked cheese scones and wearing a brightly striped blue and purple alpaca scarf.

A tractor roared down the drive, rattling the window. It was driven by a freckle-faced girl and there was a weather-beaten older man sitting next to her.

'That's Jodie Rigby and her dad, Steve,' Carey said. 'They think they can get the stone ball out of the ditch with that digger thing on the front.' He stole my coffee and washed half a cheese scone down with it.

'Right, I'd better go and see how they're getting on.' He got up again and reached for his stick.

'No, you don't!' I told him firmly. '*I'll* go down, because you need to rest. When you came in, you weren't so much limping as hopping, even using the stick.'

I was positive the accident had jarred his bad leg yester-day, and it really must have been painful, because although he grumbled he agreed to go and lie down for a while.

The Rigbys were still manoeuvring the tractor, so I took the opportunity to have a better look at the ground behind the gatepost. There, pressed into the leaves, I was sure I could make out the impression of the edge and corner of a box or crate. It was very faint, so it was no wonder I hadn't spotted it the previous day – and I didn't think the squirrel theory explained *that*. On the other hand, it was hard to believe that anyone would have deliberately rolled the stone down.

Still, I thought I'd like to know where Ella had been at the time, since she was the one with a grudge and a dodgy tem-per, and also she had been listening at the door when Carey was discussing the codicil leaving Mossby to her. Call me a nasty, suspicious person, but maybe we should find a way of letting her know Carey had changed his mind about that.

I had to admit it all seemed a bit melodramatic and unlikely in the bright light of day, so having watched the successful recovery mission and chatted to the Rigbys about the alpacas and the ghost trail, I returned to the house and went up to check if Carey was awake and ready for a cup of tea and something to eat.

When I quietly opened his door he was lying on his bed, fast asleep, and his face looked smoothed out, innocent and pale as the dawn, just like it had when we were small chil-dren. I brushed a lock of burnished red-gold hair off his forehead and then tiptoed away.

That afternoon when I suggested that we take some time off to explore the village of Halfhidden, Carey didn't put up much of a protest.

'I'll drive,' I said firmly. 'And we're not going to trek

254

round any of the ghost trail this time, we'll just chec
place out.'

'When we clear the back gate, we'll be able to drive o
that way, if we want to.'

'We'll have to see how many farm gates, if any, there are
along it to open first,' I suggested as I turned the car up the
lane just after the Screaming Skull, which was deserted at
that time of the afternoon.

Carey said wistfully, 'I'd love to take that trail up through
the woods from the pub to the Lady Spring, but I don't
think my leg is up to it yet.'

'Never mind, I'm sure it won't be long till you can make
it – and maybe swim in this healing spring too, when the
weather warms up?'

'I don't really expect it to work, but I suppose it wouldn't
hurt to try,' he agreed.

'Meanwhile, perhaps I can get some of the spring
water for you to drink, or pour over your leg, or whatever,' I
joked.

'I can't really see why it should do any good, but I'm willing to suspend belief and do anything that might speed up
the recovery process . . . and if we tell Nick about it, he's
going to want to film it.'

'I'm sure he will.' I carefully negotiated the narrow road,
which wound steadily upwards with the walls of the Sweetwell estate on my right and the occasional cottage huddled
in front of some heavy pine woods on the left.

It brought us to a sort of green, which I thought must be
the centre of the straggling village, for there were larger
houses and other buildings around it, including a small
church and a village hall.

I pulled in and put Fang on the lead before we looked
around. There was another of the big ghost trail information signs nearby, with a helpful 'You are here' arrow on the

though I think we could have worked that one out for
elves.

Carey unfolded one of the leaflets Lulu had given us and
e compared the two maps.

'That's Cam's gallery over there next to the village shop,
which we'd better suss out, because it's the nearest if we run
out of anything,' I said.

'There's a clock repair shop in Halfhidden too, of all
things,' Carey exclaimed, surprised. 'I hadn't noticed that on
the map before. It's further uphill, where there are a lot more
houses. This village seems to stretch right up the valley.'

'I think they call that a "linear village",' I suggested, dim
recollections of school lessons surfacing.

'Well, this is the middle and that drive over there belongs
to the big house, Sweetwell.' He swivelled round. 'There's a
garden antiques place there that sounds interesting.'

I'd been vaguely conscious of some steady barking nearby
since we arrived and now I noticed 'Debo's Desperate Dog
Rescue' on a sign just inside the Sweetwell gates, where an
offshoot to the drive veered to the left behind a neat fence
fronted by rose beds.

At that moment, Lulu walked down it, together with her
friend Izzy, whom we'd met the other night in the pub, and
a very tall, elegant woman with urchin-cut silvery hair. She
looked vaguely familiar.

Something that looked about the size of a brown bear was
following them, but when it caught up, it stopped and sat
down heavily.

'Hi, have you come to suss out the lie of the land?' Lulu
greeted us. 'You remember Izzy, don't you?'

'Only just: I think we'd all had too much of the Old
Spoggit Brown the other night,' Carey said ruefully, and she
grinned. She had an attractively pixie look about her and
was even smaller than me.

'You'll get used to it – it gets everyone like that the .
time,' Izzy said. 'This is my aunt Debo – she runs the la
chance re-homing centre for dogs behind us – and this
Babybelle,' she added, patting the bear, which was panting
and exposing a tongue like a giant flannel.

'What is it?' I asked.

'A Newfoundland. She was a rescue dog, but she's
mine now.'

'I've got one, too,' said Lulu, 'but mine's a Staffie.'

At first sight of the bear, Fang had wisely hidden behind
our legs, though I'd got a good grip on the lead anyway. I
wouldn't have put it past the stupid creature to try and bite
something twenty times his size.

'I don't suppose *you're* looking for a dog, are you?' Debo
asked hopefully. Then her eyes fell on Fang, peeping out cautiously, and her face fell. 'Oh – I see you've already got one.'

'Yes, and *he's* pretty desperate, so you can have him, too,
if you like,' offered Carey.

I gave him a look. 'He doesn't mean it. He's very fond of
Fang; we both are.'

'I might be, if it wasn't for his antisocial tendencies,'
Carey conceded. 'He's a bit of a liability.'

'He's very sweet really,' I explained to the others. 'He just
doesn't like men much, other than Carey. He adores him.'

'I don't know about adore. I think he just associates me
with food, though it doesn't stop him growling at me when
he feels like it.'

'What kind of antisocial tendencies?' Debo asked interestedly, so we told her about the leg biting.

'I know he's small, but he does have big, needle-sharp
teeth and he really goes for it, so they can be quite nasty
bites,' I explained.

'I've had a few like that, though Border collies are the
worst for nipping people's legs,' Debo said. 'You need to talk

257

.hris, my dog whisperer. I'll give you his number. He
.ally has to take them away for a few days of retraining,
.it they come back cured.'

Fang gave her an evil look, though with those protruding
teeth and slightly bulging black eyes, it was always hard for
the poor little thing to look any other way. There was something in his expression, though, that made me think he'd
got the gist of what she'd been saying.

'He looks a clever little fellow,' Lulu said. 'He'll probably
learn not to do it really quickly, and Chris only uses
kind methods, mostly talking to them and rewarding good
behaviour.'

Debo bent down and looked at Fang, and something
must have passed between them because suddenly he wagged
his tail and lolled his tongue at her in an amiable kind of
way, like a small pink flag of truce.

She patted him and straightened up. 'I think he's been
crossed with something: he's certainly not a pure Chihuahua. I'm not sure entirely what, though.'

'Werewolf?' suggested Carey.

'Just wait till Chris has worked his magic on him,' said
Lulu. 'He'll be a different dog.'

Izzy said she'd better get back up to Sweetwell, where she
had a clothes design workshop, and told us her husband ran
the garden antiques centre in the old stables. 'You should
have a look, before you go,' she suggested.

'Yes, and come and see Cam's gallery, too. He has a small
range of Izzy's clothes and scarves,' Lulu said enticingly.

'We will, but we're going to check out the village shop
first,' I told her, which we did after Debo had given Carey
the number of the dog whisperer.

The shop was surprisingly large and well-stocked, with
everything from food and drink to toys and gifts. It was
owned by Cam's mother. I was starting to think that

everyone we met in Halfhidden was related or connected in some way.

We hadn't intended buying anything but, due to the small but interesting deli counter, we came out with so much we had to stash it in the car boot before we went into the gallery.

It was light and airy inside, the whitewashed walls hung with paintings, and there was an elderly man manning a large, polished wooden counter.

A folding wooden floor-to-ceiling screen had been drawn across behind this, partially shutting off the far end of the room, which seemed to be a studio, with several people sitting or standing in front of easels, painting.

Lulu came round the corner of it with a mug of tea, which she handed to the elderly man. 'There you are, Jonah.'

'Cam's running one of his painting classes at the moment,' she explained to us quietly. 'I'd forgotten.'

'That's OK. We only wanted to have a quick look this time,' Carey said, his eyes drawn to the paintings on the wall, which were very good, and lingering, I noticed, on one that looked like shattered sunlight falling across water.

I'd have liked to have lingered over the small rack of Izzy's brightly coloured clothes, especially the padded jackets: I loved my coat of many colours, but it was getting extremely shabby.

'Another time,' Carey said, firmly dragging me away. 'This is just supposed to be a reconnaissance trip, remember?'

Outside, he unfolded the leaflet and we followed the trail up the road past the clock shop and a large Victorian house with a tea garden and a glazed veranda. The sign proclaimed itself to be open out of season at weekends, for afternoon tea.

'I wish it was the weekend now,' I said. 'I'm starving.'

'I can't imagine where you put all the food you eat, when you're the size of a sparrow.'

259

'You eat twice as much!'

'I'm twice as big, and anyway, I burn it off in hard work.' He consulted the map again. 'There's the Summit Alpine Nursery at the top of the valley and near it is the spot that the spectre of a Saxon warrior haunts, where a treasure trove was found. We can drive up there another time.'

But before we went home, he insisted we investigated the garden antiques centre. I drove up to a parking area and we walked through an arched opening into a courtyard much like the one at Mossby, where a tall, well-built red-haired woman was briskly wire-brushing the rust off some ancient and obscure piece of agricultural machinery.

Izzy was standing talking to her husband and she waved at us. 'You remember Rufus from the pub, don't you? He was dying to talk to you about your gates, Carey, but it was so noisy that night, it was hopeless.'

'We were all so blotto on the local brew, it would probably have been hopeless anyway,' I confessed.

'It tastes innocuous, but it should have a warning on the bottle!' she said.

'I'd love to buy your wrought-iron front gates,' Rufus told Carey. 'I mean, they're rusted to hell and in poor shape, but—'

'No dice,' Carey interrupted. 'They're pure Arts and Crafts and brilliant workmanship, and they belong at Mossby.'

'I thought you'd say that,' he said ruefully.

'There's a similar but smaller pair of gates at the back of the estate too,' Carey said. His eye fell on the tall redhead so engrossed in her work. 'I won't sell either pair, but I'd pay you to bring them up here and restore them for me. And I've found several pieces of Victorian garden statuary in one of my outbuildings that you might like, so maybe there's even a deal to be done?'

'Maybe,' agreed Rufus, his eyes lighting up, and they moved away and were soon deep in conversation.

'Just as well Foxy loves tackling rust and enjoys a challenge,' Izzy said drily, 'because it looks as if she's going to get one! Foxy Lane is my husband's right-hand woman and her sister is Debo's kennel maid.'

She took me up a nearby flight of stone steps to a large room above what had probably once been a barn, to her workshop, and explained that she sold her lovely clothes mostly by mail order, with a new collection twice a year.

'They're all made in India and I was inspired by the cotton dresses and padded jackets of the hippie era,' she said, then admired my jacket.

'This is a vintage one I bought from a charity shop. Or what's left of it, because I've just about worn it to death.'

'I could make you a new version, if you like?' she offered. 'I do sometimes create one-offs for special clients.'

'I'd love that. It's not dissimilar in shape to your padded jackets, is it? Only mine's velvet patchwork and in random colours.'

I'd never had anything made just for me. It was quite exciting . . . and possibly going to be quite expensive, too.

After a while, I managed to peel Carey away from his new best friend – everyone loves Carey, because he's so genuinely interested and enthusiastic about *everything* – and Rufus said he'd be coming up soon to Mossby.

'When you delve into it, there's an amazing amount of enterprise going on round here, not just the ghost trail,' I said, driving carefully back down the bendy steep bit of the road.

'It sounds like a lot of businesses have taken off because of the increased number of visitors it's brought in, so if they've been creative in adding extra ghostly happenings, you can't really blame them!'

261

'Well, at least you can't say Howling Hetty is made up!' I said.

Carey called the dog whisperer when we got back and then, losing patience with the dodgy and slow internet connection, took himself off to the pub, where he could use the free wi-fi to fire off a load of emails to contacts he was sure would love to help him renovate Mossby. And, such was his charm, charisma and popularity, I expected they would.

While he was there, he also chased up the internet provider he'd chosen, who had promised connection within a fortnight, so he hoped they'd put their money where their mouth was.

As I continued to work on my cartoon of the Lady Anne window, I slowly began to suspect that it was not the random design it seemed after all, but contained some kind of message.

It had taken me many hours to copy every detail – and a servant with a stepladder to help me get high enough to ensure I had it all accurately.

Coming down from this one day, after making a detailed drawing of the final top section, with its spiked sun, I suddenly felt strangely dizzy.

I had been so busy both in my workshop and in my copying of the window that it only now dawned on me that there were changes happening that heralded the arrival of a new addition to the family.

For some reason, this came as a complete shock to me. I had not said so to Ralph, for it seemed unnatural, but I had never yearned for children. But of course he must want an heir to carry on Mossby . . . though this could not have been his only reason for marrying me, since being so tall and handsome he could have married a far prettier girl!

25

On the Ball

Just after breakfast next morning, Rufus rang to ask if it would be all right to come over with his van and take both sets of gates back with him. He had a couple of friends roped in ready to help.

Carey went out to meet them at the top of the drive and I saw the big van go slowly up past the kitchen window a few minutes later, but by then I was talking on the phone to Molly. I'd suddenly realized that I hadn't arranged to have my mail redirected and it didn't look as if Nat and Willow were going to forward any on.

'So if Grant wouldn't mind asking Nat tomorrow if I've had any mail, that would be great,' I explained. 'Some of it might have gone straight to the workshop, rather than the cottage.'

'I'm sure he will, and if he and Ivan could come up and see the workshop on Saturday, they could bring it with them?'

'Of course they can, I was just about to suggest it. It's taken me longer than I thought to help Carey finish his inventory of the house, but I'll be down at the workshop first thing on Saturday, starting to clean it up, though it needs the plumbing and electricity updating first, really. I'm off to get gallons of white paint, rollers, brushes and cleaning materials later today, so I'm ready for action!'

'I'll follow them up in the car, because I've some apple pies and a batch of pasta sauces to put in Carey's freezer, but then I'll have to dash off to do the rest of my deliveries.'

'OK – you've got your key to the back door now, so if no one is about you can just let yourself in and we'll have a catch-up when you've got a bit more time.'

I finished my coffee and went out with Fang to see how they were getting on with the back gates. I was just in time to see them loading the second one into the van. Carey was holding one corner, but the other three were also big men, so I hoped he wasn't hefting that much of the weight.

He spotted me and looked slightly guilty, but actually, apart from the slight setback of my falling on his bad leg earlier that week, he did seem to be gaining strength in it and only really used his stick when he was tiring.

Rufus's friends, Andy and Ben, were so alike that they must be either siblings or identical twins. They closed up the tailgate and got into the cab with Rufus and we followed the van down in the buggy to the much bigger – and even rustier – front gates.

I'd thought of showing Carey the marks on the ground near the post, but when I looked, the leaves had been disturbed . . . Perhaps I had imagined them? There were lots of new small, round puncture marks, though, that hadn't been there before and I had a good idea what had caused those.

The round stone ball from the top of the column still lay at the side of the drive and it was at least handy to sit on while I watched them struggling to detach the first gate from its corroded hinges.

They were just about to lift it off when I heard a rattle and clunk behind me and turned to see the improbable vision of Vicky teetering down from the Lodge, carrying a tray of mugs and a packet of custard creams. She was a very unlikely tea lady.

She ignored me, and addressed herself to the unresponsive backs of the men. 'I saw you were all busy and thought you'd be dying for a cuppa!' she cried gaily, which I translated as her being so consumed with curiosity that she'd had to think up an excuse to come out.

The only reply she got was a Neanderthal grunt or two, because at that crucial point they were too involved in what they were doing to register anything else.

'Lower your end carefully, Andy!' Rufus said. 'Now, let's swing it down a bit so we can lean it against the gatepost for a minute.'

Vicky pouted disconsolately, so I got up and took one of the mugs, which was filled with such watery-looking tea that I immediately regretted it.

'Is that the stone ball that fell off the gatepost?' she asked as I re-seated myself. 'Dad told me and I was horrified, because it could have hit anyone!'

'It nearly hit Carey, that's for sure,' I said. 'I'm surprised the thud it made hitting the ground didn't spark off a small earthquake. Didn't you hear anything?'

'I wasn't here. I'd gone into Ormskirk for some shopping and to get my nails done.'

She twiddled them: they were a sparkly greenish blue.

'What's that shade called – glittery dead frog?' I asked, and she gave me one of her uncertain looks.

'Mum was going to come with me, but she had one of her migraines so she took a pill and went to lie down. She's out of it for hours when she's like that.'

So . . . that seemed to dispose of my main suspect for the stone rolling, and I couldn't somehow see Little Miss Sparkly Nails risking her talons on it, even if she wanted to squash Carey flat, which I was very sure she didn't. Or at least, not like that.

'It was very odd the way the stone ball simply rolled off

just at that moment, don't you think? I could see you'd been behind the gatepost, to have a look.'

She stared at me with her round, pale-blue eyes. 'How – I mean, I—'

'You left your heel prints in the ground. I haven't seen anyone else wearing stilettos round here.'

'I was curious when Dad told me, so I did have a look,' she said, then added, slightly pityingly, 'Do you *have* to wear those big, ugly Doc Marten boots?'

'I like them, and also they protect my feet while I'm working. Do *you* always wear stilettos so high they make the veins and tendons on your feet stand out like bunches of old ropes?'

'They do not!' she gasped indignantly.

'I've often noticed it with women who wear really high heels all the time.'

She squinted down at her feet, but they probably looked OK from that angle. 'I think you've got a strange sense of humour,' she said icily, and went to hang around the men. I could hear her gushing with girlish enthusiasm to Carey about how exciting the whole Mossby renovation project sounded and how she'd love to help whenever she was staying at the Lodge.

'Of course, I've got to keep my hands nice, because I sometimes get hand modelling assignments for catalogues,' she added, which seemed to rule out anything other than a decorative role in the proceedings.

The men finished loading the first gate and then finally took their mugs of tea, though from politeness, I think, rather than because they really wanted them. There wasn't a run on the custard creams. I spotted Carey surreptitiously tipping his tea out on to the grass verge a couple of minutes later.

When the second gate was in the van, Ben and Andy produced cans of Coke and sat on the open tailgate for a breather, while Carey and Rufus batted off up the drive in the golf buggy to look at the Victorian statuary in the outbuildings.

Vicky, abandoned, gave up and went back to the Lodge looking disgruntled. Not long after the front door had slammed behind her, Rufus rang one of the boys to ask them to take the van up to the stable block. It looked as if he was interested in some of the things Carey had found in the outbuildings, at least.

I had a little walk along the lane, then turned up a track marked Moel Farm, which eventually brought me back to the gap where the back gates had been. The alpacas were looking over the wall again, but they didn't spit. In fact, they just looked amiable and inquisitive.

Carey was in the kitchen, brewing a pot of strong coffee, which he said he hoped would take the taste of Vicky's disgusting tea away.

'What on earth do you think she did to it to make it taste that awful?'

'At a guess, put one teabag in a large cold pot, poured not quite boiling water over it, and then filled the cups before it had brewed,' I suggested. 'Was Rufus interested in some of the things in the outbuildings, then?'

I'd had a quick look at the statues myself and they were all ghastly: simpering naked maidens, holding wisps of material over their faces, or coyly looking down and sideways, as if suddenly aware they'd forgotten to put their clothes on. One of them was sitting nude and blindfold on a ball, which was a fairly weird idea.

'Rufus wanted all the statues and he took about a mile of cable-edged terracotta garden edging tiles, too. He knows someone who'd probably make me a good offer for the old carriage and he'd buy the trap himself, but I'm thinking about that. There are all sorts of old gardening tools and wheelbarrows and stuff that I haven't had a chance to sort properly, but when I do, I'll give him first refusal on any I decide to part with.'

'Those gates looked worse once you'd got them down, so I hope his assistant really does like scrubbing rust off things.'

'According to Rufus, she can hardly wait to get her hands on them. And we've done a deal, so cleaning the gates isn't going to cost me much . . . if anything.'

'Well, that's good,' I said. 'Who were those two nice boys, by the way?'

'Benbows from the Summit Alpine Nursery – cousins of Lulu, I think. They are really interested in what I'm planning for Mossby and they're going to come down and help out whenever they have a bit of free time. They both work in the nursery with their dad. It's a surprisingly big affair and they send alpine plants all over the country.'

Already I could see that Carey was doing his usual thing of attracting people, like a magnet pulling in iron filings. Only Vicky might be a bit of a dud, unless she could scrape paint and sand wood with her tongue, seeing she had to keep her hands nice for modelling.

On my way out to my car to get all the painting and cleaning materials I needed for Saturday, Ella passed me, heading for the Elizabethan wing. Her face looked like an angry, bitter mask carved from granite and she cut me dead. I don't know what *I'd* done to deserve that?

On Friday, the day of the big spring clean, the usual team of cleaners had been augmented to the point where you couldn't turn round anywhere in the house without finding a young man up a ladder dusting light fittings or a sprightly grey-haired lady steam-cleaning bathroom tiles.

The specialists who handled historic house cleaning were a married middle-aged couple called Mitch and Jenny, and

I showed them round the old wing because Carey was in the studio, about to do a telephone interview with a women's magazine. A photographer had arrived and was waiting to take the pictures for it when he'd finished, so I hoped there would be one clean and unoccupied room in the main house they could use for background by then.

Carey's agent had set up the interview, having learned of the new documentary and become enthused . . . or perhaps he was trying to redeem himself for not spotting the small print in Carey's previous contract. At any rate, there was also talk of a Sunday supplement spread.

'It's the human angle – the accident, being dumped from your old series and then getting – quite literally – back on your feet again,' the agent had told him persuasively.

'But I don't want to be a sob story,' Carey had protested to me afterwards.

'You won't be, just bravely picking yourself up and stoically getting on with life,' I said. 'The readers will love it and there'll be a bidding war for the *Mansion Makeover* rights, so Nick will be delirious with excitement.'

He grinned. 'So will I – I've got shares in Nick's company, you know!'

'There you are, then: you need to raise your profile, then the series and the spin-off books will be a huge success and keep Mossby going for years.'

'I suppose you're right,' he said, and then after the interview was done and the photographs taken, the electrician arrived to carry out a survey and estimate, and they vanished down into the cellars.

I suppose they had to start somewhere.

While they were still down in the depths, Mitch came over from the old wing, looking slightly worried.

'A woman called Ella's turned up. We were working and

270

then I turned round and got quite a shock, because she was just standing there watching us and we hadn't heard her arrive.'

'Oh dear – she does seem to specialize in sudden, silent appearances!'

'She told us she was a member of the family and she'd always looked after the old wing herself, and was very particular about the panelling.'

'She's a connection of the family by marriage and used to be the housekeeper,' I explained. 'She seems to have a compulsion to clean that panelling and when she gets to the end she must start again, like painting the Forth Bridge.'

'It's certainly the only thing in there that's been properly cleaned in living memory,' Mitch said critically. 'I thought I'd better check with you if you want us to leave that to her. Only if so, we've got a better polish, one of the Stately Solutions brand that Dolly Mops orders specially for historic homes.'

'If she isn't being a nuisance, then I'm sure leaving the panelling to Ella, using the new polish, will be all right with Carey,' I told him and he looked relieved.

'Just as well, because I don't think it's going to be possible to stop her!'

'Carey's just showing an electrician round and he'll be coming into your wing soon anyway.'

'Good, because there are a few things I'd like to discuss with him when he does: you've been pretty lucky with moth damage, but I'll put some moth traps down and I can give him the details of a good place to clean and restore the tapestries and bed hangings.'

'I suspect that will be expensive, so possibly it'll have to wait a bit,' I said, and he went off back to his cleaning.

Later, Carey said he and the electrician had come across Ella in the muniment room and he was sure she'd been trying to get in the locked bureau, though she'd pretended to be polishing it when she saw them.

'Not that there's anything of any importance in there, anyway. But it was odd: when I spoke to her she just ignored me as if I wasn't there.'

'I think she's sent us both to Coventry,' I said, and told him about Mitch coming over when she'd turned up and what she'd said about the panelling. 'So I told him to let her get on with it, as long as she used the special polish.'

'I suppose it won't do any harm ... though actually, when we left the room she was rubbing the linenfold panelling so hard it'll probably look more like flat bedsheets when I see it again,' he said gloomily. 'I'm starting to think she's a sandwich short of a picnic.'

'I think she's a sandwich, two sausage rolls and a jam tart short of a picnic,' I told him. And when he'd signed his new will, I'd make sure he left a copy in the bureau, so she'd know exactly what was what!

Apart from a couple of walks on his lead, Fang had been confined to the kitchen for most of the day and although he'd seemed happy to welcome the female cleaners when they came down for their elevenses, he'd taken exception to the three male ones and been banished to the housekeeper's parlour till the coast was clear again.

It did make things difficult, so it was a relief when Chris, the dog whisperer, called just after everyone had finally left, and whisked Fang away.

'I'll ring you in a few days, when he's ready to come home – don't worry, he'll be fine,' he assured us, but the house seemed very empty without Fang. He might be small, but he made his presence felt.

And the house not only seemed empty, but amazingly, dazzlingly clean, too.

When I said so, Carey remarked wryly that he was going to have a dazzling bill to match.

'Never mind – the house will never be quite that filthy again,' I consoled him.

I kept my condition to myself for as long as possible, not wishing for any fuss, but since I had discovered it so late there was no hiding it for ever, so eventually I had to tell Ralph. He was quite overjoyed and kissed me, something that had not happened for so long that I felt quite shy.

But unfortunately, once the first rapture had worn off, his delight expressed itself in a desire that I should do nothing but sit like a pudding till the baby was born, perhaps with little airings in the pony and trap with Honoria as a treat!

However, I was not one to be inactive or wrapped in cotton wool and, apart from that one spell of dizziness, felt perfectly well. I was determined to carry on working until my girth made it impossible!

Father was pleased at the news and Lily, who was herself in the family way, agreed that there was no need to mollycoddle oneself, and she passed on to me much of the sensible advice her mother and older sisters gave her.

26

Redirected

I was already in the workshop when Ivan and Grant arrived next day. They'd brought Louis with them.

Molly, who'd gone on up to the house to stash the latest fruits of her labours in the big freezer, tooted her horn as she passed on the way down again.

'This is a bit of all right,' Ivan said, wandering round the big workroom. 'Needs some putting to rights, but seeing it's been used for the purpose in the past, it couldn't be better.'

'It looks just like a slightly smaller version of Julian's place inside,' Grant said, putting a paper carrier bag down on one of the long glazing tables.

'It's probably about the same age, and brick-built construction, but they must have stuccoed the front to match the house later. Is that my mail in the bag?'

He upended it and a small pile of envelopes slid out.

'That's it, though most of it's catalogues and other sales stuff.'

'Well, those might come in handy, because I'm still compiling a list of what I need to buy for the workshop. But I was hoping there might be some replies about those two designs I sent in for competitions last year. I don't suppose I've won either of them, but I'm really keen on the Brisbane one because I worked so hard on the *Big Wave* idea.'

'It's a good design, so it'll come in handy for something else, even if you don't win it,' Grant said. 'Can you remember the closing dates?'

'No, but I think they were sometime around now. As soon as we get broadband I'll check, because we're on dial-up at the moment and the minute I get anywhere, it disconnects.'

I'd used the address of Julian's studio and the website email for anything work-related, so I couldn't now access the latter. But if there was any news, I expect they'd write to me, too.

'Oh, well, never mind. My main concern at the moment is to get the business up and running. I'm dying to get back to work. I've given my new contact details to the Crafts Council, the British Society of Master Glass Painters and a couple of other places, so hopefully I'll get some commission enquiries before long.'

'Sure to, lass,' Ivan assured me.

'You've got that old window to mend for Carey first, haven't you?' Grant asked.

'Yes, and I'm still a bit worried about it because it really should be a job for an expert. I'm going to ask that friend of Julian's who works in glass restoration in York for advice, but it'll probably be "don't touch it!"'

'Julian mended one or two really old windows when he was first starting out,' revealed Grant, which I hadn't known.

'But there wasn't so much fuss about it then,' Ivan put in, coming back from an exploratory circuit of the room. Louis had vanished, presumably to inspect the back premises.

'If I set myself up repairing glass, I'll concentrate on the more modern stuff,' Grant said.

'Are you still thinking about it?'

'Unless I get a good offer from a firm within driving distance, because we don't want to move house. I'll stay put for the moment, though I'm not doing the job of three people, like Nat seemed to expect when he got rid of the rest of you.'

'I don't blame you, but I'm glad Julian's window went off all right,' I said. 'I'll go and see it when it's installed. I suppose Nat will continue making windows in his style, but they won't be the same.'

'That seems to be the idea, and he's got all Julian's designs, cartoons and drawings to mine for ideas.'

I sighed. 'Oh, well, it often happens. How's Willow coming along? Has she got a flair for stained-glass design?'

'I haven't seen much of her. Nat said she'd had deadlines for those comic book things.'

'Manga,' Louis reminded us, coming back. 'She's done a graphic novel, too. This place is cool,' he added. 'There are loads more rooms – you wouldn't think it to look at the front.'

'I know. It's because it does a left turn and backs on to the courtyard buildings behind. Come on,' I said to the other two, 'I'll give you a guided tour before Carey turns up. He's supposed to be getting his ladders out of one of the stables, though he might have got distracted by something else and forgotten. We'll chase him up if he doesn't come back.'

I turned to survey the room and said, 'This room's the biggest and they've obviously used it for drawing up cartoons and cutlines as well as leading-up – you can tell from the tables now I've brushed the dust off. The nearest one is smooth and well away from the other two.'

'Plenty of room in here to do both,' Ivan agreed. 'That loft over the far end will be handy for storage and there are workbenches and a sink, too.'

'*And* they've left the shelving for sheet glass and some lead calme storage troughs,' Grant observed.

'There's more storage for lead calme underneath the big central table,' I told him. 'The leaded light maker who rented it in the thirties seems to have left a lot of his stuff.'

277

'There's an old lead mill in one of the back rooms, and a melting pot and ladle, too,' Louis put in. His idea of a high treat had always been to help melt lead and cast it into blocks, ready to mill into new calmes.

'You've got lots of storage drawers and big cupboards, but there's been a mouse problem at some point and they've chewed up any paper they can find into confetti,' Ivan said, opening doors in the far wall one after the other.

'Shame, there might have been something interesting, like old cartoons or cutlines,' Grant said.

'Better put traps down just in case they try and move back in,' Ivan suggested, and I shuddered at the thought.

'I wonder if those electronic repellers work?'

'I'll google them,' offered Louis. 'See what the reviews are like.'

'You're worth your weight in lead calme,' I told him, and he grinned.

'It doesn't need much doing in here, barring a good clean and painting,' Grant said.

'I'm going to have the walls white, to keep things light, but I want floor-to-ceiling corkboard on that stretch there, to the right of the door, so I can hang big cartoons up if I want to.'

'Good idea, and you could do with some more adjustable easels over the windows to try the coloured glass against,' suggested Ivan.

I led the way into the next room. 'This is the office/studio/staff room – though I've got a big studio space up at the house, too, so I'll probably do a lot of designing there.' I opened the door to the chilly toilet. 'All mod cons . . . almost. I need a plumber to put a little sink in and some heating everywhere. I mean, I don't want to be toasty when I'm working, just not frozen.'

'Those new electric storage heaters are good,' suggested Ivan.

'It's a thought. And I'll have a gas cylinder for my soldering iron, because I prefer that to an electric one. I'll have to buy an electric kiln, though, because there's no mains gas here.'

'They're more temperamental,' Grant said.

'Maybe, but there's no alternative. I want you to help me choose one later – open or closed, I can't decide.'

I explained where I thought I'd do the cementing and cleaning of the panels, with an overhead air filtration system, and use the smaller room off it for acid etching. 'There's a door in the room that backs on to the courtyard buildings, but it just leads out to a patch of gravel between that and the workshop. I'll put a bench there in spring, so I can take my coffee out when I need a break.'

'You've got it all worked out,' said Ivan.

'Not quite! I've still got a ton of equipment and supplies to get in, and an electrician's coming on Monday before he starts rewiring the house. That's going to be a major expense for Carey, but it has to be done and even he can't persuade someone to carry out a job that size for free ... though maybe he'll get a discount if the electrician gets a plug in the new TV series!'

'Grant told us about the new series – sick!' Louis said, though this seemed to be a term of approbation. 'I didn't know who Carey Revell was when I met him the day he came to Julian's workshop, but I've looked him up. He knows how to do stuff like fell trees and carve stone.'

'Yes, he does tend to go around soaking up practical skills like a human sponge.'

'He hasn't updated his website for months,' Louis said, 'but I saw online he'd had a bad bike smash.'

'That was a few months ago, but his right leg was really badly broken and he was in hospital and rehab for a long time. Then they dropped him from his *Complete Country Cottage* TV series and hired an actor to present it instead.'

279

'Molly and I watched it,' Grant said, 'but it's just turned into another of those shows where they do up houses with cheap tacky stuff that will look even shoddier inside a week.'

'Yeah, the ratings for the first show were crap,' agreed Louis, who seemed to have developed a sudden interest in Carey to near-stalking point.

He and Grant went out of the side door to see if there was any sign of Carey and, once we were alone, Ivan said he was glad to see Louis taking an interest in something again, because he'd been so down after Julian's death.

'You know he'd been counting on Julian taking him as his apprentice when he left college this summer.'

'Yes, but didn't Julian persuade him to apply to art college first? It's a good idea to learn about designing and new techniques.'

'He applied, but he was really keen to get down to work. It's all he's wanted to do since I first took him to see the workshop years ago, when he was a little lad. He's been really depressed since Nat told him he wasn't wanted and my daughter's really worried about him.'

He shook his head, but then brightened. 'Still, Julian would be that proud of you, setting yourself up on your own like this, and who knows what will come of it?'

I blinked away a sudden tear. 'I think he would be pleased, don't you? And it's thanks to Carey I've got this chance.'

'Did I hear my name?'

Carey stuck his head in, his hair adorned by a large cobweb, which I brushed off for him. I was glad it didn't still have an occupant.

'I was just telling Ivan what a slave driver you were, making me trudge all over the house, taking notes and holding your camera and tape measure.'

'I've got another slave at the moment: Louis is coming round to the stables with me to help carry the ladders.'

'Great, then we can finally get going!'

'So, what do you want us to start with?' asked Grant, who had followed Carey in.

'A big clean down, ready to begin painting the walls, doors and window frames,' I said. 'But first, there's a box of cups and two big Thermoses of coffee in the studio. Let's start with that.'

After the coffee, Carey and Louis went for the ladders and were gone for so long that I assumed they'd got distracted by something, but we began the great clean up without them. When finally they did return, though, they started cleaning out the gutters and washing down the outside paintwork, a cold and messy job.

Louis came back in when that was done and told me Carey had gone up to the house. 'And he said I could come to Mossby any time I wanted, to help out with the restoration.'

'How generous of him,' I said, but the sarcasm went over his head. I suspected there was a touch of hero worship developing, though Carey wouldn't notice: he assumes everyone he talks to shares both his enthusiasms and his knowledge.

'Carey says . . .' Louis started again, and this was clearly going to be his new catchphrase.

'Carey says going to art college is really useful, because you can try your hand at all kinds of other things, not just your main subject,' he said now, casually. 'If I can get on a course, then he thought you might let me come and do work experience with you in the holidays.'

'Of course I would, Louis, and I'll help you with your college application too, if you like? You've had lots of relevant experience; they should jump at offering you a place.'

'That would be great, thanks, Angel.'

'And *I*'ll be here as often as I can make it, helping you get

281

the workshop ready – *and* after it's open,' Ivan said. 'If you'll have me, that is? I don't care if you can't pay me till the business gets going, because I'm bored to death doing nothing – just like Louis is bored to death being a teenager.'

'Oh, Granddad!' Louis sighed long-sufferingly.

'You know I'd love your help, Ivan. I'd have already asked you, except I didn't want to take advantage when I couldn't pay you. How about I give you petrol money, till the business starts to earn out?'

'And a bottle of Old Spoggit Brown every day, to go with my sarnies?' he suggested cunningly.

'Done – it's a bargain!'

'And you know you said you needed a plumber? Well, I think I can help you with that one,' Ivan said, and tapped the side of his beaky nose mysteriously. 'I'll make a call.'

It's amazing what you can accomplish with help – *and* it makes everything a lot more fun – so we'd already made quite a difference by the time we finally adjourned to the house.

It was later than we'd thought, so Carey suggested he show Louis and the others the windows I'd been telling them about another day. Louis seemed more interested in the cellars and the haunted wing, anyway.

I spread out my brochures and the list of workshop equipment and materials on the kitchen table, among the coffee cups and a big plate of amazingly delicious custard-filled chocolate choux buns that Molly had left, with a note taped to the box saying, 'Eat Me'.

'I know what I want with the air filtration system,' I said to Grant. 'A smaller version of the one Julian had. It's the kiln I'm not sure about. There seems to be a huge choice these days . . .'

We pored over the catalogues while Ivan, his lips moving, read through the long list.

From time to time he'd exclaim, 'Wire brushes!' or something else I'd forgotten, and then scribble in the margins.

When we'd decided on the best model of kiln for my purposes, I told Carey that Ivan knew a plumber.

'That's right. Officially retired, like me, but still working because he'd be bored sick doing nothing all day and though you can *exist* on a pension, it's not a lot of fun,' he said. 'He's a good plumber.'

'Ivan rang him from the workshop and he's coming tomorrow to see about putting a small sink and electric water heater in the cloakroom,' I said. 'And he'll check out the rest of it, to see what else wants doing. He's going to cut me a good deal – or rather cut *you* a good deal, since the plumbing must be your department.'

'In cash,' Ivan nodded.

'How retired is he?' asked Carey, a familiarly keen expression in his eyes. 'I mean, could he do a bit of updating in the house and fit me a shower in one of the rooms, perhaps?'

'He could do that, all right,' Ivan agreed. 'You'd need an electrician as well to sort the shower wiring and fuses, mind.'

'That's OK, I've got one of those, recommended by the people at the pub down the road.'

'You'd better have a word with him when he comes tomorrow, then,' Ivan said. 'Me and Louis will be back, too, but Grant's got plans.'

'Yes, though I'll come up and give a hand whenever I can, Angel, and you can always ring me if you want to discuss anything,' he said.

'I'm just grateful you all came over today,' I told them. 'It's made all the difference.'

Next morning Carey came down to meet Ivan's plumber friend, Garry, who told him he'd sort out what I wanted at the workshop, no problem, and would come up another day to see what was needed at the house.

After that, Carey took himself off to the big attic, because the dealer friend who liked high Victorian furniture was coming over later with a large van.

Louis spent hours outside the workshop removing the old paint from the window frames with a small flame gun, which he seemed to regard as extremely enjoyable, while Ivan and I started painting the big room. Or rather, I went up the tallest ladders to paint the tops of the walls, while Ivan held the bottom and droned gently on about football, in which I had no interest whatsoever. I just said 'um' occasionally and let it flow on uninterrupted. It was very pleasant and peaceful.

When I looked out later to see if Louis wanted a drink, he was down at the corner of the building, talking to Vicky, of all people – in fact, they seemed to be getting on like a house on fire and, going by their stance, were inputting each other's numbers into their phones.

Then she gave him a flirty look and tottered off down the drive, while he gazed after her with a slightly dazzled expression. I suppose she was terribly sexy really, and Louis was of an age to be flattered by the attentions of an attractive older woman . . .

He was a nice boy, but I wasn't sure what she was going to get out of it. Perhaps she was just being nosy and pumping him for information about what we were doing, and the flirtiness was incidental.

We saw a vast van drive past in the late morning and when I took Louis and Ivan up to the house for a belated lunch and to show them the Jessie Kaye and Lady Anne windows, three burly men were loading monumental bits of mahogany into it. They'd had to park on the drive at the side of the servants' wing, since the van wouldn't fit into the courtyard without demolishing the fishy fountain and the lollipop topiary.

Carey looked pleased as the van filled up. I wondered how there could have been so much weight up there without the ceiling coming down.

When they'd driven off, we all went up to the attics to see what was left and I appropriated a couple of battered but comfortable chairs for the workshop and a pretty desk in a light maple colour for the studio-office downstairs. I'd carry on using Carey's battered old kitchen table for working on, though.

Carey had already spotted a few treasures that he was sure would find their place in the house when it had been renovated, and Louis and Ivan stayed up there helping him to pull things out, while I went down to cut a plate of sandwiches and heat soup.

Then, just as I was about to summon them down to eat, footsteps thundered down the stairs and Louis burst into the kitchen, saying excitedly: 'We've found something in the attic and Carey says you need to come and see it!'

Ralph showed me the first two rooms beyond the baize door on the upper floor of the servants' wing, which he said he had designed with a nursery in mind. We discussed furnishing it in the modern style and it was just like old times, before Mr Browne came back, when we would talk about all manner of things with interest and enthusiasm. It was decided I would design three Aesop's fables-themed top window panels to replace the plain glazing, and would commission Lily to make a matching embroidered hanging for the wall.

A whole morning had slipped by pleasantly in this manner and we went down to lunch still debating the finer niceties in the way of curtains and carpets, only to find Mr Browne had arrived for lunch, though I am very sure he was not invited. But then, he does not seem to wait for invitations but turns up whenever he pleases.

He ignored me in the rudest fashion, engaging Ralph in conversation on the subject of the latest house he had been commissioned to design, in the Lake District. Now that Mossby was almost finished, apart from some grandiose schemes for the gardens, including a hothouse in the small walled fruit and vegetable garden beyond the stables, there did not seem to be much to hold his attention here.

I began to hope he might move to the Lake District permanently and, when I expressed this thought to Honoria, she earnestly agreed with me.

27

Positively Wired

I found them at the furthest end of the attic, gathered round a long, painted metal box. The lid was thrown back and they were all directing their torch beams into it like a scene from an Indiana Jones movie.

'Come and look at this, Angelique!' Carey said excitedly.

I bashed my leg on the corner of something and stopped to rub it. 'I will if I can get through all this stuff – I haven't got a torch.'

One of them lit the way and I hobbled on more carefully. Carey's idea of what was exciting was not always the same as mine anyway, so when I got nearer I said brightly, 'I know what it is – you've found a body, haven't you? How lovely for the documentary!'

Carey grinned. 'No, it's a treasure trove– just wait till you see *this*!'

'Is it the Jewel of Mossby?' I said more eagerly.

'No, it's not any kind of jewel, though you'll think it's as good as one,' Ivan assured me.

They made way and I stared down into the box at long rolls of paper.

'We seem to have found a cache of drawings and cartoons belonging to Jessie Kaye – but when we unrolled a bit of the first one, it looks like she's made a full-colour cartoon of the Lady Anne window.'

'Oh, happy day!' I cried ecstatically and fell to my knees, carefully unrolling the corner and seeing the familiar basket-work edging and diamond panes, each with its odd circular central motif.

'I can't see properly up here,' I said, frustrated. 'Could we carry the whole box downstairs? And thank God it's tin,' I added devoutly, 'so no mice or damp have got in.'

'They seem in pristine condition to me,' Carey said. 'It's all dry as a bone up here anyway. Come on, Louis, you and I can carry it down between us – it's not heavy.'

I tested the weight of one end and I couldn't have carried it myself, so I made no objection as they picked it up and bore it through the attics like a small coffin, with myself and Ivan following, though as celebrants rather than mourners. It was a bit awkward to manoeuvre down the stairs, but finally they got it to the studio. I darted ahead and spread newspaper on the floor and fetched a duster, so I could clean if off before we opened it again.

At some time, the box had been painted a celestial blue, both inside and out, and had probably been specially made to hold rolls of cartoons. Maybe they had a mouse problem down at the workshop even then?

We carefully unrolled everything, spreading each sheet out on the desk, table and floor, weighting the corners down with whatever came to hand.

As Carey had guessed, the outer one was a large and exact full-colour copy of the Lady Anne window.

'That's going to be vital when I do the repairs, because I can see exactly how it looked before it got broken,' I said, gloating over it. 'The bit that got knocked out entirely looks like a spiky star, but it's yellow, so I expect it's supposed to be the sun.'

'It's a strange window for the time,' Ivan said, studying it.

'How do you mean?' asked Louis.

'You look up seventeenth-century windows on your internet thing, and you'll see,' he told him. 'They don't look like patchwork quilts, as a rule.'

'That's interesting. It reminded me of a sampler, Ivan,' I said. 'Pretty, isn't it, even if some of the motifs are a bit bizarre, like that open eye?'

'I think it's all about Mossby – the sun shining down on the house and everyone going about their usual business,' Carey suggested. 'The various symbols that look random to us presumably meant something at the time.'

There was a full-size cartoon and the cutline of Jessie Kaye's landing window, too, with a sheet of her original design ideas and notes written on the edge in a bold hand, though the ink was a little faded.

The final roll was for the inner hall windows, the design of which had been repeated in each panel.

'That's it,' I said, 'no more. Perhaps the rest of her cartoons and cutlines were stored in that big cupboard in the workshop and the mice ate them.'

'I could line that cupboard with sheets of tin, if you like,' offered Ivan. 'I did that to the inside of my shed years ago to keep out the vermin and there's still a few sheets laid by.'

'That would be a great idea, just in case,' I enthused, because I didn't want my cartoons turning into rodent confetti.

Later, after Ivan and Louis had gone home, I went straight back to the studio, where Carey helped me to flatten out the cartoons and put them up round the walls, with the one for the Lady Anne window directly opposite my worktable.

Carey's voice jogged me out of the trance I'd fallen into.

'Right: that's enough for tonight. We're both tired and a

bit filthy. A shower and something to eat is called for: tomorrow is another day, Scarlett!'

'Don't tell me *Gone with the Wind* was on the hospital library trolley, too?'

'No, I've seen the old film,' he said. 'I thought it was a load of rubbish at the time, but it sort of stuck with me. That Scarlett seemed to love Tara to the point of obsession.'

'I think you're heading the same way with Mossby,' I told him. Then, with a last glance back at my treasures, I reluctantly headed off to shower and change. He was quite right, because I was stiff and tired as well as filthy, but it had been a long and fruitful weekend.

When I went down into the kitchen on Monday morning, Carey reminded me that it was the day the sale of his flat was completed and the money would go into the bank.

'Just as well, since the electrician's starting on your workshop today. I think he sees updating all the electrics at Mossby as his life's work and perpetual income,' he added gloomily.

'But it urgently needs updating and extending, because it's a fire hazard as it is, so you may as well bite the bullet and get everything done while you've got the money.'

'You're right, and I'll ask him to extend the lighting into the attics and all the cellars and outbuildings, while he's at it . . . And come to think of it, I've no idea what state the wiring at the Lodge is in.'

'That's a point. You're probably responsible for repairs to the Lodge, so you ought to see over it.'

'I think I'll leave it for now, unless they actually complain about anything. I've got enough on my plate as it is.'

I ate my slab of bread and honey standing in front of the Lady Anne cartoon, but had to tear myself away eventually so I could let the electrician into the workshop and discuss what needed doing.

He was a small, wiry, energetic man who nodded briskly at everything I said, though his eyes were roving around, taking in the archaic ceiling lights, the old fuse box with the door hanging off and a few anonymous cables pinned along the walls in loops.

He poked and rummaged about and came back just as Ivan arrived in his old car. 'Accident waiting to happen, all that old wiring,' he said, shaking hands with Ivan, man to man.

'I know it all needs replacing and I'll want lots of wall sockets, too. I'll show you where,' I said briskly. 'And much better lighting over the tables.'

'There's going to be two little electric water heaters to be wired in, as well,' Ivan reminded me.

'Yes, the plumber's getting those and a small hand basin for the cloakroom, which he's going to fit later today.'

'That's no problem,' the electrician said, scribbling in a ratty-edged notebook.

I explained about the air filtration system and big kiln that would be arriving later, and that I'd be using electric storage heaters to keep the place warm. I could see pound signs shining in his eyes like stars.

'I'll get going then,' he said, finally. 'I'll be off to get a few things, and then I'll be back to make a start this afternoon.'

I hoped he meant it and wasn't going to disappear for a month, like many workmen I'd employed in the past . . . until I remembered what Carey had said about Mossby being his bread and butter till he retired.

I showed him and Ivan where I'd hidden a key to the side door, so they could let themselves in when I wasn't there, until I got more spares cut.

Actually, it was practically standing-room only at the workshop that afternoon, what with the electrician, the plumber and his hulking and almost silent assistant. As I painted walls and Ivan made endless cups of tea for everyone, the plumber held rambling conversations with anyone who'd listen about his racing pigeons.

Carey popped down with some cheese and pickle sandwiches and stayed on for ages, fascinated by the arcane intricacies of plumbing and wiring.

'Did you ask the pub if they could get us a regular crate of Old Spoggit Brown, for Ivan?' I asked.

'Yes, and I can pick up the first tomorrow. And my agent rang to say the studio had asked for my new forwarding address last week, so they could finally send on my fan mail. I assumed everyone had forgotten me, once the initial interest in my accident had worn off.'

'*I* didn't,' I said. 'I bet the Post Office will need to lay on a special van for it all.'

Clem was passing later when I was outside undercoating the side door, and said Vicky had gone back to London for a catalogue shoot, but he expected she'd be back again before long, unless her agent came up with something better.

'Her mother misses her,' he said. Just then Ella rounded the bend and passed us on her way up the drive towards the house, ignoring us as if we weren't there.

Clem looked embarrassed. 'Ella's still upset about losing her job. She'll get over it, but she's always spent a lot of time in the old wing of the house and I don't think she can break the habit.'

'Evidently not,' I agreed.

'She's at a bit of a loose end, without anything else to do.'

'Carey really doesn't mind if she wants to go up there and . . . potter about,' I assured him. 'But the specialist cleaners will keep the place in order now.'

'She's looked after it perfectly well single-handedly all these years,' he said stubbornly.

'Of course, and I'm sure she's done her best, but I think a building of that age and size needs a bit more attention than one person can give it.'

I was quite proud of that bit of tact.

'I did see Ella letting herself into the old wing earlier,' said Carey, when I relayed this conversation and her snub. 'It looks like she'll carry on haunting the place with the other ghosts, whether we like it or not.'

'Well, I suppose it's a harmless obsession, and the door from the muniment room is usually locked from this side, isn't it?'

'Yes, and the door from the tower on the upper floor, too. So, since she doesn't have those keys, she can't haunt *us*!'

After dinner, which I whipped up from Molly's delicious selection of healthy ready meals, we both went into the studio to do some work, only I got distracted again by the cartoons. This time, though, it was the ones for Jessie Kaye's own windows. There was such a contrast in style between the earlier, more stylized roses of the hall panels and the much freer form of the later window.

The latter carried on the same rose theme, but with the unusual juxtaposition of deep gold-pinks and amber and the flowing lines that made her later work so instantly recognizable.

The notes she'd scribbled were about the meaning of flowers, especially the different colours of roses. I had a little book about it somewhere – the Victorians were very keen on that kind of thing.

Carey was still working away on his laptop when I emerged from my reverie, updating his notes and photographs – *and* his thoughts, because they would all go to make up the first of *The Mossby Sagas*, an upstairs/downstairs epic in which we played all the main roles ourselves, with a fluctuating cast of extras.

Unfortunately, he hadn't forgotten that the second of *The Complete Country Cottage* programmes was on that night, and insisted we both go into the sitting room to watch it, though I knew it would only infuriate him – and it certainly did that, all right.

In that evening's instalment, they exposed a section of ancient wall that had faint traces of painting on it – and Seamus announced his plans to remove it, so that two small rooms could be turned into one, with the central fireplaces left back to back as a feature.

'And,' he added complacently to the camera, 'a fragment of the painted wall will be framed and hung in the new room.'

'Noooo!' groaned Carey, running his fingers through his burnished hair so that it stood up wildly. 'It's probably medieval! It's sacrilege! It should be left where it is!'

But the cottage wasn't listed and no one seemed interested in stopping Seamus from doing anything he liked to it.

Carey was so furious that he tried to ring the director, though he hadn't been answering his calls since the accident. When that didn't work, he rang Daisy, who *did* answer, though after listening to Carey's rant on the atrocities Seamus was committing, she probably wished she hadn't.

I could only hear his side of the conversation, but I could fill in the gaps for myself.

'You can't let him go on doing these things! It's criminal!'

She must have reminded him that the whole of this series was already in the can, so she couldn't stop him even if she wanted to, because he said, 'Then stop him destroying any other wonderful old buildings in the next series.' And then he abruptly ended the call and sat there breathing heavily through his nose, like a dragon about to emit fire.

'I think we'll go to the pub now,' I said quickly. 'I'll drive, so you can anaesthetize yourself with Old Spoggit Brown.'

Mr Browne and Ralph decided between themselves, without consulting me, that the workshop exterior and the square of barns and stables behind it should be stuccoed white to match the Lodge.

I thought this a needless expense, since they could not be seen from the house or terraces, the shrubbery hiding them — and also, I was starting to become increasingly alarmed by Honoria's hints that Ralph was running through his fortune at an astonishing pace.

I knew that his father had been a wealthy man when he married the last of the Revells and took her name, but surely he must have left Ralph a great fortune, to enable him to have carried out the rebuilding of Mossby?

But I could see Honoria was becoming ever more worried with every lavish extra expense . . . and I began to worry, too. There was also the coming child to think of now . . .

28

Joy in the Morning

Soon after I'd arrived at the workshop the following morning, Carey rang my mobile and said the postman had just delivered two sacks of fan mail and a huge parcel containing seventeen more jumpers, hand-knitted by fans.

This is what happens when you mention in a programme that the unusual jumper you're wearing had been an unexpected gift from a viewer . . .

'And there's one woollen legging,' he added. 'Muriel of Leicester, aged eighty-six, knitted it for me to wear under my jeans to keep my bad leg warm.'

'That was really sweet and thoughtful. I think I should send her a picture of you wearing it, without the jeans.'

'No chance!' he said, then added that Mr Wilmslow had rung up too and was coming to Mossby that afternoon, about four.

I said he'd probably be expecting a proper tea at that time of day, not just a cup of, with a biscuit, so in the early afternoon I left Ivan and the workmen to get on with it and baked a batch of sultana fairy cakes, which are something I enjoy making . . . and eating . . . Then I cut a plate of triangular sandwiches spread with Gentleman's Relish. Carey had developed a taste for it after a grateful client sent him a Fortnum & Mason hamper some years previously, and now seemed unable to live without it.

When the solicitor arrived Carey took him into the studio to see the cartoons we'd found, while I made the tea and carried the tray through to the sitting room.

They soon followed me and when Mr Wilmslow was seated in front of a blazing log fire with his cup and plate on a small pedestal table next to him, he said, 'This is remarkably nice of you!'

'We should have tea like this every afternoon, Shrimp: it's very civilized,' Carey said.

'I'd usually be working away and forget the time – and so would you. But maybe we could get into the habit of having a proper afternoon tea on Sundays?' I suggested. 'That would be fun!'

'It's a date,' he agreed, and when the inner man had been slightly satiated with sandwiches and fairy cakes, he described to our visitor how the Parrys had taken the news of the changes to their employment, not to mention the way Ella had cut us dead ever since, while still haunting the old wing at increasingly random times.

'How difficult!' he said. 'As you know, she lived here only briefly as a child and her mother was sickly, so the girl spent much of her time with the old nanny. I'm told she was so gaga by then that she filled the child's head with all the stories about ghosts, hidden treasure, lost jewels and priest-holes, so perhaps that was when Ella's interest in the Elizabethan wing was first awoken?'

'You could be right,' Carey said. 'Though you'd think it would have given her nightmares and put her off that part of the house instead!'

'Some of it probably sounded romantic, like that Cavalier ancestor who was killed fighting for the King, while his young widow waited for news that never came,' I suggested.

'Yes, sad indeed. As was the untimely death of Ralph

Revell, the husband of the Jessie Kaye you are so interested in, my dear,' he said to me.

'That was an accident, wasn't it?' I asked.

'Yes, a fall from the terrace outside these very windows.'

'I didn't realize it happened here!'

'It did indeed, and it was a double tragedy, for his friend tried to stop him falling when he lost his balance and was pulled over with him.'

'How horrible – it's quite a drop to the next terrace from the first.' I shuddered. 'Did you know about this, Carey?'

'No, no idea,' he said. 'Another fascinating snippet of history to tell Nick!'

'His wife, who was expecting their first child, witnessed the fatal fall.'

'Poor thing! It's no wonder she based herself back in London after that,' I said.

'I believe the boy's aunt, Honoria, had most of the care of him and, of course, he went to boarding school and then university. He was sickly and bookish, and though he outlived his mother, married and had children, he didn't make old bones.'

'I suppose he'd be my grandfather,' Carey said. 'Dad was so much older than my mother, it feels as if there should be another generation in between, somehow!'

'It's all a bit sad,' I commented. 'Aren't there any happy stories about Mossby?'

'Well, the estate nearly passed out of the family after Ralph Revell's death, because he'd spent almost his entire fortune on the rebuilding. But by a stroke of wonderful luck, his widow unexpectedly came into a large inheritance and put the estate back on a solid footing again.'

'She must have had some feeling for the place, then?' Carey said.

'Or for her son's legacy and out of affection for her husband?' Mr Wilmslow suggested. 'She did not marry again.'

Having studied her body of work and what little information there was available about her private life, I had a strong suspicion that she had been solidly wedded to her craft after the accident, but the solicitor seemed to have a surprisingly romantic streak, so I didn't disillusion him.

Later, some friends of Carey's just turned up, like the first swallows of summer heralding the arrival of the rest, and spent two days happily removing the ghastly dark brown paintwork on the upstairs landing, appearing only at mealtimes and for snacks. Carey did some of it, too, but having found a large wall clock in the attic, he became occupied in taking it to pieces on the kitchen table, cleaning it and then began putting it back together again. I don't know why it had to be the *kitchen* table.

I spent most of my time in the workshop, though it was still full of men shouting, hammering, whistling and generally pulling things about. Ivan appeared to have shed ten years and was energetically scrubbing the grime of ages from worktops and tables, when he wasn't nailing sheets of tin inside cupboards.

It was a far remove from the normal working atmosphere that I loved, with only the dull thud as a horseshoe nail was driven in to hold the pieces of the panel together as it was leaded up, or the fine scrunch of the cutting wheel incising the surface of a sheet of glass, followed by the sharp tap underneath and the crisp snap as the piece of glass divided.

But that would come – and soon, the way things were going – so I felt positive and happy.

The only slight fly in the ointment came when Grant rang me to say that Nat had finally gone to look for something in the locked cupboard in the loft and discovered that several of my cartoons and cutlines had been removed.

'He said they were there when he locked it up, so you must have somehow broken in and stolen them. I told him not to be daft: the spare keys to all the padlocks were hung in the office.'

'I left all the designs, cartoons and cutlines for commissions that belonged to the workshop behind. The rest were my personal property.'

'Yes, it was understood that you could take personal commissions for anything that wasn't going to be made in Julian's workshop, and I've already told him so. Ivan would bear me out.'

'Why was he looking for my cartoons, anyway?'

'I think he wants Willow to try and copy your style, though from what I've seen, she hasn't got the faintest idea. Nat's following up some of the enquiries Julian got at the end of last year, so he means to carry on producing windows in his dad's style, which he's quite capable of.'

'Yes, and he's a good craftsman. They'll just lack that spark of originality.'

I was glad I wouldn't be there to see that happen.

Chris brought Fang back on Wednesday evening and I'm sure Carey had missed him as much as I had. I only hoped it had been worthwhile . . .

Fang, wearing a quiet and thoughtful air, followed Chris into the house but he seemed delighted to see us, wagging his ratty tail and exposing his long sharp teeth in a vulpine grin.

'I don't think you'll have any more trouble with him now,' Chris said, accepting both a cup of coffee and a sizeable cheque. 'He may still growl to warn you when someone's about, especially if he doesn't like that person, but he won't bite. Well, not unless they're attacking you.'

'I don't think we've got any homicidal neighbours,' Carey said. 'They all seem very nice.'

301

'*Most* of them,' I amended, because I thought Ella was looking increasingly homicidal. And I did still occasionally wonder about that stone ball, even though I told myself I was being over-imaginative.

Maybe Chris should take her away and see if he could do anything to sweeten her temper a bit?

While we were chatting, I explained that I'd never had a dog, because of the glass in the workshop cutting their feet, and he said trained search-and-rescue dogs often wore heat-proof boots for searching buildings and perhaps they were made in Fang's size.

'Some of the search dogs are spaniels, and Fang does have surprisingly large feet for his size.'

'That would be a good solution if I needed to have him down there with me a lot, because Carey was away or something. I'll have a look on the internet and see what I can find . . . if you think he would let me put them on and not immediately chew them off again.'

'He's a changed dog,' Chris said. 'Anyway, he can always come back to me for a couple of days and I'll whisper him into his boots.'

Oh, joy in the morning! At last we finally had working broadband.

The first thing I did was redirect my mail from both my old home and Julian's workshop to Mossby, while Carey was checking what the viewing figures were like for the new *Complete Country Cottage* series. They seemed to have slumped radically for the second episode.

'That's not a surprise, seeing he's just vandalizing the cottage. They should have experts to stop him ruining it and wiping off great chunks of history.'

'He *is* supposed to be the expert,' I pointed out.

'Only because he presented one series about historic buildings in Scotland!'

'If the viewing figures don't pick up, then they won't ask him to do another series – but they might try and get *you* back,' I suggested. 'They were a bit hasty ditching you and now you're almost as good as new, they probably regret it. The slight limp and the black cane are all a bit alluringly Mr Rochester – the maimed but romantic hero.'

'Ho, ho,' Carey said. 'And there's no way I'd go back now . . . though I suppose they might want my Mossby series when they find out about it. But there's an email here from Nick saying the opposition are seriously interested and negotiating for it. I must let my agent know.'

'It's wonderful to have broadband again, but we've both got so much to catch up on,' I said. 'I'm going right down my list of tools and equipment later and ordering everything, even if it is going to bust whatever's left of the budget after the kiln and filtration systems. I've just got to get back to work as soon as possible and have some commissions coming in.'

'Nick will want to film the workshop being fitted out and finished, and he wants us to restage finding those cartoons in the attic.'

'I am *not* taking them off the wall and rolling them up!'

'You won't have to, Shrimp: you can just put a couple of rolls of cartridge paper in the box, instead.'

'I suppose so, though I was going to take the metal box down to the workshop. I'd better wait till Nick's been now.'

'I'm going to carry on working on the landing upstairs. I've got the undercoat, but I'm still trying to find the right shade of white paint,' Carey said. 'I found some early photos of Mossby in my uncle's desk, showing how light the house used to look – and there was a family tree, too. Jessie Kaye's husband seems to have died within a year of their marriage, so they didn't have long together.'

'Mossby should have a sad atmosphere, with all these tragic tales, but it doesn't,' I said. 'Well, the old wing does a bit, but part of that's probably because it's so gloomy.'

'When the panelling was first put up in there, it could well have been painted in bright colours.'

'That would have livened it up a bit – and I expect you're right about Lady Anne's window being a celebration of her married life at Mossby, too. It's not cursed at all, she just wanted to make sure it stayed there for ever, as a memento of her happiness.'

'I think I can hear you saying that to camera – Nick'll adore it!' Carey teased me.

'I'll have forgotten it by then.' I got up. 'Better go down to the workshop and see what's happening. What are you going to do?'

'The electrician's starting here some time today and one of the Benbow twins from the Summit Alpine Nursery rang and said he had a day off and he'd come and give me a hand. I thought he could start stripping the woodwork in one of the bedrooms, while I'm painting the landing.'

'It's amazing how many people are gluttons for punishment,' I said, and he grinned.

'But it's all fun . . . and speaking of fun, I think I'm going to sell the golf buggy and get one of those quad bikes and a little trailer, like the Rigbys have up at the farm.'

I felt he was safer pottering about on the buggy, but it has to be said that it did struggle a bit back up the hill with more than one person in it.

Also, he was throwing off his invalidism faster than a dog shakes off water, and soon there would be no holding him at all.

'I quite like driving the golf buggy,' I said wistfully. 'And

I thought it would be nice for taking picnics down to the lake in summer.'

'Then we'll have both – the buggy wouldn't fetch much if I sold it anyway,' he said and gave me the sort of smile that, even after knowing him my whole life, still sagged my knees and made me putty in his hands.

In the evening I went online, gritted my teeth and blew most of the rest of the budget, ordering everything I needed for my workshop from the long list in one massive splurge, then started building myself a website, based on a handy template similar to the one I'd used to create the Julian Seddon Architectural Glass site. I had my pages from that one copied and saved, so that speeded things up a bit. I had to update my autobiographical section, saying I'd worked for Julian Seddon for twelve years.

I had a quick look at Julian's website, but Nat didn't seem to have altered it much, apart from adding his own page, bigging himself up in the process.

After that, I made a Facebook page for Angelique Arrowsmith Art Glass, and then opened a Twitter account, both to be linked to my new website once it was up. I'd need to be out there and visible as soon as possible, to bring in the work.

Inspired, Carey asked me to help him design a website for Mossby, too, which could be linked to the ghost trail one, when they'd added the new spectral attractions, so by the time we went to bed it was very late indeed.

But now I'd sent off my big order for workshop materials I felt things were really moving along – and I was even back to bouncing out of bed at the crack of dawn. The old Angelique was resurfacing, boots and all.

Ralph and Mr Browne went off together to the Lake District soon afterwards – and I overheard him suggest that he should have a house built there, too, as if Mossby was not enough! But Ralph is deeply rooted at Mossby, so I hope nothing will come of it.

Ralph had seldom been around to notice that his wishes in the matter of my mollycoddling myself were not being attended to, for I carried on very much as usual.

Father and I now have an excellent system set up using the rail service for the dispatch of racks containing trays of painted glass for firing, though I hope eventually to set up a kiln of my own at Mossby.

Work goes to and fro, as do supplies of Antique glass and other materials.

I designed and made the windows for the nursery, based on three of Aesop's fables: 'The Town Mouse and the Country Mouse', 'The Lion and the Mouse' and 'The Tortoise and the Hare'. I exchanged many letters with Lily about our shared theme and the progress of her embroidery.

Later, I sent the cartoon of my window down to Father and he believes he has obtained a commission for me for something similar, so that I and my workmen will begin to be even busier.

I often think how much easier it would be were I still in London, but I know I am lucky to be able to carry on working. Besides, I made my bed and must now lie in it.

29

Whitewashed

The next morning I decided to start painting the corkboard wall in the workshop, which had been installed the previous afternoon by Carey and Rufus, who'd called to see him about something and been roped in to help.

I sat at the top of the tall ladders, rolling on a soft white to match the rest of the workshop, though eventually, of course, it would be pocked with drawing-pin holes and scarred where strips of masking tape had been ripped off. Still, by that point everything would be starting to look familiar, well-used and workmanlike, so I wouldn't even notice.

Despite the frosty chill in the air, Ivan had donned his bobble hat and donkey jacket and gone out to buff up the old brass lock on the double doors. But now he hobbled back in and stood looking up at me like a disapproving gnome.

'I told you the cold would get your arthritis going,' I said.

'That's not what's brought me back in – and you shouldn't go right to the top of these old ladders unless I'm here to hold the bottom of them,' he told me severely. 'Anyways up, you'll have to come down now because I've just seen Nat's car stopped by the Lodge, and that Ella was talking to him through the window, so he'll probably come straight here.'

'It *can't* be him!' I exclaimed, dismayed. 'There are loads of big four-wheel-drive cars around. Even Ella's got an old Range Rover.'

'Not as big as a truck and as black and shiny as a hearse, there aren't. It's him, right enough.'

'Oh damn.' I put the roller back in the paint tray and carried it down. 'What can he want now, a pound of flesh?'

'It'll be nothing good, knowing him.' Ivan pulled off his woolly cap, so that his thick silver hair sprung up in a crest like a cockatoo. He went to hang his coat up in the studio, leaving the door ajar, and I could briefly hear the voices of the plumber, Garry, and the electrician, who seemed to converse in shouts even when they were only feet away from each other. Then Ivan came back, closing the door, and took up a position just behind me, like a bodyguard. He obviously felt I needed back-up.

An engine roared up, a door slammed heavily – then in burst Nat in full Mad Bull mode. He came to a sudden stop a couple of feet away, glowering at me belligerently from under his thick, dark eyebrows.

'There you are!' he said accusingly, as if I'd been hiding. 'The woman at the Lodge said you'd be here.'

'Yes, here I am – and there *you* are,' I said lightly.

'She told me you're turning this place into a stained-glass workshop.' He glanced round the room and, as his eyes took in the big central glazing tables, the racking for glass and lead and the wooden easels over the windows, ready to hold sheets of plate glass, he looked taken aback.

'Luckily for me, it already was one, so I'm just renovating it.'

'*You've* fallen on your feet!' he sneered, recovering from his first surprise. 'I suppose you think you can set yourself up in competition with me.'

'There's no question of competition. I'm going to be doing my own work, while you're presumably carrying on Julian Seddon Architectural Glass along the same lines.'

I thought I'd put that with supreme tact, because what I'd really wanted to say was 'ripping off and recycling Julian's ideas and creativity for the rest of your working life'.

'Not that it's any business of yours what I'm doing anyway,' I added, 'so I don't know what you're doing here, unless it's just sheer nosiness? In which case, perhaps you'd like to push off again.'

'I do have business here, because my workshop will be carrying out any projects designed by you that were commissioned while you were still on the Julian Seddon payroll,' he said, and I stared at him blankly.

'But there wasn't anything outstanding, only enquiries. We finished the last commission to my design before I went to Antigua and Grant told me Julian's window for Gladchester had been packed off.'

'When you left, you took cartoons, cutlines and design work from a cupboard I'd locked up, including two recent designs submitted for competitions.'

'Oh, you're not at that again, are you, Nat?' I sighed wearily. 'We've already had this out and you've been told repeatedly that Julian was happy for me to take private commissions or submit designs for windows and installations that weren't to be made in his studio.'

'That's right,' agreed Ivan from behind me, and Nat gave him a dirty look.

'I might have known *you'd* be here.'

'Why shouldn't I be? You fired me, didn't you?' Ivan demanded.

'You can't fire someone who isn't employed by the business – you'd retired . . . and I bet HMRC would like to know Julian was still paying you while you were drawing a pension,' he added nastily.

'I didn't do it for money, just for love of the craft – and you try proving different,' Ivan said. 'And don't think to stir up trouble for Angel, either, because she's paying me a bottle of beer a day and the tax man won't thank you for reporting that.'

'A bottle of beer? I think you're barmy!' Nat said, thwarted, then turned his attention back to me.

'I've spoken to my solicitor about the items belonging to the business that you've taken—'

'If by solicitor you mean Mr Barley,' I interrupted, 'then he told me he wasn't going to act for you in any capacity once Julian's estate had been wound up.'

'That old fool should have retired long ago! No, I've got a different solicitor now. So you'd better return what you've stolen, or you'll be hearing from him.'

He looked around, eyes narrowed suspiciously. 'I expect you've got them stored here somewhere? If so, I'll take them back now, and there were portfolios in the loft that are missing, too, not to mention all those sketchbooks from the studio cupboard.'

'My sketchbooks? Are you mad? They date all the way back to my early teens and my whole life's in there. They're *private*,' I declared so fiercely he took an involuntary step back.

'I'd *burn* them before I let anyone else have them! And those and the artwork in my portfolios would be useless to you, because you can't design windows in my style. It's distinctive enough to be recognized if you tried to make something similar.'

'That big roll of artwork and cartoons is my main concern – if you give me those now, then I might reconsider letting you keep the rest,' he said magnanimously. 'But I'm not going away empty-handed. *Have* you got them here?'

'No, and I wouldn't give them to you if I had!'

'You're a cheeky bugger, young Nat,' Ivan put in scathingly. 'She's giving you nowt.'

'You keep out it,' Nat told him. He spotted the cupboards at the far end of the room and started forward. 'I bet they're in there – and there's nothing to stop me taking my own property.'

'*I'll* stop you,' I said, leaping in front of him and furiously brandishing the dripping paint roller. 'Unless you want to be striped like a zebra, you'd better shove off back where you came from.'

'Garry – Vic!' suddenly bellowed Ivan at the top of his voice. 'Get in here, quick!'

From the way all the workmen piled into the room, I suspected they'd been listening, just the other side of the door: Vic, the electrician, and his mate, who were both necklaced in loops of cable, while the plumber, Garry, brandished an antique and dripping ballcock. His large and silent lad followed him in, carrying a huge spanner. They lined up on either side of me. It was like having my own personal A-Team.

'Are you going peacefully, or shall I get my lad to put you out?' asked Garry, making a sweeping and slightly threatening gesture towards the door, though I think he'd forgotten he was holding the ballcock.

Nat's eyes swivelled from the large spanner to Garry's face and he must have decided discretion was the better part of valour. He slowly backed away.

'I was prepared to be reasonable,' he told me. 'But you'll be sorry, when you hear from my solicitor!'

After he'd gone, we celebrated our victory with tea, while Ivan gave everyone a potted history of Nat's perfidy, which I hope made his ears burn. Then I went up to the house to wash and change, seeing as the paint from the roller had run down my arm inside my jumper.

The cleaners were just driving off as I arrived there, so

everything was sparkling clean except me. I went up the backstairs to my room, but once I'd changed I came down the main one, where I found Carey sitting on a step, sanding the banisters, watched by Fang.

I sat down next to him and Fang clambered on to my knees and tried to lick my chin.

'I've just had a frightful scene with Nat,' I said, and while describing what had happened I found myself shaking with anger all over again.

He put his arm round me and gave me a hug. 'You should have rung me – I'd have come right down, and sorted him out.'

'It all unfolded so quickly, though it could have got nasty if I'd been there on my own. *And* messy,' I added, thinking of the paint roller. 'I don't really think he's got a leg to stand on – it was all empty threats – but all the same, I think I'll give Mr Barley, Julian's solicitor, a ring and run it past him,' I said, and Carey agreed that was a good idea.

Mr Barley was quite horrified when I described Nat's visit and his demands that I should not only return my recent cartoons and artwork, but my portfolios and sketchbooks too.

'He said he had a new solicitor and I'd be hearing from him!'

'I was aware that he was placing his affairs in someone else's hands, but in any case, I would not have wished to act for him.'

'I feel I've been scrupulously fair in only taking what personally belonged to me, both in the cottage and the workshop,' I said. 'He even wanted the artwork for two recent designs I submitted to competitions, but I've witnesses to prove that Julian was happy for me to take personal commissions and enter competitions for windows that wouldn't be made in the workshop.'

312

'Most fortuitously, I can confirm that,' Mr Barley said. 'Julian and I had discussed how that aspect might change, should he make you a full partner or director in the company. He further mentioned it in a note to me, regarding the terms of his will.'

'Then that must be conclusive? Nat has no entitlement to them?'

'No indeed, though I suppose the portfolios and sketchbooks might be a grey area. Are they perhaps very personal to an artist?'

'The sketchbooks are all very small – A5 – and date back to my early teens, so there are dozens of them. They're more like visual diaries than anything, full of drawings, paintings, notes, cuttings, dried leaves, photographs of things I've found interesting . . . just reflections of what I was doing or thinking at any given point.'

'A diary certainly wouldn't belong to the workshop, so it's an interesting point,' he said. 'Does anything in the sketchbooks directly relate to window designs?'

'No, that's not how it works, though things in them might inspire a train of thought that leads to a design idea.' I paused, and then confessed, 'I use much bigger sketchbooks too, sometimes, where I do more detailed work towards a particular window design. I always tear the pages out and put them in portfolios as I go along. But Nat will never need those because I've left behind the actual finished cartoons and cutlines for all the windows I designed for Julian.'

'In that case, I think Nat would be foolish indeed to try and take legal action to recover any of those and I expect if he really has consulted a solicitor, then he will have been told so. However, do let me know if you have any further communication with him.'

I felt more relaxed after talking to Mr Barley and I hoped I'd heard the last of Nat, but all the same, I decided I'd keep my portfolios and sketchbooks in the studio at the house, except the most current ones, just in case . . .

Carey and I spent a quietly companionable evening in the house studio, where he added the day's notes, observations and pictures to his laptop and I checked up online about what I had to do to register my workshop for business, health and safety regulations and insurance.

Of course, having worked with Julian for twelve years, I already knew quite a bit of this, but I'd never set up my own workshop from scratch before.

Then I turned to googling glass suppliers. A whole host of firms making, importing or selling sheet glass had sprung up when the famous Hartley Wood glassmaking firm had ceased business years before and we'd had to find other suppliers. Some of the best flashed glass still came from Germany, though.

Like Julian, I wasn't keen on mechanically produced glass: it seemed soulless, even though it could look quite clever in modern installations. But on the other hand, I was quite intrigued by the more frequent use recently of fused glass, where either pieces of different coloured glass were melted together at high temperature in the kiln, or as blobs fused on to the piece of glass already cut to shape for leading-up. It had always seemed to me to be fraught with possible future problems like weakness and fracture, especially if the glass wasn't annealed properly, but maybe I'd experiment with it in the future.

I'd already had an email giving the shipping date for my kiln and it would soon be on its way . . . and suddenly I wondered if it would fit into the back room of the workshop without widening the door!

Louis came over with Ivan on Saturday and he seemed gutted to have missed all the excitement of Nat's visit.

I told them what Mr Barley had said and then we went and measured the doorways into the room designated for the kiln, to see if it would go through. It would be a very tight squeeze indeed. The frame of the inner door might even have to come out.

They left at lunchtime to go and watch some game – rugby, I think, though I hadn't really been listening. I had lunch with Carey, once I'd winkled him away temporarily from his endless banister sanding. I had to admire it, first, though there's not a lot you can say about sanding, except: 'Oh – smooth!'

Then I returned to the workshop to start unpacking my little hoard of Antique glass, which I'd been looking forward to. I held each sheet up to the light to see the colours and then wiped it, first with a damp cloth and then a dry one, before placing it in one of the large pigeon holes in the special wooden shelving unit. I made little labels for each one: Streaky Grey, Pot Metal Emerald Green, Flashed Ruby Red on Clear . . . an interesting Medium Blue Over Very Pale Green.

It all took time, since every treasure had to be gloated over. I hadn't even looked in some of the tea chests of glass I'd bought as job lots from firms closing down. In fact, I'd only just emptied the first box, when Carey rang me to ask if I was staying in the workshop all night, or intended going back for dinner.

Ivan helped me unpack the rest of the glass next day, but Louis vanished after a while with Carey – a couple of his tree surgeon friends had arrived early that morning and they intended cutting up some of the fallen trees in the woods round the lake and trucking the logs up to the courtyard, where they could be stacked in an empty hay barn to season. Louis obviously thought this would be much more fun than washing glass, painting walls and window frames, or scrubbing shelves, and after a while I realized Ivan had taken his coat and vanished, too.

I went out of the workshop and followed the sound of powerful saws down to the woodland, where I found all the men, including Clem, had formed a merry lumberjack party.

There's nothing like the sound of a chainsaw to attract the other sex: it's like a bright light to moths.

And since Carey's fan mail arrived, anyone turning up to help outdoors was issued with one of his splendid collection of hand-knitted jumpers or tank tops to keep them warm, so the whole scene looked a bit like a page out of a book of knitting patterns for men, *circa* 1973.

I did not enjoy the constrictions pregnancy increasingly imposed upon me and would be glad to have it over with, though I was starting to feel a certain curiosity about what my child would be like. Ralph only spoke of it as if it was a boy, but I would be just as happy with a girl.

Honoria took a huge interest in the forthcoming child and was sewing a layette with the most exquisite skill. I wished Lily could see it, but since we were both in the same interesting condition, neither of us was able to travel.

I found time to put the finishing touches to my coloured cartoon of the Lady Anne window. I still had no idea what the significance of the figures in the quarries around the central depiction of the old house could be, though I hoped it was more cheerful than the man in the flames at the bottom suggested . . .

I might, perhaps, be wrong about that and it was a hayfield after all – and about the window having some kind of message. Yet surely those repeated sequences of motifs – like hanging drapery and flat roses in circles – must mean something? They did dimly make me think of something I'd seen in the old wing of the house . . .

30

The *Big Wave*

Nat must have contacted his solicitor the moment he left me on Friday morning, possibly even from the car before he drove home, because I got a very scarily official letter on the following Monday, threatening legal proceedings if I didn't return all the material belonging to Julian Seddon Architectural Glass that I'd removed.

It was just as well I'd talked to Mr Barley, or it might have thrown me into quite a panic. As it was, it still slightly put me off my breakfast.

I read it aloud to Carey and he said Nat was a fool to have wasted his money paying his solicitor to send such a letter.

'I'll post it on to Mr Barley, but I think I'll just ring him first to let him know it's on its way,' I said, which I did as soon as his office opened. I felt rather guilty that he'd previously declined my offer to pay him for his help, but he'd assured me that he saw it all as part of the settling up of Julian's estate.

He told me that there was nothing to worry about. 'Once I've explained the situation to Nat's solicitor, and that I have written proof of Julian's attitude in the matter, you are unlikely to be troubled in this way again.'

'I hope you're right,' I said, but I still worried that I might be on slightly shakier ground when it came to some of the more recent sketchbooks and portfolios. I even contemplated hiding the lot in the attic, but I do like to have them handy, and anyway, Carey pointed out bluntly that I was making much ado about nothing.

'Nobody's going to turn up with a warrant to search Mossby and take them away,' he said. 'Even if Nat was stupid enough to tell the police you stole them, they have more important things to do than arrest you for taking your own sketchbooks.'

'It does sound silly when you put it like that,' I agreed.

'From what you said, Nat seemed to be keenest to get hold of the artwork for the two competitions you're waiting to hear about, Shrimp,' he said thoughtfully. 'Have you wondered why?'

I stared at him. 'You mean . . . he might know something about one or both of them that I don't? But I checked their websites the day we got broadband and neither of them had put the winners up.'

'I expect they'd write to you, or email you the results too, wouldn't they?'

'Yes, I suppose they would . . . and I'd have used Julian's workshop address. So, if they have, then Nat hasn't passed the letters or emails on.'

'Come on, let's check them out again,' he said, leading the way into the studio and standing behind my chair while I opened my laptop and turned it on.

'Which one first?' he asked.

'The children's library transom window, because if I haven't won that one, the design will be really easy to adapt for something else, so I won't mind not winning so much. They wanted the subject to be Noah's Ark, so Julian and I were both working on Noah-themed ideas at the same time.'

It was just as well that I didn't really mind not winning that one, because the prize-winner's name *was* up – and it wasn't mine.

'But I know his work and he's very good. He deserves it,' I said. 'Perhaps your theory was wrong, Carey, and Nat's just being bloody-minded?'

'Well, get up the website for the other, and then we can be sure.'

'I hardly dare to look – it's for that installation in a Brisbane shopping mall and I *really* want it.'

I reached the site and scrolled down . . .

'Well, that's lucky, because you've won it!' Carey said, leaning over my shoulder.

I opened my eyes and my name danced in front of me – and when you're called Angelique Arrowsmith, there's never any mistake: it had to be me!

'Congratulations, Angel!' he said, scooping me bodily off the chair and whirling me round.

'Be careful – your leg!' I exclaimed, and laughing he put me down again and hugged me. 'You're as light as a feather – and aren't you the clever one, winning the prize!'

'I can hardly believe it.' I went back and stared at the screen, where my winning design was displayed in miniature under my name.

'It looks interesting,' Carey said, 'but it's too small to really see any detail. I assume you've got a copy of the design?'

'Of course, much larger and in full colour. I'll have to turn it into a cartoon and send it to them, then someone else will interpret that into a cutline,' I said, my mind straying ahead to the practicalities of turning my idea into a reality. 'The cartoon will be rectangular, but the freestanding frame it's to be set into will have a gentle wave in it, which sort of goes with my design.'

'So, it's a free-standing sculpture, really?'

'Yes, or a screen. It's at the centre point where four arms of the mall come together and light will come from the glazed doors at the end of each of them, as well as from above, so it'll change from whichever angle you view it.'

I clicked on the webpage email address and said, 'I'd better contact them right now and explain that I've moved to my own workshop since I entered.'

I also added that I'd entered the competition in my personal capacity, with the full agreement of my former late employer, Julian Seddon, just to make things clear.

And that, I hoped, would take care of any contact they might have from Nat.

'So you were right about Nat: he must have known I'd won,' I said, finding the right roll of cartridge paper from the unsorted heap in the corner. I spread it out on the big table, weighting down the corners with an empty coffee cup, my piece of lucky amethyst rock and two bottles of drawing ink.

Carey stared at it and gave a long whistle. 'That's absolutely brilliant – no wonder you won!'

'I was quite pleased with it myself,' I said immodestly. 'I put so much into it.'

My design, at first glance, looked as if a Hokusai-type wave was pulling the sea away from a beach, exposing all kinds of crabs, shells and seaweed, while underwater it dragged fish, octopus and long tendrils of seaweed in its wake.

But once you looked closer, the body of the wave was a blue whale, twisting upwards, the spout forming the snowy crest as it curled back towards the beach. The foamy edge broke away, turning into the fluttering, swooping shapes of white birds against a blue sky.

'The eye really follows it right round in a great twisting sort of loop,' Carey said.

'Well, that's the Golden Mean for you,' I told him. 'I wish I could make the window, not just send the cartoon and notes, and the temptation is always to do the cutline, too.

But then that hampers the person making it, so it's usually better not to.'

'You get a trip to see it when it's made, don't you?'

'Yes – you'll have to come with me!'

I sighed happily. 'I feel as if it's set off a sudden creative explosion in my head, a whole host of ideas, and now I want to work on lots of sea-themed windows. I just need some suitable commissions!'

'They'll come,' he said. 'In the meantime, you could make some free-hanging roundels on that theme, couldn't you?'

'I could. They always sell well . . .' I agreed, then broke off as an email pinged into the mailbox: it was the Brisbane organization, thanking me for contacting them.

Apparently, they'd both posted and emailed me the notification several days before and had been surprised not to hear back from me before now. But of course, they said, they now understood the situation and Julian Seddon was a huge loss to the profession.

'Julian would have been so proud of me,' I said, tears coming to my eyes.

'*I'm* proud of you, too, Angel,' Carey said, and enveloped me in one of his warm and loving hugs.

By then the morning was getting on, but before I finally went down to the workshop, I rang Nat's mobile and told him I knew he'd been opening my post and reading my emails, and had kept the news of the competition win back.

'I'm perfectly entitled to open anything addressed to the workshop,' he said defensively.

'Not when it has my name on it. But it's clear now why you wanted those designs back. Well, you haven't a hope in hell. My solicitor will be in touch with your solicitor,' I added grandly. 'And don't bother contacting the

322

competition organizers, because I've already explained the situation to them, so it isn't going to get you anywhere.'

I ended the call while he was still gibbering with fury.

'I hope that's the end of him and I'll never hear from him again,' I said to Carey.

'No, I don't think even he will try and pursue it further,' he agreed. 'I'll book a table in the restaurant at the pub tonight, because this calls for a celebration!'

'It certainly does – I've just remembered how much money I'll get for winning!' Visions of endless packing cases full of expensive Antique glass filled my head with joy.

'Will you ever award me that look of stunned wonderment?' he asked, amused. 'You're seeing the world through gold-pink glass spectacles, aren't you?'

'Yes,' I admitted but I didn't tell him he always looked as glowingly wonderful as any Pre-Raphaelite stained-glass angel: perhaps that was part of why I loved him so much?

I wasn't expecting Ivan that day, but the first deliveries from my huge shop were due to arrive that very afternoon – exciting packets of tallow sticks and thin rods of solder, plastic sacks of plaster of Paris and whitening, and tubs of ready-made glutinous glazing cement.

It was only a fraction of what was to come, but I ticked them off and filed the delivery notices in the office bit of the back room.

After that, I unpacked a bit more sheet glass before returning to the house, intending to have a good stare at the Brisbane cartoon, but instead I got hijacked by Carey into helping him finish sanding banisters.

We had a lovely meal at the Screaming Skull and afterwards, in the lounge, we found Lulu, Cam, Rufus and Izzy. When we told them what we were celebrating, Lulu produced a bottle of champagne on the house, which, since we'd already had one bottle with dinner, went rather to my head . . .

I seem to remember describing my winning design with great arm gestures and knocking a rack of local tourist leaflets off the wall, but not a lot about subsequent conversations.

Rufus, who was not a great champagne drinker, drove us home: I'd have to walk back tomorrow and pick my car up, but it had been worth it.

And, as a bonus, while we were out we'd missed the third Seamus Banyan *Cottage Catastrophe* programme, so Carey remained cheerful and his blood pressure quite normal.

I hoped he didn't sneak off to watch the repeat . . .

The win not only ignited a whole seething mass of creative ideas in my mind, but also spurred me on to get the workshop finished as quickly as possible.

It seemed to inspire Carey with the desire to demolish something – in this case a door-sized hole in the wall dividing the small room that backed on to the stable block behind the workshop, where he'd established a sort of man cave, with all his benches and tools and various bits of equipment. He'd thought it would be nice if we could come and go between the two without walking all the way round.

With Carey, thought quickly becomes action, so in no time at all I was talking to him from my side of a large hole, as he loaded debris into a wheelbarrow.

'I think it'll take a couple more weeks before the workshop's finally fully functional,' I told him, batting away a cloud of cement dust. 'I'll have to test the new kiln too as soon as it's in. They all fire differently.'

'Maybe we should have a party in the glazing room to celebrate, when it's all finished?' he suggested.

'A party? Well, I suppose we could,' I agreed. 'In fact, it would be the only time it's feasible, because a working glass studio isn't really a good venue for food, drink and revelry – all that sharp glass and toxic substances like acid and lead about.'

'Let's pick a date now, and work to it?' he suggested. 'How about Saturday the fourteenth – Valentine's Day?'

'Sounds good to me.'

'Want to come out to an architectural antiques place I've found, to look for a good old door for this hole?' he asked enticingly.

'Only if you wash the filth off your face first, and change out of the Postman Pat jumper, because on that scale he's a bit scary,' I said.

'I'd better get down to the workshop early,' I told him next morning. 'They're bringing the heavy-duty vinyl flooring and starting to lay it today. Are you going to come down and put in that nice old door and frame we found?'

But no, it seemed he was still in masonry demolishing mode.

'I might get down later, but first I'm going to knock a hole in the wall between the back gate and the stile – or where the gates will be when they get back from their beauty treatment.'

'What do you want a hole there for?'

'To put in a small gate, for any ghost trail walkers who can't get over the stile. I mean, if they've got gammy legs like me, or pushchairs or something, it would be a bit difficult, and I don't want the big gates left open.'

I hoped he wasn't overdoing it with the heavy work, but he seemed to be increasingly glowing with health and enthusiasm, and his stick now spent most of its time propped nearby, just in case.

I remembered that years ago he'd learned walling, including the intricate art of dry-stone walling, and loved it, so he was probably giving himself a treat.

'Have fun,' I said. 'I might come up and see it later.'

A team of burly men arrived at the workshop in a large van just after I did and made short work of moving the heavy furnishings and laying the dark grey heavy-duty vinyl. Ivan kept their strength up with vats of builder's tea and a box of assorted biscuits I'd laid in specially.

He offered them a lot of unwanted advice, too, while I pottered about filling in the random grooves and channels left by the electricians.

Once the flooring was down there was only really some touching up of the paintwork to be done in the glazing room and a few other small jobs. Soon I'd be ready to pin up the *Big Wave* design on the corkboard wall and think about scaling it up to full size.

But first, I was going to blow some of the competition money – even before I got it – on better door locks and a burglar alarm system.

Nat's threats had made me permanently edgy.

One day, idly looking among the books in the muniment room, I discovered a slim, calf-bound and handwritten tome, which briefly narrated Lady Anne's story.

She was a noble but impoverished widow with one daughter when she married Phillip Revell in the seventeenth century, having made an unfortunate runaway match the first time and been left penniless. She and her daughter had been grudgingly given a roof over their heads by her uncle, so I expect she was glad to exchange that situation for a good, if not grand, marriage.

The Civil War divided many families and her new husband fought on the King's side, while her uncle almost immediately switched to the Parliamentarians.

After Phillip was killed in battle, she bore a son and continued to live at Mossby while, as I had already heard, the daughter of her first marriage subsequently went to live in some kind of Protestant religious order abroad.

I showed it to Honoria, who said she had read it, but there were family traditions that there had been more than met the eye in this dry outline. 'There may be something more among the papers in the Spanish chest in the muniment room,' she added.

'Which chest?' I asked puzzled.

'Oh, it is hidden in a secret place – the old house is supposed to be riddled with priest-holes, for the Revells were secretly papists a long time ago.'

She told me that although she had seen inside the concealed place in the muniment room, only Ralph knew how to open it, the secret having been passed down to him.

I had not before thought of there being secret hiding places at Mossby and found the idea very intriguing.

31

Mixed Messages

The end of January was surprisingly mild, but February roared in with an arctic blast, so it was lucky we'd finished stripping and undercoating the workshop's outside paintwork, unblocked the gutters and mended a few cracks in the stucco, ready for it to be repainted white when the house was done in spring.

As the days passed, I heard nothing more from Nat and my life with Carey at Mossby began to settle into a basic pattern that was constantly overlaid by the interesting comings and goings of workmen and the friends and acquaintances who lent their help, and very often their specialist skills, for a few hours or even a day or two.

The electrician had moved his operations into the house, while Garry the plumber was installing a shower cubicle upstairs in a small room formerly used for making hot drinks and storing equipment by Carey's uncle's carers.

Garry and his silent lad had begun to appear frequently on Nick's film, but in the guise of friends merely helping out. I'm sure Carey was often complicit in helping some of the workmen to cheat HMRC, but mostly he got the help he needed by bartering, of one kind or another, rather than the exchange of hard cash, so I don't think he actually saw it like that.

But I decided that when *I* was in a situation to start

paying Ivan for his time, I'd get him to find out how much he could earn before it affected his pension and then put him on the official payroll.

As well as all the workmen and visitors, there was a constant flow of delivery vans trundling up and down the drive. Much of it was for the workshop, where we stacked everything in the back room next to the newly installed door to Carey's realm, ready to be unpacked.

Ivan and I were like children with Christmas presents, not knowing which box or parcel to open first: small packages of glass paint and silver stain, a big box of shiny new horseshoe nails, a crate of imported German flashed glass in interesting colour combinations . . . ginormous rolls of wide cartridge paper – you just never knew what you'd discover next and everything found its rightful place in the workshop.

I'd bought one small light-box, but Grant and Ivan were constructing a larger one on wheels in Ivan's shed, as a gift to the new workshop, along with a set of wooden battens in different sizes for edging the panels as they were being leaded up. It's the small things that tend to get overlooked – Ivan had cut some small spare lathekins, the pointed and smoothly shaped pieces of wood we used to open out the flanges of the lead calme as we worked and, one weekend, Louis sandpapered them smooth.

Every morning I'd get up in the early hours, as I always did before Julian's illness, and go down to the studio next to the kitchen to work for a while. Then, when Carey came down for breakfast, we'd discuss what we were each doing that day. Sometimes we'd have lunch together, too, or he'd bring sandwiches down to the workshop, but if not, we caught up at dinner, when it might be just us – and Fang – or quite a crowd if there were helpers staying and perhaps Nick and the crew up filming. The big drawing room would come into its own on these occasions and the old billiard table got a bit of use. I could see what a lovely room it would be in summer, with the doors from the little veranda wide open on to the terrace and that wonderful view down to the lake and the trees.

Catering was easy enough. Molly kept the freezer stocked up, and now we had broadband the supermarket shopping took minutes. We'd found a choice of delivery takeaway meals to choose from, too, for the days when we were too tired to even open the microwave door.

But Carey's interest in cooking was rapidly reviving and he bought a bread-making machine. Soon the smell of freshly baked loaves drove me wild every morning and, given the number of calories I was consuming, if I hadn't been working so hard I'd probably have been spherical and could roll down to the workshop every day.

After dinner we quite often went to the pub, especially when we had visitors, and Carey now walked there and back. He seemed to be gaining strength in his bad leg every day and though he always had his black stick studded with shiny silver skulls with him, it seemed now to have become more of a habit, rather than something he actually needed. Once his new series aired, he'd probably start getting walking sticks by every post, as well as the hand-knitted jumpers.

Carey and I were both happy and excited about what we were doing. It wasn't that I'd forgotten Julian, or didn't mourn him, but the Julian I'd fallen in love with had vanished with his first stroke and I'd already done my grieving for the life we'd shared together, long before the second . . .

Fang, due to the dog whispering, trotted docilely about after me or Carey without biting anyone. The only person he really growled at was Ella.

And who could blame him? She was still being really odd and spent hours in the old wing – sometimes at very strange times of day – obsessively polishing the panelling, or communing with the ghosts, or whatever it was she did. She certainly made a point of being there on Fridays, when Mitch and Jenny were cleaning, jealously watching to make sure they didn't encroach on what she clearly considered to be her own special task.

'Jenny said Ella now chats to them a bit sometimes,' I told Carey one day, when I'd been up at the house while the cleaners were having a cup of tea. 'So it's just you and me she's ignoring. And Mitch said he didn't like to tell tales, but while he was walking along the passage to the muniment room earlier, he was sure he could hear the roll top of the desk going down – and when he went in, she seemed to be locking it.'

'Remember that other time, when it looked as if she was trying to open it? Perhaps she's got hold of a key,' he said, then got up. 'Come on, let's go and have a look.'

We went through the house to the muniment room, where everything looked the way it usually did, except cleaner.

'You *did* put the copy of your will in there, like I suggested, didn't you?' I asked as he produced his own key and rolled up the top of the bureau.

'Yes, and it's still there, but in a different pigeon hole to the one I left it in!'

'Are you sure?'

'Yes, positive. It was in the right-hand cubbyhole and now it's in the one next to it, with the writing paper and envelopes.'

He smiled wryly. 'Well, you did say it would be a good idea if she knew about my will, in case she'd overheard that conversation with Mr Wilmslow about a codicil leaving her the house and decided to poison me or something equally Agatha Christie!'

'I did. And I wish she'd found out earlier, because I still

have a sneaking suspicion that she had something to do with the stone ball nearly killing you.'

'Oh, come on, Shrimp,' he said incredulously. 'Even if she spotted us from the Lodge, and decided to creep down through the shrubbery to listen to what we were saying, why would she be carrying some kind of box around with her to stand on? Or even know the ball was loose, so that there might be a chance of pushing it off on to my head? It doesn't add up.'

He had a point; several, in fact.

'It does sound ridiculous when you put it like that,' I admitted. 'But somebody *had* stood on a box behind that pillar, because I saw the marks.'

'There's probably a perfectly simple explanation. It was only a couple of faint lines, wasn't it? Someone could have propped a bike there or something.'

I didn't point out that bike wheels didn't have corners.

'Anyway, Ella knows now that there's a brand-new will, so she's got nothing to gain by bumping me off,' he said.

'No . . . I suppose she wouldn't do it just for a few thousand pounds, or simply because she resented your existence.'

'Depends how dippy she is, but probably not. I have to say, she does look increasingly strange and I've had enough of being cut dead on my own property: I'm going to have to have a word with Clem.'

But when he reported back on the conversation, it didn't seem to have gone terribly well.

'I told Clem that we were finding Ella's behaviour disturbing and hinted that perhaps she might have some mental health issues she should talk to her doctor about and he was quite indignant,' Carey said.

'But then,' he added ruefully, 'I've started to think that Clem is just as obsessive, in his own way. He spends almost all his time keeping the terraces immaculate, while the grounds go to pot.'

'He keeps the courtyard and the topiary trees in perfect order, too,' I pointed out.

'Yes, though I'm not sure I really want my trees trimming in the shape of slightly lewd lollipops.'

'I don't know, I've seen lots of topiary gardens and I think Lewd Lollipop has been a favourite shape for centuries. He's just following tradition. And he probably thinks keeping the terraces in order is the most important part of his job. It certainly must be hard work and time consuming, going up and down all those steps.'

'I suppose you're right. The terraces and the Arts and Crafts façade of the house are the first things you see as you approach Mossby, but in any case, he puts in such long hours that I can't really complain,' Carey decided, and we left it at that for the moment.

Perhaps Ella was just working off a fit of high dudgeon at losing her job and would come round, eventually?

By the time the fourth of the new *Complete Country Cottage* programmes had aired, viewing figures had slumped to such a low level that Carey said he'd started to feel sorry for Seamus Banyan, though that didn't stop him continuing to be infuriated by his actions.

But meanwhile, he was totally engrossed with his own project at Mossby, and Nick and the crew swooped in and out to film all the important moments – or, if they missed them, the re-enactments.

They were there when Carey's wood sculptor friend came over to turn a huge piece of log into a weirdly carved bench inspired by the legend of the Sweetwell Worm, which looked as if it would writhe its serpentine coils around anyone brave enough to sit on it.

Carey roared up and down to the barn on his new quad bike, the trailer laden with the offcuts for the wood store and, it being the weekend, Louis was roped in to help.

At first, it had puzzled me how Vicky almost always seemed to be visiting her parents at the Lodge when the film crew was about. Then I sussed it: Louis was her mole. He constantly got texts from her, which we knew because he'd innocently impart exciting bits of information to us, like that she'd had two days' work as an extra on some big film.

'That Vicky seems mighty friendly with Louis: I don't know what a woman of her age wants with our lad,' Ivan said one day, having caught sight of the two of them together outside the workshop. 'If she's not sending him messages, then they're meeting up and she's all over him like a rash.'

'I think that's just her natural routine with any man, and he's a handsome boy, after all.'

But Ivan didn't look convinced and when Louis came in he said directly, 'I don't know what you and that Vicky find to talk about.'

Louis flushed slightly. 'Films, mostly. And being an actress she's interested in Nick and the crew and how they're shooting the documentary.'

He must have felt some criticism in the air, because he added quickly, 'She doesn't ask me anything about the workshop.'

'Just as well, because Angel doesn't want you discussing her business with anyone else,' Ivan told him severely.

'I haven't really *got* any business so far, Ivan,' I said.

'You soon will,' he assured me.

I hoped he was right.

There were lots of big projects that would keep Carey occupied – and the film rolling – for years and years.

There were the buildings round the courtyard, for a start, which could one day be developed, not to mention the old walled garden beyond it, a tangled Sleeping Beauty's bower. Carey did remove the padlock from the gate one day, aided and abetted by Nick and Jorge, and ventured in, but after a couple of feet you'd have had to slash your way through with a machete so they had to give up.

I suspected that would be the next year's big project and would involve sunburn, backache, nettle rash, blisters and a lot of thorns.

On evenings when we hadn't got anyone staying with us, Carey and I often worked together in our shared studio at the house. He inputted all the information about his day's work into his computer, a sort of diary with photographs, which eventually would form the basis of his books.

I'd begun to go through all the material I'd amassed on the subject of Victorian female glass artists, most of which didn't make it into my college dissertation. I certainly had enough for a book, and Jessie Kaye and her work would form the heart of it. I'd be able to include new material on the Mossby windows, and if living here and working in her studio didn't inspire me to write it, then nothing would!

The cartoon of the Lady Anne window still hung opposite where I sat, so that I often found myself idly gazing at it . . . and slowly I began to wonder if Carey and I had misread the meaning of it and it *wasn't* commemorating a short but happy married life at all.

By now I'd found a sampler of a similar age to the window in the darkest corner of the muniment room, which bore some striking similarities to the window, including featuring the old house in the middle. But there was no clue to who had made it, or whether it predated the window and might have inspired it, or vice versa.

'It might even have been sewn by Lady Anne herself,' I suggested when I showed it to Carey.

He looked from the sampler to the cartoon. 'They both have the house and the three women, with the figure of the man in the cornfield below . . .'

'But he's dressed as a Cavalier – he can't possibly be cutting corn in that outfit!' I objected. 'And anyway, if he's supposed to be Phillip Revell, then he wouldn't be doing manual work himself at all, would he?'

'I suppose that is a bit odd, Shrimp – and if he's Phillip, then you'd expect him to be part of the group by the house, with the rest of his family, wouldn't you?'

'It's very curious,' I said, but if there was a puzzle there, a message to be understood, I had no idea what it could be.

Mr Browne being away the following day, I asked Ralph about the secret cavity in the muniment room and he said that indeed there was one, just big enough to hold an ancient Spanish chest, in which were stored many old papers relating to the family.

He told me, as Honoria had said, that the secret was handed down to each heir, but then added quite casually that since it would be a pity if the way of opening it should be lost if some mischance befall him, he would show it to me.

It was very ingenious but not terribly exciting, being a space just large enough to hold the old chest containing the papers. But then he took me to see another in the Great Hall, the trick of which was common knowledge, and this one was quite large enough to hide a man.

Ralph says there are supposed to be more, to which the secret has been lost, for one of the foremost makers of these ingenious hiding places was known to have worked at Mossby.

As you might imagine, this gave me very much to think about — and to wonder if Lady Anne might have concealed some secret or item of value in one of them, and this was the message she was trying to convey in her window?

338

32

Fired

Carey had been to a couple of Halfhidden regeneration committee meetings and was now firmly committed to Mossby being on the ghost trail. Suddenly we realized how little time there was to get ready, because Easter was in early April that year.

Things had not improved with Ella, so Carey was reluctantly forced to have yet another word with Clem, pointing out that if she continued to avoid all contact, he would not only cease allowing her free access to the Elizabethan wing, but also assume she wasn't interested in the seasonal position of tour guide when he opened it to the public.

This seemed to have been passed on with some effect, because Ella suddenly agreed to meet us to discuss things, which took place in one of the rooms at the back of the Great Hall.

Her manner remained wooden while Carey explained his plans and she neither displayed any enthusiasm, nor even made eye contact, which wasn't encouraging.

But then when he added that the room we were then sitting in would be used as a kind of office, to keep the cashbox, float, account book and supplies in, rather than in the main house, she suddenly perked up.

It appeared that when she worked at a National Trust

property, they counted the stock of items for sale every morning and evening, right down to the last pencil, and compared it with the takings. This seemed a bit excessive, but since the thought of doing it that way at Mossby appeared to buck her up no end, Carey told her she could organize it along the same lines if she wanted to.

'One of us will come over at closing time to help cash up and so on,' he added. 'We won't want to leave anything more than the next day's float in the till, or cash drawer, or whatever it is we have.'

This too must have been in line with how it was done at the National Trust property, for she didn't make any objection.

'If that's it, then, I'll be off,' she said, getting up abruptly and striding off, and when we heard the slam of the heavy front door, we looked at each other.

'Well, that went better than I expected,' I said. 'Though it was a bit disconcerting, the way she didn't make eye contact and talked without moving her lips.'

'The visitors aren't exactly going to find her a vision of cheery welcome if she's like that with them,' he agreed. 'We'll just have to see how it goes, and of course I'll be on hand for the first few days after we open to the public, making sure everything's OK. If she has some kind of meltdown, or doesn't show up, I can take over.'

'I don't mind doing the tour guide thing occasionally, too,' I offered. 'It's only going to be afternoons anyway, isn't it?'

'Yes, two till four, Fridays to Mondays inclusive, to start with. Then we'll see. I'll think about allowing coach parties too, possibly on a separate afternoon, but our facilities are a bit basic: we've no toilet or refreshments on site.'

'I expect the visitors won't mind. After all, it won't take them long to go round the house and buy a few postcards and souvenirs. If they've walked down from the farm, Lulu said they were serving refreshments in season, so *we* don't need to.'

Carey had ordered more of the little brass stands and ropes to cordon off access into some of the rooms, a postcard rack and a trestle table for the souvenirs and guidebooks . . . which we hadn't yet had printed. Cam, who apparently is an ace photographer and took the pictures for all the postcards that are on sale up and down the ghost trail, had offered to do our postcard photos and then we could use some of them in the glossy brochure. Carey was working on that. There was already a free leaflet, but it wasn't very illuminating.

Cam's mum, who had the village shop in Halfhidden, sent us the details of the firm who supplied the small souvenirs she sold, since she did a good trade in those. We decided on the usual range of rulers, bookmarks, pencils, pens, keyrings, etc., all with 'The Haunted Elizabethan Wing, Mossby' printed on them.

Carey and Clem had started erecting wooden posts on either side of any path or part of the drive that we didn't want the visitors to go down, so they could be quickly roped off on open days, and several sign boards had been ordered.

'Though there'll always be some visitors who ignore the "Private – No Entry" signs entirely and wander off,' he said pessimistically.

'Well, if they wander off into the lake, or off the edge of the top terrace, you'd better make sure your insurance covers it, like Molly said,' I pointed out practically. 'Fire, theft, accident and imbecility.'

We both took one morning off and drove up to Halfhidden together, because Carey wanted to see how his gates were coming along and Izzy had rung me to say my new jacket was ready.

We found Foxy in the Sweetwell courtyard, painting the

341

iron hoops on an old half-barrel, and she told us she'd had a great time working on Carey's gates. They were now finished, bar a second coat on one of the back ones and a little gilding.

Hearing our voices, Rufus came out of one of the stables and he and Carey vanished into the barn to have a look at the gates, while I went upstairs to Izzy's workshop and knocked on the door, feeling quite excited to see my new jacket, the first bespoke garment I'd ever had!

And when I did, I was absolutely stunned, because it was simply beautiful! It was sewn in squares of embroidered or patterned velvets in bright, jewel colours: rich reds and greens, amber and darkest rose. It was so gorgeous that when I put it on I was speechless, so for a minute Izzy was afraid I didn't like it, but didn't know how to tell her!

'Just as well you do like it,' she said, when I finally found my voice, 'because I got carried away and made a dress to go with it, though of course, you don't have to buy it if you don't want it.'

It was a tunic style, the sleeves and body in plain dark green velvet, but with a long trail of tiny tumbling diamonds in the same jewel colours as the coat. They ran from one shoulder down and across and round in a great sari-like swirl that finished at the hem. When I put it on, I thought I looked quite transformed, even if I was still wearing my jeans and big black boots under it.

'You're so petite that you can take that design, and I haven't made the squares very big in either jacket or dress,' she said, critically admiring her own handiwork.

'Oh, I love both – and of course I want them! They're worth every penny and I'll wear them to death, like I do all my favourite clothes.'

'I'll give you a discount: mate's rates,' she said with a grin. 'They've given me an idea for a whole new collection of jackets and dresses for next winter, too. Yours are one-offs, so they won't be exactly the same, just running with the appliqué velvet idea.'

'I'll probably be back for more,' I said, then invited her, Rufus and Foxy to my workshop opening party on the 14th at six o'clock, for drinks, nibbles and a cake.

It sounded terribly civilized, though if Nick and the gang came up for it, it probably wouldn't stay that way for long.

The day after the fifth of Seamus Banyan's programmes aired, Carey's agent called and told him that since the current series was bombing, they wouldn't be renewing Seamus's contract.

'And they wanted to know if I'd go back,' he said, relaying this conversation to me. Then he explained, immodestly, 'My many fans are clamouring for my return.'

'So . . . are you thinking about it?'

'You have to be joking, Angel, after the way they dumped me!'

'Yes, they were a bit hasty, to say the least. But I suppose they thought that even if you recovered, it would be a long time before you were ready to work again.'

'They made a snap decision and there wasn't a thing I could do about it, because of that clause they slipped into the contract,' he said, and it was clear this still rankled.

'Did you tell your agent you're not interested?'

'He didn't really expect I would be, because ITV are definitely taking the new series.'

'Really? Oh, that's *great* news!' I exclaimed delightedly.

'It will be, if it's a success.'

'Of course it will be. It'll run for years and years. When will the news be out?'

'As soon as the contract's been drawn up, I suppose,' he said. 'That'll ruffle a few feathers!'

*

Daisy must have been delegated to change Carey's mind about going back to do a new series of *The Complete Country Cottage*, because she rang up that evening while we were in the studio. He'd just been talking to his mum on a faint and faraway line to Arizona, so the phone was turned up to max volume and she came across loud and clear.

'Carey?'

He grimaced at me and made 'stay put' gestures when I would have tactfully retreated.

'Well, this is a surprise, Daisy,' he said. 'Where did you get my number from?'

'You rang me from it a few days ago, remember? I rang your mobile first, though, and sent you loads of texts, but you didn't answer.'

'I forgot to charge it – it's still plugged in in the kitchen, come to think of it. What was so urgent?'

'Well . . . it's this way,' she began in soft, persuasive tones. 'Carl, *The Complete Country Cottage* producer—'

'I know who Carl is,' Carey interrupted. 'The slight concussion didn't affected my memory.'

'Right . . . Anyway, he – we – just wanted to say how disappointed and surprised we are that you don't want to return for the new series. Naturally, we only saw Seamus as a temporary replacement until you were ready to return, but perhaps we didn't make that clear enough?'

'No, perhaps you didn't,' he agreed drily. 'Or perhaps you didn't mean that at all, but now you're regretting ditching me so fast, because the series has bombed without me.'

'You have such a big fan base and there's no one quite like you . . .' she said. 'You're quite irreplaceable.'

'Only the best butter,' I muttered, and he grinned at me.

'I do wish you'd come back, Carey, and not just for the sake of the programme: *I* miss you so much, too,' she cooed. 'Letting you go was a big mistake.'

'You didn't so much let me go as drop me like a hot potato,' he pointed out. 'But that's not important any more, because I've moved on – and in more ways than one. Nick's made the pilot for a new makeover series and sold it to ITV.'

There was a stunned silence, then she said sharply, 'But you can't do that! We have the rights to the original title and format and—'

'You don't have the rights to my life,' he said gently. 'And that's what the new series is all about: my life here at Mossby.'

There was another pause, while she regrouped. 'I saw a magazine article about you. It said you'd inherited an old house from a rich uncle – is that Mossby?'

'Yes, though my uncle was far from rich and the house and gardens are very run down. Lots of scope for my skills here.'

'Look, maybe I could come and discuss things with you, before you actually sign anything?' she suggested persuasively.

'It wouldn't be worth your while trekking up here to west Lancashire, because I've made up my mind.'

'I'd forgotten the article said the house was in Lancashire – but you're surely not going to stay there permanently, are you? Won't you just do the house up and sell it?'

'No way! This is my home now and I love it. And Angelique's staying with me and setting up her own stained-glass workshop on the estate.'

'*Angelique?*' she repeated sharply, then lowered her tone with an obvious effort. 'Well, business aside, I'd love to see you again – *and* dear Angelique, too, of course.'

Anyone would think we'd been best friends, whereas I'd only met her a few times and she'd seemed to loathe the sight of me.

I made gagging gestures and Carey gave a thumbs down in return.

'I'm afraid we're really busy right now, Daisy, and it

345

wouldn't be worth your while coming anyway,' he said ambiguously, then cut her off mid-protesting bleat.

He looked across at me, with one raised eyebrow and a glint in his violet-blue eyes.

'My bet is she just turns up on the doorstep one day, like a stray cat,' I said.

The big kiln arrived and was manoeuvred into its designated room with some difficulty and the temporary removal of the inner door and frame.

Only when it was in place did we add a sturdy bench and the bag of plaster of Paris that was used to line the metal trays that would be slid in and out of the kiln using a special tool that I'd hung on the wall.

I had a selection of cones that melted at different temperatures and Ivan and I would carry out a series of test firings at some point, to see if there were hot and cold spots. I knew Grant would want to have a go too, one weekend: he'd always been the self-proclaimed kiln-firing expert.

The special boots I ordered for Fang arrived and he seemed to acquire a slight swagger when he was wearing them. He also had a cushioned basket under my desk in the back room at the workshop, which served as the staff room as well as being a kind of office-studio.

The angel's head I'd painted from Julian's drawing had been turned into a little stained-glass roundel with a flowered border and now hung in the window over the sink, casting a soft yellow, pink and mauve-blue motley over my desk when the sun caught it.

Modern, streamlined storage heaters now took the worst of the chill from all the rooms and with the floor covered in thick, heavy-duty vinyl and the cracks round the window frames filled in, the workshop was quite cosy.

346

In the big glazing room, sheets of heavy plate glass had been placed on the easels over the windows, bundles of lead calme lay in the wooden troughs, ready to be stretched and used, and the sheets of Antique glass slumbered in the deep, dark recesses of the labelled unit, until it was their turn to come to life against the light.

Really, the workshop was almost completed – just a little more unpacking and the finishing touches, then it would be done . . . and so, unfortunately, would be my savings.

I'd simply *have* to drum up some business as soon as possible!

As soon as the burglar alarm was fitted and new locks (I knew it was entirely irrational, but I still expected Nat to suddenly break in and steal my work), I pinned the Brisbane design up on the corkboard wall in the glazing room and started to scale it up to full size. The installation, when put in place, would be a gentle S-shaped wave, divided into tall narrow rectangles, so it would be as if you were looking through multiple windows, or perhaps through a series of those sea zoo windows that are half under water and half above.

I'd put up on my website more examples of my work and also the winning design for the competition. I updated my details on one or two other databases, too, and found I'd had a couple of initial queries about commissions, which was encouraging. There was also an invitation to submit a design for a side chapel window in memory of a child – and since no subject was specified, I could possibly adapt my Noah's Ark design for it. Most children loved the story of the animals going in two by two. It would be cheerful and hopeful and bright.

I'd make a few changes to the original design, though: my train of thought since I'd won the Brisbane competition had run on the idea of dual worlds, both under and above the sea, and eventually, I might have triple worlds, with the stars and moon and clouds.

For the moment, however, two were enough and Noah's Ark would be followed underwater by all manner of paired sea creatures.

It had been sheer coincidence that Julian and I had been working on our different Noah's Ark designs last year, but in very different forms – he for his last commission and me for the competition.

I'd never be able to listen to Benjamin Britten's *Noye's Fludde* again, though. The associations would drag me right down into the depths of the past, where the light never penetrated.

I remembered a story, told to me by Honoria soon after I arrived, of a splendid jewel of great value that Queen Elizabeth had bestowed on the then Revell heir when he briefly caught her fancy. There was indeed a portrait in the Long Gallery of a handsome young man wearing it, and a huge and unwieldy ornament it looked to be! But all mention of this bauble had ceased at about the time of the Civil War . . .

While I was working I often looked up at the cartoon of the window and began to wonder if what I had thought to be a spiky sun shining down could instead be the Jewel? Or was my imagination overly stirred by the romantic histories I had learned and I was reading into it what I wanted to see?

33

Queen of Hearts

The morning before Valentine's Day, preparations for the party were well underway. I baked some jam tarts with the last of the previous year's bramble jelly that Molly and I had made together, making little heart-shaped pieces of pastry for the top using an old metal petit four cutter I found in a drawer.

Carey had already discovered a huge punch bowl, of the type with small cups hanging from it all around the rim and, inspired, had gone out to buy the ingredients he needed. There would be an alternative non-alcoholic version too, though in a less swish large glass mixing bowl.

My tarts looked pretty and so did a batch of fairy cakes in their heart-patterned paper cases – there was a bit of a theme going on there, but then, it was almost Valentine's Day and the shops were full of heart-shaped everything.

Even Carey had impulse-bought several strings of heart-shaped fairy lights while he was out, and he went down to the workshop to fix those up, as well as covering the long glazing tables with plastic cloths to keep them safe from spills and accidents.

Molly was making a special cake. It was her gift, so I had no idea what form it would take. I was going over to fetch it next morning, along with a lot more party food . . .

Nick and the gang were arriving around lunchtime and intended to film the party, or at least the start of it. Carey said they'd help him fix up some music, too, and I was just thinking that everything was organized when it suddenly occurred to me that perhaps I should give Carey a present of some kind. Not quite a Valentine's present, but something in general appreciation of everything he'd done for me.

I made a card with a little cartoon doodle of Fang, wearing his boots and looking smug, then shrugged into my lovely new coat of many colours and dashed in the car up to Cam's Hidden Hoards gallery in the village, where I lavished a considerable chunk of what little remained of my savings on the picture Carey had admired so much. Cam wasn't there, but the extremely ancient gentleman behind the counter, his great-grandfather Jonah, proceeded to make a pretty parcel of it in silver tissue paper.

When I'd paid, I impulsively invited him to the party, too. 'And do bring anyone you like with you,' I added.

'Izzy mentioned it to our Tom – he keeps the Lady Spring now, like I used to,' he said. 'He can drive me down. I'd like to see this haunted wing that's going to be in the trail.'

'Carey could probably take you up for a quick look during the party,' I suggested. 'It's not far from the workshop.'

'I've seen the outside of it, right enough. Time was, the Revells used to join in with local festivals and such, so we'd go there carol singing every Christmas Eve. The family would gather in the porch of the new part of the house and there was hot rum punch and mince pies afterwards.'

'Carey will be fascinated if you can tell him about old traditions like that,' I said, then noticed the time and, tucking my parcel under my arm, dashed back to the car.

When I arrived home the Raising Crane Productions van was already parked in the courtyard and, having hidden the picture in the housekeeper's parlour behind some of my still unpacked boxes, I found everyone in the warm and slightly steamy kitchen.

Preparations for lunch were underway. Jorge appeared to be filming Carey in the final stage of making a seafood sauce to go over the mound of spaghetti that Nelson was draining in the sink. Sukes was laying plates on the long table, Fang was attempting to trip everyone up and Nick was leaning back and comfortably observing everything.

'So sorry we forgot to get you a director's chair with your name on it,' I told him, and he grinned.

'I doubt this scene will make the director's cut anyway,' he said, but he got up and opened a bottle of rosé, which he said was now extremely trendy again.

'I just thought it would be nice for the party tomorrow, being pink, so I got a few bottles,' Carey said.

My workshop-opening party seemed to be turning even more into a Valentine's extravaganza!

When we'd demolished the huge vat of pasta I, for one, would have loved to have slept it off for a bit. But the effect on Nick and Carey was to reactivate them to fizzing point and soon we were all trooping down to the workshop for some before-party filming.

It already looked strangely dressed and expectant, with festoons of heart-shaped fairy lights around the door and hanging from the edge of the loft storage space. The glazing benches were covered with red vinyl tablecloths and there were cellophane-wrapped packages of napkins, paper cups and plates.

'You seem to have gone a little overboard with the hearts,' I remarked to Carey. 'Didn't they have any matching plastic cutlery?'

'They were all on special offer, because of Valentine's Day, so they cost less than the plain ones,' he explained. 'But with the main lights off for the party, you won't notice all the hearts.'

'If it's only going to be lit by the fairy lights, you won't notice anything at all,' I pointed out, but Nick said they'd sort out a bit of ambient lighting next day, along with the music.

'And you can all help bring things down, too,' Carey told them, 'while Angel's off collecting the rest of the party food from her friend Molly.'

'Who's coming to the party?' asked Sukes.

'Lots of interesting local people,' Carey said. 'You've met some of them at the pub – Lulu and Cam and their friends Rufus – who renovated the gates – and his wife, Izzy. And Molly and her husband, Grant . . . Oh, and I bumped into Debo, Izzy's aunt, the other day,' he said to me. 'I invited her and her friend and anyone else she wanted to bring.'

'Izzy said Debo used to be a famous model in the sixties and she still gets some work and the odd cameo role in films,' I told him. 'That's why she looks so familiar.'

Nick looked alert. 'Isn't she the one who runs the dog rescue place in the village? If she was a famous model, that could make a good piece for the series.'

'You can talk to her about it at the party,' Carey said. 'And I felt I had to ask Clem if he and Ella might like to come.'

'If she does, she'll be the spectre at the feast,' Nick commented. 'I've never seen such a gloomy woman. When we were filming in the old wing last time we were here, she followed us round as if we'd gone in to steal the silver.'

'Yeah, and she didn't say a word, even when we spoke to her,' agreed Nelson.

'Oh dear, we thought she was getting better,' I sighed. 'By the way, I think I saw Vicky going into the Lodge earlier – perhaps you'd better invite *her*, too.'

'Why bother?' said Sukes. 'She turns up whenever we're here anyway.'

'That's true, and I expect she'll just assume she's welcome to come,' I said. 'And I seem to have invited pretty much everyone I've bumped into in the last couple of days, just like Carey has, so it's going to be open house, really!'

'I doubt it'll go viral on the internet, so we're inundated with teenagers wanting our fairy cakes and cheese straws,' Carey said.

'I do a great retro canapé hedgehog,' Nelson said suddenly, and we all stared blankly at him. 'You know – lumps of cheese and little pickles and pineapple cubes on cocktail sticks, stuck into half a grapefruit.'

'I didn't realize you had these hidden depths,' Carey said. 'I think you should go for it!'

'We've got loads of cheese, but that's about it,' I said dubiously.

'I bet the shop in Halfhidden has all the rest,' Carey suggested. 'I'll drive you up there first thing tomorrow.'

Jorge, eyeing the heart-shaped lights as if he'd had a light-bulb moment himself – probably of the kind where you realize you've forgotten to buy your partner anything for Valentine's Day – said he'd go with them for the run.

'Well, let's get things wrapped up here, before the light goes. I want Fang wearing his boots and some footage of Angel standing in front of that wonderful cartoon on the wall, as if she's working on it,' Nick said more briskly. 'It's a pity Ivan isn't here today, though, because he's such a character and the camera loves him!'

I didn't break it to him that Ivan hated being filmed, which is why he was such an old grump when they were there. But Old Grump seemed to be his allocated role in the series now.

I stood in front of the *Big Wave*, mahlstick in hand, and

354

pretending to draw, before we moved into the back room where, as a finale, they filmed me standing next to the angel roundel, my translucent twin.

It was almost dark when I locked the workshop door behind us and we set off back to the house. Fang hadn't wanted to take his boots off and it was freezing out there, so I supposed they would at least keep his feet warm.

'I can hear a car in the courtyard,' Carey said as we turned the corner into it and a taxi briefly illuminated us in its headlights as it drove out past us.

'Someone's arrived – I wonder who?' Carey began. 'I'm not actually expecting anyone but . . .'

His voice petered out and we all came to a sudden halt, staring at the familiar figure standing under the porch light, a flowered suitcase at her feet.

'Thank God you're here, Carey, darling!' called Daisy. 'I thought the taxi must have brought me to the wrong place. This is the middle of nowhere!'

Then she seemed to take in the rest of us, hovering like rent-a-crowd behind him and did a double take.

'What on earth are you doing here?' said Nick. 'Carey, you haven't been having second thoughts about signing up for another cottage series and invited her, have you?'

'Not me,' he said. 'I've told them I'm not going back.'

'I just thought I'd pop up and see Carey – I said I would.' She gave him an intimate smile as she came forward to offer her cheek for his reluctant kiss. She looked up at him winsomely. 'You know how impulsive I am, darling.'

'Yes I do, don't I?' he said shortly, disengaging himself. 'So, where are you impulsively going to be staying tonight?'

'But . . . I assumed you'd be able to fit little me in somewhere in this vast pile of yours? Preferably not in the Grimm's fairy tale bit, though.'

'We don't use the Elizabethan wing. And I'm afraid I've got a full house all weekend – no beds, unless you can persuade Nelson or Nick to share?'

Actually, since Jorge and Sukes shacked up together, and I didn't think anyone else was staying tonight, there probably *was* a spare room, and lack of bedrooms hadn't ever stopped Carey inviting people before: some mornings you'd fall over bodies in sleeping bags in practically every room.

'I know you're just saying that because you don't want me to stay, but I really didn't think I'd hurt you so badly that you couldn't bear to have me under the same roof!'

'Look, he doesn't want you here because we're filming a series for ITV, right?' Sukes told her. 'We don't want any BBC moles trying to find out what's happening.'

'You mean . . . you've already signed a contract with ITV?' Daisy exclaimed.

'No, but we're definitely going to,' Carey told her.

She looked crestfallen, but then rallied. 'Right . . . but you did tell me that the new series was different, just about you living and working here at Mossby, and it's on such a huge scale! So there's no reason why you couldn't do both series, is there?'

Fang, who had been sniffing in the shrubbery, made a belated appearance just then and, spotting his former mistress, greeted her with the return of his old aggression, so that I had to grab hold of his collar. He probably thought she was going to snatch him away.

'That's never Tiny!' she gasped. 'He's turned into a monster!'

'We call him Fang and we've been feeding him a bit more than miniature portions of pedigree mush,' Carey said.

'And . . . he seems to be wearing boots.'

'They're a fashion statement, Daisy,' I said shortly. 'You know all about those.'

Daisy looked as if she was about to do battle, but Carey sighed in a resigned kind of way, took my elbow and urged me forward.

'We can't stand out here in this freezing wind for ever; we'd better go in.'

Daisy took this as an invitation and followed us. Then, a couple of minutes later, when it became obvious that no one was bringing in her case, she went back out to fetch it herself, along with a carrier bag that clinked.

The bag contained a peace offering intended to pour liquid balm over any slight awkwardness her arrival might have caused: a bottle of super expensive spiced rum and another of some rarefied whisky that Carey drank on high days and holidays . . . if someone else was paying.

Of course, the crew broke into the rum with cries of loud joy even before the takeaway we'd ordered arrived, and a bit of a thaw soon set in.

Sukes offered to bunk up with Jorge, which she was doing anyway, so Daisy could have her room for the night.

'But only tonight,' qualified Carey. 'You'd better look trains up for tomorrow.'

'Of course, darling,' she said, and added that if she was staying, she'd love to go and freshen up.

I took her up in the lift, since it was evident that she couldn't carry the case, only trundle it. God knows how long a stay she'd intended making!

I pointed out the bathroom opposite, next to my room. Then she asked casually where everyone else was sleeping and said she supposed Carey had the best bedroom. So I told her he did indeed have the biggest one, the last on the right . . .

When she reappeared, she'd changed into a jumpsuit that was tight round her scraggy butt and baggy above, where she didn't have much in the way of boob. But I have to admit black did set off her Nordic, almost other-worldly fairness, with her lint-coloured hair and glacier-blue eyes. I'd forgotten how breathtakingly pretty she was.

I'd forgotten how amusing she could be, too – *and* indiscreet. By the time we'd relaxed in the sitting room with the takeaway and the bottles, she'd shared several very funny stories about how Seamus made increasingly bizarre demands during filming. 'Having a certain brand of Nepalese herbal tea, brewed in his own glass teapot, constantly on tap, was only the start of it.'

'Weren't you living with him, though?' asked Nick bluntly. 'You must have already known all his little ways.'

'Oh, not really. I mean, I needed somewhere to stay and he totally got the wrong idea,' she lied quickly. 'I had to move out again almost right away.'

I looked at Carey once or twice, to see how he was taking all this, but his expression remained withdrawn and non-committal, so I'd no idea how he was feeling. But her lights were certainly all turned on for him, and they made quite a blaze.

Of course, it was inevitable that at some point the party was mentioned and she said wistfully that she'd love to stay for it.

'No dice,' Carey said curtly.

'Anyway, we'll be filming it for the new series, so if you were in it, it wouldn't go down well with your boss,' Nelson pointed out.

I was sitting at one end of the velvet sofa with Fang curled on my knee, and every time Daisy spoke, he lifted his lip in a silent snarl, which she seemed to find disconcerting. Or maybe, after a glass of spiced rum, I was doing the same . . .

I'm not sure what kind of scenario Daisy had envisaged would develop when she arrived with her two bottles. She'd known I'd be there, so perhaps she'd intended laying me out with one, then rendering Carey resistless to her charms with the other?

But she hadn't reckoned on the crew, who demolished the rum, but left the whisky to Carey, who had one small tot, then put it away in the cabinet in the corner. I had coffee after my solitary drink: I didn't want to spend tomorrow nursing a hangover.

I was just drifting off to sleep that night when there was a sudden rumpus somewhere at the other end of the landing. I slid out of bed and opened the door a crack – and there was Daisy, clad in something diaphanous, backing out of Nick's room.

He appeared in the doorway, looking slightly sozzled and amused.

'Sorry I wasn't who you expected, but I'll give it a go if you like?' he called after her retreating form. 'I don't mind.'

'In your dreams, buster,' she snapped. 'Stay off me!'

'I never touched you. You're the one who threw yourself on me,' he pointed out. 'In fact, I was trying to protect my virtue.'

'I wish you'd protect it quietly, I'm trying to sleep,' said Nelson, popping his dreadlocked head out and staring at them, especially the transparently clad Daisy. 'It's hardly worth wearing that thing, you know,' he added to her, then went back in and shut his door.

Daisy, her face scarlet, made a furious hissing noise and rushed for her own room, though unfortunately forgetting the two steps down and up, where the stairs rose to the landing. She fell heavily, floundered back up again and staggered on.

I silently closed my door just as another opened and Jorge's voice said, 'What the hell's all the racket?'

It was just like an old-fashioned farce.

Daisy's door slammed resoundingly. There'd been no sign of Carey, though I was sure he couldn't have slept through all of that.

As my shape changed and my slender body grew ever more rounded, it seemed to me that both my husband and Mr Browne regarded me with increasing distaste. Indeed, though Ralph was punctilious in enquiring after my health, he seemed to find me physically quite repugnant and avoided even kissing my cheek whenever he could do so, let alone according me any more intimate demonstrations of affection.

I confided these concerns in a letter to Lily and she replied that she had heard that some men did find pregnant women unappealing, even the most loving of husbands, but she thought his affections would soon rekindle when the child arrived.

I hoped she was right . . . but I now suspected Ralph and I would never draw close again while Mr Rosslyn Browne was planted firmly in our midst. Even when he had to go away on business, Ralph would often go with him, so we rarely spent time alone together.

Honoria and I both feared that one day Ralph would return from one of these excursions and inform us that he had purchased land in the Lake District on which to build a house . . .

34

The Morning Chorus

My inner alarm woke me at five and I got up, and then shivered under the antiquated shower next door, a brass arrangement that sprouted like a strange steampunk flower from one end of the bath. Daisy was in the room opposite, so my bathroom reeked of something delicately exotic – though her snores were not delicately anything, but of the more homely snort-and-whistle variety. I was tempted to record them for posterity . . . or blackmail.

She wasn't the sole emitter of nocturnal noises, because there was a positive symphony of snores as I tiptoed along the landing with Carey's card and painting tucked under my arm, like a slightly Goth and out-of-season Mother Christmas. Silently I cracked opened his bedroom door and listened: he sighed gently and turned over, so I quickly slid the envelope and parcel in and closed it again.

Downstairs, once I'd let Fang out for his morning watery communion with the fishy fountain, I made a mug of coffee and took it through to the studio. This was probably going to be the only quiet time to myself that I'd get that day and I had the two enquiries about possible commissions to think over and reply to. Then, I wanted to start designing a series of free-hanging roundels, based on the under-and-over the sea idea, like portholes. I could sell that kind of thing for a good price very easily, through galleries and online.

And maybe some more angels . . . starting with one of Carey. Not that he was any kind of angel in reality, and nor was Daisy, despite her other-worldly beauty. Last night he hadn't shown any signs of falling for her all over again, but she'd certainly done her best to make him.

Perhaps he was still attracted by her, but too proud, or afraid of being hurt again, to show it.

Deep in thought, I'd been sitting at my worktable staring blankly at the wall opposite for ages, coffee in hand, before I registered the brown paper package leaning against it. An envelope bearing my name was stuck to the front. And even without the unmistakable writing, the style of the wrapping was typical of Carey: his presents were always covered in recycled brown parcel paper, turned inside out, or odd wallpaper samples.

I got up and when I pulled off the envelope and opened it, I found inside a slip of paper that said:

Here you are, Angel, my little Heavenly Host all rolled into one –
Happy Valentine's Day!

I had no idea what Carey meant by that 'heavenly host' bit, but I carried the package over to my table, cleared a space at one end and laid it down flat. From the sheer weight and feel of it, I had a good idea of what it was, though not what form it might take, so I ripped off the paper eagerly.

Inside was a fragment of a stained-glass window, the empty flanges of surrounding broken-off lead calme splayed out around it. It was bound with clingfilm to a piece of square board, which I removed, my eyes fixed on the painted face beneath. It was as if my earlier thoughts had conjured up the haloed head of an angel, Pre-Raphaelite in style and brilliantly painted and stained. There was a hint of celestial blue robe in one of the remaining pieces and the feathered top arch of a wing behind the head.

That was all that remained intact – the head and three other pieces – then the torn protruding bits of empty calme where the window had been knocked out. I'd seen it happen many times before, but never with glass of this quality. It was a miracle that someone had at least thought this fragment worth preserving, perhaps worth a few bob.

I grieved for the window that had been lost, even while I rejoiced in the part that had been saved.

The door opened and Carey entered, carrying the painting and card, which he set down on his desk before picking me up and giving me a bear hug and a smacking kiss.

'Thank you, Shrimp, you couldn't have given me anything I'd like more!'

'Ditto, though I wish I had the rest of the window,' I said breathlessly when he put me down. 'It's so beautiful, they must have been mad to smash it.'

'I know, but I expect it was just workmen doing what they were told. I found that piece mixed in with a box of loose squares of that pink and blue machine-made glass you hate, in the architectural antiques place. They couldn't remember where the box came from and they'd had it for years. I had to buy the whole lot, so the rest of it is in one of the stables.'

'It'll come in handy for Grant, if he sets himself up doing repair work,' I said, then looked down at my angel's head again. 'I think this is – or was – an important window.'

'That's what I thought, too. You can't mistake the full, sulky-looking mouth on that angel, beautiful as she is in her way,' he agreed. 'Pre-Raphaelite – maybe even Burne-Jones?'

I nodded.

'What will you do with it?'

'Take it apart and then re-lead the remaining pieces into a roundel, I expect. I meant to make some more angel ones anyway – just for me, not to sell.'

'You could hang some in the windows in here,' he suggested. 'And I'll have my painting in here, too, so I can contemplate it when I need inspiration.'

'I think right now you'd better get inspired about cooking breakfast, because I can hear the thunder of hoofs on the trail.'

'So there is,' he said, but instead of heading out to the kitchen, he stood looking down quizzically at me, his large, warm hands gripping my shoulders. 'I'm sorry about Daisy turning up, Angel. I just couldn't shove her out into the cold and dark last night, but I'll send her on her way this morning, even if I have to drive her to the station myself!'

'I don't know why you're apologizing to me – *I* don't care whether she's here or not,' I said untruthfully. 'But now she's got wind of the party, I doubt you'll dislodge her before tomorrow.'

'Limpet' was probably her middle name.

'Just watch me,' he said, then added, still looking down at me and raising one quizzical eyebrow, 'You know, I could have sworn I heard her and Nick arguing on the landing in the middle of the night. It sounded as if she'd walked into his room and woken him up.'

'Did she? Perhaps she was looking for the bathroom,' I suggested, with limpid innocence.

After breakfast, I drove over to Molly's to collect the cake and the rest of the party food. Daisy still hadn't put in an appearance, which was probably just as well, because there was much ribald joking about the bedroom farce in the middle of the night. Nick was pretending that she'd fallen suddenly and passionately in love with him and he'd had to fight her off to preserve his honour.

As usual, the crew were none the worse for the rum, though slightly sleepy. Carey, Nelson and Jorge were to go up to the Halfhidden shop while Nick and Sukes took some shots of the alpacas in the field behind the back gates for, as he put it, a bit of quirky local colour.

I left them discussing it, hoping that dumping Daisy at the station with her huge suitcase would be part of Carey's plan. Fang had wanted to come with me, but since I might have to put some of the food on the back seat of the car, that wouldn't have been a good idea. He's such a glutton.

Molly had iced a big rectangular cake like a stained-glass window and lettered 'Angel Arrowsmith Art Glass' on to a scroll in the middle. You could have leaded up that design quite easily, so Grant must have had a hand in it.

There were biscuits with stained-glass middles made of melted brightly coloured sweets, as well as some more mundane offerings like mini sausage rolls, cheese straws, quiches and savoury tartlets.

'I've marked anything that *isn't* vegetarian,' she said. 'If you've invited any vegans, then they're on their own.'

'I don't think I have – but they could eat the crisps and nuts, I suppose.'

We had coffee and a slice of carrot cake before it was time for her to load her deliveries into her little van. I told her about Daisy and the bitch that barked in the night.

'You're a terrible woman!' she said, laughing. 'Do you think she'll have gone by the time you get back?'

'I don't know. Nor do I know how Carey really feels about her now. You haven't seen her, but she's almost unbelievably pretty,' I said gloomily. 'He says he's totally over her but . . .'

'Oh, don't be daft – even I can see he's not looking for someone else!' she said robustly. 'The two of you are having too much fun together for him to even think about it.'

'It has been fun – like old times – but I'm being selfish not wanting him to meet someone else just yet. I mean, I couldn't very well carry on living at Mossby, if he married, or moved a partner in, could I?'

'Oh, Angel!' she said, looking at me in a strangely exasperated way. 'That's really not going to happen. Now he's got you, why would he want anyone else?'

'But that's different! We've known each other so long, we're like brother and sister.'

'Not like any brother and sister *I've* ever known,' she said drily. 'And I suspect you haven't always thought of each other that way, have you?'

'Well . . . in our last year at university I did think our relationship was starting to change,' I admitted. 'But then I caught him snogging yet another blonde at a party, so I knew it would be better to keep things as they'd always been.'

'Then you met Julian soon afterwards anyway,' she finished.

'Yes, and Julian and I fell in love at first sight, so it was obviously meant to be.'

'But now you and Carey have both had to move on into a new phase of your lives and you *need* each other,' she said. 'Things change.'

'They do, but we're destined to remain just best friends for ever.'

'Yeah, right,' said Molly sceptically.

'No, really, we are,' I insisted . . . but then into my head popped the recollection of that very unbrotherly kiss he'd given me, right after the stone ball almost fell on him, and I could feel myself turning slightly pink.

I got up. 'I'd better leave you to it. See you later at the party!'

When I got back, Carey helped me unload the food on to the cold slate shelves of the larder and told me that Daisy had

367

disappeared. It seemed that having come downstairs so late that she found herself alone in the house, apart from a sneering dog, she'd ignored the note he'd left suggesting she ring for a taxi to the station and vanished into thin air instead. Unfortunately, she'd left her suitcase behind, which wasn't a hopeful sign.

It was a puzzle, but one we soon forgot about while we set to and finished the preparations for the party. Nelson, assisted by Sukes, produced his hedgehog canapés, while Carey cut and buttered thin triangles of a kind of fruit loaf he'd made in the bread maker. Finally, everything was ready and it was time to ferry it all down to the workshop and arrange it, under its clingfilm wrapping, on the tables.

Nick buzzed in and out with a camera and finally informed us that he'd just seen Vicky stopping her car at the Lodge, and Daisy getting out of the passenger seat and going in with her.

'The plot thickens,' Nelson said, in his deep and wonderfully plummy voice.

And then she rang Carey's mobile and told him her old friend Vicky Parry had called at the house this morning to ask if she could come to the party and had been totally surprised to find Daisy there – wasn't that an amazing coincidence?

'Then she said Vicky would put her up tonight and, since she had to get back to London tomorrow herself anyway, Ella would drive them both to the station.'

'So she's not coming back here tonight: what's the catch?' asked Nick.

'She hoped I wouldn't mind if she just popped briefly into the party later to say goodbye, and she wants me to drop her suitcase off at the Lodge.'

'Now?' I said. 'We're all about to change for the party.'

'I'll take it down – I'm beautiful enough already,' offered Nick. 'But if she grabs me and I scream, you've all got to rush to the rescue.'

I would have liked to have travelled to London to visit Father, so that I might see Lily, but Ralph wished me to wait till after the baby had arrived.

Instead, Father paid us a visit, bringing gifts and messages from Lily, as well as the completed nursery embroidery, which was quite delightful.

I showed Father my finished cartoon of Lady Anne's window and told him of my increasing conviction that it contained a message, possibly relating to some hidden treasure. However, he said he could not see any such meaning in the random motifs and he supposed pregnancy had rendered me fanciful!

35

Illuminations

I put on the lovely new dress Izzy had made for me and some black tights. Then I dithered between my usual Doc Marten boots, or the black suede ballerina pumps I kept for smart occasions. The tunic dress was quite short, but then, so am I . . . and I do have very nice legs.

I wore the pumps, even though I knew I'd freeze on the way down. When Carey saw me his eyes widened and he said I looked beautiful, while Nick wolf-whistled.

'I'd forgotten you had legs, Angel.'

'Ho, ho,' I laughed hollowly. 'I assume, since you're here, the man-eating spider-woman didn't gobble you up when you dropped off her suitcase?'

'No – I dumped it on the doorstep, rang the bell and drove off again,' he admitted cravenly.

'Coward,' Nelson said. 'We know she wants Carey really, but I'm sure you'd do if she was desperate.'

'It's hard to imagine anyone *that* desperate,' put in Sukes, but Nick just grinned.

I'd been putting Fang's blue boots on and someone had tied a blue and white spotted triangular scarf round his neck, so he looked quite festive.

We all walked down together, except for Carey, who'd gone ahead to switch on the lights. The room was lit only by

370

the heart-shaped ones, the workbench lamps and a series of tea lights up the centres of the long glazing tables. Jorge put on some soft music while we uncovered the food and Carey mixed his punch. I now had a small fridge in the back room, so we'd crammed extra ice cubes in the top compartment and fruit juice in the rest.

'It looks magical, doesn't it?' I said, gazing round the workshop. 'Thank you, everyone, for all your help.'

'It does look great,' Nick agreed.

'We'll shoot a bit of film now, then more when the guests start arriving . . . and it's almost time,' Jorge said.

'I didn't show you what Jorge gave me for Valentine's Day,' Sukes said, exhibiting a small jade heart, edged in silver, on a long chain. 'It's my favourite colour – and I didn't know he had a romantic bone in his body!'

'You'd be surprised,' he said.

I was sure I'd seen the pendant among other luscious jewellery in Cam's gallery, and since Sukes habitually dressed in shades of green, like the floaty tunic she was wearing over her jeans now, guessing her favourite colour hadn't really been a mind-stretch.

They did a bit of filming and then, as at all parties, just when you're wondering if anyone's going to turn up, the guests arrived all at once. They milled about just inside the room, like a slightly confused shoal of fish, before sorting themselves out.

Rufus and Izzy had brought me a gift – a small wooden sign for over my door, lettered in gold with 'Angelique Arrowsmith Art Glass'.

'Carey told us what you'd called the business,' Izzy said.

'You know, a sign for outside is something I'd totally forgotten,' I said. 'I'll have it fixed over the side door, so it faces the drive.'

Cam and Lulu had collected Jonah and Tom Tamblyn on

371

their way, and Tom gave Carey a big glass bottle of water from the Lady Spring.

'Do I drink it, or pour it over my leg?' Carey asked, thanking him.

'I'd drink it, but as soon as the weather's warm enough, you should come and swim in the pool.'

'It's big enough to swim in?' he asked, surprised.

'Oh, yes – though not huge, just a couple of strokes each way,' Izzy said. 'I start going in quite early in the year, because it never seems anywhere near as cold as the air around it.'

Then she said her aunt Debo and Judy were coming once they'd finished the evening kennel round, bringing the kennel maid, Sandy, with them and her sister, Foxy.

The room by then was getting quite full, and noisier as the level of the punch bowl went down. There were Molly and Grant, Ivan and Louis, the Rigbys from the farm, Chris, the dog whisperer, with his teenage daughter, Liz. She was a pretty girl with soft brown hair framing a heart-shaped face and big dark eyes. I noticed that she and Louis naturally gravitated towards each other, as the youngest people there by a mile.

Fang happily hoovered up dropped crumbs, pausing only when the door opened on a cold blast of wind that blew Vicky and Daisy in.

Everything seemed to freeze for a moment – even the music – and I have to admit they looked quite striking. Both were tall, pale blondes, though Daisy's more ethereal beauty made Vicky look a bit sturdy and wholesome.

Daisy was wearing what I think they call a Bombshell Dress: tight, low cut and producing curves she didn't really have. She certainly looked as if she should be mooing into a microphone at the front of a forties dance band. Vicky was clad in something like a bandage wrapped horizontally round her from mid-thigh to just above her bust, and both wore killer heels, which I hoped wouldn't kill my new vinyl flooring.

For a minute the two pale figures stood in the doorway like twin vampires in a low-budget horror film, then everyone got back to whatever they were doing before, which in my case was standing with Carey behind the cake, about to cut it, while Molly and Grant were handing round the glasses of bubbly for a toast.

Camera lights flashed as I plunged in the cake knife. I pretended it was Daisy, which made it even more enjoyable.

'Toast!' called Carey. 'Here's to the new workshop. Every success, Angel!'

'And here's a toast to the success of Carey's new TV series. ITV have taken it and we hope it's going to run for years!' announced Nick, and everyone clapped.

'Hurray!' chorused Ivan, Jonah and Tom, who were sitting in the corner with plates and glasses fully charged.

'Eat, drink and be merry,' said Carey, and Jorge turned the music up. It was rather as if he'd turned the conversation up too, because the noise level rose so quickly.

'Vicky was right behind you while Jorge was filming you cutting the cake,' Carey said into my ear.

'She'll be a happy bunny if she's finally got herself in the series,' I said.

Nick, reaching over for a slice of the cake, said, 'Actually, you'd be surprised how many times she's got herself in the background when we were filming, without us noticing till too late. But no starring roles.'

'Have you noticed there's no sign of Clem and Ella?' I said.

'Clem *was* here earlier for a few minutes; you must have missed him,' Carey told me. 'He said he wasn't much of a party animal, but had just looked in to wish you success. Ella's got one of her migraines.'

One or two people had begun to dance in the clear space under the loft, where the only light was the glimmer of the heart-shaped fairy lights.

'There you are, Carey!' Daisy exclaimed, as if he'd been hiding, which isn't possible even in a crowd when you're six-four and have a head like burnished red gold. She linked her arm in his and, looking up at him, made big kitten eyes. 'Come and dance with me, darling.'

'I was never much of a dancer and I don't think my leg is up to that kind of thing yet,' he said, disengaging himself.

'*I'll* dance with you,' offered Nick heroically. 'And if you want to come back and share my room tonight, I promise not to scream this time.'

She gave him a look. 'I'll stay at the Lodge, thanks. And just make sure I'm not in any of the film you've taken tonight,' she added brusquely, before turning her back on both of us and moving in on Carey again. This time she got up on tiptoe to murmur in his ear, but whatever she said didn't ring his bell, because he walked off even while her mouth was still moving and went into a huddle with Rufus and Cam.

They were probably discussing a much more exciting topic, like the best way to add ghosts to your postcards, or what kind of wood chipper to get.

I sipped the remains of my bubbly and did a bit of people-watching. Vicky, who'd looked totally disconcerted when she'd found Louis was totally ignoring her in favour of a teenager, and presumably conceding defeat where engaging Carey's interest was concerned, was now eyeing up the other possibilities.

But before she could make any move, she was buttonholed by Debo, who appeared to be working the room. She'd arrived still wearing her dungarees and made even those look so elegant that Nick filmed her from all angles like a

374

paparazzo, until he abandoned any more filming in favour of getting down to some serious drinking and eating.

'Debo's got great social skills,' I said to Izzy. 'I think she's talked to practically everyone here.'

'That's because she's trying to get them to adopt one of her dogs,' she said. Just then some slow and smoochy music came on and she dragged Rufus off to dance. Vicky, having now escaped Debo's clutches already, was with both Benbow twins. Two for the price of one, as it were.

'Come on,' Carey said, suddenly appearing at my elbow and, removing the glass and plate from my hands, put them on the table behind us. 'They're playing our tune.'

'We haven't got a tune – and you told Daisy you weren't up to dancing.'

'I wasn't up to dancing with Daisy and, anyway, I'm not about to launch into a jig. I'll just sway about a bit.'

So we did and, since I'd had rather a lot of bubbly and a glass of fairly potent punch by this point, I subsided against him as we swayed and turned.

'Oh, this is nice,' I sighed.

'You and me, always, Angel,' he agreed and, tightening his arms around me, rested his cheek against my hair.

After a while, when the music went up tempo again, we separated. Carey had promised to show Jonah the Elizabethan wing in all its ghostly evening glory, and Nick and Jorge tagged along, hoping to get some footage of a ghost, should one obligingly appear.

They were away for only about twenty minutes, so when they returned I was still slowly circulating among my guests. I was trying to have a word with everyone, though the noise level was now such that it was hard to hear myself speak.

But they all seemed to be having a good time, just as I was . . . until I walked into the back room to get some more

375

ice and found Daisy and Carey entwined and mid passionate kiss. It was just a brief glimpse, because I immediately turned and blundered blindly back into the other room: it was déjà vu, a repeat of that time at university, when I'd thought our relationship had changed, only to be disillusioned.

And in one blinding stroke it revealed to me the depths of my jealousy. My love for Carey had at some recent point changed its nature and what I most wanted to do at that moment was go back in there, seize Daisy by her pale-gold hair and bang her head repeatedly on the worktop.

But then, it took two to tango and Carey hadn't exactly looked as if he was fighting her off.

I stood in my dark corner, getting my face and my slightly homicidal impulses under control and then went to sit with Molly.

But I can't have done that good a job of it, because she said in my ear, 'What's the matter? I just saw you come out of the back room looking as if you'd seen a ghost.'

'I did,' I said with a shaky and unconvincing laugh. 'The ghost of parties past: Carey and Daisy were in there, having a smooch.'

She stared at me. 'It can't be what it looked like,' she said flatly after a minute.

'It looked to me like he still can't resist her and perhaps they'll get back together.'

'There has to be an explanation,' she insisted. 'I mean, a *different* explanation.'

'It doesn't matter. But you see, I was right about me and Carey. We're just best friends and that's how it will always be, nothing more.'

Molly looked troubled, but didn't say anything else, and when Carey reappeared there was no sign of Daisy – other than a raspberry-red streak of lipstick on his face.

*

When I came back in after waving off the last of the revellers, Molly and Grant had already packed away the small amount of leftover food, while the crew had helpfully drained the last of the punch and the dregs of the open bottles.

Jorge and Sukes were tossing the debris into a big black plastic bag and I hoped someone other than me was going to sort that into the recycling bins tomorrow . . .

'You've gone very quiet,' Carey said to me, putting his arm round my shoulders and giving me a searching look, which I avoided. The lipstick had quickly vanished – someone must have told him about it – but I still felt Daisy had put her mark on him.

'Oh, I think I've just had too much to drink – but it was a great party.'

'Why don't you go up to the house and make some coffee and we'll follow you up in a minute? We can clear everything else away in the morning,' he suggested.

'Good idea,' I said, and on the way scooped up Fang, who was fast asleep under one of the tables, his small tummy round with leftovers.

The cold night air cleared my head a bit, though even the icy wind couldn't scour away my emotions.

Molly and Grant went home after the coffee, saying they felt tired, and once the warmth of the kitchen had hit me I'd suddenly felt as limp as a bit of chewed string, too. But the crew seemed to get a second wind and decided to go back into the old wing and ghost hunt in Lady Anne's bedchamber.

'Sooner you than me,' I said. 'It's cold as ice in there, even with the electric storage heater going.'

'You coming, Carey?' asked Nick, as they headed out.

'I'll catch you up. I'll just take Fang into the courtyard first,' Carey told him and then, when they'd gone, looked

377

down at me and said, with that irresistible smile, 'Why not come out and see the stars, Angel?'

I hardened my heart and told him it was too cold and I was so tired I only wanted to go to bed.

'OK – and happy Valentine's Day,' he said softly and I managed a smile.

'I've had a wonderful day, from the stained-glass angel onwards,' I told him, though I didn't add that it had all shattered in one awful, illuminating moment and I needed time to reassemble my love for him to the old pattern.

My husband and Mr Browne were away when Father visited, but when they returned I thought they had been quarrelling again.

I believe Mr Browne now wishes to permanently leave Mossby and move to the Lakes, where he is sure of getting more commissions.

I hope he does so and there is a final break between them: I believe it would be for the best.

Somewhat irked by Father's opinion of my mental faculties, after he had returned to London I began a systematic search of the old wing for anything that might appear among the motifs in the window. I was by now rather too large and cumbersome to do anything more useful! I wrote jokingly to Lily that since this was clearly a honeymoon baby, I should call it Paris . . .

36

Down Time

I woke as early as usual next morning and opened my window on to still, crisp, cold, starless darkness. Shivering, I closed it again and quickly dressed in jeans, black sweatshirt and my boots.

I felt like me again: no nonsense.

Downstairs I drank some coffee and then, standing by the open fridge door, grazed on a cold vegetarian sausage roll and two cheese and tomato sandwiches, as you do when there are leftovers. It's as if there's some guilt involved and you need to be ready to slam the door and hope no one notices the crumbs round your mouth.

I didn't go into the studio after that, but instead put on my cheering coat of many colours and set off for the workshop. I asked Fang if he'd like to come with me, but he was still curled in his basket by the stove and only opened his eyes long enough to give me an 'At this time of the morning – you can't be serious?' look before firmly closing them again.

I'd remembered that the workshop needed to be cleaned and ready, because Grant and Ivan were coming over after lunch with their long ladders to remove the Lady Anne window and bring it down. I wanted everything straight and workmanlike for them . . . much as I intended my relationship with Carey to be from then on.

Firmly back on the old footing.

When I got there I found there wasn't too much to do, since most of the debris had been taken up to the house last night. I wiped down the plastic tablecloths and folded them up when they were dry, rounded up a few missed empty paper cups and plates and swept and mopped the floors. Then I only needed to take down the fairy lights and it was as if last night's party was but a slightly bizarre dream.

By then, a bright, wintry sunlight was pouring into the room, lightening my mood and making me count my blessings: here I was in my own workshop and living in a lovely house with my very best friend. How lucky was I?

And if things changed . . . well, I had yet to explore the chauffeur's flat over one of the stables, but whatever state it was in, I was sure it could be updated so I'd be able to move there when Carey found someone else to share Mossby with.

Lunch up at the house was a scratch meal of the last of the party leftovers and lots of coffee to wake Carey, Nick and the gang up: they'd stayed up late in the old wing, waiting for an apparition that never appeared, while telling each other ghost stories so they jumped at every creak the old house made.

But they quickly revived and were ready to film the Lady Anne window being removed, once Grant and Ivan had arrived.

I was on tenterhooks watching as they carefully removed the three panels of the tall, narrow window and laid them on a board, even though putting in and taking out leaded lights was something they were well used to. Grant had previously measured the window opening and brought a sheet of plain glass to keep out the weather, until the old window was reinstalled.

While they had the ladders up, Grant checked the tie bars, wires and mortar on the side windows, too, some of which were loose.

'But they don't look too bad at all. I think someone's been

up here and done a few repairs at some point. And the condition of the glass is surprisingly good, given the age.'

'I expect the way the hill rises behind this wing protects it from the elements a bit. These panels certainly don't look as if they've been exposed to the elements since the seventeenth century,' I said, anxiously hovering over my treasures. 'Well, apart from the hole the bird made.'

'At least that's in the small triangular top panel, so there's just that one to repair,' Grant said. 'And now you've got the original cartoon, it should be a doddle.'

I wasn't entirely sure 'doddle' was the right word when it came to repairing priceless old windows, but I'd have to do my best. Carey helped me to transport it down to the workshop in the back of his estate car, leaving Ivan and Grant to finish glazing the empty window.

Once the three precious panels had been transferred to a glazing table, I quite forgot I had an audience of Carey and the film crew and I took a rubbing of it to show the position of the leading. Then I propped each panel carefully against the clear plate glass on the easels over the studio windows and stood back to study them.

'Everything's watertight and shipshape up at the house, Angel,' Grant's voice announced, breaking into my reverie.

'Oh . . . are you back?' I said, turning round to find not only Ivan and Grant, but the film crew lined up watching me. 'Thank you both for doing that.'

'It was nowt,' said Ivan. 'Shall I make us all a cup of tea?'

'That would be lovely, thank you. I don't know where Carey's got to.'

'I think he went through the back room into his workshop,' Nelson said. 'I'll give him a shout when the tea's up.'

'What exactly are you going to do with the window?' asked Nick.

'As little as possible. I only want to repair it, conserving what's left and I have no intention of doing anything that can't be undone later. An expert in glass restoration is coming over tomorrow to have a look at it and perhaps give me some advice – and by the way, I emailed and checked with her if she'd be happy to appear in the documentary and she said no, so you can't film in here tomorrow.'

Nick looked resigned. 'Oh well, maybe we'll do a bit more in the old wing instead – that priest-hole in the Great Hall, for a start.'

'This window's not in poor shape at all, considering,' Grant said, having a closer look at the panels on the easel. 'But you might as well re-lead all of it while we've got it down.'

'Yes, I suppose so,' I said. Taking an old window apart isn't always the easiest of tasks. Sometimes you're in luck and the lead and cement simply gently peel apart from the glass, or the cement has turned to dust and crumbles easily away. But occasionally it's solidly accreted on and then you have to painstakingly remove it with a sharp blade, without damaging the glass.

I hoped this would be an easier one.

Over the tea, Carey promised to do his best to record the various stages of the repairs when the crew were not there, on the camera Jorge had loaned him. His filming had been a bit hit and miss so far, since when he's flown with enthusiasm for something he entirely forgets to record it.

Grant and Ivan went home after the tea, but I have no idea where the others got to. I went up to the house to make an exact black and white copy of the Lady Anne cartoon to take down to the workshop and saw no one.

It was strange that the bird that'd broken the window appeared to have burst right through that strangely spiky sun, as if it had aimed for it.

Perhaps it had.

*

Next morning, Ivan and I began the task of carefully taking the panels apart, but it was slow work and we hadn't got far by the time the expert arrived.

She was a middle-aged woman, with curling ash-blonde hair, piercing light blue eyes and a severe and humourless manner. I was sure she knew her stuff, but suspected that the joy of working with coloured light had never touched her soul.

While she was examining the window, I sent Ivan to winkle Carey out of his man cave next door, since any decisions on what to do with it were up to him. He came through, wiping his hands on an oily rag.

'This is Grace Jakes, an old friend of Julian's, who's going to give us some advice,' I said, introducing them. 'Carey Revell, who owns Mossby.'

'I've been cleaning up the pikes from the display in the Great Hall, so I'd better not shake hands,' he said, but after a brief nod, she'd already turned back to the business in hand.

'You have a very interesting window here, Mr Carey – unusual for its time in that it was designed by a woman and different in style to others of that period,' she began.

'Call me Carey,' he suggested, giving her one of his blinding smiles. She blinked, as if a sudden flash of light had hurt her eyes, but was only briefly deflected from her lecture.

'It's therefore an important window and by rights, it should come to us to be properly restored and conserved by experts in the field.'

'No chance,' he said. 'Anyway, I don't want it restored, or glued together, or whatever else you experts get up to. Angel says there are a couple of cracked pieces, plus the shattered one, which luckily is cleanly broken into three, so she can lead it back together.'

'That's the old way, of course, using very narrow calmes,

384

but the lines of the leads are intrusive,' she said, then turned to look at the broken pieces of the sun, which I'd laid out on the small light-box. 'However, if edge-to-edge bonding with resin was used instead, then it would look exactly as it was made.'

'That's not something I feel competent to do and, anyway, Julian said even the new resins would go yellow eventually,' I objected. 'We both actually preferred to see old windows repaired with lead calme – it added to the charm somehow, rather than detracted.'

'I'm afraid I can't agree with you there, but on the other hand, if you decided to send the panel for professional restoration at some future point, there would be no problem undoing what you'd done.'

'Yes, that's what I thought.'

'The glass is in surprisingly good condition – almost no pitting or discoloration.'

'The hillside rises behind that wing, so it's sheltered. It's a mystery how a bird managed to fly into it at all, unless it had a death wish,' Carey said.

'Unfortunate. Do you intend attempting any kind of cleaning process before you re-lead the glass, Angelique?'

'Not really, I thought I'd just wash it with distilled water and dry it.'

She briefly closed her eyes, as if in pain. 'I brought some ionized water in the car, in case you hadn't got any.'

I shook my head. Not only did I not have any, I had no idea what it was.

She fetched it in just as Carey vanished back into his cave and, though she seemed inclined to follow him in order to make a further attempt to persuade him to let her take the window away, I told her it was pointless.

'Once he's made his mind up, he's totally stubborn. And also, you see, he's a Revell, so I think he really *believes* the family would be cursed if you did that.'

'I don't hold with superstition,' she said austerely, then went disapprovingly away.

'Has she gone?' Ivan whispered, sticking his silvery head round the door of the back room. 'I took a scunner to her: she was just like my maths teacher when I was a boy. She tried to beat fractions into me with a ruler.'

'Grace didn't attempt any physical violence, but we've got to wash the pieces of the window glass in this special water.'

'Eh, whatever next?' he said.

We carried on gently taking the panels apart, placing each piece of glass in its right position on the black and white cartoon I'd made and laid out on the other glazing bench.

I continued for an hour or so after Ivan left, reluctant to stop, before locking up and returning to the house. There I found everyone in the kitchen as usual, with an open bottle of wine and the menus of the three local takeaways that delivered.

'There you are,' said Carey, looking up and smiling at me, as if my arrival was the only thing needed to make his life perfect, though, actually, that's pretty much the way he always *does* smile at me.

'We're ordering food and then flagellating our artistic souls by watching the last of the Seamus Banyan *Complete Cottage Catastrophes*,' he said. 'Indian, Italian or Chinese?'

Later, we all walked to the pub, where the crew described how Ella had almost caused them to have a mass heart attack earlier in the day, when they'd opened the priest-hole in the Great Hall and found her sitting there.

'I mean, Carey showed us how it worked and it swung open, and there was this tall, dark figure with a white face and burning eyes, staring back at us,' Sukes said.

'What on earth was she doing in there?'

'Cleaning, she said,' Jorge put in. 'But unless she was dusting the stone walls with her hands, I don't know how.'

'She grows stranger by the day,' I said. 'It's beginning to get worrying.'

'Jorge started filming her,' Carey said.

'Automatic reflex,' he explained. 'But she pushed past us without a word and went out of the front door.'

'It was a bit . . . bizarre,' Nick said. 'Great bit of film, though – couldn't have set it up better if we'd tried.'

We had a pleasant evening at the pub and then, while walking home, Carey took my hand, which was nothing out of the ordinary. Holding hands, putting his arm round me, casual kisses . . . I told myself that it was all part of his tactile nature and meant nothing more than it ever had.

Next day, after a couple of phone calls, there was a sudden change of plan and Carey went back to London with Nick and co. Apparently, there were things to sign, agents to see . . . and perhaps he'd meet up with Daisy, too? He hadn't mentioned her since the party, but that didn't mean he wasn't *thinking* about her.

Anyway, it wasn't any of my business. It was just as well I'd realized the change in the way I felt about him wasn't reciprocated, before I made a fool of myself and ruined our perfect friendship.

'I'll be back tomorrow,' he told me when they left. 'Will you be all right on your own?'

'Of course! I'll be far too busy with the window to even register you've gone, though Fang had better put his boots on and come to the workshop with me,' I added, 'otherwise, I might get so engrossed I forget to go up and let him out.'

*

387

I *was* so engaged with my work that I hardly missed Carey at all during the day. It was different in the evening, and Fang kept looking at me reproachfully, as if it was my fault he wasn't there.

But he returned on the train next day, saying everything was settled, though not whether that encompassed Daisy, too. Perhaps he hadn't fallen under her spell again and it had just been a random kiss. But it had served to remind me that if it wasn't Daisy, he'd soon fall for another leggy blonde in the same mould.

Ivan and I had totally dismantled the Lady Anne window in his absence and over the next few days we cleaned each piece of glass.

Ionized water seemed much like any other.

There were thankfully no breaks anywhere except in the top panel. The cracks could be fixed with narrow ribbon lead calme – and so could the broken pieces of the sun, for the longest break helpfully ran along one of the spiky arms, making the mend less obtrusive.

'We'll need to trim the edge flanges a little bit to ease it in when it's fixed,' Ivan said, as we discussed it, 'but that's no great problem.'

'That sun's very odd when you really look,' I said pensively gazing at it. 'It's more like a star . . . or a sparkling jewel.'

'It all looks odd to me, what with these little bits of pattern and pictures painted in circles in the centres of the diamond quarries,' Ivan said. 'I've never seen owt like it: fiddly, I call it!'

My head was so full of my work that I was probably boring Carey senseless with it, though he never *looked* bored. He popped in occasionally to film a bit of the process, but otherwise was engaged in his renovations – stripping the wallpaper in my bedroom and prepping it for painting. He'd sold his uncle's old car to a nearby garage called Deals on

Wheels and put the money towards his own camera. I just knew he'd permanently add his new skills to all the others.

We'd settled back happily enough into our life together, immersed in our own affairs during the day, though each was interested in what the other was doing. Then, if no one else was staying, we'd often spend the evenings working in the studio. I was getting design ideas ready to submit for those two commission enquiries, as well as working on a series of sea-themed free-hanging roundels, so my book idea had been pushed temporarily on to the back burner.

It was idyllic: a temporary idyll, perhaps, but all the more to be treasured for that.

At last the glass was cleaned up and Ivan and I were ready to re-lead the three panels.

The wooden side and top battens for each one were nailed to the glazing benches, the wide calmes for two sides of the borders cut and laid against them – and we were ready to begin.

Soon, the only sound to be heard was the tapping in of the horseshoe nails that held each piece of glass firm, while we placed the next.

Ivan worked on one panel and I the other, at adjoining tables, though I reserved the top and trickiest one for last – and it was somewhat of a joint effort, with Ivan standing by like a nurse in an operating theatre, ready to hand me the right size of calme, a horseshoe nail, or the next piece of glass as I worked towards the centre. There, the narrowest of calmes held the broken parts together, within the original boundary of wider lead that defined the diamond quarry – and the sun (or whatever it was) became whole again.

I soldered all three panels with my new gas-cylinder-powered iron. I *adore* soldering – tinning the end of the iron, cleaning the lead joints with a wire brush, rubbing them with a tallow stick and then placing a neat round flat cap of solder on top of each. And this time, it was a real labour of love.

When they were finally completed, we carried them with great care through to the cementing room at the back of the building, because there's a lot of bend in a glass panel before it's cemented and allowed to dry out.

The thickly glutinous black mixture was brushed under the flanges of the leads, then a pointed stick run round the edge of each piece of glass to remove the excess. After that, whitening was sprinkled all over the panels to soak up the remains and then scrubbed off with a brush.

The finished panels, clean and shiny, went into a rack, to harden: one small window, so much work, but enjoyable and worthwhile. We felt we'd done a good job and we raised a toast in Old Spoggit Brown before Ivan went home for a well-deserved weekend off.

Even on a sunny day it was gloomy enough to need a lantern in some of the rooms of the old wing, to which Ralph's gas lighting had not reached.

Nonetheless, I continued my search until one day, when I was in the room called Lady Anne's bedchamber, examining the linenfold panelling, the folded top point of which was a frequently used motif in the window, I noticed that the bosses running just above it were carved with roses, another frequent symbol!

But if the room concealed a hiding place, which of these to press, turn, or pull when the panelling went right round the room, was the question!

In turning to survey the rest of the walls, my light happened to fall directly on to the massively carved bedhead, which I now saw depicted Adam and Eve in the Garden. What's more, Eve seemed to be carrying a woven rush basket, presumably to hold the apples she had just gathered, one of which she was offering to her spouse.

This was not a biblical story I was generally much in favour of, since it neatly unloaded the blame for the ensuing evils created by generations of men on to the shoulders of the innocent daughters of Eve.

But now I peered closer, running my hands over the design.

A circle containing just that very basketwork pattern had always appeared in the window quarries next to an apple. I set down the lantern next to the bed, kneeled on it and tried pressing and prodding and turning both . . . until finally, with a faint creak as of something long unused, the central panel slid aside revealing a dark and musty cavity.

37

Treasure Fever

The next day being a Saturday, Louis turned up at the workshop to admire the windows on his way up to the house. He was going to help Carey with his various projects most weekends, until I had more work coming in and needed him.

He'd brought with him Liz, the dog whisperer's daughter, having picked her up in the car that Ivan had bought him when he passed his test – some quite ordinary little hatchback, which he'd tarted up with bold stripes up the side and an oddly large and protruding exhaust.

It was a day for brief visitations, for soon after they'd gone, Molly dropped Grant off so *he* could admire the finished Lady Anne windows too, while she was stocking up Carey's freezer after the film crew's latest depredations.

Grant slid each panel cautiously out of the rack, holding them to the light. 'You've made a good job of this, Angel – but the design is even odder when you look at it closely, isn't it? I wonder what the significance of all those little pictures and bits of pattern in the centres of the quarries is . . . if there is any.'

'I know. The more I worked on it, the odder it seemed. Most of the motifs seem entirely random, but in places they're repeated in sequence. See here, where there's what looks like the top point of a linenfold panel three times in a row, followed by one of those flat Tudor roses.'

'It's hard to see any meaning in that, so perhaps your sampler idea was right and she just drew whatever came into her head to make a pretty pattern.'

'It's a mystery,' I said, then showed him the fragment of the Pre-Raphaelite angel that Carey had given me, which I'd begun taking apart.

'That's really fine painting,' he said appreciatively. 'What are you going to do with it?'

'Oh, lead it up into another roundel, I think. I won't attempt to replicate any of the missing original pieces, other than letting the lead calme outline where the wings and robe would have continued.'

Then I asked him how he was getting on with Nat, now that the dust had settled slightly.

'I think he's realized he's shot himself in the foot, getting rid of you and Ivan, because I'm not busting a gut to do all the work, even if he is paying me more. And he's very much the boss and I'm the employee. It's not the same as when we all worked together as a team: you, me, Julian and Ivan.'

'I know what you mean. I miss that, too, though at least now I've got Ivan during the week. And of course, Carey's often in his workshop next door and comes through for a chat, or a cup of tea, so I'm not isolated.'

'Willow's come up with a couple of weird-ass designs for windows, but she won't try her hand at cutting, or leading-up. She says she's not getting her hands cut and filthy on glass and lead, so she's not really got a feel for what is and isn't possible.'

I looked down at my hands, which are small, long fingered and not at all smooth and ladylike. 'You have to suffer for your art. But someone might like her designs, Grant, you never know.'

'Nat's still got a grudge against you for taking those cartoons, but at least he seems to have accepted he's not going to get them back.'

'Yes, Julian's solicitor said it had all been dropped now and I could forget about it.'

Molly beeped her horn and I went out to talk to her through the car window while Grant got in.

'Everything fine?' she asked, with a searching look.

'Great,' I said brightly. 'Now I've mended the window, I'll finish the Brisbane cartoon off and get that away. Then I've had a couple of enquiries about possible commissions that I'm working on.'

'Well, that's not quite what I meant,' she said, 'but I've just seen Carey scraping down the paint in the inner hall as if it was something he'd been looking forward to for ages, so you're obviously both happy in your own way.'

Then she passed me a large chocolate chip muffin in a cellophane bag, saying it would sweeten me up a bit, and drove off.

Left to myself, I finished unleading and cleaning up the bits of angel, before I laid the pieces on a sheet of white cartridge paper and set about incorporating them into a roundel. Then I spent a happy hour choosing and cutting glass for it, before being summoned for a soup-and-sandwich lunch with Carey, Louis and Liz.

I decided I'd finish cutting the glass that afternoon and then leave it for Ivan to lead up on Monday while I was putting the finishing touches to the Brisbane cartoon.

After dinner that evening, while I was sitting at my worktable in the studio absently staring at the colour cartoon of the Lady Anne window, instead of getting on with the design for a half-finished fishy roundel, Carey came in.

'Interesting . . .' he said looking over my shoulder. 'I don't know how you're going to translate the translucent rainbow effect of the jellyfish into glass, though.'

'Easily. I found a random sheet of clear Antique glass streaked with several colours in one of those tea chests. It must be an old bit of Hartley Wood glass; they made the occasional curious sheet.'

'So the glass inspired the jellyfish, not the other way round?' he said, then asked me what I had planned for the next day. 'Only Louis and his girlfriend are doing something else, so I wouldn't mind a hand sandpapering the panelling in the hall, ready to paint.'

'No chance,' I said firmly. 'I'm going to the workshop in the morning, then spending the rest of the day getting those designs for the two possible commissions ready to go. In fact, I meant to do that this evening, but I got sidetracked by my jellyfish idea.'

'Oh, well, the Benbow twins said they might come down – it's quiet at the Summit Alpine Nursery at this time of year,' he said resignedly.

On Monday, when Carey appeared with a booted Fang under his arm, I was halfway up the ladder in front of the corkboard, contemplating the *Big Wave* cartoon. Ivan, who had just leaded up the Burne-Jones angel, was about to carry it through to be cemented.

Carey admired what we'd done with the angel and then said, 'I've just been in the old wing, looking at those suits of armour. My ancestors must have been midgets!'

'I think people have just grown taller over the centuries,' I suggested.

'I haven't,' Ivan said.

'*You* don't seem to have, either, Shrimp,' agreed Carey. 'Perhaps you're both throwbacks to some ancient hobbit-like race.'

'Why were you looking at the armour, particularly?' I asked.

'Because I've been searching online to see how you should look after it properly. I've been resisting the urge to spray the moveable parts with general-purpose oil. I thought they might need something a little more specialized.'

'You're not going to take *those* apart on the kitchen table, are you?' I asked in some alarm.

'No, I need more space and it'll take quite some time, so I'll do them on the big bench in my workshop next door,' he assured me. 'It was while I was examining the visor on the suit of armour at the bottom of the stairs, that I felt someone was watching me.'

'A ghost?' asked Ivan eagerly.

'No, it was Ella. She was sitting in one of the carved chairs in the dark corner by the fireplace and I've no idea how long she'd been there.'

'Did she say anything when you spotted her?' I said.

'Yes, quite a lot for Ella: she gave me to understand that removing the window from the house was a bad idea and we were all doomed – or something like that.'

'Cheerful as always! What did you say?'

'That it would be back before long . . . and also that I'd rather she confined her cleaning activities in the old wing to set days and times. But she didn't reply, just got up and went. I'm going to have to talk to Clem yet again, though that hasn't had much effect so far,' he said gloomily. 'By the way, when can we put the Lady Anne window back? It looks odd without it.'

'The glazing cement needs to totally harden and then the first weekend that Grant and Ivan are free, they'll replace it. Long before the wing is opened to the public at Easter, at any rate,' I added. 'And nothing dreadful *has* happened since we took it out, so if that's a curse, then mending it in the workshop didn't count.'

'I thought we'd decided that wasn't a curse anyway, it was only that she wanted it to stay at Mossby for ever?'

'I know, but I was talking to Grant on Saturday about the odd way some of the motifs in the quarries are repeated, and it got me thinking again. Perhaps it *does* mean something, and if I could find the same sequences in the old wing . . .'

'Then you might also discover hidden treasure behind the panelling?' he finished, looking amused.

'Well, it's worth a try,' I said defensively. 'And I don't think that *is* a sun at the top of the window now, after all, but a representation of the Jewel of Mossby.'

'Yeah, right,' he said disbelievingly. 'The Mossby Jewel being this huge baroque pearl and enamel thing on a ruby necklace and the picture in the window showing a spiky sort of star shape?'

'I said it *represented* it. She wouldn't want to have given the secret away that easily.'

'If there was anything to give away in the first place, Angel, but it's all too Enid Blyton for me.'

'I don't think it's Enid Blyton at all! I'm convinced that Lady Anne is trying to tell us that after her husband's death she hid the Jewel away. Maybe it was for safekeeping, or just that she thought it had brought bad luck – and if she did, it's probably still here.'

'Eh, it's just like that Dan Brown book with the weird clues that Grant lent me,' Ivan said, enthralled. I'd forgotten he was still there.

'Isn't it just?' Carey agreed. 'You know, Angel, you've got a much more romantic imagination than I'd thought!'

'I'm not romantic at all!' I protested indignantly.

'Well, if you think you really do have a clue to finding the Jewel, help yourself to the spare keys to the old wing and go right ahead and search. I'm sure you'll have hours of harmless fun even if—'

He broke off abruptly as a sharp rap sounded on the door and it swung open. He mustn't have shut it quite to when he came in.

Clem popped his head round. 'I thought you might be here, Carey. There's a man come to collect some wood – the sycamore put aside for a sculptor? He's parked down by the Lodge.'

'I'll be right down, thanks, Clem.'

'You don't think he overheard what we were saying, do you?' I whispered, as soon as the door had closed behind him.

'I expect he'd only just got here. But it's a pity he *didn't* hear the bit about Ella because it would have saved me another awkward interview with him,' he said, then added, 'What I *really* came down to ask was whether Fang could stay with you for a bit.'

'OK, but if he gets underfoot, I'll banish him to his basket in the back room.'

This wasn't much of a banishment, because it was Fang's favourite position anyway. He could comfortably keep the biscuit tin in direct view and, since Ivan was addicted to digestive biscuits and generous enough to share, make his move as soon as Ivan appeared.

Despite throwing myself into my work during the next few days and producing several more free-hanging pieces of stained glass, which would find a ready market online or in galleries, Treasure Fever had me in its grip.

I drew the two frequently repeated sequences from the window and was sure I was right in thinking one of them *was* the pointed top of a linenfold panel repeated three times, followed by some kind of Tudor rose.

The other sequence was more baffling, being a circle filled with what looked like basket-weave, followed by an apple. It was always preceded by an open eye, but whether that just meant the onlooker should open their own eyes and see the message, or was simply the all-seeing eye of God, I had no idea.

I popped into the old wing on my way back to the house one late afternoon, wandering about in the dim light – the electrician hadn't got that far yet. It was a bit spooky, especially upstairs, where I felt I was being watched, even though whenever I turned there was nothing and no one there.

I wondered if Ella had sneaked in to see what I was up to, which wasn't a very comfortable thought. Ghosts would be preferable.

I narrowed the linenfold and rose sequence down to the muniment room and Lady Anne's bedchamber. The roses were actually carved bosses on a horizontal board above the panelling. But I was totally stumped about the apples and basket-weave.

And even though I'd narrowed the search area down to two rooms, if there was a secret chamber, then discovering the right method of twisting, pulling, turning or pressing whatever it needed in the right order, could take a long time . . .

Then I suddenly remembered we'd been told that when Ella was a small child, the old family nanny had filled her head with stories of ghosts, secret chambers and lost jewels. Could it be that she was also convinced there was another secret chamber and her obsessive polishing of the panelling had a slightly more rational explanation?

But if so, and she hadn't discovered it after all these years, what hope had I?

I felt disheartened: maybe Carey was right and I – and possibly Ella – were engaged on a wild-goose chase. But I wasn't prepared to give up *quite* yet.

*

I thought about it overnight and then went back to the old wing the following afternoon to have another look in the muniment room. I didn't really think they'd have put the entrance to two secret chambers in there and also, I wanted to compare the rose bosses to my drawing again, because I thought they might be a little different. If so, I'd be able to eliminate that room and concentrate on the bedchamber.

I went in by way of the Great Hall and unlocked the door to the muniment room, which was only opened on that side when the cleaners were in.

The roses *weren't* quite the same, but I thought I'd have a little search anyway, and had just started fingering the top of the third panel of linenfold carving to the right of the fireplace, while simultaneously trying to turn or push the boss above it, when I felt, more than heard, a movement behind me.

Turning quickly, I found Ella in the doorway, watching me intently.

'What on earth are you doing here at this time, Ella?' I demanded, my heart thumping. 'You gave me such a shock, creeping in like that!'

'I might say the same thing about you, sneaking about and poking around where you've got no business to be,' she said insolently.

'I was not sneaking about. Why should I, when Carey is happy for me to go anywhere I want to and has given me a complete set of keys?' I said.

'I suppose you're looking for the secret hiding place in here, though I'd have thought Carey would have shown it to you, if you asked him *nicely*,' she said, with a wealth of unpleasant innuendo. 'I know there is one – not a room, just a space. But I don't know *where* it is. They give the secret to the boys of the family, not the girls.'

I relaxed slightly: she meant the window seat opening with the chest inside, and I didn't point out that since

401

Carey's uncle hadn't considered her to be a member of the family at all, he wouldn't have told her the secret anyway, female or not.

'I wasn't actually looking for anything, I'm just interested in the different kinds of panelling,' I said lamely, and she gave me a contemptuous look.

'But you must know they often hid the way of opening priest-holes in the panelling,' she said, watching me closely from eyes as dark and flat as a snake's.

'Of course – and perhaps there *are* others still to be found, who knows?' I said, as casually as I could.

'If there were, I'd have come across them by now, including the one in here, if the room hadn't been kept locked up all the time. And you needn't carry on pretending that isn't what you're looking for, because Clem overheard you talking to Carey about it.'

Actually, the mechanism for opening the hidey-hole under the window seat was so ingenious she might *not* have found it, even if she'd had the run of this room. And if the same master craftsman had designed another chamber elsewhere, then she could well have missed that one, too, even if she had polished every inch of the panelling for the last fifteen years!

Of course, she hadn't had the advantage of the clues from the window – if they were clues – and I hoped she hadn't got them now. I couldn't exactly remember what I'd said to Carey, but even if I'd mentioned them, since the window was currently in the workshop, they were out of her reach.

But now my overwhelming urge was to get rid of her unwelcome presence, so I said casually, 'I expect you're right and it would be pointless even looking.' Then, since she still didn't show any signs of moving, I added, 'What *are* you doing here at this time anyway, Ella?'

'Why shouldn't I be? It's not late, just dark. When I saw the lights on, I came to see who it was.'

The only place she could have seen the lights was from the courtyard . . . unless she'd already been in here. I said firmly, 'Well, I'm going to go through this way to the house to change and have dinner — but I'll just see you out first.'

'I can find my own way out,' she snapped, but to my relief turned and strode away down the passage, clicking off the wall lights as she went, until the distant narrow view of the Great Hall also vanished into darkness. I heard the bang of the big oak front door and the heavy rattle of the lock and knew I really was alone at last.

I locked the muniment-room door after her and went through the tower into the house, which seemed a haven of light, warmth and normality after the old wing, even without the added advantage of not being infested by madwomen.

Of course, when I went downstairs I poured the whole tale into Carey's ears and he had to admit that Ella and I seemed to be on the same treasure hunt, though that still didn't mean the treasure actually existed.

He can be so stubborn sometimes!

'But I'm getting really worried about Ella and this is the last straw,' he said. 'I'll give Clem an ultimatum tomorrow. She needs to see her doctor and get some professional help, because her behaviour just isn't normal. And until she does, I'd like back her key to the old wing.'

I shivered, remembering her expression when I'd turned and seen her watching me.

'I think you're right,' I said. 'But will he make her do it?'

Until that moment, I don't think I'd entirely believed in my own theories so I sat there quite stunned for a moment until the guttering and sudden extinguishing of the candle in the lantern recalled me to my senses.

It was almost time for luncheon and soon Honoria would be in search of me. I could do nothing without a fresh candle, so I managed to close up the panel after a small struggle, then went through the turret to the house, intending to return as soon as I could.

I could hardly contain myself during lunch, and when I was supposed to be lying down on my bed for an hour to rest (at Honoria's insistence — she took great care of me and, I believe, looked forward to the arrival of the baby more than I did!), I instead sneaked off back into the old wing with a fresh candle in my lantern.

38

Black Holes

Carey went to find Clem right after breakfast next day, wanting to get the unpleasant interview over, but when he reported back later, it hadn't gone down that well.

'He's still insisting there's no problem and Ella just has a bit of a bee in her bonnet about the old wing. He said the thought of what damage the electrician was going to cause when he started work in there soon was preying on her mind, too.'

'Did you tell him how she behaved towards me yesterday, suddenly sneaking up and then being so rude?'

'Yes, but he thinks you misunderstood her.'

'Yeah, right!'

'I explained that we both thought she was becoming increasingly disturbed and her visits to the old wing at odd hours weren't something I was prepared to allow any more – it *is* part of my home, after all – and I wanted her key back.'

'What did he say to that?'

'He started to get angry and insisted I was being unreasonable, because she wasn't doing any harm. It was all very difficult,' he said heavily, running a hand through his redgold hair. 'In the end I said if she handed back her key, then I was prepared to allow her to go in on Fridays when the cleaners were there.'

'That seems reasonable to me, though I doubt if she'll see it like that.'

'Until we do get her key back, I'd feel happier if you did any treasure hunting in daylight, Angel. I'm not saying she's dangerous, but she does seem unbalanced and might make herself unpleasant again.'

'OK. I've come to the conclusion it needs a methodical search in daylight anyway,' I agreed. 'And I'm pretty sure now that the clues refer to Lady Anne's bedchamber, because the carved bosses look more like the Tudor roses in the window than the ones in the muniment room.'

'Perhaps we should both take a few hours off later in the week and I'll help you to look?' he suggested. 'Then we can decide if you're on a wild-goose chase or not.'

Even if he wouldn't admit it, I could see a touch of Treasure Fever was sneaking up on him, too!

I'd really been tinkering with the Brisbane cartoon for the last couple of days, reluctant to let it go until it was perfect.

When Ivan arrived the following morning, I asked him what he thought. 'I'm not sure about that bit at the top, where the first bit of white foam is turning into a bird,' I said. 'Maybe I should just—'

'No, lass, you leave it alone,' he interrupted me. 'It's finished.'

I sighed. 'I suppose you're right. Come on, let's take it down. I've got a big cardboard cylinder ready to pack it in, with a letter and some notes, though I'll have to leave that till later, because I've got to go back up to the house first.'

'I'll pack it up for you,' he offered.

'That would be great, if you don't mind – and then could you work on another of the roundels till it's time to leave? I know you're going home at lunchtime today.'

'That's right, it's the Senior Citizens' trip to Blackpool and I'll not be back in till Monday, but I'll have plenty of time to sort the cartoon and start the roundel before I go.'

'I'll leave you to it, then. And if I'm not back by the time you leave, just lock up when you go, because I'll be down later and I'll see to the alarm then. And have a lovely break in Blackpool!'

'I'll bring you a stick of rock,' he promised.

Carey had set off early that morning for an auction on the outskirts of Liverpool, where a couple of nice pieces of Arts and Crafts furniture were coming up, so I'd offered to be there when the workmen came to service and update the lift.

In fact, the two men from Elevated Ideas arrived at the house just as I did and I took them through to the tower, where the electrician was already at work. He has a key, now he's practically part of the family.

I left them at the bottom of the lift shaft, deep in a discussion involving words like 'motherboard' and 'fail-safe', while I went to the kitchen to make tea. Fang was shut in there, just in case he took a dislike to the new workmen, though he rarely blotted his copybook these days.

When I'd taken the tray through, I went back and had a cup of coffee, wandering into the studio with it and standing in front of the Lady Anne cartoon.

Those flat, stylized Tudor roses were, I was sure, much more like those in the bedchamber . . .

It was broad daylight and there were several workmen around, so the fear of being shut up in the old wing with Ella seemed suddenly slightly absurd. On impulse, I decided I'd pop through the upper tower and check those bosses out then and there.

*

The bright day didn't appear to have made it as far as the old wing, because even with the blinds up and the curtains drawn back, the haunted bedchamber was still gloomy and, as always, struck chill.

I realized too late that I should have brought a torch. There was a tiny one on my keychain but the battery was dying, so the bulb had about as much power as an anaemic glow-worm.

Still, I could see enough to tell that the bosses on the horizontal boards above the linenfold panelling *were* exactly the same as in the window, so presumably I needed only to find the correct sequence of three linenfold panels and a boss . . .

That wasn't going to be as easy as it sounded, but the sequence had to start from some point, so I followed the panelling round the room with my glimmering light and noted that the run was broken by the fireplace, the two doors and the substantial headboard of the bed, which seemed to be fixed to the wall. That narrowed the search down a bit.

Despite what Carey had said about us searching together, it was too irresistible not to have a little *try* and I'd just decided to go back to the kitchen for my big torch when the dying flicker of the one I was holding caught the knobbly carving of figures and a tree on the central panel of that huge wooden bedhead.

Hadn't Carey told me it looked like a man and a woman in a garden, when he first showed me round the house? How could I have forgotten that? Of course, it must be Adam and Eve! And now I was nearer, I could make out the sneaky serpent, too . . . and that the female figure – Eve – was holding out an apple to her spouse, which she seemed to have taken out of a very domestic-looking rush basket.

Apples, basketwork . . . it was the missing sequence!

The almost useless torch gave up entirely at this moment, but in rising excitement I kneeled on the bed and, putting

408

my right hand on the apple and my left on the basket, tried twiddling, turning and pressing both until finally, with a creak of long disuse, a panel slid open in front of me and I was facing impenetrable darkness.

I sensed there was a large cavity there, but in frustration realized I'd have to go back for the big torch before I could see anything.

I hesitated – the door to the rest of the wing was locked, but even so, I thought I'd better close the panel again before I left the room, in case the workmen delayed my coming back. It was a bit of a struggle, more from disuse than anything, I think, but I managed.

Back in the turret it was like a different world. I could hear voices and the lift door opening below, so the men were still at it. I hurried along the landing and down the back-stairs to the kitchen, where I'd grabbed a torch and was just about to run back, when the phone rang.

I hesitated, but it was just as well I answered it, because it was Carey and the moment I heard his voice I excitedly poured out what I'd found.

'I only came back for a torch, so I could have a look if there's anything in there.'

'I should be back in just over an hour, Angel. Couldn't you wait till then? Or is that too much to hope for?' he added, sounding amused.

'I *can't* wait,' I confessed, 'but I'll only shine the torch in and if there's anything there I'll leave it where it is till you get back.'

He laughed. 'I doubt there will be anything there at all, so don't get your hopes up.'

'There might be, because after all, Lady Anne put the clues in the window that led me there.'

'True, but her idea of what was important enough to conceal might not be valuable jewels,' he suggested. 'By the way,

'I've bought that bed frame and two of the chairs I wanted and I was only ringing you because there's a small lot coming up soon that you might be interested in. A couple of broken Victorian leaded light panels with some very pretty moulded opalescent glass flowers in the central section. Would you like it for the pieces if it's cheap?'

'Yes, please,' I said, momentarily distracted by a different kind of treasure.

'Right – better go. Back soon.'

Since it was his house and would be his treasure, should anything be there, I knew in fairness I really ought to wait for Carey before opening the panel again, but I simply couldn't resist any longer!

All was quiet in the turret room, though I could hear voices moving away, so the workmen were probably going for a break and we'd just missed each other.

I noticed Fang was following me only when I opened the door into the haunted room, because he started whining on the other side when I shut it. There was no point in opening it for him, though, because he wouldn't enter the old wing.

Perhaps he knew something I didn't.

The room was much as I'd left it, with the curtains drawn and the blinds up, though a weak wintry light was now banding the wooden floor.

I kneeled on the bed and opened the cavity quite easily this time, before shining the powerful torch into it.

It was larger than I expected, perhaps five feet square, so a man could have crouched there to hide, even if not in any comfort.

At first glance it seemed disappointingly bare. I directed the bright beam into every corner and finally along a kind of step or shelf just below the opening . . . and there, at the back, spotted a long, narrow shape – a package of some kind. I reached down and picked it up, finding it disappointingly light. It certainly wasn't the Jewel! I shoved it down my dungaree bib before leaning in further to see if there was anything else I'd missed, perhaps hidden by the jut of the shelf.

Behind me, Fang's whines turned all at once into a volley of sharp barks. Then suddenly my legs were grabbed and I was violently tipped forward into the hole.

For a brief instant I seemed to fly. Then my head hit the far wall and everything went black.

I managed to open the panel quite easily this time and shone my light inside, finding it to be quite large. At first it appeared to be entirely empty, until on looking downwards I saw a small packet resting below the opening on a stone shelf.

I seized it, but it was disappointingly light – certainly not heavy enough to contain the Jewel! In fact, it felt more like a roll of paper sewn into a wrapping of some thick material.

It was quite dampening: Father might have been quite right about my pregnancy giving me fantastical notions after all, though at least I had found something!

I cast the lantern about once more, to be certain there was nothing further there, and then closed the opening.

Until I'd examined my find further, I didn't want to share my discovery with anyone so, tucking it beneath my shawl, I made my way back to my bedchamber, where I snipped the stitches of the wrapping, revealing, as I expected, a roll of paper. It was long, and covered on both sides with writing in a fine italic hand, though in an archaic form, with many strange spellings, that was at first difficult to decipher. But eventually I made out at the top the words: 'Being the true confession of Lady Anne Revell, in the year of our Lord, 1655.'

I could not imagine what Lady Anne might have had to

confess, unless they were sins of a religious nature? I determined
I would secretly decipher and copy it out in the evenings after I
retired to bed, the only time when I was sure of being
undisturbed.

39

Down and Out

I don't know how long I was out for, but I woke in a crumpled heap in utter darkness, dazed, confused and with a grazed forehead.

After a few minutes I pulled myself together and sat up, my back against one wall, and waited for the dizziness to pass. Then I explored with my fingertips for the torch, but it wasn't there – whoever shoved me in must have taken it . . . and suddenly I wondered if they'd taken anything else? But no, the mysterious package, which felt like a roll of paper wrapped in stiff fabric, was still tucked into the bib of my dungarees.

I didn't need evidence to feel totally certain that it was Ella who'd tipped me in there. She must have had a key to the room and had crept in while I was leaning right into the hole, searching the further corners. Presumably she'd thought I'd only just that minute found it and must have been disappointed not to find any hidden treasures once I was out for the count, though at least that meant she hadn't thought to search me.

She'd managed to shut the panel and then left me there . . . for ever?

Suddenly a wave of panic swept over me – the ghastly, buried-alive feeling of nightmares. I felt the heaviness of the walls pressing in and wondered how much air I had left to breathe.

Then I remembered that Carey was probably already on his way home and if there was no sign of me waiting for him, he'd surely come looking?

Very, very faint and far off, I heard a sharp yapping. 'You tell them, Fang,' I muttered and the panic receded slightly.

I groped my way dizzily upwards and kneeled on the stone shelf, fingering the very thick wooden back of the headboard. I didn't rap on it, in case Ella was still in the bedchamber – I mean, how horrible would it be if she rapped back . . . or *something* rapped back? But I did explore it with my fingertips, to see if there was a way of opening it from this side, though eventually I gave up this fruitless search and slumped back into the corner.

That was when my mind *really* began to play tricks on me. I was sure I could hear stealthy movements in the room beyond the panel and voices muttering . . . and finally, a faint, dreadful scream that was quickly and horribly cut off.

I expect I was wide-eyed with terror and pale as a ghost myself when suddenly the panel opened and I found myself looking up into Carey's beloved and anxious face.

'Shrimp!' he exclaimed, his expression changing into one of heartfelt relief. I put up my arms and he reached in and hauled me out, holding me close. This was just as well, since my legs seemed to have turned to jelly.

'What did I say about waiting for me?' he said severely, then turned my face up and kissed me, and there was nothing remotely fraternal about it, *or* my response.

'You're filthy, darling, and also, you're crackling,' he said, when eventually our lips parted. My knees were now totally jellified on two counts and Fang was whirling round our feet like a small dervish, yapping.

'You say the nicest things,' I murmured, my arms around his neck.

'I like filthy girls. Not too sure about the crackling, though.'

'It's a packet I found in the hole. I shoved it down my dungaree top so I could check if there was anything else in there. But while I was leaning right into it, someone grabbed my feet and shoved me in. I banged my head.'

'So I see. There's a graze on your forehead and you might even end up with a black eye. And when I find whoever did this, they'll be sorry!' he added grimly.

'But it must have been Ella – who else is loopy enough to do something like that?'

'I suppose so, but if it was, how was she to know anyone would find you in there? It was a sheer fluke that I happened to ring you earlier when you were in the kitchen and you told me what you'd found, and then Fang was trying his best to show me where you were, too. When I opened the door from the tower he shot past me, jumped on the bed and barked his head off.'

'That was very brave of him, because he's scared of this room.' I shivered and tightened my grip on Carey. 'I think I am now, too. And what if Ella's still lurking about, feeling a bit homicidal?'

'I'd better check the rest of the wing while you stay here with Fang for a minute,' he suggested.

'No way – we'll wait for you in the tower,' I said firmly.

It seemed wonderfully bright and warm in the tower room and the lift repair men were back on the job – or at least, having a nice chat about football with the electricians downstairs.

Carey returned quite quickly. 'I've been right through and there's no sign of her. The front door's locked, too, so I think she's long gone.'

'What are we going to do about her?' I asked. 'I mean, we

416

can't just let *this* go, can we? I don't think she's responsible for her actions, and even Clem must agree she needs urgent help now.'

He took my hand. 'Come on – you need to get cleaned up and changed, and then we'll discuss it in the kitchen over a good hot cup of coffee.'

'With all the lights on?'

'It's the middle of the day, even if it is a bit gloomy now it's clouded over, so it'd be a waste of electricity.'

'This is no time for economy,' I said sternly, and gave him the package to take down with him.

I felt much better once I'd washed off the dust and the blood from my grazed forehead and changed into clean jeans and a warm knitted tunic. Looking in the mirror, I thought Carey might have been right, and I'd have a black eye tomorrow.

With the memory of that passionate kiss still tingling on my lips, I felt strangely shy when I entered the kitchen, though of course, relief can make us do all kinds of strange things . . .

But there was more than just relief in Carey's eyes when they met mine. He gave me a wordless hug and then made me sit down before putting a mug of coffee laced with rum, and a cheese sandwich cut into small triangles in front of me. He added two aspirin and a glass of water.

'There, if you get those down you, you'll feel a lot better. I've eaten my sandwich.'

I hadn't thought I was hungry, but once the rum stopped the shivering I found I was and wolfed down the food.

'What have you done with the packet?' I asked, when I'd finished it.

'It's on my desk in the studio. I think it's a rolled document of some kind, but it can wait till you're feeling better, *and* until we've sorted out what to do about Ella. If it *was*

417

Ella. Like you, I can't really imagine who else would have done it.'

'And I definitely didn't fall in by accident, bang my head and close the panel up while unconscious.'

'I think we can rule that scenario out.'

'I suppose we *could* report it to the police and they might find her fingerprints on the bedhead, but that wouldn't prove anything anyway, would it? It would be my word against hers.'

'That's what I thought, and that the first thing to do was to let Clem know what had happened,' Carey said. 'I rang him at the Lodge while you were upstairs and he said there was no sign of Ella, even though she's always got his lunch ready by now. Her car was still there, though.'

'Did you tell him exactly what happened?'

'Yes, and at first he tried to insist that she wouldn't have done anything like that, and you'd just banged your head and imagined the rest.'

'Yeah, right!'

'I told him that was impossible and he'd better find her, so we could sort this mess out once and for all, and get her the help she needed. It was that, or call the police in.'

'It had to be her – we know it and Clem must know it, too.'

'I'm sure he does, he just doesn't want to admit it. But he begged me not to call the police and said he was going to search the grounds and any unlocked outbuildings. Vicky'd just arrived, so she'd help.'

A nasty thought struck me. 'You don't think she's done anything stupid, do you? Perhaps we should go and help look.'

'Clem's ringing back when he's searched, and you need to sit quietly and recover for a bit. You might even have concussion. Maybe I should have taken you straight to hospital?'

he added, looking at me anxiously. 'How many fingers am I holding up?'

'The one with the Greek seal ring on it, you imbecile,' I said. 'Of course I'm not concussed! In fact, I feel fine now, apart from a slight headache.'

And also an unusual disinclination to be on my own . . .

I began to write out Lady Anne's confession that very night and quickly became accustomed to her erratic spelling and odd – to my modern eyes – turns of phrase. The beginning only described her first marriage and how she came to marry again – which was as far as I got before overwhelmed by sleep. These sudden descents into the arms of Morpheus seem to be yet another annoying effect of pregnancy . . .

Next day, there had evidently been yet another breach between my husband and Mr Browne. Ralph flung himself about the house all morning, restless and ill-tempered: he is such a different man from the one I married!

Later he spent several hours closeted with his man of business, which did not sweeten his mood. Perhaps if the breach with Mr Browne were to be permanent, then he might listen to good advice? There is the child to think of now, after all. Yet I do not know what is to come of us if, as I now suspect, Ralph has run up so many debts that Mossby may have to be sold.

Having started in a straightforward way, Lady Anne's tale took a strange and disturbing turn that evening! I could hardly believe my eyes . . .

Though shocked and upset, I would have read on despite my

tiredness and physical discomfort, but sleep soon set my head nodding, whether I would or no.

Mr Browne returned from wherever he had spent the night – as I came downstairs this morning I heard him talking to Ralph and again attempting to persuade him to build a house in the Lake District. Ralph, to my relief, was adamant that he could not afford to do so – and at this juncture they caught sight of me and turned and moved away with one accord, as if my advanced pregnancy might be some vile and contagious affliction.

40

Broken

I wandered into the studio with my second cup of coffee to look at my find and Carey followed. 'It's not the Jewel – it's too light to be anything but papers.'

'I came to that conclusion when I found it. It's been sewn into a sort of heavy linen material,' I added, turning it over in my hands. 'It's odd that two different shades of thread have been used to sew it up. See, this side is a slightly darker colour.'

'She probably ran out of the first one – assuming it *was* Lady Anne who hid it there.'

'Who else, since it was her clues that revealed where it was?'

'I wonder what was so private that she felt the need to hide it at all – an important letter, perhaps?' he suggested, and I could see he was dying to find out, just like I was. But we had the Ella situation to resolve first. Just then, Clem rang back.

'He hasn't found her,' Carey reported. 'There was no sign of her in the woods or by the lake, and he and Vicky have checked the stable block. Now they want to go over the old wing again, even though I told them I'd searched it.'

'Well, I suppose she might have left once she'd shoved me in the hole, but then slipped back in again?'

422

'Very true. I'll go and let them in, but you'd better stay here, Angel.'

'Not on your life! I'm coming with you!' I said firmly.

Clem and Vicky were standing in the doorway of the old wing, but were hardly recognizable as their former selves. Clem's usually ruddy face was pale and drawn, while Vicky looked totally distraught. I'd never suspected her of being capable of any deep human emotion, so I'd obviously badly misjudged her.

'Mum *must* be in there. There's nowhere else she could be,' she said. 'She wouldn't have left Mossby unless she was in the car.'

'I think she might have come back here – perhaps when she realized what she'd done, so she could let you out, Angel,' Clem said, which was a tacit admission of her guilt. 'She's not responsible for her actions.'

'We'd already figured that one out,' Carey said, unlocking the door, then standing back to let us in.

'Have you hurt your ankle, Vicky?' I asked. 'You're limping.'

'I broke the heel of my shoe off – got it stuck down a grating in the stable yard,' she said, stopping and removing both shoes.

Without the stilettos, she was suddenly not much taller than I was, though still leggier.

Carey clicked on all the lights in the Great Hall. 'We'd better search in pairs,' he'd begun, when I suddenly shushed him.

'Listen!' I hissed. 'Can you hear that?'

Into the silence fell a sort of faint, faraway babbling that rose and fell, rose and fell . . . but never ceased.

With a sudden exclamation, Carey strode over and opened the priest-hole in the opposite wall – and there, in the furthest corner, sat the hunched-up figure of Ella, with her face hidden on her knees. She was rocking and muttering very, very fast, the words running together so that it was hard to make sense of them – if there was any sense to be found.

'It wasn't there it wasn't there all these years mine my jewel mine mine all these years my jewel mine . . .'

'Oh God!' Carey said blankly.

It was some considerable time later.

A doctor had been out and given Ella some kind of injection and then rung around to find an emergency psychiatric bed. Then she'd been gently removed in an ambulance and Clem and Vicky were about to go down to the Lodge to get a few things for her and then follow on.

'Poor Mum – this isn't the first time this has happened,' Vicky said, 'though she's never been *this* bad. Usually we know when she's about to have another episode, because she talks faster and faster . . . and then Dad rings me and I come up if I'm not working.'

'You should have let us know she'd had previous problems when Carey told you he was getting worried about her mental state, Clem,' I said. 'We knew something was wrong.'

'But she seemed all right, not like she's been in the past when she's been ill. I *was* a bit worried about her increasing fixation with the old wing; she was never quite so obsessed until your uncle died, Carey.'

'Yes, it was when your uncle told her about the will and that he was leaving Mossby to you that it started,' Vicky said accusingly, as if it was all Carey's fault. 'She hadn't even realized you existed before that and she was so distraught she got in her car and drove straight down to my flat in London. I don't know how she got there safely. I was gobsmacked when I realized it was you who'd inherited, Carey. I mean, anybody might be called Revell so I'd never connected you with Mossby.'

424

'I had no idea about the connection until after my uncle died, either,' he said, then added, grimly, 'but I've finally remembered where I've seen you before – and it *wasn't* at Gino's Café, though it was in Dulwich. You were looking out of the side window of the car that hit me: a big silver four-wheel drive. Ella's?'

She sighed. 'Yes . . . but we hoped you wouldn't remember.'

'But, Carey, we know the car that knocked you off your bike was turning sharp left in front of you,' I began, puzzling it out. 'So if you could see her looking at you through the side window, Vicky must have been—'

'In the passenger seat,' Vicky finished. 'Yes, I was. Mum was driving.'

'Oh God!' Clem cried, covering his face with his hands.

'But she didn't *mean* to hit him, Dad,' Vicky said quickly. 'I'd just told her to take the next left turn when I spotted him and said, "That's Carey Revell there, on that bike, Mum!" That made her swerve, then she realized she'd almost missed the turn and turned sharply.'

'And, having sent me flying into a parked car, kept going,' Carey finished for her.

'We thought she'd only just clipped your bike. We didn't think it was serious,' Vicky said. 'Honestly, when we found out how bad it was later, we were both really upset.'

'Well, that's very consoling,' Carey said drily. Maybe he was wondering, like I was, if it really *had* been an accident.

'I knew nothing about all this,' Clem said, dropping his hands and showing us a harrowed and anguished face. He seemed to have aged ten years almost in an instant.

'So . . . we might buy the idea that that one was an accident and Ella didn't swerve into Carey on a sudden homicidal impulse,' I said, summing things up. 'But she certainly tried to dispose of me and I'm wondering if she could have been responsible for the stone ball that nearly killed Carey?'

425

'No, that was me,' Clem admitted shamefacedly, and Carey and I stared at him in astonishment.

'I'd noticed it was loose the day before, so I'd taken an old beer crate down to stand on, so I could have a look. Then you turned up to see the film crew off and I was just standing there . . .'

'Listening?' I suggested, but he continued as if he hadn't heard.

'I lost my balance and the ball slipped and rolled off . . . and my heart nearly stopped until I heard you both speak,' he finished.

'Yeah, ours did much the same,' Carey agreed blandly. 'It didn't occur to you to come and see if we were OK?'

'No. I panicked, picked up the crate and beat it.'

'You must have run like hell, because we spotted you on the terraces a few minutes later,' I said.

'I should have owned up to it. I'm sorry.'

'Your family seem to have it in for me,' Carey said.

'*I* haven't,' Vicky protested. 'Neither has Dad, really. He's told you it was an accident. And Mum isn't responsible for her actions.'

'Oh, well, that's all right, then. Let's just call the whole lot acts of God and forget they ever happened, shall we?' Carey said sarcastically.

'You're sooo kind,' Vicky said, taking him seriously and giving him a watery smile. 'Come on, Dad, we'd better go.'

'Take the buggy down,' I suggested. 'We'll pick it up from the Lodge later.'

It would have been a long hobble down the drive in broken stilettos.

I was afraid to read the rest of Lady Anne's confession that night, and yet I felt impelled to go on and on to the end . . .

And what an end! I could hardly believe that the terrible events it described had really happened!

Despite my weariness, all hope of immediate sleep was dispelled. I longed for a hot drink to warm my chilled heart, but did not wish to ring for a maid at that hour, so decided to go downstairs myself.

But I was no more than a pace or two along the passage when I heard a cry from my husband's room and, without pausing to think, opened the door and looked in.

I don't think I will ever forget the sight that met my eyes: the firelight cast its glow over the entwined limbs of the two men, naked on the bed.

I must have made some small sound, for Ralph looked round and saw me . . . I fled back to my chamber where I must have fainted, for I awoke in my own bed, with Honoria and the maid flapping about in a great fuss.

'Send the maid away, Honoria,' I said. 'I must talk to you.'

I could not believe that I had been both so innocent and so blind – but my revelation came as no surprise to Honoria. She said she had hoped marriage would change his ways . . . until the return of Mr Browne.

'*I suppose he married me because he wanted an heir,*' *I said bitterly, and she asked me what I would do.*

'*Keep to my room tomorrow, perhaps, until I have my ideas in more order,*' *I said.* '*Later – I must see Ralph.*'

I slept little for the rest of that night. Now my eyes were opened, I understood Mr Browne's jealousy and Ralph's despair when his friend seemed set on moving away from Mossby. They had loved each other – perhaps still did, despite the ever more frequent arguments and reconciliations.

How much I had learned and understood since yesterday! Yet, compared to the awful events that had befallen Lady Anne, my discovery paled in comparison, though of course mine affected me more nearly.

I had no appetite to eat breakfast but, quite worn out, meekly accepted the cup of hot milk Honoria brought me, and then fell into a deep sleep, while outside the warm early September sun shone and the birds sang, as if there were no cares in the world.

41

The Skeleton Key

When we went back into the warm kitchen, it felt like a million traumatic years had passed in one day.

Fang, who had been curled asleep in his basket, got out and slowly stretched.

'Fang's a search-and-rescue dog: he deserves an extra special dinner tonight,' Carey said, bending down to give him a pat.

'We all do, but even though I feel totally limp and I've still got my headache, I want to know what's in that packet I found first!'

He grinned. 'Me, too. Look, let's order a takeaway and then open it. And then later, some more headache pills and an early night.'

He didn't specify in which room I'd be spending my early night, and I was starting to wonder if I'd imagined that passionate kiss after he'd rescued me!

While he rang to put in the food order, I fetched my nail scissors and then we snipped apart the threads holding the binding and carefully began to unroll the brittle paper within.

'It's quite long and written on both sides,' he said. 'But then, good-quality paper was a luxury at that time.'

'If Lady Anne wrote this, then she must have been well educated, because the writing is quite elegant.'

'Yes, I think it's what they call a fine italic hand,' he agreed, as we flattened it out and weighed down the corners. 'And it is hers; it says so at the top.'

He read it out in his lovely, honey-over-gravel voice:

Being the true confession of Lady Anne Revell, in the year of our Lord, 1655.

He paused, and then carried on very slowly, stopping from time to time while we figured out the obscure bits, for the spelling was odd and inconsistent, and she had a strange way of expressing herself.

I hope to bring ease to my mind by writing this account of the death of my husband, Phillip Revell, in 1644, for the awful circumstances leading to this event lie heavily on my soul.

But then it will be best to hide it in a place known only to myself, though I have caused a window to be made that will reveal all, should any have the wits to discover it long hereafter.

I looked at Carey, puzzled. 'Her husband was a Cavalier and killed in battle, wasn't he?'

'So I've been told. I wonder what on earth these mysterious circumstances could be.'

'Well, go on reading it aloud and we might find out,' I urged, though when he did, it appeared that the lady was now skimming through her earlier years:

I must go back a little way, to tell how I came to marry Phillip Revell, a childless widower who owned the small but ancient estate of Mossby, in west Lancashire.

I was of noble birth but, being an impetuous and romantic girl, I made an imprudent runaway match at fifteen, instead of the advantageous one planned for me. My family cast me off and my husband's likewise, so that our means were very straitened. My husband's fondness for me quickly waned after the birth of our only child, Lydia. He was carried off by a grievous ague in her tenth year, leaving me lacking any means of sustenance, so that I was forced to beg my uncle, who had succeeded to my father's title and property, for help. He grudgingly took us under his roof and Lydia shared the schoolroom with his daughters, while I became little more than a servant, constantly at my aunt's beck and call, expected to show gratitude for every morsel of bread that passed my lips.

This miserable existence might have continued for ever, had not a party of visitors arrived to stay, bringing Phillip Revell with them. Although I did not put myself forward in any way, he seemed to well like my company and oft times joined me when I walked in the garden. This much displeased my uncle and his wife, who pointed out what I well knew: that a handsome man of comfortable means could have no serious intentions towards a penniless widow.

But when he professed his love for me and did offer marriage, they pressed me to agree to the match, seeing it would spare them the expense of keeping me. I was nothing loth, especially since he spoke with kindness to Lydia, who was then a very pretty child of twelve and said she would be as his own daughter.

'Cinderella,' I said, looking up. 'Though sadly, the prince gets killed fairly soon afterwards, so they don't live happily ever after for very long.'

'That doesn't exactly sound the stuff of confessions,' Carey pointed out, before going on:

Mossby was a strange house, the main portion being in the old black and white style and, being built at the time of Catholic persecution, had many secret ways and chambers within the walls, for the family at that time were papist.

There had been earlier dwellings in that place, though little remained other than a stone tower. But various additions to the house had been made piecemeal, which had enlarged it without adding greatly to its convenience.

I had been allowed to bring with me Dorcas, the faithful maid who had been my prop and support throughout all my misfortunes. She was now of middle age and of severe manner, but sincerely attached both to myself and Lydia.

The other female servants at Mossby were none of them young and not overly friendly, so I was glad of Dorcas' company. Phillip, however, was most attentive and kind and I hoped soon to form pleasant acquaintances among the other local families, especially those with daughters of an age with Lydia.

We had been married some months when I told my husband that I was with child. He expressed great delight at the thought of an heir, so that I worried that I might prove to be carrying another girl . . . but then, all men seem to desire a boy to carry on their line.

When I went to tell Lydia, she asked me if I was happy in my marriage, which I thought strange, but assured her I was. Then when I told her she was to have a little brother or sister, she kissed me and said she was glad, though I noted that she was very quiet thereafter.

My husband ceased to come to my bed, once he knew I was with child, though he continued to be kind and concerned for my good health. Dorcas, in whom I confided all, told me that many men were thus, but all would be well again after the baby's arrival.

It was about this time that I noticed Lydia seemed to have taken my husband in sudden dislike, though he positively doted on her, and gave her many gifts including a fine grey pony. I thought perhaps he teased her too much, for she was a young lady of thirteen now and more conscious of her dignity. But I was engrossed with Phillip, my growing babe and my household duties, so that it was some time before I began to worry that something ailed her, for by then she had grown thin, pale and nervous.

Her antipathy towards Phillip grew and I could not understand it, especially when he was so kind to her, nor would she explain herself when asked.

How blinded by love I was!

'I'm starting to have a bad feeling about where this is heading,' I said. 'It all started out so well, with Cinderella rescued by the handsome prince, but now . . .'

'I know what you mean – though I'm hoping I'm wrong,' Carey agreed.

There was increasing unrest and conflict in the country and while Phillip and my uncle had once both declared for the King, my uncle had now changed his mind and thrown in his lot with Cromwell. Many families were thus divided in loyalty during this time.

Phillip prepared to answer the King's call to arms when it came – indeed he showed some relish for the thought of fighting – and said he would leave me in charge of Mossby when he should be absent. To this end, he showed me the way of opening those secret ways and passages in the house that could conceal any fugitive requiring concealment. Some valuable trinkets, including a fabulous jewel bestowed upon one of his ancestors by Queen Elizabeth, were hidden in one of them, the opening cunningly built into the carved head of my bed, which was in the chamber next to the old tower.

Another place of concealment and escape also opened from this room. On pressing a certain part of the panelling to the right side of the fireplace while twisting a carved boss above it, a door would open on to a narrow stair that led down to the cellar – and from thence, via a tunnel, to one of the lower terraces. But should the boss be turned to the left rather than the right, the topmost step would fall away, so that anyone standing there would be precipitated straight down to the cellar. When Phillip told me this, I shuddered.

One night soon after he had showed me these things, I was awoken by a dreadful scream and started up, as did Dorcas who, since I had been feeling often sickly in the night had been asleep on a truckle bed in my chamber. I knew my child's voice instantly and throwing on a bedrobe hurried to her room. A candlestick on the press inside showed me Phillip standing over the bed, my daughter hysterical and wide-eyed. He explained that he'd heard the scream and hurried hence, but thought it perhaps a nightmare and would leave Dorcas and I to calm her fears.

434

When I asked her why she had screamed, she said it had been a night horror and I took her to my bed for the rest of the night. Next day, Dorcas suggested she should continue in this until my time was near, which seemed meet to me.

Lydia has had no return of the night horrors, but is become like a small, nervous ghost of her former lively, cheerful self. My first husband was subject to fits of the melancholy, in which I hoped my child had not followed him and wished a doctor to see her, but Phillip said it was merely the megrims and would pass . . .

But Dorcas was as concerned as I, and watches over her as much as her duties allow.

I wished our neighbours had been more willing to return my calls, for then Lydia might have had some young company to cheer her.

When Phillip received a messenger and told me he was off to fight the very next day, he seemed both excited and pleased. But my mind was filled with fear and turmoil, so that instead of resting in my chamber that afternoon, as he suggested, I persuaded Lydia to take a turn on the terrace with me.

The wind proved sharper than I expected and she went in to fetch a warm cloak for me – but when she did not immediately return, I followed her in – and thence, hearing a muffled cry and the sound of a struggle, to the muniment room, where a most terrible sight met my eyes.

Lydia, Phillip's hand covering her mouth, was attempting to escape from what were clearly the vilest of intentions on my husband's part. His face, thickened with lust, was one I had never seen before . . .

The scales fell from my eyes in an instant and I realized that my husband was the vilest of monsters.

'Phillip, what goes on here?' I exclaimed, and on an instant he had let her go, his face changing to the bright, open expression I had known and loved so well.

'Thank God you are come, my love,' he said. 'Lydia was faint, so I brought her in here and she began to cry out as she came round. I start to think she must be prone to fits where her wits are disordered and if so, we must keep this very quiet, if she is to find a husband.'

'A husband of her own?' I heard my voice say.

'Mother', cried Lydia, her face ashen, 'I—'

'Hush,' I said, gathering my child into my arms, close against her unborn sibling . . . the child of this monster. 'Come, we will go to my bedchamber.'

I didn't look again at my husband, but late, when I left her in Dorcas' care, Phillip did his utmost to persuade me I was the monster for imagining such terrible things. I was unmoved and at last he grew angry and declared that when he returned from the fight, he would know how to deal with me.

I felt then my helplessness: for I was his wife, his chattel, and who was there to take my part?

I barred the chamber door against him and did not open it again until assured that he had ridden off to join the King's army.

'Unfortunately we weren't wrong – poor Anne!' I said. 'And that poor child, too! It seems there were monsters even then.'

'Yes – and now we know why the local gentry weren't so keen to visit Mossby, or have their daughters become friendly with Lydia,' Carey said grimly.

Dorcas tells me the servants, overhearing some of what went forward, now speak of what they have kept secret since our arrival: that my husband has a fancy for very young girls and no cottager's child has been safe from him . . .

Lydia told me that, though fearful of being believed, she had meant to reveal to me what was happening on the morning when I had told her I was with child. I remembered then how she had asked me so strangely if I was happy in my marriage.

Love makes us blind, it seems . . . but no longer, and now I began to scheme to send her safely away. I had no other course than to write begging my uncle that she might make a visit to him for the air of Lancashire did not agree with her and also, she was missing the company of her sweet cousins.

But I knew I must stay at Mossby and await events. My feelings of anguish over the possibility of my husband's being injured or killed in battle had now turned to an earnest desire that he should perish, God forgive me – and him.

'And he was, wasn't he?' I said, as Carey paused. 'If all she had to confess was that she hoped he died, then that seems very natural to me!'

News came at length that there had been a great battle at Aughton Moor which had gone badly for the King's side. I gave instructions that food and drink be given to any fleeing from the battlefield who might make their way hence, even though I heard rumours of bands of Parliamentarians in search of such fugitives. I was still firmly for the King's cause . . . though that would not prevent me using my uncle's high position with Cromwell to protect my household, if necessary.

I bethought me to show the way to open the hiding place in the Great Hall and the secret stairs in my bed-chamber, to both Lydia and Dorcas, so they could succour or assist to escape any persons sheltered there, should I be indisposed. Lydia shuddered when I warned them to take care turning the carved boss to the right, not the left, or it would cause whoever stood on the top-most step to plunge to their deaths in the cellar below, but Dorcas was hardier.

There had been no word or sign from Phillip, but a gentleman of his acquaintance sent me word that he had seen my husband struck down during the battle at Aughton Moor, he thought mortally.

After a few more days, I dared to hope that it might be so . . .

'Good,' I said, as we reached the end of the first page and delicately turned the yellowed sheet over.

'I feel there's a bit more to come, somehow, Shrimp . . .'

'Well, it can't be any worse than what we've already read . . . can it?'

'We'll soon find out. And I can't say I'm feeling exactly happy about having Revell blood running in my veins at this moment,' he admitted. 'But on we go.'

One evening, when I had retired to my bed early, feel-ing most unwell, I woke suddenly to find my husband standing over me in the act of shutting the secret cavity behind the bedhead, from which he had taken the bag of jewels. Beyond him, the panelling near the fireplace gaped open, showing how he had gained entrance.

He warned me not to cry out — and indeed, I was silent with horror to find him thus alive. He looked gaunt and wild, with one arm tucked into his coat and explained that he had been laid up in a hayloft, with a wounded shoulder and a raging fever, unable to get back before now. He feared there was a troop of Roundheads hard on his heels . . .

Then he sneered at my silence and ordered me to get up and fetch him some food and drink, telling me he would take the bag of jewels and had a passage arranged on a ship if he could get to Liverpool before dawn.

Just then, the sound of loud hammering at the door of the Great Hall silenced him.

Lydia came in hurriedly, saying, 'Mother, there are men at the door demanding entrance though I have told them—'

At this moment she saw my husband and a look of horror appeared on her face. 'I had hoped you were dead!' she told him.

'Ah, my loving daughter,' he said with sarcasm.

There was a further clamour below and I heard Dorcas calling as she approached that the Parliamentarians were in the house and I must come at once.

Phillip was across the room and stepping back into the cavity by the fireplace, even as she entered. She stared at the unwelcome apparition, but he ignored her, solely addressing me.

'You'll have to close up the panel, Anne. I can't manage it from this side with one hand. Then get down and get rid of them — and none of you need think of betraying me, or you will be sorry for it,' he added.

He gave Lydia a leer. 'You can come down and bring me food and clothes, when the coast is clear.'

I suppose he thought I was the only one with the secret of how to close the panelling, but as I reached up and pressed the top of the third section of linenfold carving, I heard hasty footsteps come up behind me and a hand reached over my shoulder and twisted the boss above it sharply to the left.

There was a dreadful cry – and then, as the panel shut . . . nothing.

I turned and looked at Dorcas, aghast, but then pulled myself together and told her to see to Lydia, who was now faint with horror, and make sure there was no trace that Phillip had ever been there, should the Parliamentarians search.

Then I put on a heavy robe and went downstairs . . .

Our eyes met in mutual horror.

'Are you sure this is a *real* confession and not part of some Gothic novel, hidden away later?' he asked.

'It has to be real – look at it!' I told him. 'And anyway, think of the clues she left in the window. No, it's genuine.'

It was daylight before the troop of soldiers rode away, finally convinced that I harboured no King's men. I made great play of my uncle's name and gave them to understand that I was of his political persuasion.

I do not know how I managed not to appear distraught before them. While I provided food and drink, the loud howls of the wind down the great chimney sounded to me like the cries of an injured man . . . though I knew my husband could not have survived such a fall.

All was quiet after they had left: the wind and the howling had long died away. Dorcas had given Lydia a draught and she slept in her old chamber, where I joined her, for the thought of mine made me shudder.

My husband was assumed to have died on the battlefield and his man of business proved a staunch support, giving me much wise advice until my son, Edmund, was of age. Our investments prospered beyond expectation.

I caused the door of the great bedchamber to be locked and never used again and soon the servants were declaring it was haunted and avoiding that part of the passage . . .

Perhaps it was.

I often shudder at the thought of what lies down there in the darkness at the heart of the house, but I do not feel it weigh too heavily on my conscience, except that I would wish I had earlier understood what ailed my poor daughter. I failed her in this.

But I expect she and I will long have been dust ere anyone reads this, and will not judge Lydia's action too harshly: for terror made her turn the carving and consign Phillip to the depths.

It affected her mind, so that in time I acceded to her wishes and got her to a Protestant nunnery in the Lowlands, where she could do penance for her sins, though to my mind, when the truth is weighed in the balance, I believe God will judge her not to have been the sinner.

Signed this day, 14 June 1655
Lady Anne Revell

'Well,' I said to Carey, 'I didn't see that last bit coming. I thought it was the maidservant, Dorcas.'

'Me too – but the poor child must have been terrified and he deserved everything he got.'

'Including the everlasting flames of hell – that's how she portrayed him in the window,' I said. 'But whatever happened, he brought it on himself.'

I awoke to the sun streaming through the open window and the curtains stirring gently.

On the terrace below, I could hear voices raised in argument — my husband and his lover. I slipped out of bed and looked down on them: Rosslyn Browne sat on the stone balustrade while Ralph stood facing him. Their voices carried clearly and Ralph sounded as if he had been drinking heavily.

'I tell you, she knows everything — what if she spreads the tale?'

'She wouldn't be believed if she did,' his friend said with a short laugh. 'In any case, I'm leaving, so it's not my concern.'

'Leaving? You mean . . . for good?' Ralph took a hasty step forward. 'No — you've threatened often enough, but you always come back.'

'Not this time — and since you say Mossby will have to be sold to meet your debts, there won't be anything to come back to,' he said cruelly.

'I can mortgage it, I'll find a way . . .' began Ralph desperately.

'I hope you do — but believe me, it's over between us.'

Ralph went very still. 'You've found someone else, haven't you?'

'As a matter of fact, yes. It was good while it lasted but now you can play happy husband and father and forget I ever existed.'

He got up and flicked the end of his cigar over the edge of the terrace. 'I'm off in the morning. Everything at the Lodge can be

442

packed and sent on.' He looked up at Mossby's white façade but I am sure he didn't see me watching him for he said, as if to himself, 'Mossby is beautiful, but I want to be remembered for designing many houses, not just one.'

He was off guard when Ralph, with an indescribable howl of anguish, threw himself at him – I don't know with what intent, but both staggered back against the stone balustrade and vanished over the edge. The scream, I am very sure, came from Mr Browne – and then there was silence.

42

Written in the Dust

Later, after we'd eaten a meal neither of us had much appetite for any more, we discussed the rather gruesome idea that Phillip Revell's skeleton was most probably still mouldering in the secret cellar below the tower.

Then Carey suddenly exclaimed, 'Just wait a minute! I've thought of something and I need to check it.'

Baffled, I followed him into the studio, where he turned the confession over and silently read the second side through again.

'I thought as much,' he said finally, looking up with a gleam of excitement in his eyes. 'Lady Anne said he'd taken the bag of jewels and was holding them while he was talking to her – but then there's no further mention of them. So, if Phillip Revell is still down there, the jewels presumably are, too. There's been no family record of them since.'

I stared at him in astonishment. 'You know, you're quite right! But is it possible that no one has discovered the secret stair in all these years?'

'If they had, I expect they would have passed the secret on within the family, like the priest-hole in the muniment room.'

'And since they haven't . . . he and the jewels *could* be still there.'

We gazed speculatively at each other.

'There's only one way to find out, Angel, but not tonight. I think we'd better go to bed. Come on,' he said, pulling me to my feet.

'Oh, Mr Revell, this is so sudden!' I said and he stilled, looking down at me and frowning.

'You know, that's exactly what I've tried my best *not* to be,' he said. 'I didn't want to rush you so soon after you'd lost Julian – but my feelings towards you have changed so much, it was impossible to stop myself kissing you earlier. I'm so sorry.'

I looked up at him, surprised. 'But I'd already told you that I really lost the Julian I was in love with long before he actually died and had come to terms with that. It doesn't mean I didn't love him and I often miss him now, but I've already moved on. And,' I added boldly, 'if you remember, I kissed you back!'

'So you did!' he agreed, his wonderfully blinding smile lighting up his handsome face, and then kissed me all over again.

'I'd like to sweep you up and carry you upstairs,' he said, finally releasing me. 'But I'm not sure I'm quite fit enough yet. I might have to work up to it over several nights, one or two steps at a time.'

'The lift is working again – you can sweep me upstairs in that,' I suggested demurely. 'And after the hell of a day I've had, there's no way I'm sleeping on my own tonight, especially after reading that horrible confession and knowing there's probably a body in the cellar.'

'It'll only be bare bones by now: the family skeleton you thought we might find.'

'I didn't mean literally, though,' I said.

'Well, never mind, I'll just be your comfort blanket tonight,' he promised . . . but then, he always was.

*

445

Next morning I woke up in a strange room with a familiar man. I hadn't spent the night in the same bed as Carey since we were about seven, which wasn't at all the same thing . . .

My best friend . . . and now somehow about to be permanently transformed into my lover. It seemed strangely right, as though we'd met at the heart of a maze after several wrong turnings.

I slid out, trying not to wake him, which was difficult since there was more of Carey draped over me than duvet.

He opened one drowsy, violet-blue eye. 'It's early – come back?' he suggested.

'Today we're treasure hunting, remember?' I reminded him and he snapped awake.

'You know, for a minute there, I'd forgotten. Something must have put it out of my mind . . .'

I threw the cushion from the chair at him on my way out to shower and dress: I've always had good aim.

We seemed to have simply slid seamlessly from one close relationship into another – or perhaps we'd just added an extra layer, for apart from a tendency to smile at each other a lot, on the surface nothing much appeared to have changed.

Carey was determined to eat breakfast before we did anything else, while I was almost too excited – or maybe that should be too nervous – to manage anything more than one slice of toast.

Luckily my headache had gone, though the bruise on my forehead was an interesting violet blue, spreading into the eye socket. I didn't think it'd develop into a complete shiner, just look as if I was wearing weird eye shadow on one side.

I gave my crusts to Fang, informing him if he ate them he'd get curly hair, just like my granny used to tell me, then we began equipping ourselves with torches and one of those battery-powered storm lanterns.

We were just about ready when the phone rang, and I snatched it up impatiently, to find it was Vicky.

She told me that Ella was being moved from the emergency bed to a ward in a psychiatric hospital, and gave me the name of the ward, though considering I had a bump on my forehead the size of a hen's egg, I was hardly in the mood to send flowers.

'Dad's visiting her there later and I'll probably go with him,' she added, before asking me to tell Carey she was very sorry, though not what for.

I relayed all that to him.

'I like her much better now she's showing she cares for someone other than herself,' he commented.

'You'd better not start liking her *too* much,' I warned him, 'because I know what you're like with leggy blondes, and from now on I'm not having any of them coming within ten paces of you.'

'Spoilsport!'

'And now I come to think of it, I'd like to know why you were kissing Daisy at the party. I saw you, so you can't wriggle out of it.'

'I wasn't kissing her, she was kissing me, and you obviously didn't hang around long enough to see me push her away and tell her I wasn't interested. Nelson told me I had lipstick on my face when I went back in the other room, but I thought you hadn't noticed.'

'With that hair, raspberry red is so not your colour,' I told him.

'On the other hand, jealous green suits you,' he returned, then grabbed my hand. 'Come on, we'd better get a shift on, because I've just remembered Nick and the gang are driving up today and I want to look in that secret chamber before they get here – if we can discover how to open it.'

'The directions in the confession were clear enough: we

447

find the top of the third linenfold panel to the right of the fireplace and then a carved boss above it.'

'Nick's going to love the story about finding the cavity behind the bed panel . . . suitably edited to protect the guilty party, of course,' he said.

'He'd like us to find a grisly skeleton and a bag of jewels even more,' I pointed out, and with Fang firmly shut into the kitchen we hotfooted it to the haunted bedchamber.

It certainly haunted me more than ever now. The sounds I'd heard when I was locked in that cavity might have been the product of concussion and panic-induced imagination, but I'd never quite forget those muttering voices, the footsteps and the one, quickly cut-off scream . . .

After all Ella's years of fruitless searching, it proved surprisingly easy to open the door to the staircase, though you had to press the correct side of the panel while at the same time pushing and turning one of the rose-carved bosses.

'But it needs to be turned to the right only,' Carey said, suiting his action to the words, and a whole section of panelling moved away, revealing the top of a stairway.

It was intact. I suppose when the panel was shut again, the top step slid back into its original position. I shuddered slightly, though that might have been the cold, dank air wafting up out of the darkness.

Carey went down first, and I gingerly followed him, loath to tread on that first step, even though he'd tested it before putting his weight on it.

But it held firm and the staircase wound tightly down through the thick walls of the old tower. The ceiling was low and Carey had to descend in a half-crouch, so that I ran into the back of him when he finally reached the bottom and immediately stopped to straighten up.

He held up the lantern and slowly turned, revealing a square room of the same size as the ones in the tower above . . . *and* the glimmer of white bones on the stone floor, some way from the wall.

I shone my torch on it with dread, and was horrified to see not the huddle of bones I expected, but a skeleton that appeared frozen in the act of trying to crawl away.

Carey stooped over it. 'He's quite a distance from the opening to the shaft he fell down, so it looks like the poor devil wasn't killed outright in the fall, doesn't it? He's got shattered bones, but he's tried to pull himself towards that door over there, which must lead to the tunnel.'

I shivered again, and not just from the cold. 'And no one came back, so he died in the dark, alone and in agony.'

'He certainly paid for his sins. But since he's here, then the jewels should be scattered around him somewhere. We'll go over the floor with our torches and—'

'Carey, look!' I exclaimed, for as I'd turned away from the gruesome sight, my torch had revealed an ancient, dust-furred table with a not-so-ancient tin box sitting on it. It *was* old and slightly rust-spotted, but a picture of a simpering little girl holding a kitten and the word 'Bonbons' were much more Victorian than seventeenth century.

'What the hell . . . ?' began Carey, putting down the lantern next to it and then, with some difficulty, prising off the lid. Inside was a small leather-bound book wrapped in some waterproof fabric, and pasted inside on the marbled endpapers a letter written in a familiarly bold and spiky hand. The words at the end danced before my eyes:

Jessie Kaye Revell
Mossby
1914

'My God, Jessie got here first!' I gasped.

'So she has – and perhaps we've been following in her footsteps all along. Remember the way the cover of the confession had been sewn up in two different threads?'

He turned and played the beam of his powerful torch across the floor. 'She was probably on the same errand as us, too, because there's no sign of any jewels.'

'I'm sure you're right, but I wonder what she did with them,' I said, then sudden illumination struck. 'Do you remember Mr Wilmslow telling us that after her husband's accident there were a lot of debts and it looked like the house might have to be sold – until Jessie unexpectedly came into a large inheritance? I bet there wasn't one: it was the money from the sale of the jewels!'

'It does all hang together,' Carey agreed. 'And if you're right, I suppose there wouldn't still be a Revell at Mossby if she hadn't found and sold them. Now it's up to us to make sure it stays in the family for ever.'

'Yes, but—' I began, then broke off as he got down on one knee in the dust. I looked at him in astonishment. 'What on earth are you doing?'

'Proposing: let's get married! Mossby should be a happy-ever-after family home, not a mausoleum.'

'But, Carey, you know my views about marriage being an outdated institution . . . and anyway, you can't *possibly* propose to me next to a skeleton!' I protested, casting a nervous eye at our silent witness. He still looked as if he was about to crawl off. I was almost sure I'd seen him move out of the corner of my eye. 'Can we get out of here, now?'

'Only if you say yes.'

'Yes!' I snapped, but when he got to his feet he paused to stoop again over the collection of bones.

'I think Jessie missed something – that's a signet ring on his finger,' he said interestedly.

450

'I don't care what it is, it can stay there for ever, as far as I'm concerned,' I snapped, then tucked the bonbon tin under my arm and made for the stairs.

'I must nail that top step down as soon as possible, so we don't have any accidents,' Carey said, as he emerged into the bed-chamber after me and closed the door to the staircase. 'But first, I think I should ring the police and notify them about the skeleton, even if we're sure it's been there for centuries.'

'I suppose so – and what a lot of exciting revelations we've got for Nick and the gang when they get here,' I said. 'But I absolutely refuse to go back down there and pretend to find that ghastly skeleton again on camera.'

'OK, if necessary I'll pretend to find it on my own,' he said equably.

'You know, if Jessie Kaye went down there by herself, then she was quite a woman,' I said thoughtfully.

'So are you,' he said, putting his arms around me. 'And now you're all mine!'

I was the object of much compassion when I gave my account of this tragic accident, especially when my child was born early, soon afterwards – a son, Joshua.

While I was recovering from this, I reread Lady Anne's confession very carefully: how sadly, in some ways, our lives mirrored one another in misfortune, though her husband's crimes were heinous, while I cannot find it in me to hate Ralph for what was in his nature, even though he was cruel in marrying me to attain his own ends.

Once I was well again, I sewed the confession back into its original wrappings and replaced it where I had found it. Then, since my husband's death had encouraged rather than deterred his creditors from seeking payment, I summoned his man of business and revealed that I might be about to come into an inheritance . . .

Of course, there was no inheritance, but it had struck me that in Lady Anne's confession there was no further mention of the bag of jewels her husband had been holding when he fell, so that they could very well still be in the secret room below the turret . . .

I may be small, but I am neither imaginative nor cowardly. I thought of my child's future, and of Honoria's, and then, taking a small lantern, opened the secret place in the bedchamber next to the tower, testing the first step gingerly despite knowing

I had turned the boss only to the right. I descended the narrow winding stair that seemed to go on for ever, till I emerged into a square chamber below.

Next to where I stood was the opening through which Phillip Revell must have dropped ... but there was no huddle of smashed bones at the bottom of it. Instead, the lantern showed his shattered skeleton, seemingly still trying to creep away towards the door that must lead to the passage and help. It was all too awfully apparent that he must have spent his last hours alone here in agony. Retribution for his sins, indeed!

Shuddering and averting my eyes from these broken relics, I began to cast my lantern around in ever increasing circles from the foot of the stairs – until, at last, the light caught and flickered on something that shone deep red. Despite my resolution, my heart beat faster for a moment, until I told myself that this was not blood, miraculously preserved over aeons, but that which I sought. The bag must have burst asunder and rotted, for the jewels lay scattered and dusty on the flagged floor. I began to pick them up and put them into my shawl: a monstrously formed pearl and jewelled ornament of the kind men wore in old paintings, on a heavy ruby necklace, the stones large and cold to the touch. There was also a sparkle of diamonds in a twisted brooch and the dull glow of dark emerald earrings.

When I was sure there were no more to be found, I knotted the shawl and carried my treasures back up to the bedchamber. You can imagine with what relief I closed the panel to that dread place behind me.

I wrote to Father and he brought Lily to stay with me for a few days, before returning to town with the precious cargo. He has acquaintances who can ensure a fair price, with no questions asked, though in truth the jewels belong to my son, so I do no wrong in using them to preserve his heritage.

453

43

Casting the Bones

Nick and the crew arrived just after we'd got back to the kitchen and Carey gave them a condensed version of the events of the last twenty-four hours, including Ella's assault on me, the breakdown and the cellar full of bones.

'So now I'm about to ring the police and notify them of the skeleton,' he finished.

They'd listened to him with eyes wide and stunned expressions, but now Nick said quickly, 'You can't ring them till we've filmed down there!'

'Why not? You couldn't use the footage anyway, because it would be too gruesome and horrible,' I said, with a reminiscent shudder.

'But maybe Nick's right and we *should* have a record of it, Shrimp,' Carey suggested. 'Then perhaps later there could be an edited version for the series. And I might as well ring the police now, because they're hardly going to race up here with their sirens on for an ancient skeleton, are they? It could be days before they turn up.'

'When they do, they're bound to notice that there've been loads of people down there,' Sukes pointed out. 'Perhaps we'd better say we all found it together, like the Famous Five.'

'Six,' I said, 'and Fangy the dog.'

'Good thinking, Sukes,' said Jorge, and Carey picked up the phone.

I wasn't going down those stairs ever again and anyway, Jessie's little journal in the bonbon tin was calling to me. I wondered why she'd chosen to leave it down there.

Once the others had gone, I settled myself in Granny's rocking chair by the stove with Fang snoring comfortably, if heavily, on my feet, and began to read.

I'd finished by the time they returned, slightly cobwebbed and over-excited, but it was just as well they *were* back, because the police turned up with amazing alacrity and Carey had to descend into the depths all over again.

In fact, he seemed to be doing guided grisly tours all day, though mostly just to the top of the no-longer-secret stairs, before leaving the various officials and experts to get on with it. But finally, once a pathologist had officially declared life extinct (I could have told them that) and the bones very old, the skeleton was taken away for examination.

Carey, of course, hadn't mentioned the Confession, or Jessie's diary, for those were family secrets. He'd simply explained that he and his friends had come across the staircase when searching for more priest-holes.

It looked like the whole affair was officially destined to be an unsolved mystery and a gruesome page or two in the guidebook, which would have to be hastily revised before printing.

Nick and the gang had only really meant to call in on their way elsewhere, so eventually they reluctantly tore themselves away, but not before Carey announced that we were getting married.

'At last!' said Nick. I don't know what he meant by that, unless he had a crystal ball.

'Let Revells commence,' joked Nelson, in his lovely, plummy deep voice.

'I only said I'd marry you so I could get out of that hideous cellar. If you love someone, you don't have to tie the knot officially, just because of some old traditions designed to hand women over like so much merchandise,' I said stubbornly.

'I want to tie you to me with as many knots as possible, traditional or otherwise,' Carey said. 'I'll even promise to love, honour and obey you, if you like: you always boss me around, anyway.'

'I felt just the same as you about getting married, Angel, until Jorge proposed to me at your party,' Sukes said, taking me totally by surprise. 'But I'll do it, if you will.'

Jorge gave me a pleading look from under his fringe.

'There we are: you can have a double wedding and we'll film it,' Nick said. 'All sorted!'

'The film crew filming the film crew getting married?' said Nelson.

'And the main subjects of the TV series the film crew are filming,' agreed Nick. 'It'll be a *winning* episode – the viewers will love it.'

'My mother will probably have other ideas about the venue,' Sukes said firmly.

'And I'm not sure either of us want to get married just because it makes good TV,' I said, but I don't think anyone was listening. Carey certainly wasn't.

'I think you should have one of those Victorian rings with a band of coloured jewels that spell out a message,' he told me, slipping his arm around my waist.

'Help?' I suggested, but under the onslaught of his blindingly wonderful smile, the last of my resolve was melting away faster than a snowball in summer.

*

456

When we were finally alone again, which felt like the first time for at least a week, I told Carey he should take Jessie's memoir into the sitting room and read it, while I broke out one of Molly's seafood paellas for dinner.

'It's quite short, so it won't take you long, but there are a few surprises in there – and one or two disturbing revelations.'

'Oh, no, I'm not sure I can take any more family skeletons at the moment,' he groaned, but did as I suggested and had just turned to the last page when I took the tray through, laden with two plates of paella and a couple of glasses of rosé.

'I see what you mean,' he said, looking up. 'I've skimmed the earlier bits but read all of it from when she gets to Mossby.'

'It's a sad story really, but she was happy in her work and I think she understood and forgave Ralph,' I said.

'It must have been a shock to her when she realized he was homosexual – and of course at that time, it was a crime. But what really seemed to hurt her was that he'd only married her because he wanted an heir for Mossby.'

'Yes, that was cruel,' I agreed. 'Honoria lived to a good age and seemed to adore the boy, though – your grandfather, you said?'

'That's right.'

'The note she's added at the end of the journal is illuminating, isn't it? I think Jessie loved her son, but she loved her work more, so she was happy to spend most of her time in London working with her cousin.'

'The boy not being interested in glass must have been a disappointment, but I expect he was brought up a gentleman like his father, and was more a Revell than a Kaye,' Carey suggested. 'You know, having Revell blood in my veins doesn't really seem to be anything to be proud of now!'

'But there must have been many perfectly decent Revells, too, and I think there's a lot of the Kayes in you,' I told him.

'You're certainly not a typical Revell in any way that I can see, except in looks.'

'And my love of Mossby . . . though I love you more,' he said, pulling me down into his arms. 'And now I've got you for ever, I can have my Angel cake *and* eat it!'

Mossby, 1914

I ceased my journal at this point, having much to occupy me, but the story of an unexpected inheritance from a godmother was accepted. My husband's debts were cleared and the remainder of the money invested securely, since when we have gone on very well.

Despite his early arrival, Joshua has thrived under his aunt's care at Mossby, dividing his holidays there, or at my London home, though to my disappointment he has shown no interest in the business . . . or indeed, in any business. In appearance he is very much a Revell, having his father's red-gold hair and deep blue eyes, but bookish and will shortly be going up to Oxford.

Honoria is fit and well, and, though Papa has gone before me, Lily and Michael and their children live happily on in my old home and the business flourishes. Mossby has been a place of holiday to them and the company of his young cousins has been good for Joshua.

I will be sad to leave him at such a tender age . . . but so it appears it must be. I have secured his comfortable continuation at Mossby and the rest is up to him.

I intend to seal up this account in a tin and make one final brief trip to that dreadful room below the tower. Perhaps one day someone will follow the same path I took and discover it . . . or perhaps not. I leave that to fate.

My own legacy lives on in my work, my proudest achievement. God gave me the gift of painting with light, and I hope I have used it well.

Jessie Kaye Revell

44

In the Light of Day

I was standing in the courtyard by the fishy fountain on Good Friday, when for the first time, the big oak doors to the Elizabethan wing were thrown open to the ghost trail visitors.

Although only early April, there was warmth in the sun that slanted down through the Lady Anne window and cast a diamond pattern across the stone flags below.

Somehow, the whole of the old wing seemed to have grown lighter and warmer once that terrible scattering of shattered bones had been removed and buried in the Halfhidden graveyard . . . though *not* in the family vault.

The macabre story of their finding – suitably edited – had been included in the guidebook and was also scheduled to feature in the next series of the *Mansion Makeover*, should the first one be a success, which I was positive it would be.

Ella was reportedly improving and Clem had decided to semi-retire to his native Devon and become a jobbing gardener. He thought that when Ella came home, a fresh start in a new area would be good for her.

As for Vicky – well, there she was right in front of me, becomingly dressed in Elizabethan costume and welcoming the visitors at the door. She seemed set to become a permanent character in the TV series and at the moment was living

461

in the Lodge . . . and so, to my great surprise, was Nelson, whenever the crew were up here. It seemed a most unlikely pairing, but then, the ways of love are often very strange.

I mean, take Carey and me: if he'd been able to prevent blondes throwing themselves at him and I'd not thought the worst each time, we'd have realized we loved each other long ago.

But then, I suppose I wouldn't have had the happy years with Julian, so I can't really regret that. And I was certain Julian would be happy that Carey and I were forging a future together – and delighted that Angel Arrowsmith Art Glass was flourishing to such an extent that I'd soon be able to offer Grant a full-time job in the workshop.

This was just as well, since a few days ago Grant had broken the sad news that Nat was selling up the business and moving back to the south.

Apparently, Willow had loathed living in Lancashire and threatened to leave him: the worm had turned.

He was going into partnership with another stained-glass artist and I hoped for his sake that it was one who could design a decent window, since they intended continuing to use the Julian Seddon Architectural Glass Studio name.

But whatever they did, Julian's legacy would live on unspoiled in his wonderful work and his memory in my heart.

This was not a day for sadness and looking back, however, when the future was so bright with promise.

Carey, who had been in the old wing checking that Louis and his girlfriend, Liz, who were manning the souvenir and guidebook table, had everything they needed, now came back and slid his arm around me.

'I *love* the sound of that cashbox rattling,' he said, his hair a nimbus of red-gold in the sunlight and his wonderful violet-blue eyes shining, as always, with enthusiasm. 'Especially since I've just had the final bill from the electrician.'

'Well, at least he's finished now,' I consoled him. 'And he's made a wonderful job of it. Those torch sconces in the Long Gallery look almost like the real thing.'

'Speaking of the real thing,' Nick put in, from his precarious perch on the edge of the fountain, from where he could watch the crew circle the visitors like persistent wasps. 'I'm so glad Carey persuaded you to get married in that really picturesque church in the village – a little Halfhidden wedding will be perfect.'

'You old romantic,' I teased him. 'But I know what you really mean is that you're glad because it will look good on film. Still, at least it will be a small affair . . . and you're not coming to Brisbane with us on our honeymoon.'

'Too late to back out of the wedding now, anyway,' Carey told me. 'I've asked Fang to be pageboy and he'll never forgive you if you ruin his big day.'

Fang, who was sitting at my feet watching the queue file in with the benign expression of a dog who would never, ever bite anyone's ankles, lolled his tongue and looked up at me with his best vampire smile.

'OK – I'll go through with it for him,' I said gravely, and Carey laughed and pulled me closer.

'Smoochy kiss for the camera!' called Sukes, and when we obliged, the stream of visitors queuing behind her broke into spontaneous applause.

Recipes

Angel cake

When I was little I used to love the sweet lightness of an angel cake, baked in a loaf-shaped tin, which we would slice and then butter. The slightly salty butter on the sweet cake was delicious. When I was thinking of a recipe to include in a book featuring a character called Angel, I knew this had to be the one.

Ingredients

180g (6 oz) plain white flour
30g (1 oz) cornflour
350g (12 oz) white caster sugar, plus extra to prepare the tin
12 egg whites
1 tsp cream of tartar
1 tsp vanilla essence

Method

1. Preheat the oven to 160°C/fan 140°C/gas 3. Get your loaf tin and butter it, then dust with a layer of caster sugar.

465

2. Sieve the flour with the cornflour and add 275g (10 oz) of the caster sugar. Mix to combine.
3. In a separate bowl, whisk the egg whites with the cream of tartar until soft and frothy, then add the rest of the sugar and the vanilla essence and whisk to stiff peaks.
4. Sift the flour mixture into the egg white, folding it in gently with a balloon whisk or metal spoon, then pour into the loaf tin.
5. Bake for about 45–55 minutes, until the cake has shrunk slightly from the edges and is golden on the surface. Cool in the tin for 10 minutes before turning out.

Stained glass window biscuits

These are fun biscuits to make, especially with children, at any time of year, though you can easily adapt them to be pretty Christmas decorations too: simply pierce the top of the biscuit with a plastic straw or skewer before baking, then tie a ribbon on once they're cool and hang on the tree.

Ingredients (makes around 20 biscuits)

175g (6 oz) butter, softened
100g (3½ oz) caster sugar
225g (8 oz) plain flour
About 20 colourful boiled sweets. Fox's Glacier Fruits work best.

If you're making festive biscuits, you might like to add 1 teaspoon of ground ginger and the zest of one orange to the mixture. You will also need Christmassy shaped cookie cutters!

Method

1. Preheat the oven to 160°C/fan 140°C/gas 3. Line two baking sheets with greaseproof paper.
2. Combine the butter and sugar in a bowl and beat by hand until smooth. Then add the flour (and ginger and orange if using) and, by hand, bring the dough together, making sure not to overwork it. If it's a hot day you can chill the dough in the fridge for half an hour before rolling it out.
3. Roll out on a lightly floured work surface, to a thickness of about 3cm/1¼ inch. Use cookie cutters, or the rim of a glass or mug to cut out the biscuits. Then cut out the middle of each shape, leaving a good thick surrounding edge. Arrange on the baking sheets – at this point you might want to make a small hole for threading the ribbon through, if you're doing that.
4. Separate the boiled sweets into their colours and put them in plastic bags – one colour per bag. Crush using a rolling pin, then pour the grains into the middle of each biscuit.
5. Bake in the preheated oven for about 12–15 minutes or until the biscuits are a pale golden colour and the sweets have melted to fill the holes. Don't overbake, they'll continue to harden as they cool.

Bramble jam

Years ago I went through a phase of making jams and pickles, and this blackberry jam was one of my favourites. Plus, if you can find a local hedgerow groaning with ripe fruit, it's practically free!

Ingredients

1kg (2¼ lbs) blackberries
900g (2 lbs) preserving sugar
Juice of 3 lemons
You'll need some clean, sterilised jam jars – this recipe makes around a kilo (2¼ lbs) of jam.

Method

1. Place 2 or 3 saucers in the fridge to chill. Wash the blackberries well. Tip into a large, heavy-based saucepan or preserving pan, add 400ml (14 floz) cold water and bring to the boil. Reduce the heat, cover the pan and simmer gently for about 20 minutes, or until the fruit is soft. Remove the lid, add the sugar and lemon juice and heat

gently, stirring all the while, until the sugar has dissolved (about 4–5 minutes).

2. Bring to a vigorous boil and cook for 15 minutes. Be careful that the mixture doesn't boil over or spit on you – it will be very hot!

3. Remove the pan from the heat and test to see if the jam will set by spooning some on to one of the chilled saucers. Let it cool for a few seconds, then touch the syrup with your fingertip. If the surface wrinkles slightly, it's reached setting point. If not, boil for a further 2 minutes and test again. Repeat if necessary until setting point is reached.

4. Position a large metal sieve over a large mixing bowl. Fill the sieve carefully with some of the blackberry mixture and using the back of a large, metal spoon, push the fruit through the sieve into the bowl. When you've extracted as much syrup as you can, throw away the seedy pulp left in the sieve. Continue until you've strained all of the mixture.

5. Spoon the strained syrup into the jam jars and seal.

The Little Teashop of Lost and Found

Trisha Ashley

Alice Rose is a foundling, discovered on the Yorkshire moors above Haworth as a baby. Adopted but then later rejected again by a horrid stepmother, Alice struggles to find a place where she belongs. Only baking – the scent of cinnamon and citrus and the feel of butter and flour between her fingers – brings a comforting sense of home.

So it seems natural that when she finally decides to return to Haworth, Alice turns to baking again, taking over a run-down little teashop and working to set up an afternoon tea emporium.

Luckily she soon makes friends – including a Grecian god-like neighbour – who help her both set up home and try to solve the mystery of who she is. There are one or two last twists in the dark fairy tale of Alice's life to come . . . but can she find her happily ever after?

A Leap of Faith

Trisha Ashley

Sappho Jones stopped counting birthdays when she reached thirty but, even with her hazy grip on mathematics, she realizes that she's on the slippery slope to the big four-oh! With the thought suddenly lodged in her mind that she's a mere cat's whisker away from becoming a single eccentric female living in a country cottage in Wales, she has the urge to do something dramatic before it's too late.

The trouble is, as an adventurous woman of a certain age, Sappho's pretty much been there, done that, got the T-shirt. In fact, the only thing she hasn't tried is motherhood. And with sexy potter Nye on hand as a potential daddy – or at least donor – is it time for her to consider the biggest leap of all? It's either that or buy a cat . . .

A Good Heart is Hard to Find

Trisha Ashley

Cassandra Leigh has woken as if from a bad dream: forty-four, childless and twenty-plus years into an affair with a married man. Max assures her that one day soon they will be able to marry, but Cass is desperate for a baby and running out of time. Maybe Max is not the only man for her?

There's her friend Jason – though he's perhaps a little too rugged, and there's something strange about the way his wife disappeared. Or there's Dante, the mysterious stranger she meets on a dark night in his haunted manor house . . .

Cass must throw caution to the wind and claim the life she's always wanted. Suddenly, it's a choice between Mr Right, Mr Wrong or Mr Right Now . . .

Did you love this book?

Sign up to Trisha Ashley's newsletter
for a look at the new book, chapter
samplers, competitions and the chance
to read before anyone else!

Dive into Trishaworld, where there is
always a warm welcome.

To sign up, search for Trisha Ashley on
penguin.co.uk and sign up on her page.